MISSING WHITE WOMAN

MISSING WHITE WOMAN

KELLYE GARRETT

MULHOLLAND BOOKS

LITTLE, BROWN AND COMPANY

New York Boston London

Mulholland Books / Little, Brown and Company
Hachette Book Group
1290 Avenue of the Americas, New York, NY 10104
mulhollandbooks.com

First Edition: April 2024

Mulholland Books is an imprint of Little, Brown and Company, a division of Hachette Book Group, Inc. The Mulholland Books name and logo are trademarks of Hachette Book Group, Inc.

The publisher is not responsible for websites (or their content) that are not owned by the publisher.

The Hachette Speakers Bureau provides a wide range of authors for speaking events. To find out more, go to hachettespeakersbureau.com or email hachettespeakers@hbgusa.com.

Little, Brown and Company books may be purchased in bulk for business, educational, or promotional use. For information, please contact your local bookseller or the Hachette Book Group Special Markets Department at special.markets@hbgusa.com.

ISBN 9780316256971
LCCN 2023941823

Printing 1, 2024

MRQ

Printed in Canada

To Mallory, Julian, and Ian

I call it the missing white woman search syndrome. If there is a missing white woman, you're going to cover that every day.

—*Gwen Ifill*

MISSING
WHITE
WOMAN

ONE

I was going to jail.

    I knew it. She knew it too. I could tell by the way she looked over at me—or rather didn't. We were the only two people on this block of fancy-schmancy row houses. A thin sliver of grass and a fence at half-mast separating the two of us.

When she came through the wrought-iron front gate, I was already feeling as lost as Dorothy in Oz and ready to give anything to snap my <u>ASICS</u> together to get back to Maryland. So I was *excited* when I first heard the gate slam the next house over. I'd even smiled initially when I looked back at her, convinced her sudden appearance was a good thing. That finally there was someone who could help me. My Glinda.

I couldn't see much of her. Not at first with the sun being long gone and the darkness turning her into just a skinny blob. She didn't take human form until she passed through the remnants of the floodlight from the house attached to the other side. And even then, I couldn't make out more than a square inch of her face. Blame a face mask as red and sparkly as a pair of ruby slippers. But I didn't need to make out a nose, a pair of eyes, perfectly contoured cheekbones, blond hair, to tell she was pretty. The accessories filled in the blanks. Black jumpsuit.

Rose-gold hardback suitcase. Stilettos. She even somehow managed to not look ridiculous wearing sunglasses at night.

She looked like she belonged there. Like *she* was the one taking a long weekend jaunt with her new boyfriend to a city she'd never been to, with keyless door locks, four-story row houses, and unobstructed views of the Manhattan skyline.

I, on the other hand, looked like someone standing in the dark outside a place I didn't belong, trying to get in without a key. It was exactly who I was and what I was doing. My outfit was wrong. *Target.* Suitcase was wrong. *Amazon.* Skin was wrong. *Brown.* Hair—kinky and getting bigger by the second—was definitely wrong too. The most expensive things on me were my sneakers.

She didn't look in my direction for more than a second, pulling her oversized purse closer to her, quickening her step up the stairs to her pitch-black stoop—or whatever they called it in fancy-ass neighborhoods like this one. But a nanosecond was probably all she needed.

Good thing I was already about to cry.

Blame the damn door and my inability to get it open. I'd tried three times already. Put in the code Ty had given me. Hit the Key button. Jiggled the knob like it needed some complicated handshake. I did it a fourth time, only to yield the same result. The only change, the new audience of one, looking like she wanted to boo me off the stage like this was the Apollo.

I braved another glance over. I was quick, but she was quicker, turning her head away so fast the crystals on her protective mask looked like sparklers as they caught the light. She'd been watching the latest attempt. Even from a distance—even in the dark—I could make out the pale white manicured hand gripping her cell phone like the weapon it could be in these situations. At least for people who looked like me.

I pulled my own phone out—this one a lifeline. Ty picked up on the second ring.

"Be there in fifteen," he said.

"You're in the Uber?"

"Not yet, but I will be. Packing up now."

My phone said it was already 10:46. He'd sworn he'd pick me up from the train station. Then sworn he'd meet me at the house. He'd been wrong on both counts.

"Oh." It was just a syllable. One I didn't even say that loud, yet he still heard it.

"Everything okay, Bree?"

I glanced over. She was still there standing with the screen door open. Pretending not to watch as she took her own time going inside. "Yeah." I wiped my eye as I spoke. It wasn't the first time I'd lied to him. "It's the code. It doesn't work."

"Really? It worked this morning when I checked in—1018."

"It's 1019." That was the one in the text. The one I'd plugged in four times.

"I'm pretty sure it's 1018. Let me check."

But I didn't wait for him to answer. Just tried the door again, but 1018 this time. It buzzed practically before I hit the Key button. The knob turned as he spoke again, realizing. "I sent you the wrong code."

"It's fine." Another lie.

I glanced over, hoping to catch her watching me again. Nodding as she realized she was wrong. That I wasn't some thief in the night. That I did belong here. That my boyfriend had given me the wrong code. But of course she'd finally disappeared inside.

I shook off the unease and turned my attention back to Ty.

"I'll make it up to you," he said.

He'd been saying that a lot since he'd come up to New Jersey on Monday for work, the routine we'd established over the past three months immediately shot to hell. No nightly FaceTimes. No long-winded responses to my texts. And when he did respond, it was just hitting the Heart button or one-word replies sent so late that I'd damn near forgot what he was responding to.

Work.

Always work. Some intense finance job that took a lot of time but also paid a lot of money. Some new project that was dominating most of his working hours and almost as many out of the office as well. It was only after I suggested maybe this weekend wasn't a good time to come that he'd called. Said he still wanted me to take the train up.

Lucky for him, I wasn't one to make a big deal.

"It's fine," I said again as I finally opened the door. It was cold enough inside to give me goose bumps if they hadn't already been there. "I blame those big-ass hands of yours." I was proud of how I sounded. More teasing than annoyed.

He laughed then, the first time I'd heard him do that all week. I was glad too because I loved how it sounded. "Oh, now you have a problem with my big-ass hands. Last week it was—"

I laughed too. "I'm hanging up now."

"Wait."

"Bye, Ty." I tried to stifle a yawn.

"You're gonna wait up for me, right?"

"Bye, Ty."

"Right?"

"Guess you'll have to get here and see."

But we both knew I would—in no makeup but also no bonnet. Happy to see him. Like always.

We both said goodbye and I finally stepped inside, thanking the heavens there wasn't an alarm and that snoop of a neighbor hadn't dialed 911. The cold air felt better than any jail cell I'd been in.

* * *

This trip had been planned for a month.

Ty had rolled over on a lazy Sunday morning when my mom would've wanted me to be two hours deep into worship service and casually asked if I'd ever been to New York. His spontaneity was one of the many things I liked about him—already loved about him, though I hadn't said the words out loud yet. And neither had he. It'd only been a few months since we met jogging.

We were at the "Let's take a trip" stage. Technically, it was a two-week work trip for him. One he took every couple of months to his company's Jersey City office. I was just tagging along for a weekend.

Ty had been here since Monday, but he'd been staying at a hotel until today. The plan was for me to come up Friday evening, then we'd stay in an Airbnb and spend the next two days in New York City before I went back home in time for my own job Monday afternoon. Of course mine was nowhere near as fancy. I was a manager at a stationery store.

I'd never been much of a traveler, but still I was excited when Ty turned toward me that morning. So excited that I'd even purchased new Kenneth Cole luggage and packed the good panties—even though my mother spent the entire month strongly disagreeing with the trip. That was the great thing about being over thirty—even if I did still live in my college studio. Your mother kept giving advice; you just didn't have to take it.

My maternal line was that of a mighty few. Only children begetting only children. All girls. My grandmother was in her nineties, battling dementia like she'd battled everything else life had thrown at her. Yet she'd gotten worse right before my mother retired from her position as a head of marketing. Taking care of her had become my mom's full-time job. And my part-time one. I was off Thursdays and Fridays, so I would drive forty-five minutes to my mom's house to give her a break.

My mother had a million and two questions when I'd told her about the trip. She'd sent them in a string of single text messages over the course of five excruciatingly long minutes. The English major in her not accepting a single typo no matter what the medium.

What about COVID?

The numbers were down.

When are you going?

Last week in April.

That's soon.

It was a month away.

My relationship history was mainly made up of a series of first dates. Ty was my first serious boyfriend in over a decade. I was going to enjoy my first couples vacation just like I was going to enjoy my first time ever in New York. Even if my mother wanted to ruin it one text at a time.

Initially she'd sent me articles about how dangerous New York City was. When I pointed out I was staying in New Jersey, she just switched to sending articles about there. Shootings. Break-ins. Assaults. Her latest was about some pretty blond white woman who'd gone missing.

I didn't click a single link. Just promised to bring the Mace she'd gotten me.

And when she wasn't bothering me about the dangers of the big city, she was bugging me about where I was staying. After a few weeks, I mentioned the house, but not Ty's job chipping in for it. New York City wouldn't be my only first. I'd also never stayed in an Airbnb. I'd been excited about that too. At least before I encountered the key code.

Her last string of texts had come just as I was getting off the train.

I can't believe you're going someplace you've never been with a stranger.

But that was the thing. He was only a stranger to her. I'd met his mom, Ms. Patty. He just hadn't met mine. And it wasn't something I was looking forward to.

I just think it's premature, Breanna.

My mother thought a lot of things. So did I. So did the entire world. The rest of us simply didn't feel the need to share them all.

It'd just been the two of us since my dad unexpectedly died of a heart attack when I was in grade school. My memories of him were fleeting at this point, but one of the things I would never forget was how he used to look at me and my mom. I'd never felt more loved—more safe—than when he was smiling at me.

I pushed the convo out my mind as I took in my home for the next two days. I dropped my "weekend tote" a few feet into the first-floor open-concept living area.

110 Little Street in Jersey City.

I felt like one of those kids the first time they stepped inside Willy Wonka's chocolate factory. I didn't know what to look at first, what to touch, where to sit. I was afraid to even put my bag on the glass entry table, which looked so simple it had to cost more than a month of my paychecks.

Ty had made his presence known. There were dishes in the sink and he'd left the big-screen TV on mute. I didn't recognize the news anchor, which meant it had to be a local station.

I put my phone up and slowly did a 360, taking photos of the exact same things in the pics he'd screenshotted from the Airbnb listing. The entry table and stairs a few feet away from me. The living room couches and oversized rug the same dark gray as the walls. The all-white kitchen in the back of the house. The entire garden through the windows behind it.

My shots were nowhere near as pretty, but they'd do. Finished, I sent the lot of them to my mother with two words: Made it!!!

Ty had done good. I wished it wasn't so important to me that my mother see that.

By the time she responded, my Kenneth Cole and I had made it up three flights of stairs to the "owner's suite." Of course I stopped on floors two and three to take more pics. Sent those to her too. She got the office, the gym, and both spare bedrooms. All varying grades of gray. All fancier than anything I'd seen on some decorating show. But if the rest of the house was HGTV, the fourth floor was *Architectural Digest*.

The bedroom took up the entire floor. When I finally willed myself to look away from the bed, I noticed the floor-to-ceiling windows. The skylight. The Keurig twinkling on a marble counter, joined by a sink and a mini fridge. Guess when you're rich, you don't go downstairs for midnight snacks.

I took another photo in front of the "beverage center"—this one a selfie—then sent that one to her too. My phone buzzed just as I was realizing that the green blob I saw out the back window was the Statue of Liberty.

I smiled, for once excited to see what she had to say. There was nothing she loved more than a good marble countertop. She had to appreciate this house. There wasn't a single thing bad even she could say about it.

I unlocked my phone and opened the text. Her response was simple.

You let your mystery man see you looking like that?

* * *

He'd lied about being on his way, but then I did too when I said I didn't mind that he was still stuck at the office. It was a gorgeous house, and I forced myself to enjoy it. I haphazardly unpacked, hanging up the lone dress I'd brought in the walk-in closet. It had a safe, but I didn't own anything worth putting in there.

Unpacking didn't take long, which meant I had time to do a quick face-mask treatment. I ran downstairs to see what was in the fridge. Ty had gone shopping. There were eggs, oatmeal, yogurt, and honey— perfect for a quick facial. I mixed and matched until it was ready to go. Then slathered it on my face, waited the requisite ten minutes, and went upstairs to shower.

Once in there, I took my time, pressing buttons and turning knobs at will. All while pretending not to be surprised—and excited—by what each one did.

My studio in Baltimore was in an old building and I paid all utilities, which meant I wasn't used to anything more than quick showers. Lukewarm ones at that. I kept expecting the water in the Airbnb to get cold. Someone to bang on the door to tell me to hurry up, like my mom would do when I was a kid. That I was wasting all that good water, like she used to say. But it didn't happen. Made me want to stay in there forever, the steam keeping the rest of the world—and the problems that came along with it—at bay.

When I got out, I was going to go downstairs. Wait for Ty there in as little clothing as I could manage. But then I opened the door. Saw the inky blackness below. Turning out the lights and the TV when I'd come up to shower had been a mistake. I'd never been afraid of the dark, but it sure hit different in my six-hundred-square-foot studio than it did being solo in a four-story row house.

I came back into the light, shut the door, then burrowed myself under the heap of covers and sheets that felt softer than my legs after a fresh run of my razor. I checked my texts again. Nothing from Ty. Guess he was just as tired of his lies as I was. I tried to turn on the bedroom television and failed miserably. But who needed it when you had thousands of online videos to keep you company? Not as good as Ty, but still.

When it came to social media, I was familiar with the usual suspects, using them all differently. Facebook was for birthday reminders. Twitter, or whatever it was called now, was for news and outrage. Instagram was the one I used most. I didn't have to dance or edit thoughts down to 280 characters. I didn't even have to put a caption if I didn't want to. I could just upload a photo and call it a day.

My page wasn't private but it might as well have been. There were less than 100 followers. My life consisted of two things: working and running. The closest thing I had to friends were my coworkers—a conveyor belt of college students too self-involved to ask me much about my personal life or past. I had to admit I liked it that way. Surface conversations. Only going out to celebrate birthdays, new jobs, and, most often, graduations.

No one told you how hard it was to make friends outside of college—especially when you didn't try that hard. I was crap at keeping in contact with folks—especially the ones who knew me *before*. Just like with dating, my last close friendship had ended in college. A childhood-turned-college friend who had been the closest thing to a sister. And that breakup with Adore had been just as painful as with any college boyfriend. Needless to say, I spent a lot of time online.

Of all the apps, TikTok was still trying to figure me out. I hadn't committed to following many accounts. A few Black skin-care influencers and The Rock, because who didn't follow The Rock? The result was an algorithm as much a mess as my desk at home—videos with a #BlackSkinCare hashtag and any other thing with a ton of views.

I opened the app on my iPhone and prepared for the onslaught of the first automatically loading videos on my For You page.

A somber-looking blond white chick popped up under four words: *Where is Janelle Beckett???*

Though the name was slightly familiar, I didn't stick around to find out. Just thumbed to the next video, this one a Black woman with deep brown skin as clear as glass. I sat back and watched.

I was five videos and three products-I-need-to-buy-right-this-very-moment deep into her TikTok when the door banged open. I screamed, then reached for the Mace in my bag, all while praying I'd remember how to actually get it to work. Only one thought went through my head.

Of course my mother was right.

I just hoped it wasn't my last.

"Bree, it's just me."

Ty stood frozen in the doorframe in his dress shirt, a hint of muscle caressing each sleeve. He was tired, the bags under his eyes a dead giveaway that this wasn't his first late night at work.

"I called out when I came in," he said.

I forced myself to relax, deep breaths in and out like right after I finished a run. After a good ten inhales, I was finally able to speak. "I didn't even hear you come up the stairs. It's like the whole place has been soundproofed or something." I paused, then took him in again. "Not necessarily a bad thing."

He laughed, and when he stepped inside, I could practically see him shedding the stress. "I missed you." He sounded like he meant it too.

"How was work?"

But he was shaking his head before I even got to the *w*. "No work talk. Please."

"Fine," I said. "This place is gorgeous. Have you stayed here before?"

"Nope. First time seeing it in person was when I checked in this morning. Found it online. I'm just glad the pics did it justice."

He stopped a foot from my side of the bed, taking me in from head to toe to head again. I wished I'd struck a better pose than just sitting up against the upholstered gray headboard. At least I'd touched up my makeup. Damn my mother.

He bent down to kiss me and had the nerve to try to stand back up, but I wouldn't let him. Just cupped his face in my hands, wiping off traces of my Dope Taupe Mented lipstick from his dope medium-brown skin. Because I had missed him too.

Even with the bags under his eyes, he was divine, but I shouldn't have been surprised. He somehow got more beautiful the more I looked at him. Ironic, considering I hadn't paid him any attention when we met.

We'd been on the same weekend running schedule even during the winter. Both of us preferred the same trail. He claimed we passed each other for two straight Saturdays before he told me my shoe was undone. I hadn't noticed it, just like I hadn't noticed him. I definitely did after. It took another two weeks before he asked me out. I immediately said yes, assuming it would be another one-and-done. Except I enjoyed myself so much that I didn't make an excuse when he asked when he'd see me again.

And now here we were.

My mother would find flaws for sure, but she'd have to look hard as hell. He was tall, attractive, but not intimidatingly so, with both a decent job and decent teeth. And he had no kids despite being thirty-two and everything I just mentioned. If I weren't already dating him, she'd want to set me up.

He finally retreated, going for the bag he'd left in the doorway. "I know being this late that I couldn't come up in here empty-handed."

I feigned confusion. "Jewelry stores aren't open this time of night…"

"It's even better. Close your eyes."

I made a big production of slapping both hands over my eyes.

When he spoke again, it was from a few feet away. "Hold out your hand, but keep your eyes closed."

I did as told. After a second, I felt a bag, then smiled and opened my eyes. Sure enough, it was what I'd thought. "Muddy Buddies."

My snack of choice. Luckily cookies and cream since he was allergic to peanuts. He shook his head as I tore the bag open and shoved a handful into my mouth. "Gross."

I leaned forward. Smacked my lips. "Let me give you another kiss hello."

"Not with that Muddy breath."

"Come here."

He did, pretending to be disgusted as I pecked at him like a bird. Finally I retreated, and he sat a few feet away at the edge of the bed, casually rubbing my leg through the covers.

"The good news is that I'm done with work. I'm all yours this weekend."

He better have been. "Promise?" I said.

"On my mama."

I smiled then, even though I didn't believe him for one minute. I said nothing as he began to get undressed, starting with his shirt. He zoned out for a second as he undid the buttons, lost in thought as he scratched the scar on his stomach. I should've asked what was going on. Instead, I enjoyed the opportunity to take him in. I was smiling when he zoned back in and noticed me looking. "You're admiring my skin, aren't you?"

"Something like that."

"Thanks. Been using this gunk my girlfriend made for me."

The "gunk" was a recipe of essential oils and shea butter I'd whipped up in my sliver of a kitchen. I didn't know if I was more pleased that he actually was using it or that it was working so well on his hyperpigmentation. "Gunk, Mr. Franklin?"

"Gunk." He got serious as he took off his shoes, then pants. "Did you apply for that grant yet? Deadline's coming up."

I hadn't, but at least the printout was in my suitcase. I'd been "meaning to" mail it for two weeks now. I searched for any excuse. "I still need a name for my product line."

"I just gave it to you. Gunk."

"It is catchy."

"The name doesn't have to be final for you to apply," he said.

I didn't want to keep talking about it so I went for a subject change. *"Hamilton."*

"I like the name Gunk better," he said.

I ignored that. "You got us tickets to *Hamilton.* And you want it to be a surprise. That's why you haven't told me what we're doing tomorrow."

"I'm not telling that easy. You follow my packing instructions?"

"Of course. Brought lots of 'nice shit.'" I used quotation marks.

"And the shoes?"

"Two pairs. Cute but walkable." I'd even done a test run. *"The Lion King."*

"The movie? If you want to Netflix and chill, then we can do that."

"Of course it could also be that place where they shoot *Saturday Night Live*…"

"Rockefeller Plaza."

"Yes. Are we going there?"

He shrugged.

"You gotta give me a hint."

"Sure. It'll be in Manhattan."

I lobbed a pillow at him. "Thanks."

TWO

When we finally got to sleep, it felt just as amazing as the events prior. The mattress was big enough that I barely knew Ty was in the bed. I'd gone to sleep tracing the Kappa Alpha Psi tattoo on his chest. When I woke up the next morning, he wasn't there. I lay there listening for him and not hearing a thing.

He didn't answer when I called out his name. I might as well have been yelling into the abyss. Finally, I glanced at the clock moonlighting as art on one whole wall: 9:34 a.m.

Early for me—especially since I didn't have to work. Sophomore year at Morgan State I'd taken a retail job at a stationery store a few miles from campus. Thirteen years later I was still there, having "moved up" to afternoon manager.

I needed to call Ty, but first I needed to find my phone. There were few things more constant in my life than never knowing where my cell was. A coworker said I needed an Apple Watch. Claimed it had a function that made your phone beep. I couldn't afford one, though. My salary hadn't improved much in thirteen years either.

I finally found it in the bathroom, hidden among the skin care I'd brought with me and already scattered all over the counter the night before. My mom had texted, but I ignored it to call Ty.

He was the first number in my favorites. During the first night I'd spent over at his place, he'd jokingly taken my phone and changed his name from "Ty Franklin (Run)" to "Darius Lovehall," after the main character in the movie we had watched that night. I was listed in his as "Nina Mosley." I hadn't changed his name back.

His phone rang and rang. I hung up right before the voicemail kicked in.

Like my mom, Ty was an early riser. He just wasn't as judgy about it. He'd let you sleep in. He was probably downstairs catching up on CNN while waiting patiently for me to get up.

I wondered if we'd have time for a run. I dug through my things until I found my running gear, resisting every urge to throw my clothes every which way like I did at home. My tote wasn't the only new thing I'd gotten for the trip. My latest pair of Gel-Kayanos were black with hot-pink soles. I made sure my shorts and tank matched. It was as stylish as I got these days—though I could still recognize Chanel. Blame the internet.

Once I was dressed and laced up, I jogged down the three flights of stairs, expecting to find Ty in front of the television. Though it was on, he was nowhere to be found. The bedroom doors had all been open on the way down so I knew I hadn't run past him. The bathroom door was open as well.

He had to be somewhere. I opted for the front door first, cracking it open just enough to peek outside. Three people were huddled on the sidewalk in front of the house. All of them white. I'd been quiet but not quiet enough. They all turned to look at me. I should've waved like I belonged here. Instead, I slammed the door shut and backed up so quick I almost hit the glass entry table. *Smooth.*

It took me a few seconds, but I shook it off, heading toward the kitchen area. There was a door back there too. I could make out the back of Ty's low-cut fade through the glass. He was on the deck, talking on the phone.

He turned just as I opened the door. Smiled when he saw me as he spoke into the cell. "Call me so I know everything's all set like discussed." He hung the phone up, then addressed me. "Someone I'm working with has gone radio silent on this project due Monday."

Work. Always work.

"If you need to work, I can go for a run on my own."

He smiled as he started jumping up and down as if warming up. "Not a chance, Wright. In fact, I figured maybe you were pretending to sleep because you didn't want none of this."

He turned some jumping jacks into a full production. I smiled. "Or maybe you were afraid to wake me up because you knew what would happen."

He stopped. I could see him huffing and puffing like he was going to blow the row house down. Too bad for him it was brick. "Maybe," he said as his phone beeped. And that made him once again jump.

I watched him struggle to not look. "You can check it," I said.

He shook his head. "Or I could go for a run with you. I'd follow you anywhere when you look like that in those shorts."

My turn to smile. "We don't have to run. We can just skip it and do breakfast."

"No, you like to run first thing when you wake up."

I'd done it damn near every day for the past eleven years. If I was being honest, it was the only way my life had improved since *that* night.

"Then let's run," I said.

He walked past me. "Let me go change," he said. "Loser makes breakfast."

I made a smile appear like it came out of a hat. "Perfect. I've been wanting your French toast."

* * *

The street looked like one of those movie sets masquerading as an "urban street." Ten row houses lined each side and had the same base ingredients. All tall and narrow with four floors, three windows on each. A large staircase leading up to a front door. But the owners had taken liberties with their exteriors with no thought of cohesiveness. There were enough colors along the street to make up a rainbow.

I thought the group had dispersed, but once I stepped out the front door I realized they'd just moved farther downfield. Two houses away, to be exact, so lost in their conversation they didn't notice me when I came out the gate onto the sidewalk. At first I wanted to retreat, but I heard a voice just as I did.

"Don't worry. They don't bite."

I turned to find an older Black woman with salt-and-pepper locks that cascaded down her back and a deep brown face that was much lighter around the mouth and nose. Her skin was smooth, and I bet it was all natural. Like she just slapped some Vaseline on her face each night because that's what her grandma did when she was little. She wore a sundress, which showed off arms and legs that looked the same. I recognized it as vitiligo. She came toward me, clutching a stack of pink paper to her chest with one hand while holding a leash with the other. It was attached to a small brown dog.

Ty could talk to a wall. He was that friendly. Me, not so much. It took me a good four meetings to warm up to someone. Most people didn't want to wait me out. I smiled tentatively as she approached, even though I was happy to finally see another Black face. She stopped a few feet away as I instinctively knelt down to say hi to the dog. They were always friendlier than the humans they came with. "Your dog's adorable," I said. "What's the name?"

"Her name is Chelsea," she said. "And yours?"

I took my time standing up. "Bree."

"Bree. You're prettier than he even said."

Of course Ty had already made a friend.

"Your skin is glowing," she said. "He said you're working on a skin-care line?"

"I wouldn't call it a line. More just some stuff I whip up in my kitchen."

I'd given some of it to Ty and he'd run with it, finding Phenomenal Woman, a grant for local, Black-owned businesses named after that Maya Angelou poem. He even had me convinced to apply. I'd gotten as far as printing out the application and reading it over—always stopping when I saw the mention of a background check.

"Have you thought about doing something with sunscreen?" she said.

I was about to answer when the trio moved back toward us. Two women and a balding man in a bright orange shirt. I could tell he was the ringleader because he was half a step ahead. Now that they were closer, I could see they also had pink flyers. "You coming, Morgane?" the man said. "We're going to hit the next block over."

He didn't even look at me. The woman—Morgane—barely gave him a glance. "I'll meet you over there, Drew."

One of the women, a redhead, spoke up. "We're not going to wait for you."

"Which is why I said I'll meet you over there, Krista."

Even though they weren't looking at me, I was definitely looking at them. It was clear Krista wanted to say something in response. Instead, Drew spoke up. "Let's go."

"Friendly." I said it more to myself, but the woman heard me anyway.

"They usually aren't that bad, but everyone's on edge with Janelle missing."

I turned to her abruptly. "Who?"

"Janelle Beckett." She handed me a flyer.

"Missing" was in big bold letters. The name "Janelle Beckett" right underneath it. She'd been last seen Monday in the Journal Square section of Jersey City. What followed next was a photo. She looked how I'd wanted to growing up. Beautiful. Blue-eyed. Strawberry blond. Her hair casually flung up in knots on both sides of her head. Space buns that I couldn't get away with even when I had my hair in braids. A glance at her physical description confirmed she was as tall and as skinny as I'd immediately suspected. A contact number ran across the bottom of the page.

I'd seen the pic before—on tweets as I'd scrolled through my newsfeed and on the newscast before I'd turned to another channel and on the TikTok I'd ignored last night. Even a text my mom had sent. I hadn't paid much attention beyond registering she was pretty, blond, and white. I hadn't even realized she'd been missing in New Jersey, much less in Jersey City.

"She disappeared from here?" I said.

"Not this neighborhood. About fifteen minutes away in Journal Square, where she lives."

I racked my brain for what I remembered. "She disappeared Monday evening…"

"That was the last time anyone saw her," she said. "She did her normal dog walking that day. And it was the last time I saw her myself. She never showed up on Tuesday, and a few of us grew concerned. Drew went over to her place Tuesday night, but her landlord wouldn't let him in. So Wednesday he went to the police. She's local but doesn't have any family here. Parents died. She has a sister somewhere, but Drew hasn't been able to contact her. The police were dragging their feet until some big-name TikToker or something Janelle followed posted about it."

"I'm so sorry." I didn't take my eyes off the photo. "Are the police looking for her now?"

Out the corner of my eye, I saw her nod. "Yes. And I guess now she's gone viral. That's what my niece tells me anyway. So they're getting pressure. It hasn't helped, though. No one's heard from her since Monday night. Or seen her since Monday morning. I'm the only dog owner on the block who doesn't have to work anymore. She's been walking everyone else's for years, so we'd see each other at the dog park and just on the sidewalk. Keep each other company for that half hour. We'd only chat then, but it was something I'd look forward to. She was funny, easy to talk to, and remembered everything. My birthday. My *dog's* birthday. She even gave Chelsea a present. She seemed fine Monday, but not showing up for work on Tuesday without any warning isn't like her. Drew says her phone is going straight to voicemail and her texts aren't being delivered."

I shuddered, then glanced at the phone again. No one under forty went anywhere without keeping their phone on.

"Ms. Morgane with an *e* at the end." Ty's voice came out of nowhere and it felt like he magically appeared beside me. He immediately draped his arm around my waist. "Bree, I see you met my friend, Morgane Porter."

"I told you that you should just call me Morgane," she said.

"And I told you that my mother would whoop me if I did that," Ty said. Mine would too. Putting a "Ms." in front of the name of an older Black woman was a sign of respect.

They both turned to look at me. I had other things on my mind besides names.

"Did you know that woman who's missing is from near here, Ty?" Now that I knew about her connection to this neighborhood, I suddenly was interested in the case.

Ty's eyes widened at my outburst. "I had heard. I'm sure she'll be found soon."

"It has to be the boyfriend, right?" I turned back to Ms. Morgane. "It's *always* the boyfriend."

"She never mentioned dating anyone," Ms. Morgane said.

"A friend maybe," I said.

"Bree…" Ty's voice trailed off, clearly not happy that I suddenly wanted to play detective. "This is someone Ms. Morgane knows."

He was right. I was treating it like some Netflix true-crime documentary. Janelle Beckett was a person. I needed to show respect. "I'm so sorry," I said.

"It's fine," Ms. Morgane said. "So when are you going to—"

Ty jumped in. "Where we're going."

"Oh, right. She doesn't know."

I looked at Ty.

"Yep, I told her," he said. "Everyone knows but you." He turned back to Ms. Morgane. "We're gonna run a few miles, then she's going to make me breakfast after I beat her."

I playfully rolled my eyes.

"You taking her to the waterway?" she said.

He nodded. "Of course. Gotta start off the trip trying to impress her. It'll give us plenty of time to get back and dressed and head into the city."

"PATH or ferry?"

"Definitely taking the PATH," Ty said.

It was like they were speaking a foreign language. Ty must've seen my eyebrows furrowing because he finally addressed me. "It's like a subway except between New Jersey and Manhattan."

I nodded. Now that he'd translated, it wasn't much of a surprise that we weren't taking the ferry. Ty wasn't a water person. Some bad experience at Chesapeake Bay as a kid. He hadn't shared much more than that, and of course I didn't pry. Just like I never asked him about that scar on his stomach. Because me asking questions about his past would only lead to him asking questions about mine.

"That'll put you closer"—Ms. Morgane glanced at me—"to wherever you're going."

My eyes narrowed as I looked at the two of them. After a moment, they both burst out laughing. Ty spoke first. "Let's get this run over with before she breaks up with me."

"Smart man," Ms. Morgane said.

"It was nice meeting you, Ms. Morgane," I said.

"Same."

Ty produced a card from somewhere in his running pants and handed it to her. He'd done the same when he'd met me. I still had it where I'd thrown it on my dresser. The cardstock was 100lb. gloss. Thinner than other types but also more durable.

"In case you were serious about investing in Ethereum," he said.

I snorted because I knew nothing about it other than it was some form of crypto. Ty had tried to explain it to me more than once. I was glad Ms. Morgane was more interested in it than I was.

"I definitely will..." She trailed off as she looked behind us. I glanced back to see the man in the orange shirt on the corner. Even from a distance I could see he was staring. "You know what?" Ms. Morgane said. "Let me give you both my number."

* * *

The rest of the day was a fairy tale, complete with a whole horse-and-carriage.

We didn't run to the waterway as originally mentioned, instead sticking closer to Little Street. The entire neighborhood was equally as gorgeous. More row houses that hadn't been chopped and screwed into multiple apartments. Each one looked more taken care of than a twenty-five-year-old Sugar Baby. The only indication of the age of a house was the size of the trees in front of it.

Our race didn't truly start until we were a block from our Airbnb, and then it turned into an all-out sprint. Ty had speed, but I had endurance.

I won.

I got dressed while he got started on breakfast.

Once we'd eaten and he'd dressed, we headed for the PATH and took it under the Hudson River into Manhattan. I was expecting to hit all the tourist traps. Ty had something much better in mind. We walked the city, hitting the places he loved the most. We started high, some place called Washington Heights, at this botanical garden by the same people who did that fancy celeb party every year. Then we made our way down, hitting his favorite cookie spot (Levain) and bookstore (Kinokuniya), before eating dinner in the outdoor space of his favorite restaurant (Scalini Fedeli).

He tried to stay present, but I'd still catch him on his phone tapping furiously when I came back from the bathroom or spent too much time browsing bookshelves. He always put the phone away as soon as he noticed me noticing.

Despite the test run, my feet were killing me by the time we made it back up to Central Park. So I was especially happy when Ty took us right to the line of waiting horse-and-carriages. Our driver was named Bill. Though I didn't have glass slippers, he had on a top hat. We both jumped when Ty's phone rang when we were about a half hour in. Bill was in full tour-guide mode. "We're coming up on a great place for photos."

Ty was a vibrate person. It was the first time I'd even heard his ringtone. He quickly checked the phone, then glanced at me as if remembering his promise to not work. He gave me a tight smile, then put it away.

We'd been taking pics all day, mostly solo shots of each other or selfies with the two of us to add to our couple shot collection. None of them had made it online. We weren't "Instagram official." Not yet. When it came to twenty-first-century dating, that didn't happen until after we both said an "I love you." There was no worse feeling than dealing with a breakup and having to delete dozens of pics from your social media. Or so I'd been told.

We'd just stopped at the lake when Ty's phone rang again. "This is Cherry Hill," Bill said. "We'll stop for a few minutes so you can get some beautiful photos. I'd be happy to take one of the two of you by the fountain."

I spoke as we got out of the carriage. "Work again?"

"Client," Ty said. "It's fine."

But I could tell by his voice that it wasn't. I nodded and then: "Ian gonna get mad?"

His boss.

"Probably," Ty said.

"Don't you have that meeting with him when you get back home?"

Ty was up for a promotion. I didn't understand any of it but didn't have to in order to know what a big deal it was. I could see it in his eyes. He wanted it. Bad. And I would be damned if he didn't get it because I was looking at lakes in Central Park.

Ty loved his job. Make that his career. Because that's what it was. He was a numbers person who had always been good with money and had parlayed that into a career at one of the biggest finance companies in the world.

My job paid enough to keep me fed, even if it didn't keep me happy. Five-year-old Breanna never saw herself in a dead-end job. She'd wanted to be a lawyer like her dad, and the feeling only intensified after his death. College Breanna had even signed up for the LSAT and was supposed to take it—until that night.

It was why I was so proud of Ty. So determined to get this promotion. Follow his dream. "You should answer," I said.

He kissed me so quick I wasn't even sure it had happened. His phone was already at his ear as he started to walk away for privacy. "Hi, this is Ty—" He pulled it away to stare at the now-black screen. "It died. It's fine."

But once again, I could tell it wasn't. "You can always call them back with my phone. I'm at, like, at least fifty percent."

He turned to look at me as I held my own up, complete with a photo of the two of us on our rare-for-me second date. "You don't want photos of us in front of Cherry Hill?" He motioned to Bill at the ready a few feet away.

"We'll take them after you call your client back." I handed it over. "Hurry up, Mr. Future Vice President."

The second kiss was much longer.

THREE

Ty wasn't in bed when I woke up, and he didn't answer when I called his name. I glanced at the wall clock: 11:06 a.m.

That was more like it when it came to my sleep schedule. My train wasn't until 7 p.m. It left plenty of time to explore either the city or each other.

My phone wasn't on the nightstand or in the bathroom. After searching for a few minutes, I found it under the bag I'd abandoned by the door in our rush to get into bed the night before. A few texts from my mom and my latest work bestie—an eager college senior named Alyssa. I ignored them both as I grabbed a handful of Muddy Buddies from the nightstand. Breakfast of Champions.

After some creative begging on my part, Ty had finally relented last night and told me the plan for today: the tourist hot spots we'd missed the day before. I was more excited than I wanted to admit to go to the top of the Empire State Building.

The skylight clued me in that it was another beautiful day. I threw on some fresh running gear, laced up my sneakers, and went down a flight to find the office door open and my boyfriend inside.

Ty had made himself right at home, or should I say work. His laptop was open. A mishmash of numbers filled a complicated spreadsheet with more shades than a Benjamin Moore paint palette. The desk beside him was clean except for a mouse, what looked like a jump drive, and a glass of amber liquid that had to be Coke. Ty was addicted. He was in some large captain-style black chair, typing away with his back to me, when I came up from behind and put my arms around him like this was some cheesy commercial.

His fingers didn't stop moving, but he leaned back into me. "I was hoping to get this done before you woke up."

"It's fine. I'll go for a run."

He smiled, fingers still going at it. "Oh, you don't want a rematch of yesterday, huh?"

"You're the one who made breakfast."

"Yes, but I had you there when we got to the corner of our block."

"You mean before we started sprinting?"

"Touché," he said.

"I mean, if you want a rematch…"

"I would, but I have to work."

"Right." I kissed his cheek. "Be back in, like, forty-five minutes."

"I'll be done by then. Promise."

"You can make breakfast if you aren't. This time I'm thinking omelets."

"On it." But his voice was already distracted, lost deep in the spreadsheet rainbow.

Future Vice President.

The smile stayed with me down both flights of stairs and into the living room to do my usual pre-run stretch. It was still with me a few minutes later when I went outside. But then I saw the group gathered on the sidewalk next door, and my smile up and disappeared. Five people huddled this time. I recognized just one, though he'd switched his shirt from orange to yellow. The others clustered around him like he was relaying an offensive play.

He glanced in my direction, then abruptly looked away like he hadn't seen me at all. I hesitated, immediately wanting to retreat. Then realized how silly that was. What would Ty do? *WWTD?* He'd walk down the stairs, give them a grin, then start his run. But by the time I smiled, they'd all turned away.

I walked toward the sidewalk, their voices at library level but getting more clear as I got closer. The ringleader moved his hands as he spoke. "…the detective told me to call their tip line."

An older woman with her hair in a bun chimed in. "Maybe she just needed to get away…"

The man—Drew—glared at her. "She loves Puffy. She'd never up and leave him like this. Have Lori or Rod seen her? She and Lori are close."

The one in the bun glanced at me, then stepped closer to Drew. I took off on a light jog. "They're out of town at that convention he goes to, but I spoke to her before they left. Lori was just as worried as the rest of us."

Drew's voice trailed after me. "I'm gonna try her landlord again."

I followed the same path as the day before, because it didn't require me to think. The time flew by, probably because I was too busy wondering about Janelle Beckett. The neighbors had been hard at work. Pink flyers were tacked to every street sign I passed and more than one tree, Janelle Beckett smiling at me in each one.

It had to be a boyfriend. That's what the true-crime shows said, right? It was always the partner. But then I remembered what Ms. Morgane had said about Janelle being single. That made it scarier. If it wasn't a boyfriend, that meant it could be anyone and it could happen to any of us.

When I got to the next red light, I stopped abruptly instead of jogging in place like normal. I didn't start moving again until I got my Mace out of my running belt and it was securely in my right hand.

The football huddle was gone by the time I got back. It actually made me more afraid, and for once I was happy to pick up the pace until I got back to 110 Little Street, rushing inside like this was some horror movie and not the nicest house on some expensive block. Ty wasn't downstairs when I slammed the door shut. I immediately felt silly about it all. It was broad daylight. Even though I was tired, I bounded up both flights of stairs, calling out to Ty as I reached the third-floor landing, hoping all traces of ridiculous fear were gone as I spoke. "I don't smell any bacon..."

The office door was closed.

After the briefest of hesitations, I kept going to the primary suite.

*   *   *

The door stayed closed for the next two hours. Didn't even open for a bathroom break. I knew because I walked by several times, hoping it'd magically open and there he'd be. Ready to spend time with me before I had to go.

I wasted time in the living room, catching up on what had happened to Janelle Beckett. It wasn't a hard thing to do. CNN was my gateway drug. Like Ms. Morgane said, the disappearance had gone viral to the point that it had made national news. The television had been on and muted when I came downstairs. Still, I saw the headline: *New Jersey Woman Still Missing.* I fumbled around until I found the remote just in time to hear the anchor say the local police were asking the public for help. They included the number for the tip line.

I was already tumbling down the rabbit hole by the time the show cut to commercial. Information was everywhere. And like with all good stories, it was important to start at the beginning. It took a while, but I found the first post about Janelle going missing. Like Ms. Morgane said, it was on TikTok. An account named A Brush With Billie featuring a white woman as blond and pretty as Janelle. She had pink highlights. Apparently, Janelle was one of her followers, and an online friend had asked

Billie to get the word out, which she did in a stoic close-up with tears running down her cheeks that somehow didn't mess with her makeup.

"My name is Billie Regan. Normally I talk to you about makeup, but not today. One of my followers, Janelle Beckett, is missing, and we need your help to find her. Her last known location is Journal Square. That's in Jersey City, which is right across the water from Manhattan. She texted one of her dog-walking clients Monday, saying she lost her wallet and asking if they'd seen it. This was at 8:45 p.m. No one's heard from her since. A neighbor says they heard someone leaving her apartment around ten and thinks it may have been Janelle. The client even stopped by her place. No answer, and the stupid super wouldn't let him in even though he *told* him he knew Janelle."

Billie paused, eyes looking down in a way that I knew meant she was reading comments. "The police have been alerted but apparently are dragging their feet on looking for her."

Billie stopped to give the camera a look letting us know exactly how she felt about that, then continued on.

"My follower asked me to get the word out. So y'all go ahead and signal boost."

There were over 2 million views.

Billie Regan had posted regularly about Janelle in the days since, with random updates, memories, and pleas for folks to message her if they had any info. She also shared more about Janelle, echoing much of what Ms. Morgane had briefly told me. Janelle had grown up around Jersey City. Graduated college nearby at someplace called Montclair State University. She had dreams of doing Broadway but had yet to get her big break so she was still walking dogs to pay the bills.

Her parents had died in a car accident a few years back, and there was a sister in Rhode Island, but so far she hadn't done any interviews—even refusing to talk when a local news reporter came to her house, chasing her and her two kids from their car to the front door. That didn't stop them from filming her tear-streaked face through the glass. Billie found the harassment appalling. Each of her videos ended the same, with the promise that her "DMs are open."

I only stopped watching when I stumbled upon something else that grabbed my attention. The link to Janelle's Instagram—her profile pic the beautiful double-bun photo I'd seen tacked to every tree trunk in a five-block radius. There were lots of pics of dogs in parks, but the last post was of Janelle, still in space buns, pretending to eat chocolate cake. The caption read: *I want someone to look at me the same way I look at chocolate cake.*

She'd tagged a place called Bunz. I struggled to remember if I'd passed it on either of my runs or when Ty and I were heading to the PATH train. It didn't ring a bell. It had almost half a million likes, and the comment section was chock-full of theories and arguments. I wasn't the only one who thought a boyfriend may have done it. But others had their own speculations. The worst were the ones blaming her for what had happened—making Superman-sized leaps about her putting herself in danger. The top comment was someone who went by Rachhhh with even more numbers after it. *A woman goes out in the middle of the night by herself in a city to "find her wallet" and disappears. Shocker!! Ladies, we need to stop putting ourselves in these positions!!!*

It had more than 10,000 likes and 300 responses.

I felt for Janelle at that moment. We didn't know much about what had happened to her, but one thing was clear: something did happen. She was a victim at the mercy of strangers' assumptions. I knew how that felt.

I resisted the urge to respond. Instead, I just liked every comment calling Rachhhh every name in the book.

Two hours later and I was as convinced as half the internet that it had to be someone Janelle knew. A friend or an employer—maybe even someone on this block. They could've watched me as I ran by. It was enough to make me shiver. I was two degrees of separation from a missing woman and I didn't like it at all. It made me feel vulnerable in a way that I hadn't felt in over a decade. It made me want to become a couch sleuth—desperate to find some clue about what exactly had happened to her so I could feel some sense of control.

I only put my phone down when the sound of my stomach was louder than the bajillionth Janelle Beckett missing theory video I watched. It was then I realized Ty still hadn't left the office. He had to be as hungry as I was.

My knock was tentative at first. He mumbled something from the depths. I took it to mean "come in." I plastered on a smile as I opened the door—not wanting him to know I'd spent the last couple hours scaring the hell out of myself. He was right where I'd left him, still in the black office chair, his fingers across the keys the only thing moving. He didn't turn as I approached, so I spoke.

"Hey, you. I know you have to be starving. Figured I could whip up some eggs or maybe we can do something simple, like Mexican. I ran by a taqueria this morning."

He said nothing.

"Okay," I said. "No Mexican. Pizza? Chinese? Burgers? Stop me when I get to something you want. I could go on all day."

Still nothing. I leaned on the desk next to him, trying to be sexy. Instead, I knocked over the glass of Coke from the morning. It didn't look like he'd taken more than a sip. "Crap," I said and reached for it, hoping to minimize the damage.

Ty looked over like he'd been hit with a defibrillator. He immediately grabbed for the jump drive as I righted the glass, then used my T-shirt to sop up the mess, catching the stream mere centimeters before it reached a haphazard pile of paper. He didn't say anything at first. Just sighed. Way worse than yelling.

"I'm sorry," I said. "I just wanted…"

He was examining the jump drive like it owed him money. And that's when I realized.

"That's one of those crypto things, isn't it?" I didn't understand any of it. Just enough that if I'd ruined the drive, someone would lose a ton of Bitcoin. And it would be all my fault.

"It's fine," he said. "I know I've been stuck in here all day, but I only need thirty minutes. Please."

"I just wanted to know if you're hungry." I dabbed at the desk just to give myself something to do other than make eye contact.

"*Thirty. Minutes.* Breanna. Can't you just give me thirty minutes?"

I finally stopped moving, my arm frozen mid-mop. Then slowly I pulled my hand away, my T-shirt snapping back to its rightful position touching my body. I ignored the wetness when it reached my stomach, just like I tried to ignore the tears that were forming. Then I turned and left. Not because I didn't want him to see me crying. I was afraid he wouldn't care.

This was the first time Ty had so much as raised his voice to me. I'd never been good with confrontation with people I cared about. Tears always sprang as if they were a leak. I cried as much as I yelled, sometimes doing both at the same time. The more I cried over an argument, the more I cared about someone. I still remember the first time I came back from spending the night at my boyfriend's during freshman year. As soon as my best friend saw the tears, she was ready to kill. I had to tell Adore all he'd done was watch *The Walking Dead* without me.

I'd cried a lot over the past twelve years, but it hadn't been because of someone outside my family that I cared about. Sadly, this was just another indicator of how much I liked Ty. He didn't call after me, though I'd never admit I wanted him to. There was nothing but silence as I kept going until I made it down both flights of stairs and out the front door. I somehow managed to pick up my handbag on the way out.

The hotter than normal air hit me as soon as I got outside. Why had I done that? Why hadn't I just made the eggs? Why hadn't I just waited for him to come down? I stood there, questioning myself, as my middle finger and thumb rubbed my eyes to keep the tears at bay. *This is why I don't do second dates.* I stayed like that—rubbing, questioning, berating. Then I started walking.

This time I didn't notice a single pink flyer.

FOUR

Judging by the six-deep line, the taqueria was a good choice. I'd called before I'd come. Ty had a nut allergy. Even with the argument, I wanted to confirm they didn't cook anything in peanut oil. Once they confirmed it was allergy safe, they asked if I wanted to place an order for pickup. I'd said no, not in any rush to get back.

I quietly got in line, careful not to invade the personal space of the woman in the mask in front of me. I had a friend at work who had to Yelp every restaurant before she would agree to go to it and would know exactly what she wanted before she even said yes.

That wasn't me at all. Another reason I was happy with the long line: it gave me plenty of time to look at the menu plastered above the set of cash registers. I tried to focus on the options—Ty didn't eat pork, so it would have to be chicken or beef—but instead I kept replaying our last interaction and checking my cell, willing him to contact me.

Can't you just give me thirty minutes?

I was on my third replay when I heard a familiar name coming from the woman behind me. "Janelle has to be dead."

I glanced back just as her friend spoke up. "You think?"

They were both white and brunette, looking like they'd just come from Pilates. "I'd rather be dead than stuck in someone's basement. Wouldn't you?"

She had a point. I didn't say anything, just listened like they were a TikTok video. It was much easier to think about Janelle Beckett's circumstances than my own.

"I don't know," the first friend said. "I just hope they catch *whoever* did this. I was afraid to walk from my car last night."

At least I wasn't the only one scared.

The man behind them spoke up. "It has to be someone she knew. Has anyone looked into the guy who reported her missing?"

"Why would he push the police so hard if he had something to do with it?"

Another good point.

"What about one of her other clients? She walked a lot of dogs. Maybe one of them hit on her and didn't like being rejected."

I immediately flashed on the huddle of neighbors putting up the flyers. What was the name of the guy in the orange?

"You gonna go?"

I turned to see all three of them staring at me.

It was my turn to order.

* * *

I went with chicken and beef tacos. The restaurant had a lunch special. Three tacos and a drink for eight dollars. A steal. The walk back should've taken just ten minutes, but I took my time, counting the flyers as I walked by so I wouldn't check my phone for texts. This was not how I'd pictured the last day of my trip.

Ty was sitting on the porch when I finally got back. Jumping up when he saw me, he ran over to hold the gate open. He spoke as soon as I was in range. "I'm sorry."

"It's fine." Another lie. I wiped my brow.

"No, it's not. I was supposed to be wining and dining you and instead I've been working. I snapped at you for wanting to make sure I ate, for goodness' sake."

We walked up to the porch. "Is the project almost done at least?" I said.

"Deadline's Monday. It's this new client. Usually it's not such a quick turnaround and I wouldn't be working on a weekend—especially with you here. But at least it should be all taken care of tomorrow morning." He opened his arms. "You forgive me, right?"

I didn't even hesitate, just went in for the hug, letting his body envelop me.

"I'm so sorry I ruined the trip, Bree. I was gonna take you to the Empire State Building but don't think we have time if you're leaving at seven."

I took a step back. Even with the apology, I didn't want to leave things like this—didn't want to leave him. I wanted to stay. I opened my mouth to say something, then immediately closed it.

He noticed. "You're still mad."

I thought it over. *WWTD?* He'd offer to stay.

"What if I don't?" I said. When he said nothing, I pressed on. "I can stay an extra day. We both know I get up late as hell anyway. I won't even notice when you go into the office tomorrow morning and turn your project in."

He rubbed my back. "While you sleep in. I'll be done by the time you're up."

"Exactly. Then when you come home right after it's done, we can do everything we were supposed to do today."

I looked up at him in time to see the smile start to form. "So we both play hooky…"

"Correct."

I got on my tippy-toes to kiss him long and hard. And when I stepped back, he took his phone out of his pocket. "You want to message your boss first or should I?"

I thought it over. "Same time?"

Ty narrated his actions as he emailed his boss, making a point to sneak peeks at me doing the same. This was my Ty. The one I had come to visit. The tension I'd been holding in my shoulders started to loosen. "Eyes on your own paper, Tyler Franklin," I said.

"You probably never let anyone cheat off you in school," he said. "All done?"

"Yep. You do an away message?"

"On it now." He recited as he typed. " 'I'm unexpectedly out of the office with no access to email and will answer your email as soon as I return, hopefully this week.' "

I finished my own note, then hit Send. When I looked up, he was smiling at me.

"Empire State Building tomorrow?" I said.

"Empire State Building tomorrow—unless you'd like to stay in?"

"And do what exactly?"

"I can think of some things."

He laughed. I joined him. We were so loud it sounded like a truck was rumbling by.

Someone cleared their throat. We looked up. Orange-turned-Yellow finally decided to make eye contact, a handful of hot-pink flyers clutched to his chest as he glared at our happiness. The smile slid off my face as he walked by, staring us down as he did.

A woman was missing. Possibly taken right from this neighborhood. I grabbed Ty's hand. "Let's go inside."

*　*　*

Ty spent the rest of the afternoon finishing up his project. I spent the entire time downstairs on my phone. I started with Twitter, and my heart caught when I saw Janelle's name trending along with the word "Honda." I'd never clicked on anything so quick in my life. Someone had uploaded a pic of a gray Honda Civic, supposedly similar to hers, in somewhere called Hoboken, but a few more clicks let me know it was just a false alarm. She was still missing. There were no other updates.

I moved on to Instagram. There were exactly 6 likes on a pic I had uploaded from Central Park. That was good for me.

I went to Ty's page. He was more popular. Just like in real life. He'd posted only a few photographs all weekend. Another telltale sign he'd been sneak-working. The latest was just of our feet as we were enjoying Netflix. Part of me was excited to make it onto his Instagram—even if it was just my toes.

Like me, he'd chosen a selfie from the park, the location tagged in case anyone couldn't recognize it. He smiled wide, and it felt like he was looking right at me. I leaned forward to take him in without worrying about real-life him catching me ogling. I could just make out my elbow in the corner.

I hit the Heart button.

I kept scrolling until I saw the ad. That was the thing I hated about these social sites. How you could visit one site, one time, and next thing you knew, you were inundated with ads for it or something similar. The people doing the Phenomenal Woman grant had sprung for Instagram ads. *We're offering $10,000 to help you launch your business. Phenomenally. Deadline June 1.*

Instagram made interacting with their ads so easy. Just clicking on it would take me right to the website so I could *Learn More* or *Shop Now* or, in this case, apply today. And I would have—except for that damn background check.

I'd like to pretend I was happy to still be at the stationery store—that I liked dealing with entitled customers and college kids looking to supplement scholarships and student loans. I'd tried to leave once about five years ago for a job at a large athletics company. Even *got* the job—until the background check came through. Apparently, they weren't too keen to hire someone with a record—even if I'd only spent a few months in jail.

I never applied for anything else again.

Now I stared at the Phenomenal Woman post before clicking three buttons in the top corner. Then I selected Hide Ad.

"Whatcha doing?"

I jumped, then turned to see Ty standing at the bottom of the steps. I hadn't heard him emerge from his third-floor lair. The house *had* to be soundproofed.

"Didn't mean to scare you again."

I managed a smile. "It's fine. Next time wear a Jigsaw mask."

He came over and put his arms around me. "I prefer Michael Myers. You know I'm a horror purist."

"You finish your project?"

He nodded. "Just need to do the final touches tomorrow. Wanna watch a movie?"

Ty's energy was different. He was smiling more. Making eye contact. Doing all the things like the Ty I knew. It made me happy that I'd decided to stay longer. "As long as it's not *Halloween,*" I said.

We made it halfway through *Ferris Bueller's Day Off* before we changed our minds yet again. Ty wanted to break in every room in the place. We made it through two and a half floors. By eleven, we were exhausted. We played Rock, Paper, Scissors to see who got to shower first. I let him win—he always went with paper. He took his cell to the bathroom. The shower turned on immediately, then stayed on longer than normal. I checked my phone. No Janelle Beckett updates. I texted my friend to tell her I'd be out tomorrow, then texted my mom.

She'd responded almost immediately. Your boss isn't going to be happy with the last minute notice.

My boss hadn't even cared. Just told me to have a good time since I already had someone to cover for me. The lone benefit of having worked somewhere for over a decade. We went back and forth like that for a good few minutes to the point I was tired when Ty got out of the shower.

He came out in a T-shirt and shorts, cheesing it up. "I'll go in super early. Be back before you are even up. You won't even miss me."

I put my phone away. Arguing with my mother was like talking to a brick wall.

"I'll miss you less if you have an omelet waiting when I get up," I said.

"I'll throw in some French toast too."

"A feast."

"Come here, you."

And I did, snuggling into him, enjoying the scent of his soap-tinged brown skin. When I tried to pull away, he held on. "I can't be smelling that great," I said.

"Like roses."

Finally he let go, turning his body so he could fully watch me walk into the bathroom. I got inside, then glanced back, a tease of a smile at the ready. "Yes, Mr. Franklin?"

He was staring at me intently. If my smile was a tease, his was fully exposed. The expression on his face reminded me of how my dad used to look at my mom.

"God, I love—"

But then he hesitated. It sounded like he was going to say he loved me. I wasn't expecting it. Not this soon. It'd only been a few months, and though I hoped we'd get to that point, I liked that we were taking the scenic route.

He smiled at me now. "I love that you're staying."

Billie Regan sits in front of the camera. Her hair is blond with pink highlights. It's in a ponytail. Although her skin is clear, there's a bit of redness. Telltale signs of long-gone acne. She's perfectly lit, courtesy of an unseen ring light. Behind her is a gray wall where @ABrushWithBillie is spelled out in purple neon cursive lights. When she speaks, she has a hint of a Southern accent.

"Hey, Billie Bunch. I'm Billie Regan. This is my channel. Normally I do makeup, but the past few videos have been much-needed updates on Janelle Beckett, one of my followers in Jersey City who's been missing since Monday."

Behind her, a screenshot of a comment pops up from JayJay4321: *Gives a new meaning to red, white, and blue. You look great, Billie! Subscribing.*

The screen changes to another comment from JayJay4321: *Today's #MakeupMonday got me wanting to hit up my ex.*

It's quickly replaced with another comment from JayJay4321: *Cookie!! He's adorable.*

Then we're back to Billie for a moment as she speaks. "Many of you have been asking for a timeline of what's going on. I'm going to share with hopes that maybe someone saw her somewhere."

The screen flashes to an Instagram photo of Janelle Beckett kissing a doggie. "If you've been following my channel, you know that Janelle is a very popular dog walker in Jersey City. It's not a job for her. It's a seven-days-a-week passion. And we know that she did show up for work Monday morning. I've personally confirmed this with some of her clients. She had several in various areas of Jersey City—she was *that* popular—but Monday morning she was around Little Street in the Paulus Hook area."

The screen does a quick cut while Billie's background changes to another screenshot. An Instagram post of Janelle in her usual space buns pretending to eat chocolate cake.

"This is Janelle's last Instagram post. It's from Monday." Billie points to the top of the screen, where the location is listed. "Though we don't know the time she posted, we have an idea. You can see she tagged a place called Bunz—that's with a *z*. This is in Jersey City, about ten minutes from Janelle's apartment."

Another quick cut to an Instagram comment section. Billie points to one as she talks. "An employee commented on Janelle's photo that they were the one who waited on her. She was alone, friendly, and left a tip." Billie smiles at that.

"This was around one. From there, we believe Janelle hit her afternoon dog route and then went back home. If she stopped anywhere before doing so, we don't know yet. As I've previously shared, she normally shows up to my Makeup Monday Live chats, where I give both relationship and makeup advice, but that time she didn't make it. I knew something was wrong then but didn't want to say anything because she's always there. Always. She texted with one of her clients at 8:45 p.m., asking if she'd left her wallet. When the client responded she hadn't, Janelle never wrote back. Furthermore, she never showed up to work the next morning. She was supposed to be back in Paulus Hook."

Billie cuts to another Instagram account, this one of a strawberry-blond white woman. The photo is Janelle's Missing picture. Billie points to the caption, which is from Janelle's friend, sharing the latest. "This is when folks began to get concerned. One of her clients went over to Janelle's apartment to do a wellness check. As you can see from this caption, the landlord was not helpful. Even though the friend was insistent, the landlord wouldn't let him in."

The screenshot disappears and Billie is full screen again. "As I've said, no one knows where Janelle is. It's been almost a week and no one's heard from her. So if you saw Janelle at any of these locations or near these locations on Monday, please let us know. And if you've seen her since then, please DM me on Insta. Same exact handle. We need to find Janelle, so don't forget to follow me. I'll let you know as soon as I hear any updates."

FIVE

I had a shitty night. I woke up in the middle of it to a full bladder and Ty no longer next to me. The blackout curtains made it impossible to know if it was day. So I used the clock on the wall.

It was 4:34 a.m.

I'd been asleep since before midnight—with Ty right next to me, but now he was gone. He had to be in the bathroom.

But the door was open.

Maybe he'd gone downstairs for a snack.

It was fine. I'd go get him, drag him back to bed.

Before I knew it, I was through the door, and it felt like I was stepping into space. The hallway was pitch-black. I had to remind myself this wasn't some horror movie. This was an Airbnb in Jersey City. It wasn't until I got to the third-floor landing that I saw even a hint of light. He was in the kitchen. I called out. "Babe?"

He didn't answer, so I spoke again, louder this time so it carried down two flights. "Babe?" I went for the joke. "Is this about the Muddy Buddies? Because you're the one who bought them."

The light went out. I stopped short. There was the sound of steps, but he still didn't speak.

"Come back to bed. I'll make it worth it."

I passed the open bathroom door and scratched my head. That's when I realized I'd forgotten to put on my bonnet and now I was paying for it. My curls on the back of my head were flatter than a piece of paper, while the ones in the front jutted out every which way. I tried to fluff up the back and smooth down the front, but it was useless. They had a mind of their own. Usually I appreciated that. But not now, when I was trying to entice my boyfriend.

I didn't have to see myself to know that I wasn't a pretty sight. At all.

I went up instead of down, where I went hard with the curl refresher and lip gloss. Then I got in the bed. Ready.

* * *

I woke up alone and non-naked. I checked the clock: 10:08 a.m. Early for me.

I'd fallen asleep waiting for him, didn't hear when he came back up. He should've woken me. I went to get my phone to tell him just that, but it wasn't on the side table. It also wasn't on the dresser or under the bed. Had I left it in the kitchen? The morning was getting shittier and shittier.

No phone and no boyfriend—made worse because I didn't know where either was.

I was almost at the bedroom door when I located Ty—or at least remembered his approximate whereabouts. He had to work today. Promised he'd be back before I woke up.

I quickly made myself presentable—I couldn't have a repeat of how I'd looked last night. Put my hair in a head wrap and applied enough makeup to look like I didn't have any on. Luckily, I'd packed an extra outfit—if you could even call it that. Leggings and a T-shirt—Target's finest. But it clung where it needed to.

He'd said his job was close. No more than a five-minute drive. A fifteen-minute walk. And he probably assumed he had time before I was up. That he had at least a half hour to get back to serve me French toast and an omelet the size of the average male ego.

But I'd beat him to it. I didn't cook much, but I could whip up some eggs. Maybe figure out a way to repurpose the tacos we never finished last night. *Tasty* or *Bon Appétit* probably had some recipe. I'd have it ready and waiting when he got back. It might not be good, but if I looked cute enough, he probably wouldn't notice.

I was planning out what I'd say when he came back as I hit the last set of stairs down to the first floor. I felt more and more confident with each step. It was going to be a good day. An amazing one.

I was so focused on trying to manifest good vibes only, I didn't notice the shoe until I was midway down. It was mere centimeters from the bottom step. Red sole, so at first I thought it was the work of some designer. But then I realized it was blood.

SIX

Even from a flight up, the blood looked deep enough to swim in. It wasn't a pool so much as a river trailing from her head. Long thin lines jutting this way and that in the rectangular space, stopping just short of the gray wood in the living room.

Fear propelled me down the stairs, but common sense stopped me at the last step. The woman looked white, her body where the glass table used to be. She was face down among its remnants. I couldn't see anything more than strands of hair soaked wet with blood. Her hands on both sides of her head as if she'd tried—and failed—to break her fall. She wore stylish blue jeans, but her top was so soaked in red I couldn't tell the original color.

My brain finally processed what I was seeing and I instinctively retreated. Up a step. Then another and another. Staring at her all the while.

"Ty!"

I screamed it loud enough to echo throughout this cavern passing off as a house. No response. The only thing that moved, the blood seeping from the woman's head.

That's when I remembered. Ty was gone—and I was here, with the body of some woman who had to have broken in and fallen down the stairs sometime this morning while I'd been sound asleep.

What if she hadn't come alone?

Fear propelled me once again down one step, then two. My mind blank except for one thought: *Get out.*

Survival instinct propelled me down that final stretch. I didn't even look at her this time, just jumped over her body and the pool of blood that should've been inside it.

When I got outside, the street was deserted for once. *Crap.* I needed help. I immediately flashed on Ms. Morgane but didn't know which house was hers. So I just went with the one closest. I ran out the gate and right to the one next door, then up the stairs. I pushed on the doorbell, then wrenched the screen open to bang on the door.

No one answered.

"Open the door!" I yelled as loud as I could, but still no one answered.

"What's going on?"

The voice came from behind me. It was one of the women from the huddle standing on the sidewalk. The one who'd snapped at Ms. Morgane. She stared at me, annoyed, as a man walking a dog came up behind her. Orange-turned-Yellow. Today his shirt was blue. Ms. Morgane had said his name once. I struggled to remember it, happy to have something else to focus on.

I was relieved to see someone—even them. The first letter of his name was closer to the beginning of the alphabet. And it was two syllables. No, one. It was simple. I knew that. My mind went through potentials until it finally stopped at the right one.

Drew.

His name was Drew.

"Everything okay, Krista?" he said.

They kept talking while I hurried down the stairs toward them.

"I don't know. This woman"—she made it sound like the *b* word—"is banging on Lori's door."

"They're not home," Drew said.

"Which is why they didn't answer," Krista said.

Drew didn't say anything. He was too busy looking at me as I stopped a few feet from them. My fear must've shown on my face because he looked alarmed. "What's wrong?"

I shook my head. Not sure what to say. Wishing Ty was here because he would know what to do next.

Drew took me in. I, in turn, took in big gulps of air as if coming up from the world's deepest dive. The dog barked beside me. "What's wrong?" Drew said again.

I finally managed to speak. "There's a woman. A body. Inside."

It was all I could get out. So I just stood there as the gulf between us became wider than the few feet that actually separated us. My breathing sped up until it matched the rhythm of my heart.

Krista and Drew looked at each other, then at me. "Inside 110?" Drew said.

I nodded.

He looked toward 110 Little Street. I refused. Instead staring at the house across the street.

"Are you sure?" he said.

I took a step toward him. Finally looked him in the eye, my fear morphing into anger. "Of course."

Who would lie about something so horrible?

"Okay." He had the nerve to smile when he spoke.

He handed Krista the leash, then strolled to the gate of 110 nonchalantly, as if this was all some sick joke. What I did for shits and giggles. Run out of houses. Stop the first stranger I came across. Send him inside some strange house to check for nonexistent dead bodies.

As he made his way up the stairs, all I could think about was the blood. Krista didn't say anything, just silently followed Drew's progress as he opened the door, then stopped abruptly. A car plowing into a wall.

He backed up and ran down the stairs a lot quicker than he went up. But he left the door open, and the vision overtaking my head was once again a reality. The woman. The river of red. I could even make out her nails. The long juts of pale beige polish specked in what had to be blood.

He didn't say anything when he got back, just looked at Krista and nodded. Confirmation I wasn't lying. It was only then Krista gasped and stared at me. "What did you do?"

I took a step back. "She broke in."

"So you fought."

"No. I was asleep. I found her when I woke up."

I flashed again on the body. My grandmother had lived by herself for way too long, ignored all pleas to move in with my mom. The final straw was when she fell down the stairs. I had come to drop off dinner, and she had been coming to let me in. Through the window in the door, I could see her fall. Watched her tumble face down, her arms instinctively splayed out—just like that woman in the foyer. Luckily, my grandmother hadn't landed on a table.

"She fell down the stairs. Hit the table." My tone was pleading.

Krista turned to Drew as if wanting him to confirm, but he had his phone out, calling 911. Within seconds he was talking. "Yes. I'm at 110 Little Street. Paulus Hook. There's a dead woman inside."

He paused for a beat before resuming his report. "No, I didn't check her pulse, but I don't think... There's a lot of blood."

Rivers.

He listened some more. "I don't know. Let me ask." He finally acknowledged me. "What's the name?"

"Mine?"

"Hers."

My throat started to constrict, but somehow I managed to get words out. "I don't know. I came downstairs and she was there."

I sounded unsure. He heard it in my voice. I did too. But it was the truth.

"I don't know who she is. She must've broke in this morning after my boyfriend left." I finally willed myself to stop blubbering, knowing I was only making things worse. Drew didn't say anything. Just stared at me until I spoke again. "Are they coming?"

Still staring me down, he spoke into the cell. "We don't know her name."

But he sounded even less sure than I had.

After a second, he nodded. "Okay."

He hung up, then reached out his hand. It took me a second to realize it was for the leash. Krista handed it to him. "They're on their way," he said. He wasn't talking to me.

It hit me once again. *The hair. The hands. The jeans. The blood covering it all.*

I'd never seen anything like it. Even the worst fight I'd seen at the detention center was nothing like that—and that person had gotten stabbed. I lost my balance as the tears came full force. Neither Krista nor Drew tried to grab me. They were just going to let me fall, but I managed to catch myself. They watched as I wiped away tears with the back of my hand. It was okay. It was going to be okay. I was going to be okay. I just needed to talk to Ty. And to do that I needed my phone.

I didn't even think, just walked back toward the house. I had the gate open when the arm grabbed me. Drew. "What are you doing?"

The hair. The hands. The jeans. The blood covering it all.

"I need to talk to my boyfriend."

"He's inside?"

I shook my head, and Drew let out a breath. "My phone is," I said. "I need to call him."

Ty was probably still working away, oblivious to what had happened after he'd left me asleep this morning.

"It's a crime scene," Drew said. "The police will get whatever you need when they get here."

The police. Of course the police were coming. Not just an ambulance.

I didn't trust them—at least not the ones in Maryland. I highly doubted the ones in Jersey would be much better. I'd obeyed all laws since my arrest. Never went more than ten miles over the speed limit. Always used my blinker. And hadn't even thought of running a red light since that night. But still, my heart sped up every time I heard a siren or saw the strobing lights behind me. And they'd be long gone before I could breathe normally.

Drew was right in that the last thing I needed was for them to know I went back into the house.

I took a step back. He waited until I let the gate go before he crossed the street to what I now realized was his house, Krista on his heels. His was meticulous. A white stucco with shutters painted a black so shiny that it looked like they were still drying. Drew didn't go inside, though. Just went up his short walk to sit on the steps, his dog trotting along next to him like they were still on a Monday midmorning stroll. Drew hadn't invited me to come with him and I hadn't invited myself either.

I just stayed on that sidewalk outside of 110 Little Street, afraid to look back, forcing myself not to think about the body inside and failing miserably. *The hair. The hands. The jeans. The blood covering it all.*

Hoping Ty would finally show up. I would've given anything to hear his voice saying my name, feel his arms around me, letting me know everything would be okay.

But Ty never came.

Neighbors quickly started to appear, though, coming from each house as if summoned. They barely looked in my direction, much less said anything to me. They all just went over to Drew, the huddle forming once again. The only one who didn't show up was the one I'd wanted to see: Ms. Morgane. I didn't need to look at them to know what they were talking about, what they were thinking.

I didn't know how long it took the police to get there. My phone was somewhere still inside—with the blood. My mother had always told me to get a watch, not to depend on my cell for the time. I'd get one after this, though I wouldn't tell her she was right.

The neighbors didn't stop whispering until we heard the sirens. A triple shot. Even though my brain had been expecting them, my breath sped up. I had to remind myself that I could still breathe, but it took everything in me. I counted each inhale as an ambulance followed by two squad cars snaked down the street like a conga line.

In. Out. In. Out.

There was no driveway and no available street parking. So they all just double-parked in front of the row house. Side by side with their fronts to the sidewalk like some makeshift parking lot.

In. Out. In. Out.

That's when Drew finally left the huddle.

The first officer climbed out of the car, looked over at me standing in front of the house. I immediately wanted to avoid eye contact. Instead, I forced myself to look at him, only to be ignored so he could meet Drew in the middle of the street. Another cop joined them. All white. I couldn't hear them. None of them invited me into that circle either. None of them even said as much as a hello.

The other pair of cops rushed into the house, followed quickly by the EMTs. They too didn't acknowledge me, but at least they had a good reason. They thought there was a life still to be saved. I didn't say anything. They'd find out soon enough.

I turned back to watch the cops talk to Drew. I took them in. A man and a woman. Both in uniform. Each tall and good-looking enough to pose for one of those charity calendars. Drew said something. They nodded back. Friendly but all business.

He pointed at the row house and they all glanced at it—looking through me to do so. Then finally one of the cops came back outside. "Lou. Come here."

The woman ignored me as she rushed by. The man managed to squeeze in a full once-over in the second it took to pass me. Even from a distance I heard the door slam. It was just like at night, when it was pitch-black and you were scared shitless. Even the softest noise felt like it was blasting through speakers.

I turned, and sure enough, the door was finally closed. I exhaled but still saw her lying there in my mind. Drew stood a few feet away, staring at the closed door as if he could see right through it.

Before I knew it, the woman was the first back out. And this time she stopped to talk to me.

In. Out. In. Out.

Where was Ty???

"This is your place?" she said.

I wasn't under arrest. They were just asking me a question. One I could answer. I shook my head, made a point to keep my response simple. "Airbnb."

"But you were the one who found the body?"

I nodded.

"And what's your name, sweetheart?"

At least this one was pretending she was nice. "Breanna Wright."

"Spell it for me." She typed it into her phone. "Ms. Wright, you said you and the deceased had rented the place."

I shook my head too fast. It made me dizzy. "My boyfriend."

"Where is he?"

"At work. JPMorgan."

She typed that too, thumbs working fast. "So you don't know who's in there?"

I shook my head yet again. Tried to think of her as a person versus just a body on the floor.

"Or how she got inside?" she said.

"I'm assuming she broke in and fell while coming up the stairs."

"You heard her?"

"I was asleep."

"But you know she broke in?" she said. "There weren't any signs of forced entry."

I hadn't checked. Other things had been on my mind. I finally glanced at the place, saw the lock that had given me hell my first day. I turned back to the officer. "It's an Airbnb. Keyless lock. She could've known the code. She was there when I woke up."

"Did you try to revive her?"

It never even occurred to me. I just ran—only thinking of myself. "No. I got out of there. Went to get help." Not exactly true, but it sounded good. "That's when I ran into…Drew and Krista. He called you and we waited outside for you to get here."

She said nothing, just used her thumbs to note what I'd said before finally looking up. "The detectives should be here soon. We're going to need you to wait in my patrol car."

I stopped all breath. It wasn't the first time I'd heard a cop say that.

SEVEN

I t was all Adore's fault.

She was the reason I'd even gone to that party—and the reason I'd left it so quickly. We'd met in middle school when Adore got a scholarship to our private school and would travel forty-five minutes to attend class, but we really got super close when we both went to Morgan State. She was always more mature than I was, probably because she was from DC. I'd looked up to her in middle school from the moment she stood up to the class bully, and I was overjoyed to finally be her friend in college.

We were the only people we knew—and back then that was all you needed to start a friendship. Luckily, it became something more as we bonded as you can only do in college when you're experiencing so many adult firsts together.

She was the person who helped me cram for a test. The person who gave me a condom when I told her my boyfriend and I were going to finally have sex, then handed me tissues when he and I broke up. The person who encouraged me to take the LSAT when my mom made me feel like she knew I wouldn't score high enough. The one who became so close that people thought we were actually sisters—even though we were opposite in looks, personality, and focus.

It wasn't just our backgrounds—me the only child of middle-class parents, her the product of a single mother in DC. Adore was outgoing. Even then I was more quiet. I'd come to college to be a lawyer. She'd come to meet her husband.

She'd been attached at the hip to Keith since they met at the end of spring semester junior year and seemed to want to spend all summer with their tongues down each other's throats. I didn't mind much. I was too busy studying for the LSAT.

Still, I hated seeing them together. How she acted. How he acted. How they acted together. Volleying between fighting and making up like some tennis match and it was love–45.

Keith was an asshole. A cute asshole but an asshole nonetheless. A year behind us, he was the star of the football team. Not saying much considering Morgan wasn't a football powerhouse, but still. He seemed to think he was destined for the NFL. Adore did too, which was why she put up with so much of his mess. Just in case.

So I wasn't surprised they'd been fighting when I got to the party. I was more than happy to leave early—the LSAT was just a week away and I was able to take it only three times. I'd barely been there an hour when she demanded we go, dragging me to my car. We'd only driven to the corner before Keith caught up and begged her to stay. It didn't take much convincing—even though I told her not to fall for it. She was out of the car so quick, she left the bag of fries she'd brought with her.

It was all Adore's fault.

She was the reason I ran that light—too busy thinking about if she'd call again in a few minutes, begging me to turn back around. I didn't even see the police car until the lights were flashing behind me. The cop was young and white, wearing his need to be in charge alongside the badge that said DOMINGO. And I'll admit, I wasn't very friendly at first—I didn't do much to hide my annoyance. I didn't follow any of the rules my mother had told me about being stopped by the police. I had an attitude. They called it "resisting arrest."

But that didn't give Domingo the right to claim he smelled marijuana. Or to "ask" that I get out of the car. And it sure didn't give him the right to plant weed in my back seat. I'll never forget when I saw it in his hand. The Halloween baggie with an orange pumpkin on it that they sold at Target.

I was arrested and convicted of possession. The cops didn't believe me that it wasn't mine. My mother and lawyer didn't as well—all because my mother had found weed in my room when I came home after freshman year. I shouldn't have listened when they said I should cop a plea, but they were persistent. I fought them for the entire year it took for my trial date to come. Finally, exhausted, I gave in right before the trial was supposed to start and took the deal.

I never got my degree. I was in jail when my classmates were at graduation. Due to a simple traffic stop and a crooked cop, I lost everything—from my friends to my scholarship to my will to fight. I was left wearing my conviction like a scarlet letter.

And now, I wasn't supposed to be here. Not again.

Ty knew none of this—he and I had made a pledge to keep "the past in the past." His idea. I'd readily agreed.

Another reason I didn't want him to meet my mom. She'd be sure to mention it.

Thoughts bounced around my brain like a game of pinball and they all had one thing in common: fear.

Ty had to be on his way back by now. I turned to the corner to look for him. Instead, I saw a news van pull up, stopped by a police car blocking the entrance to the street. I had no clue who had called them, but it didn't matter. What did was that the camera was turned on me as soon as they could get it ready. The fear ratcheted up.

I turned to the officer next to me, the one who had claimed the detectives were on their way. "Is there somewhere else I could wait?"

There was no way I was going back into a cop car. I'd wait in the hot sun even if it meant becoming a spectacle.

"We can use my place." I had already forgotten about Drew when he spoke up.

It was also when I realized the cops had gotten rid of all of the other neighbors too—though there was no doubt they were watching from their windows like this was a new show on Netflix.

"That would be great." I was already walking before I finished my sentence, not wanting to give the patrolwoman a chance to think better of it.

Drew also had an open floor plan. Whereas 110 was all flip-or-flop grays, Drew was all beiges and woods. And I had to glance twice to realize the miniature couch in the middle of the room was for his dog.

The police took us both to the second floor and placed us in different rooms. I got what looked like Drew's office. More dark woods and thick furniture. And yet another opulent mini couch. I took a seat on the weathered leather adult-sized one next to it. It was clear Drew spent more on dog furniture than his own. One of the patrol guys kept me "company," his eyes glued to his phone. I recognized the Twitter app even from my spot across the room.

I didn't say anything. Just forced myself to breathe. I'd tell them what had happened, and if I wasn't comfortable, this time I'd ask to speak to a lawyer right away. Not that I had one, but it didn't matter. Ty would get me one. He wasn't like Adore, someone who didn't bother to show up when I needed them. And he wasn't like my mother, whose version of help was forcing me to do something I shouldn't have.

It took the detectives an hour to get to me. This pair was mixed—in gender and race. A Black man named Randle and a white woman named Calloway. She was the one with the smile. She had a large designer bag in her right hand and a water bottle in her left.

Her partner stood back, letting her take the lead, like we were at some high school party. It just made me want to hug the wall as she glided over. I knew the question she wanted to ask me wasn't if I wanted to dance.

I wiped the sweat from my palms onto my leggings. I was still dressed as a runner and I was sweating like one too.

I had to remind myself I wasn't under arrest. No one had read me any rights. I was just a witness.

Of course that didn't mean I trusted these two.

She sat down next to me on the brown leather couch. It felt sticky even with the central air, like I'd have to peel myself off it like I had at my grandma's house as a kid, where everything was covered in plastic.

Calloway took a minute to get settled, then smiled. I returned it, but mine didn't come anywhere near my own pupils.

This wasn't before. She wasn't Domingo. I was going to be nice this time. Not cop an attitude. Do what my parents had taught me about acting right.

We both kept smiling as she got herself settled. Water bottle still in hand. Bag on the floor in front of her. My mouth was too dry to tell her it was bad luck. That she'd never have any money. My lips ached by the time she stopped moving, but still I smiled. Why were the fake ones always so much harder to maintain?

"Hi, Breanna. I'm Detective Mallory Calloway. That's my partner. Detective Tim Randle. Wasn't sure if you drank coffee, but everyone drinks water, right?"

She held up the bottle. Though I was thirsty, I didn't grab it. Didn't want her to see my shaking hands. "I'm okay," I said.

She looked like she didn't believe me but set it on the table in front of the couch anyway.

"Is my boyfriend here yet?" I said.

"Not that I know of. He's the one who rented the house?" She glanced back at her partner. "Tyler Franklin?"

So that was the delay. They had been doing research. "Ty went to work this morning," I said. "I haven't spoken to him, though I'm sure he's worried about me."

"We can reach him for you. Let him know what happened. What's his cell phone number?"

I wished I knew, but this was the twenty-first century and I had been raised with the entire world a push of a button away. Ty had been number one in my favorites for a month now. If I wanted to talk to him, all I had to do was press his name.

"I don't have it memorized," I said. "But you could try his office. It's the JPMorgan office in Jersey City."

Behind her, Randle spoke, his voice surprisingly high for how big he was. "I'll call him right now. Anything you want us to tell him?"

"Just that I'm okay."

When he left, Calloway placed her phone on the table. I glanced down to see it open to some app, the same one the patrolwoman had used. Calloway was looking at me when I glanced up.

"It's some fancy new technology. Lets you take notes on your phone." She wiggled the French manicure that jutted a couple of centimeters above each finger. "You can tell it wasn't a woman's idea."

She waited for me to laugh, but I didn't give her one so she kept on.

"I just had a few questions for you, then hopefully we can get you on your way."

I nodded like I believed her. "You ID the woman yet?"

"Not yet. Unfortunately, the body is in pretty bad shape."

I was quite aware. The image kept invading my thoughts. "She must've been almost to the second floor when she fell," I said.

Calloway didn't respond. Just stared at me a beat too long before finally speaking. "You told the patrolwoman you didn't know her."

I shook my head, swallowed back going on about her breaking in.

"And you didn't see her?" she said. "She didn't stop by before this morning?"

I shook my head.

"When did you check in?"

"Friday night."

"Was Ty with you?"

I didn't like her using his nickname. I shook my head. "He's been up here all week."

"At the Airbnb?"

I shook again. "He came up early for work. Was staying at a hotel closer to work until I got here. He checked into the Airbnb Friday morning."

"What about the next day?"

"I didn't see her, but I wasn't exactly looking for someone casing the place."

"I meant what did you do? You're obviously from out of town. This your first time in the tristate area?"

Oh. "Went to New York."

"PATH or ferry?"

"PATH."

"I'm a bridge and ferry girl myself. I hate going underground. As a kid, I saw this movie with Sylvester Stallone. Guy who played Rocky. They're trapped in a tunnel and water's seeping in. I mean, Sly saves the day and all, but still. It was touch and go for a minute. I have avoided tunnels ever since. But we're all scared of something, right? What about you?"

Just one thing. Cops. I didn't say that, though, or anything, not wanting to prolong the small-talk phase like this was some date. I already knew I never wanted to see her again.

There was a knock. Detective Randle was back. He took a step inside, then stopped as if he'd hit some invisible force field. It was a good thing Calloway was already on her way to meet him. Their conversation was short and too soft for me to make out what they said.

After a minute, Randle left again, and Calloway was back, sitting down.

"You reach Ty?" I said. Anxious.

"Not yet. You go into the city yesterday too?"

"We just hung out in the house." But I was distracted when I said it. *Where can he be?*

"This must be a new relationship. I've been married fifteen years. To me a vacation is *not* spending time with my husband. He'd say the same. Something for you both to look forward to."

She casually grabbed her phone with both hands, manicured thumbs ready for action. Finally done with trying to butter me up. I braced myself, but my body still felt like jelly.

"How'd you sleep last night?" she said.

"Fine." I couldn't remember if it was even true, but it sounded good.

"Must've been a nice bed. I need a new mattress. What time you go to bed?"

I racked my brain, trying to remember. But suddenly the last twelve hours were a blur. "Midnight. Maybe a little before."

"So you were down for the count until..."

"Ten-ish."

"Wow. Must be nice."

It was, when you didn't find a dead body when you woke up. I flashed on the woman again in bits and pieces. I didn't realize Calloway was still playing good cop until she gently placed her hand on mine. I jumped at the sudden human contact.

"You okay?" she said.

I slid my hand away. "Yep. What did you say?"

"I asked if you normally sleep that late?"

I shrugged. "I work a two-to-nine shift."

"Got it. So you wake up at ten *as usual*." She smiled. "Then do your normal routine. Brush your teeth. Shower. Do your hair." She took in my yoga pants. "Get ready to exercise?"

"I went to find Ty. Like I said, he had to work this morning.

Promised he'd be back by the time I woke up. I went downstairs and that's when I...found her."

The hair. The hands. The jeans. The blood covering it all.

"Any idea how long she'd been there?" I said.

"We don't know, but early thoughts are she's been dead a ballpark of eight hours at this point. Give or take."

Drew had a clock on one wall. I glanced at it. Eight hours would be around 4 a.m., but that didn't make sense. Ty was an early bird, but even he wouldn't have gone to work at that time. He would have found her when he woke up. But he hadn't.

Calloway read my mind too, because she spoke again. "We called JPMorgan. Your boyfriend didn't go into the office today."

And that's when the room lost all its air. I struggled to breathe as Calloway stared me down.

"Any idea where he might be?"

No. Ty should've been at work, and that woman should not have been in the foyer.

Calloway kept on. "You spent every moment together until this morning, when you woke up to find him gone and a body downstairs. That's what you said, correct?"

I said nothing, but my brain was busy hurling out questions. Something would have to be very wrong for Ty not to go in. For him not to be outside right now, demanding to be let into Drew's house. *What if something happened to him?*

"And you didn't see the woman at all before this morning, when she magically appeared in your Airbnb. Dead. While you were upstairs and Ty was *not* at work." This time Calloway didn't wait for me to purposely ignore her. "Let's try it a different way. You didn't see *any* blond women the past couple of days?"

Of course I had. Blond women were everywhere. I didn't say that, though, too focused on something else. My heart sped up. *What if he had stumbled on the woman when she was breaking in?*

"You've been here for two whole days and never seen her before? Not anywhere?" She paused then, long enough for me to finally force myself to inhale. "Not even in a photo?"

And then it felt like my heart stopped. *What if she had hurt him?* It was a huge house, and I hadn't checked everywhere. He could be—

I finally spoke. "Was anyone else in the house?" The words came fast, following one another so quickly that it sounded like I'd created a new language.

Calloway was midsentence. She stopped.

I tried to speak English again. Slower this time so she could comprehend. "Was anyone else there?"

"No. Just the woman," she finally said. My heart started again as she kept on. "The one you never saw before. Not anywhere. Not even in a photo?"

"I never saw her. I don't know how she got inside. When she got inside. Like I said, I was sleeping when she fell. She must have been heading upstairs."

Calloway pushed the button on her cell. It went black. No more notes. She spoke as she put the phone back into her designer bag. Her voice was soft. "She was face down."

It took me a minute to get what she meant. The woman should've been on her back. And yet… "Maybe she realized I was home. Came back downstairs."

"Or maybe she didn't fall."

"You think someone pushed her?" I said.

And that's when I caught sight of what else was in her bag, just a quick flash of pink before she zipped it up. It didn't matter, though. I knew exactly what it was. Because, like blond women, I had in fact seen it everywhere—including on the trees smack-dab outside where I was sitting.

Janelle Beckett had finally been found.

EIGHT

As Calloway picked her bag up, my eyes followed as if Superman had loaned me his X-ray vision. They stayed there as she spoke. "I'm gonna grab a coffee. Want anything?"

But she didn't wait for an answer. Just left. Randle stayed put at the door, like some bouncer—one that wasn't letting me out instead of in.

Like most of the internet, I'd spent the last day worried about Janelle Beckett. Damn near obsessed about what had happened to her. And there was some part of me that still hoped for a happy ending. I thought of her face—the one in the pics. Not the one on the floor of 110 Little Street. And tried to comprehend how, just how, she'd gotten there.

She had to have known it was an Airbnb. She had walked the dogs of almost everyone on the block. Had she entered of her own accord? Had she been running from a house nearby? Or worse, maybe she had been dragged in there. Because someone else had known it was an Airbnb too.

I pictured a scared Janelle being pushed in. I pictured her fighting back. Her falling down the stairs. Or even more horrible, being thrown. Her head banging on the glass table, causing it to shatter.

I suddenly remembered that I'd gotten up in the middle of the night. That Ty wasn't in bed when I had.

I imagined Ty hearing something. Maybe he had still been in bed beside me? Or maybe he'd snuck down to the office to do some work. He'd have gone downstairs to check. To protect me, only to find poor Janelle dead and whoever did it looking up at him.

I shut my brain off before I could imagine what happened next. I felt nauseated even though I hadn't eaten a thing.

I needed to tell Calloway. But when I got up, Randle immediately stood at attention, hand moving closer to the gun hanging on his hip. I instinctively put my hands up, suddenly nauseated for a different reason.

I didn't move, just thought of how quickly he'd reacted, how he'd reached for his firearm. There was no way I was telling them Ty wasn't there when I woke up in the middle of the night. Not when they clearly were suspicious of him—of *us*.

Randle saw me as a threat. I was alone in a room with a cop and no one knew where I was. Even who I was.

I was hundreds of miles from home, across the street from a crime scene that still had my phone, wallet, and ID. The only person I knew in a three-state radius wasn't at work—and I couldn't even remember his damn phone number to make sure he was okay.

"Am I under arrest?" I said.

Randle shook his head. "No. We'd have to read you your rights, but you already know that, don't you, Ms. Wright?"

Guess I was wrong about no one knowing who I was. At least now I knew why he was so quick on the draw. He'd been busy typing my name in some database while Calloway was pretending to be interested in my vacation itinerary. There was only one conviction on there. One mug shot. But that was enough. It was one more than I'd ever wanted.

I glared at him as he smiled. All innocent. "This shouldn't take long. We just need your help."

I bet.

I finally sat back down.

There was a lot I remembered about my arrest—usually at the most inopportune times too. I'd be at the grocery store and think of how Domingo had made the cuffs so tight I lost circulation. Or be in an elevator and remember how the officer searching me at the station had worn the same perfume as my grandmother. I couldn't share my Social Security number without thinking about how I had blanked on the first three digits when they demanded my personal information.

But most of all, I remembered the waiting. It was like time stood still from the moment Domingo dragged me into the police station—and it wasn't just because they took my phone and my belongings. When I complained—loudly—Domingo made a joke about me having to cancel my nail appointment.

I didn't laugh. Just spit.

Now I spent the time in silence, trying not to replay my version of what had happened last night. Instead trying to figure out some other scenario where Ty was okay. Maybe he had been too late to save Janelle but had still fought the person off? Chased them out of the house? But then why hadn't he come back to make sure I was okay?

Randle and I stayed frozen in place like we were waiting for a friend to *take the picture, already.* Finally there was a knock. Randle disappeared into the hall but was back within a few minutes. This time he walked over to me, hovering until I finally looked up at him. "Your lawyer's here."

I didn't have representation. Didn't know I needed it until a couple of hours prior. There was only one explanation.

Ty.

I felt the stress leave my body like it had somewhere to be.

He's okay. He'd sent someone to take care of me. To get me and bring me to him so we could figure out exactly what the hell was going on. Together.

When the next knock came, I was ready for it. The woman who came in was Black, artfully put together like she was filming a reality show in Atlanta. Light-skinned and tall, wearing a black suit that did little to hide her curves. It was clear that was how she wanted it. She wore a lot of makeup but at least tried to make it look subtle. The exception being her red lips.

My smile up and left, but I didn't say anything. Just watched as Randle discreetly gave her a once-over, then offered his hand. "Detective Tim Randle."

She ignored it, walking past him as she spoke. "A. Kristine McKinley."

She didn't look at him either, too busy giving me a once-over of my own. Up and down and up again. We just took each other in.

"You okay?" she finally said.

I nodded.

"I tried calling you."

"My phone's still in the house. They won't give it to me."

And that's when she finally turned to Randle. "You're withholding my client's belongings?"

"It's still an active crime scene," Randle said.

"My client's phone was found next to the deceased?"

"I think I may have left it in the kitchen," I said.

She was still looking at him. "Is that where her phone is? In the kitchen?"

He nodded. I spoke up again, channeling my anger, letting it finally bubble up to the surface. "Everything else is in the bedroom. All the way on the fourth floor."

"We'll get Ms. Wright's things back to her as soon as we can," Randle said.

She didn't say anything. "Let's go, Breanna."

I got up.

"We have more questions for her," he said.

"She'll answer them when we come pick up her stuff. *Tomorrow.*"

She didn't look back when she walked through the open door, just assumed I'd follow and Randle would stay put. I started after her, but Randle's hand stopped me. He held two business cards. "Ms. Wright. Please let us know when you hear from Mr. Franklin."

I went to take them, but the lawyer intercepted. Didn't even look at either card as she put them in her bag. It was an Hermès. The same one I'd had on my vision board in college.

We went down the stairs, me staring at her red soles as she walked in front of me in my pink-soled ASICS. The suit didn't have any telltale designer signs, but I was sure it was from a fancy label just like the shoes and bag. My only critique would be the piles of makeup—but even that was probably a designer brand.

I expected her to walk straight to the front door, but she went into the kitchen. No one was there to stop us. We walked to the back door, then out into a small backyard the same size as the one behind the Airbnb.

She kept going down the stairs and onto the lawn, her heels knowing better than to sink into the grass. The backyard was gated, but there was a door that led to an alley. A shiny Tesla sat parked, not a speck of dust on it despite its location. She went straight to the driver's side. The door beeped as it unlocked. She paused when she saw me standing at the gate. "Get in," she said.

I took her in again. The hair. The suit. The bag. Thought of the way she had introduced herself. She was everything College Me had wanted to be. Owned everything I'd wanted to have.

I shook my head.

"Fuck you, Adore."

Billie Regan sits in front of the camera. Her makeup looks streaked, and wisps of hair are coming out of her ponytail. Her face is almost the same pale pink as her hair. Tears rim her blue eyes.

"Sorry, y'all, but I wanted to confirm everything before I posted. A follower in Jersey City DMed me about an hour ago to tell me that police are gathered at a house on Little Street in the Paulus Hook section of Jersey City."

She uses her left hand to put her pink hair behind her ear, but it just falls back in her eyes.

"There are reports that a woman's body has been found inside. My follower says the woman's appearance is consistent with Janelle's."

She pushes a wisp of hair out of her eyes again. They're watery.

"That same follower lives in the area. They were able to stop by the crime scene. They sent this photo."

It pops up behind her as a shrinking Billie moves to the right side of the frame. A small section of yellow crime-scene tape is large at the bottom of the screen. Farther back—smaller—are a couple of police cars. A few men and women in uniforms mill about.

"Obviously this just happened. Nothing's been confirmed through DNA or even an ID. But as much as it hurts me to say this, it does sound like our Janelle. I don't know how she got inside or how long she was there. And I don't want to speculate. Not right now."

Billie pauses before continuing. "What I can tell you is about the house. I know you're wondering who it belongs to. According to my follower, it's an Airbnb. They even sent me the listing! I'll add it to the comments, but here's a look inside."

The screenshot behind her changes to an Airbnb listing page. After a few seconds, Billie changes the screenshot to a photo of a dark gray living room with two couches and a massive gray rug covering hardwood floors.

"Of course we don't know who's renting the place now, but they have someone in custody. We don't know who. There was someone staying there, though. I'll share an update as soon as I know more information. If you know anything about who rented the house, please, please, please let me know. My Instagram DMs are open."

Billie pauses again. Struggles to get the next words out. "Y'all, I really hope this isn't our Janelle, but it's hard to be hopeful." She then looks directly into the camera. Resolute. "And if that is our Janelle in there, whoever did that to her: Please don't think you'll get away with this. She was someone's daughter. Someone's sister. Someone's friend. We will make sure there's justice for Janelle."

NINE

The last time I'd spoken with Adore Smith—now apparently A. Kristine McKinley—also had involved cops.

Domingo had done everything by the book—technically. Lots of pleases and thank-yous, but each word had dripped with condescension. Constantly asking if I was okay, then ignoring me when I said I wasn't. I'd been loud, angry, and belligerent by the time he'd dragged me in. Since he was too smart to physically harm me, he'd taken a perverse pleasure in putting me in time-out.

I stayed in the corner of that cell in central booking for what felt like forever. There was no clock. The only indication, the sunrise, not that I could see anything through the sliver of a window. It was only after they finally came to get me for my phone call that I realized it had been close to six hours. When I finally got my chance, I had two choices: Adore or my mother.

It was the easiest decision of my life.

"This is Adore," she'd said, loud enough to be heard over the bass line of the song she had playing. I recognized it immediately. Rihanna.

"It's me."

"Bree! I've been texting you all morning. Thought maybe you were mad at me. Where have you been?"

"Jail."

"What?" There was some mumbling on her end. She had to be talking to Keith because a few seconds later Rihanna immediately shut up and it was quiet. "What are you doing in jail?"

I flashed on Domingo's hands on my leg. He'd said he was searching for a weapon.

"I was leaving the party. Tired as hell. I must've run a red light because this asshole cop stopped me."

"Okay... You have some unpaid ticket you didn't know about?"

I wished it was that easy. "No," I said, then spoke loud enough for every cop around to hear me. "He said I had fucking drugs."

"You brought weed to the party?"

"Of course not. You know I've barely even drank since I started studying."

"True. Despite my best efforts." She was quiet for a moment, contemplating. "There was no way you would have any drugs on you."

"I know. But he said he 'smelled something.' Asked me if he could search the car and my dumb ass said yes."

Some lawyer I'd be.

"So then where did the drugs come from?"

"Him," I said, then louder. "The drugs came from him. Officer Domingo searched my car, then came back with a bag of weed."

"That's bullshit," Adore said. "That cop had to have put it there."

"And I'm just staring at him as he holds up this orange baggie with a pumpkin on it, of all things, trying to say he found it in my car."

Adore didn't say anything at first, obviously as shocked as I was. "That's... ridiculous."

"What am I gonna do?"

And that's when I finally started to cry. It sounded like distant thunder rolling in, soft at first before building up momentum. I wiped the snot threatening to drop from my nose and turned away from the waiting cop, who was ignoring me anyway. When I was finally able to calm myself down, I tried it again. "What am I gonna do?"

But I said it too softly because Adore didn't answer me.

I tried a third time. "What am I gonna do?"

Finally, she spoke. "This is gonna be fine, but you need a good lawyer."

As much as I wanted to be one, I didn't actually know any. I doubted Adore did either.

When I didn't respond, Adore spoke again. "Did you talk to your mother?"

"No. And I don't want to. You know she thinks I'm a full-on drug addict since she found that one bag of weed. You gotta get me out of here."

"Okay," she said. "There's that Legal Services office on campus. I'll go there and then I'll come get you."

The relief came so hard I had to sit down. "Thank you."

"I'll be there as soon as I can," she said.

Twelve years later and she still hadn't made it.

Instead, my mom showed up after two hours dressed to impress. She was in her fur and perfect makeup, eyes boring into me. I made the mistake of feeling relieved to see her, but then she spoke.

"What did you do, Breanna?"

She didn't bother to listen to my answer. Still hadn't heard it, twelve years later.

I was sure she'd thought she was doing the right thing by coming down. Bringing the lawyer. One who also barely listened to a word I said.

I'd never forget the way my mother acted, like she was disappointed but not surprised. Like I was no longer her child but a statistic. And even worse, a stereotype. She wanted me to take the plea. Do the three months. Move on with my life. She didn't care when I shared a statistic of my own. That Black people in the US were seven times more likely than white people to be wrongfully convicted.

At first I was determined. Went back to school fall semester for my senior year. It was a disaster. My grades were so bad I lost my scholarship. Everyone knew what had happened, thanks to both the newspaper and the grapevine. They saw me as a stereotype too. I didn't return spring semester. I just gave in, began to feel like a stereotype myself.

Like it wasn't already hard enough to be a Black woman in America—without a drug conviction. And it was difficult to say I didn't do it when there was proof I accepted a plea. Even if I hadn't taken the deal right away. Giving in to my lawyer and my mother had been a mistake. I never forgave myself for not fighting. And I'd vowed to never let it happen again.

Adore was one of the many people who hadn't kept in touch. I guess having a jailbird as a best friend hadn't matched her aspirations to be America's next trophy wife. She hadn't called me and I hadn't called her either. Too mad that she'd never come like she'd said she would. I didn't know she'd left Baltimore or even the DMV area. Didn't know where she lived now. Jersey was small, and Manhattan was just across the river. She could've come from anywhere.

It'd been so long ago, I wasn't even mad anymore. There was the occasional good memory when one of the girls at work talked about a good party or a bad date. Followed by a quick sense of sadness more than anything else.

So I was surprised at how angry I'd felt when I first saw Adore's face, recognized it under the layers of straight Brazilian virgin hair extensions and equally expensive makeup.

"Good to see you still have the same favorite word." Adore even smiled when she said it.

I kept it all business. I had more important things to worry about than Adore's sudden presence. And she'd gotten me away from the police.

"Have you heard anything about the cops finding another body anywhere in the area?" I said.

"No," she said. "Why?"

"My boyfriend's missing."

She took this in but said nothing. Just opened the car door.

If Ty was alive—and he had to be alive, he *had* to be—he would be as worried about me as I was about him. Since Adore had found me, the story was obviously already on the news.

WWTD?

He'd thank her and try to reach me. I started walking. "I appreciate you getting me out of there."

She called out. "Bree, where are you going?"

To look for Ty. Just like he had to be looking for me.

The alley was narrow, nothing more than gravel and city-issued trash cans. There were two exits, but Adore's car blocked the one to my left. So I went right.

I was at the cross street before I knew it. I looked left, then right, and that's when I saw the crowd. There were enough people to fill half a high school auditorium. The police had put up crime-scene tape and barriers that people pushed up on like they were front stage at Coachella. All of them white. A few had cameras up, filming. Receipts to share with friends and post online that they'd been *this close* to an accident.

No.

A murder.

I hadn't thought this through.

Luckily, none of them looked in my direction, still focused on the cordoned-off street.

"Breanna." Adore came up from behind. "You can't stay here."

She was right. I felt exposed, but I couldn't go back to the house. And it wasn't like I could just stand in the alley hoping Ty would show up. "I'll go to his job," I finally said. If nothing else, I'd leave a note.

"Why don't you just call?"

"It's not his main office. No direct line." I knew from experience.

"I meant his cell," she said.

"I don't have his number memorized." I'd said it softly. Embarrassed, I waited for the sarcastic comment, like we were still in college.

But Adore surprised me. "I don't think I ever had my husband's number memorized—his cell or his practice—and we were married five years." She sighed. "At least let me drop you off."

"Fine," I said. I had no clue where Ty's Jersey office was and didn't even have my phone to get an Uber.

I followed her back to the car.

I took a quick inventory as soon as I sat down. White leather seats. An iPad-sized tablet lodged next to a sleek steering wheel. Not a single piece of trash. It was as if she'd come straight from the dealer.

Adore threw me a tight smile as she pulled away. The inside was as quiet as a library. We turned left, slowly making our way through the crowd of people, everyone still focused on the crime scene.

I stared straight ahead, afraid that even the slightest movement would get their attention.

"You hungry?" Adore said.

Starving. "No."

Out the corner of my eye, she motioned to her cell in the cup holder between us. "You need to call your mother?"

"You still have her in your contacts?"

There was a pause before she spoke and I hoped she knew exactly what I was referring to. She opened her mouth, but nothing came out. Then she smiled yet again. "I do, actually. It helps to never delete anyone. Even my ex-husband."

I grabbed her phone. "Thanks," I said, trying my best to sound sincere but also not caring that I had failed. I couldn't deal with my mother. Not this time. She'd find a way to blame me for what had happened. The number I dialed was my own. At least I knew *that* one by heart. It rang and my breath immediately synced with it. *In. Out. In. Out. In. Out.*

I held the last one in as the automated voice kicked in. I hadn't bothered to leave my own outgoing message. And I barely checked any messages folks left me, figuring if it was important they'd text. There were two options: hit pound or star. I went with star and lucked out. A voice prompted me for my password. I plugged in the one I always used, then waited.

One new message.

Thank you, Jesus. Joseph and Mary too.

I couldn't hit the button fast enough, holding my breath the entire time. But then the voice came through.

"Breanna, it's your mother. You haven't answered any of my text messages."

I hung up. Said nothing as I put the phone back where I'd found it. We were quiet for a few lights, then Adore spoke. "The police think the body may be that missing woman. Janelle Beckett. I have a friend on the force, but he's too afraid to say much. Apparently, her face is in bad enough shape to make a visual ID hard."

Adore's source was wrong. All of her was in bad shape.

The hair. The hands. The jeans. The blood covering it all.

Now that I knew who all those images belonged to, it somehow made it worse. Even in the pink Missing flyers, Janelle still looked so *alive.*

"You have to know how this looks, Bree."

I did. A dead white woman. A missing Black man. They'd say he did it. That he was on the run. "Ty wasn't involved in this."

"Then he needs to explain that. Him leaving—with you in the house at that—doesn't look good."

I took in a breath, didn't bother to hide my sigh before turning to stare at her long white nails gripping the steering wheel. They were sharp enough to be talons. Fitting for her.

"It's an Airbnb. What about the owner?"

"A corporation."

The Tesla stopped at a light.

"We were supposed to be there," I said. "She wasn't. Yes, she's a victim, but we are too. I don't know why she was there, but she wasn't alone. That's who they need to look for. Whoever brought her there. Did that to her. And instead of treating my boyfriend like a suspect they need to be treating him like the witness he probably is. Once I find him, then we can figure it all out."

"I wouldn't suggest it."

"Right. I forgot. You don't care if someone is actually guilty, as long as the police think so."

And that ended the conversation. We hit another red light. I needed to get out of the car—away from her. "You can drop me off here," I said.

"I told you'd I'd take you to his job."

"I can walk."

"Fine, and then what if he's not there?"

I didn't tell her the police already had told me he wasn't.

Adore kept on. "You're just going to camp out in the lobby?"

I glanced around. We were next to a hotel. At least twelve floors coated in mirrored glass. "I'll get a hotel room."

"And pay for it how?"

For a second, I thought she knew all my credit cards were maxed out and I was making two hundred dollars stretch until payday. Stationery store manager wasn't exactly a top-ten-earning profession. But that was ridiculous.

"All your stuff is still in that house," she said.

"I'll be fine." I just needed to get to his job.

"Right." She drew out the word like she used to in college when we both knew I was being stubborn. "How about we do this? You go to his job. I'll go into the hotel. Get you a room for a couple of nights. If you don't use it, that's fine. But it'll be there if you need it."

"Cool," I said, but it was more just to get her off my back. I'd find Ty tonight. We'd stay somewhere *together*.

"You sure you don't want me to drop you off?"

"I'll walk." Even if it was to the end of the world.

"Great," she said.

"Great," I said.

She reached over to hand me something. "In case you need anything."

Her business card. The back was rose gold—my favorite color—with some generic legalese-looking graphic. She hadn't been lying to the cops. She was a lawyer. *A. Kristine McKinley, Esq.* I wanted to rip it into a million pieces. She noticed me noticing the name. "I told you I was divorced."

"Your husband give you the Kristine too?"

"That's my middle name."

I remembered. There was a pause as I twirled the cardstock between my fingers. It felt good. Smooth. Expensive. I continued to finger it as I finally flipped it over. The reverse side was white but with rose-gold lettering. Some foil print that I had to admit looked nice. Nicer than mine, and I worked at a stationery store.

I opened the car door to get out. Her voice followed me. "Bree, good luck."

I didn't say thanks, just stuck the card into the tiny pocket of my leggings as I walked down the sidewalk and stopped the first stranger I saw, my smile as bright and unthreatening as I could make it. I would tap-dance right then and there if I needed to. Adore and I used to call it Perky Black Girl. "Excuse me. You know where the JPMorgan building is?"

* * *

He sent me the scenic route, assuming I wanted skyline *views* when there was just one building I gave a crap about. I could make it out in the distance. Without a watch, I had no clue how long it took me to get there. It felt like I made good time, weaving past bicyclists and runners and awed tourists taking pics. When I finally got to it, the building loomed large—sleek and silver and shaped like a bullet.

And for a moment I thought of how Ty and I were supposed to see the Empire State Building today. Then I went inside.

The lobby was vast. Shiny woods and shinier floors. The elevator bank was dead center, protected by turnstiles and two old men who looked like they were using this job to supplement their retirement. There was a steady stream of people going in and out. I forgot what I was wearing until the man in the Security suite reminded me with his glance. I smiled anyway. *Perky Black Girl.* He was white and smelled like hard work and good body wash. Stray salt-and-pepper beard hair escaped from various parts of his blue surgical mask. The name tag said JERRY. No last name provided.

I was going to ask for a pen and paper, but seeing all these people gave me hope that Ty was among them. Maybe no one had seen him come in? It was a long shot, but still. "Hi, Jerry. I'm here to see Tyler Franklin at JPMorgan."

His eyes creased to indicate a smile as he picked up the phone to call the office above. "ID, please."

"Would you believe I forgot it, Jerry?"

He nodded. "That's too bad. Unfortunately, I need it for you to go up."

"Oh," I said. "I don't need to go up. I'm not exactly dressed for it. Ty's my boyfriend. I wanted to surprise him. Please tell them Breanna's here. Breanna Wright. Ask him to come down."

He hesitated, then started to dial. I nodded encouragingly as he waited for someone to pick up. "Yes, hi, I have a guest here to see Tyler Franklin. Breanna Wright."

"His *girlfriend*," I said it with emphasis.

"His girlfriend."

Good.

He listened. I waited. When he spoke again, it was to me. "Mr. Franklin isn't in today. They're not sure when he'll be back."

Calloway and Randle hadn't been lying. It was like watching your favorite sad movie. You know the outcome. The mother will die. The couple won't get together. The big, bad corporation will win the case. Yet you're still hopeful that this one time you'll get a happy ending.

I had known it was a long shot that Ty was there but still had been holding out hope. I managed to smile through my disappointment. No need for Jerry to know. "That's no prob, Jerry." I spoke like we were old friends. It was back to plan A. "Can I leave a note?"

"Don't people your age text?"

"I'm old at heart," I said. "I just need to borrow a piece of paper and an envelope to put it in. Oh. And a pen."

He laughed then. Finally charmed. The rust was completely off Perky Black Girl now. It took him a few minutes to rustle it all up. I leaned against the counter as I waited, watching people coming in and out. They all wore business suits and were in a rush. They all also probably never paid attention to the view. The higher the floor, the harder they likely worked.

"Here you go, Ms. Wright."

Jerry handed over a pink sheet blank side up. I didn't need to flip it to know what it was. The flyer.

The hair. The hands. The jeans. The blood covering it all.

Jerry noticed my hesitation but obviously wasn't a mind reader because he said, "That's all I had. Sorry."

I just smiled and took it, trying to force myself to think of what to say instead of what I'd seen. And to my credit, the note started off strong.

I'm okay. Phone still in the house.

But then I faltered. There was no way for him to contact me—unless I took Adore up on her offer and actually stayed in the hotel room she'd promised to get me. As much as I hated needing her help, I needed it. I couldn't just wander the streets. I didn't even have money to wait it out at a restaurant. And the hotel had the one thing I wanted more than anything: a phone.

Staying at the Crown. Call me as soon as you can. I'll be waiting. Bree.

Jerry had left a weathered manila interoffice envelope on the counter. I folded the note—making sure not to look at Janelle's smiling face—then put it in the envelope, wrapped the string around it until it was closed tight, and wrote Ty's name on the first empty line. Next, I handed it back to Jerry and thanked him for his help.

TEN

The Crown lobby was as gray and desolate as I felt. The only people were me and a white attendant who looked like this was her first job and she wasn't really too impressed with it. Her name tag said VALERIE. She was so focused on her phone she didn't notice me until I cleared my throat.

"Sorry," she said, though she didn't sound like she meant it. "They found Janelle Beckett dead in a neighborhood close to here. I've been searching TikTok for updates. Just saw the police are doing a press conference later."

The hair. The hands. The jeans. The blood covering it all. I pushed the image away.

Much like Jerry before her, Valerie noticed my visceral reaction. "I'm sorry," she said again, and this time it felt like she meant it. "I wasn't trying to scare you. Paulus Hook is a very safe area. What happened to Janelle was—"

"I just need my key. Someone booked me a room earlier."

"Oh, the pretty woman. Her bag was gorgeous. I've never seen a Birkin bag in real life before."

It was a Kelly. Still I didn't correct her. "The room should be under Breanna Wright."

"Right," Valerie said, but I could tell she was still thinking about Adore's choice of arm wear. "I would need an ID to give you a key, but your friend—"

"She's not my friend." It came out more forcefully than I had intended because Valerie looked at me, finally no longer focused on overly expensive handbags.

"Your *associate* explained you lost your wallet. So she just left you a 'note.'" She actually winked as she slid over a sealed envelope with my name on it.

Two key cards were inside for a room on the fourth floor. "Thanks," I said, then hesitated. "Which way is the business center?"

It was down the hall. First door on the right.

The room was small and deserted with one lone black Dell desktop waiting to be used. It looked newer than I'd thought it would be. There was no log-in page; I just tapped the space bar and the computer lumbered to life. The desktop featured a shiny, happy photo of the hotel with rows of the standard Windows apps.

I opened Chrome and immediately went to iCloud.com, cross-contaminating tech-company platforms. The page was white and spare, with blurred-out images in the background. Blue, orange, and green. There was just one box underneath a directive: *Sign in to iCloud.*

I typed my Apple ID in the white box and clicked the right-facing arrow. Another box popped up below it. This one asking for my password. I typed it in, and after a nanosecond both boxes disappeared, replaced by something else: *Two Factor Authentication. A message with a verification code has been sent to your device. Enter the code to continue.*

Crap.

I clicked on the line below it: *Didn't get a verification code?* Clicked on a few pages after it, but it was no use. I'd need my phone if I wanted to get into my account. I didn't know who I wanted to curse out more:

Apple or my damn self for being so vigilant about keeping my account secure. And of course Past Me had done the same thing with all my other accounts: Gmail. Twitter. IG. TikTok.

If I wanted to log in to any of them to contact Ty or get his info, I'd need my phone.

But if I had my phone, I wouldn't need any of the apps.

I sat back in the chair. Willed myself to think. There had to be a way to make sure he was okay. Though I didn't know his phone number, I did know his social media. Maybe I could create an account and send him a message? Hopeful, I checked his Twitter, scrolling past Ty's pinned tweet about NFTs. Didn't stop until I saw his last tweet. It was from two days ago. The selfie from the park. There were other pics from our day as well. He looked so happy. I know I had too.

Then something else caught my eye in the "What's happening" column—a name right below the mention of the Mets and Cardinals squaring off.

Janelle Beckett.

I clicked. Her name was the number-four trending topic, sandwiched between what I could only infer were baseball's finest. She was trending with "Body found."

I clicked again, then scrolled down. Farther. Farther. And farther. The tweets were all versions of the same thing. Police had found a body matching Janelle Beckett's description in the Paulus Hook section of Jersey City. They suspected foul play. Had questioned one person who was in the house. Were looking to question another.

The company that owned 110 Little had already put out a statement expressing their shock and vowing to help the police in any way they could. It'd been liked over 20,000 times.

I went to Instagram, then TikTok, only to get similar results and an array of hashtags. #JanelleBeckett, #JanelleBeckettRIP, #JanelleBeckettUpdate. And one last one:

#Justice4Janelle

If Ty was alive, he was probably just as scared as I was. Because someone had chosen to kill Janelle Beckett in our Airbnb, his life was now in danger. I just hoped he was smart enough to be hiding—at least until he got a good lawyer.

I needed to find him before he got hurt.

I exited the browser. Put the computer to sleep. I looked around, but the one thing the business center was lacking was a phone. I'd have to finally go to my room. I could call his office, force them to give me his cell phone even if it was just to get me to stop harassing them.

The walk back to the elevators was quick. There was only one person in the lobby when I got there.

Adore.

She was back and so was my anger toward her. She stood when she saw me—in one hand, a weekender bag I'd seen in paparazzi photos, and in the other hand, a paper bag of takeout. "You still love sweet-and-sour chicken?"

"Why are you here?"

"Because I figured you'd be hungry."

"You know that's not what I meant. Why are you here wanting to be so helpful?"

I left off the "now."

I wanted an apology. Instead I got: "There was a video of the cops at Little Street on TikTok this morning. There was a group of people there, but I recognized you immediately. I've been wanting to reach out to you for a long time but…"

"But you didn't. And now you're coming in wanting me to be grateful, right?"

I walked past her and she didn't attempt to follow me. I'd stay at the hotel tonight and pay her back if it was the last thing I ever did. It wasn't until I made it to the elevator that her voice carried through the empty lobby.

"Tyler Franklin. Area code 410?"

It was only then I turned. I didn't say anything as she made her way to me, smiling like she was bridging the enormous gap between us instead of just thirty feet. "I found his number," she said when she finally got to me. "Let's go upstairs so you can call him."

The elevator doors dinged. "Come on," I said.

The walk to my room was quiet. Not even small talk about the weather. Twelve years ago this wouldn't have been a problem. Our silences had been as comfortable as the oversized Morgan State sweatshirt I still sometimes wore.

Adore had gotten me a suite. It was narrow but nice. Ebony wood cabinetry. Aqua subway tile backsplash. A sink barely bigger than a brick. The view wasn't much. Just a building across the street, but I didn't care. I wouldn't be there long enough to look out of it.

Because my things were still at the row house, I had nothing besides the key card to drop on the table separating the kitchen from the living area. I beelined straight for the phone. Some black number much sleeker than it needed to be. I fumbled around until I figured out how to get a dial tone, then turned to find Adore awkwardly standing in the kitchen area, still holding both bags.

"Number," I said, then the home training kicked in. "Please."

She rattled it off. It wasn't surprising she already memorized it. Adore had always been good with numbers. I'd cribbed off her more than once in Algebra freshman year. I turned away as I dialed, needing to at least pretend I was alone. *Please pick up, Ty. Please be okay. Please know I'm okay.*

But the routine was the same as with my own phone. Four long rings. Four deep breaths. The last one stuck inside me as I waited for what came next. Again hoping for a different ending, even though I already knew what would happen before the credits rolled.

The voicemail kicked in. Unlike me, Ty had taken the time to record an outgoing message. Just hearing his voice took the wind out of me. I took a seat on the couch, ignoring Adore's hopeful expression. Happy just for a second to hear Ty's voice once again so close to my face. I could practically feel his breath tickling my earlobe.

The words tumbled out as soon as the beep stopped. "Baby, it's me. I'm okay. I'm at a hotel. The Crown. Room 408. I don't have my phone. It's still at the house. They won't give me my stuff, but otherwise I'm okay. Please call me back. So I know you're okay too..."

I trailed off then, not having anything else to say but not wanting to hang up. This wasn't an answering machine like my grandmother had when I was a kid. Ty wasn't going to pick up in the middle of my spiel, breath heavy like he'd just run in from the garage. And yet I couldn't hang up. I said nothing, just breathed. Afraid to end the call, afraid to think why he hadn't answered.

Adore finally spoke. "Bree, hang up."

And my brain jump-started like a car battery. "Please just call me. I'll be here. And...and...please stay safe."

I finally hung up, turned to her. "Can I please see your phone? In case he can't check his voicemail."

Her hesitation lasted just shy of a nanosecond, then she handed it over. There was no red bubble in the upper right of her Messages icon. Either she didn't get a lot of texts or she was particular about checking them all. I didn't bother to find out. Just went to the Messages icon, plugged Ty's number into the "To" line, and typed a variation of the message I'd already left him two times now. It's Bree. I'm okay. Crown Hotel. Room 408. Call me as soon as you get this.

I placed her cell on the end table. "Where are you, Ty?" I was talking to myself, but Adore answered anyway.

"Did he have a car? Would he drive back to Maryland?"

I shook my head. "Of course not."

"I just don't get why he hasn't reached out to the police yet."

"Do I really have to explain the optics here? Are you really asking why a Black man isn't automatically trusting the police to do the right thing? You know how this looks. Black couple. White woman. It's the reason you came to help me."

I glanced at her, the weekender bag on her shoulder making her look like a little girl playing dress-up with her mom's purse. Then I spoke again. "He wouldn't leave me."

She finally set the bag down on the end table. Took her time doing it too. I watched every move, until she finally spoke. "He already did, Bree. He left you to come downstairs and find a mutilated woman in the foyer."

The hair. The hands. The jeans. The blood covering it all.

I hoped Ty hadn't seen her. That those images weren't consuming his brain like they were consuming mine.

"He could've chased the killer off. Been wanting to protect me."

"Then why not come back? He'd have to be an asshole to leave his girlfriend to deal with it," she said.

I'd rather he was an asshole than dead. Finally, I spoke. "He's still here."

Adored sighed, like she'd forgotten how stubborn I could be. "Okay," she said, leaving off the *we'll play it your way.* "Could he be staying with a friend?"

"Maybe."

"He know anyone who lives close by?"

"I don't know," I said, then realized how bad it sounded. "I mean, no one he's mentioned by name."

"Okay…Who are his boys back home? Maybe he's reached out to them."

"There's Mo."

She smiled, relieved. Happy for something to glom on to, she picked up her cell. "That short for Mohammed? Maurice? If you just give me his last name, I can get his number too."

Her questions came rapid-fire. I'd forgotten how she got when she was excited. She looked at me and I said nothing, too busy racking my brain for an answer to *any* of her questions. I came up empty. "I'm sure he's commented on one of his posts." I motioned to the phone still in her hand. "You have IG? You can check Ty's account." I rattled off his screen name.

She nodded encouragingly, like *I* was the child playing dress-up and wanting approval. She served as her own narrator as she went to Ty's page and checked his last post. It was the one we'd taken in Central Park. "Ten comments. That's manageable."

She scrolled, spouting off each name. "You think any of these are Mo?'

None of them sounded familiar, but I'd never been the type to police my boyfriend's Instagram activity. I shrugged.

"It's cool," she said. "We can contact all ten if you want."

I hesitated, not sure if Ty would want just anyone in his business. "Let's hold off. You said I should get my stuff tomorrow. Have you heard anything more? From your friend in the police department?"

"They're looking for the murder weapon."

I jolted. As much as I'd thought about the body, I'd figured Janelle was pushed. I hadn't attached a murder weapon to the tragedy.

"And of course they're anxious to talk to Ty," she said.

"He didn't do anything," I said.

"Maybe, but he needs to tell them that. The whole thing is just strange. How she got there. Why she was there. Your boyfriend disappearing."

I couldn't explain any of it, but still I tried. "Like you said, we woke up to a stranger in our house. Ty would want to protect me. Maybe he chased the killer off. Couldn't get back inside. What if he's hurt somewhere? What if he *gets* hurt?" I flashed on the body. "He wouldn't kill anyone, Adore. Especially not like that. I know he wouldn't."

"Bree, I have to be honest. It sounds like you don't really know Ty that well at all."

I didn't want to say what I was thinking: that she was right. "We both know I haven't always been the best judge of character," I said. "But Ty's not you."

Again I was stunned at my anger. I would've sworn I'd let it go a decade ago. Adore didn't say anything for so long that I was surprised when she did. "I shouldn't have said that." It wasn't an apology, but Adore had never been good at those. "You're scared. I'd be scared too if I woke up to a strange person dead downstairs. Want to protect myself first and foremost."

"I just feel helpless. Like I'm sitting here doing nothing. I should go back. There's a Black woman who lives on the street. Maybe she saw something. Saw him."

"That's not a good idea."

"I don't have much of a choice."

"The police are still there," she said. "You don't need to be anywhere by there, especially not talking to neighbors. I'll reach out to Randle. Arrange for us to get your things first thing tomorrow morning. But for now, why don't we just sit here and eat while you wait for Ty to call back. The press conference should be soon too."

I'd already forgotten the woman at the front desk had mentioned it. My throat contracted at the mere thought. "Are they going to mention our names?" I finally asked.

She shrugged. "If they wanted to arrest you, they would have at the house. I heard they're focused on footage from one of the neighbors' Ring cameras."

I got excited. "From this morning?"

"Last Monday night around 10 p.m."

That got me even more excited. Monday at 10 p.m. I was in Baltimore. Ty was at a hotel. "What time does the press conference start?"

ELEVEN

When I got back from the bathroom, Adore was right where I'd left her on the couch. She'd figured out how to turn on the television while I was gone. She had it on mute so a solemn Black male news anchor mimed words as one sentence scrolled below him at the bottom of the screen.

Police scheduled to have press conference about body found in Jersey City.

But she wasn't looking at the television, instead staring intently at her cell.

I still remembered the excitement when I'd found out we were both going to Morgan State. That I'd know someone—Adore at that. As a sheltered suburban girl, I always had been fascinated with her. This girl who would come to school every day all the way from DC. She seemed so worldly. I was jealous. It was only after I got to know her that I discovered she was jealous of me as well.

She was my first-ever roommate. Our mothers moved us in on the same day, meeting for the first time. I still remember the way my mom's lip curled when Adore's mother told her they lived near the Benning Road Metro station in DC. I didn't fault Adore for never telling anyone else.

Her mother had been as excited for Adore to go to Morgan as my mother had been disappointed. Adore because she was the first in her family to go to college. My mom because I'd chosen a "Black school" even though it was relatively close to home. My mother had hated the very thought—wanting me to go somewhere Ivy League even though my grades made it clear I could never get in. But for the first time, I'd stood up to her.

Adore and I first bonded about not having fathers—mine had passed away when I was ten and Adore had never known hers—but then eventually we found more things in common. She had an adventurous streak that I got secondhand. Adore was always the friendly one. Always the one who got us invited to parties and lunch tables. We shared the bond that comes from becoming adults together. Making mistakes. Figuring out how to fix them. I learned more from her than I did from most of my professors, and vice versa.

A lot of my friends changed after my arrest, but if I were being honest, Adore's reaction hurt the most. I'd never fallen out with a best friend before. And though I had friendships after, there were none like I'd had in college. My arrest and plea bargain had made me keep myself closed off—dare I be judged and once again rejected.

Staring at her now, it shocked me how much I still remembered about someone I hadn't spoken to in over a decade. She was still making that face, the one I used to joke was putting on her Thinking Hat. It had gotten us out of many a problem in college, like the time we missed the bus back from Classic weekend in Atlanta with an exam at 8 a.m. Monday morning. We'd made it. Passed the test too—Adore with a much higher grade than me. She'd always gotten so serious when the hat was on, and, just like back then, I found myself wanting to lighten the mood. But I didn't. We weren't going to fall back into old roles. No matter how much Adore wanted us to.

"What happened?" I said, then didn't let her answer. "You heard from Ty. He's okay?"

She shook her head. "You still have access to your social media?"

"No. I need my phone. Why?"

She just held hers out. I took my time walking the three steps to grab it but still got there too soon. I'd been expecting Instagram or even CNN. Instead, I saw TikTok. A Brush With Billie's page was up. The profile photo was the same—some close-up of a precise makeup job—but now there was just one thing in her bio: #Justice4Janelle.

Adore spoke. "This account's been posting nonstop about Janelle's disappearance and—"

I finished her sentence like I used to. "Murder. I know who Billie is. I've been just as fascinated with Janelle's disappearance as the rest of the world. And Billie always has folks sharing stuff no one else knows yet."

Yesterday, that had been a good thing. Today, the thought made me scared. I also wanted Janelle to get justice, as long as it was directed toward the person who actually had done this.

"Click the latest post," Adore said.

"The one with 300,000 views..."

"And 5,000 comments. Though I'm sure it's gone up."

I clicked on it. "It has. By several hundred."

The video opened with a screenshot of a tweet. I leaned forward to make it out, but then I realized I didn't need to because Billie read it for me.

"Jersey City police sent out a statement that they'll be holding a press conference about the body many believe to be Janelle Beckett. Sources say that the body was in horrific condition. Beat beyond recognition."

Unfortunately, that was something I already knew.

"Beat. Beyond. Recognition." Billie started to tear up. "She was so beautiful. To imagine her beat beyond recognition. I'll be watching the press conference and will share an updated post as soon as it's done. The police haven't said anything—yet—about who owns the house, but if you've been following the Justice for Janelle hashtag, then you know that it's an Airbnb. The police haven't said if it was booked this past weekend, but we have reason to believe it was, perhaps by this man."

Ty suddenly stared back at me. It was one of my favorite pictures. The first of him I'd ever saved to my camera roll. He'd been at one of his frat's scholarship luncheons. He had on a black suit and was smiling. And for a moment—just a moment—I smiled at the sight of him alive and happy.

But then the screen switched to a close-up of the bio. *Tyler Franklin. Baltimore born and bred. UMD Man. JPMorgan Golden Boy. Ty to my friends. Mr. Franklin to everyone else.*

Even though part of me had expected this—*dreaded* it—I still wasn't prepared.

Billie spoke over it. "His last couple posts starting with Saturday have all been photos from the New York–New Jersey area."

She shared my vacation with her hundreds of thousands of followers. Even with her flipping through his posts so quickly, I recognized each place. The bookstore. The cookie shop. The restaurant. Then she stopped on one. I recognized it too. "However, it's this one in particular," she said.

In the foreground were intertwined feet on a coffee table. A frame of *Ferris Bueller's Day Off* was in the background. We'd never finished the movie.

"Tyler Franklin didn't include a specific address for the photo, though he did tag it Paulus Hook," Billie said. "Now, if you go to the Airbnb listing for 110 Little Street, you'll see this photo."

The screen switched to a realtor-like shot of a living room designed in sophisticated grays. Ty had sent it to me right after he invited me to visit.

"I'm going to zoom in here." She did. "You see that? Same TV. Same art. It seems pretty clear this Tyler Franklin and someone else were at 110 Little Street at the same time our Janelle went missing.

Unfortunately, I don't have any information on the other person in the photo. Tyler Franklin didn't tag anyone in any of his posts."

The shot switched again and Billie was back to dominating the screen, the Airbnb photo behind her. "We know that the police spoke to two people at the scene and let them both go. I don't have confirmation that one of them is this Tyler Franklin. I also heard they're looking for a third suspect. Again, I'm not saying that it's Tyler Franklin. And to be clear, I'm not saying this Tyler person has anything to do with Janelle. Though I can't help but also wonder about the woman with him."

I didn't move, not even stopping the video when it looped back to the start.

"So?" Adore finally said. "What are you thinking?"

"That I knew I should've gotten a pedicure."

"This isn't funny, Bree. It gets worse." She snatched the phone back, tapping her screen a few times, then handing it back to me. Ty's last Instagram post. "Check the comments."

The ones from his friends were still there. The folks I was embarrassed to admit I didn't know by their government names. But now there were more. A lot more.

Why did you do it? #Justice4Janelle
I hope you rot in jail. #JanelleBeckettRIP
Murderer. #Justice4Janelle

That last one already had 224 likes. Billie would have cried at the low number. I wanted to cry at the high one.

All because some woman who'd rather put on makeup than get a job had posted his Instagram handle. Not for the first time, I hated the entire World Wide Web. How you could find anything on it. Say anything too. Who needed proof when you had thousands of likes, comments, and views? I started to talk, then closed my mouth. Swallowed before trying again. I got out just one sentence, but I put my all behind it. "This is not good."

"At all," Adore said.

Then we spoke at the same time.

Me: "They know about Ty."

Her: "They're going to find you."

"What?" I said. Then: "I didn't tag anything with Paulus Hook or take any photos inside the house. It's like Billie said: they don't know who I am."

"*Yet*, Breanna. They don't know who you are—yet. They'll find you just like they found him."

I went with the joke again. "Don't worry. I don't share pics of my feet."

"You're in videos at the scene," she said.

"You said I was in a group. I probably only stood out to you because you knew who I was."

She said nothing, just motioned for her phone and I kept on.

"He didn't tag me in anything. I don't comment on his photos. He doesn't really comment on mine. At least not any lovey-dovey shit. We're not *that* couple."

She tapped her screen a few more times. "You do take photos in the same places, though."

And when she handed it back, my last Instagram post was up. The park. There were just two comments underneath it. Neither wishing me death.

I was surprised she knew my handle. For a second, I thought maybe she'd been checking up on me since college, even if I hadn't done the same. But a bigger part realized how easy I was to find online. My handle was a variation of my name. And it probably helped I hadn't changed my name or gotten a new address.

"You think Ty and I are the only people on Beyoncé's internet happy to be at Central Park?"

"No, but I do think you and Ty are the only two people following each other and happy to be at Central Park at the exact same time."

"He has thousands of followers. Thousands of people he follows. It's going to take them a while to get to me."

"But they will."

"Ty's missing. That's all I care about right now."

I handed her phone back, then walked over to the landline by the couch. Picking it up, I hit Redial. Ty didn't answer after any of the four rings. The voicemail kicked in and there was his voice. It didn't calm me this time. If anything, I wanted to record it. Upload it to Twitter myself. Tag #Justice4Janelle. Hope it went viral. So people could hear him. Be reminded he was human, not just a photo on social media for them to comment on from the safety of a device.

When I glanced over at Adore, she was busy typing away.

"This is fine," I said, even though it wasn't at all. I glanced at the clock, then at the television. The makeup-ed news anchor droned on silently. "Isn't it seven? You said the press conference was going to start at seven."

"Maybe they're running late."

"Why?"

"I don't know, Bree."

"Can't you ask your friend? What if it's canceled?"

I needed the press conference to happen. I needed them to show that video of whatever happened when Ty was miles away from Little Street in some hotel room. I needed folks to see that whatever happened the night Janelle went missing had nothing to do with him and that *they* needed to focus on someone else: the person who actually did it.

"Can you text them and ask?" I said.

"Fine."

Neither of us said much while we waited for a response. Adore stayed on the couch, munching on cold sweet-and-sour chicken like she would do the week before finals, when we were always trying to catch up on a semester of work we'd ignored. I was surprised I remembered that too.

I wasn't the least bit hungry, so I just paced back and forth in front of the television—same as I had done back then too.

And I could tell by the way she kept glancing at me that it still annoyed her. Except now she was too afraid to say anything. I only stopped moving when her phone finally buzzed. The noise wasn't loud yet I still jumped like some teenager in a horror film.

I came up to the couch until I was so close I could smell the remnants of her perfume. I didn't recognize the scent, but it was also probably above my pay grade. Adore looked up at me and spoke. "It's been pushed to eight."

"Less than thirty minutes."

I wondered how many comments would be posted between now and then. Just as I started to pace again, Adore stuck her hand out to block my way. "Enough time for you to shower," Adore said. "Get out of those clothes."

"I don't have anything else to wear."

"I brought some stuff over. You shower. I'll leave it in the bedroom." She shooed me with a chopstick.

"I smell that bad?"

"Remember that time you tried rock climbing?"

"I was nervous."

"I could tell," she said.

She started to laugh and I had to swallow back my own. We were pitiful. I'd only gotten about five feet up the wall. Adore hadn't even tried.

The shower was a walk-in with one of those fancy-schmancy rain showerheads I always saw touted on my mom's HGTV shows. It was as nice as they claimed on TV but still wasted on me. The water bounced off the tension in my shoulders like I was bulletproof.

When I got out and dried off, I finally saw what was in the bag Adore had been toting around. Clothes. In theory, as casual as the ones I'd just taken off. But when I touched the joggers, it confirmed what

I'd suspected. They were terry cloth. Probably expensive. The tag indicated some brand I was too broke to know. There was no question that she'd gotten them from her closet, which meant she was more local than I'd thought. Probably lived in one of the high-rises we'd gone past, not in a studio with old pipes, surrounded by college kids.

When I emerged, Adore was still on the couch and the television was still on the local channel—the news anchor now reduced to the left side of the screen. Next to him, in a smaller box, a different camera was trained on an empty podium.

The same words ran along the bottom like it was a race: *Police scheduled to have press conference about body found in Jersey City.*

I took a seat as the first camera cut to another scene. I recognized the house immediately. Had woken up in it just this morning, though it felt like a lifetime ago. A police officer came out the door, closing it behind him. I wondered if the body was still inside.

The camera cut immediately back to the anchor. He spoke more muted words before his little box disappeared. The press conference was finally going to start.

I grabbed the remote and unmuted the television before Adore could even ask me to.

A portly older white guy with more hair in his beard than on his head came in first, a trail of people behind him. All white. All men. All in uniform. The first guy went straight for the podium. The rest stood behind him like an offensive line. I searched for either Calloway or her partner. They came in last, Randle barely making it into the frame. They were the only ones in suits—no time to go home and get camera-ready.

I took in a breath and waited for whatever came next. The portly one cleared his throat to begin. "Good evening. I'm Police Chief David King. At approximately ten thirty this morning, 911 received a phone call about a possible dead body at 110 Little Street in the Paulus Hook section of Jersey City. Our officers were immediately dispatched to the scene, where they confirmed a woman was deceased on the premises."

I wanted to skip ahead to the video like in someone's Instagram Stories.

"There were two witnesses on the scene. Neither was able to identify the deceased. Her identity remains unknown."

I gave Adore a surprised look. She spoke. "They don't want to identify her until they have a positive ID. It could take weeks."

I said nothing, just continued to twirl the remote like some majorette as the police chief continued. "I will say that this was an exceptionally violent crime. The woman is unrecognizable."

The hair. The hands. The jeans. The blood covering it all.

"We're treating this as a homicide and will be continuing our full investigation as we work to identify the deceased. We are asking for the public's help in this matter. We'll be releasing some video footage captured in the alley behind Little Street."

That last sentence jolted me back into the present. *Finally.*

"As you'll see, there are two people alone in the alley," he said. "The man appears to be chasing the woman."

Say it. Share the date. So folks know there was no way Ty could be involved.

"The video isn't long. Just a few seconds."

Say.

The.

Date.

"However, we believe it may be related to the deceased found this morning. It was taken last Monday evening. Around 10 p.m."

Adore let out a sigh. I felt just as relieved. He'd said it.

"Again, we're asking for help identifying both people shown here. We believe the male may be a person of interest in this morning's homicide."

Yes. He straight-up had said what I knew and wanted everyone else to know too. Whoever was in that alley on Monday was the murderer.

The police chief turned to his left. Nodded. The offensive line all did too, and the camera zoomed out to reveal a large video screen. Both Adore and I instinctively leaned forward. Neither of us dared say a word. Not yet.

The footage was black-and-white, a camera trained on a square chunk of rough road. No one was in frame yet, but then a person appeared at the bottom of the screen. Her back was to us, but you could tell she was skinny. She wore no jacket, just jeans and a light-colored T-shirt. Her hair was also light. It hung straight to midway down her back. She walked quickly. No purse. Her hands in front of her like she was texting while walking.

The woman stopped, then turned abruptly and looked back, giving us a glimpse of her face. But it was only for a second because she turned back around. Took off again. She did a final quick double take back at the video's edge, her pace so quick that she was out of frame within a nanosecond.

A moment later, another body came into frame, just as she had. But this one looked taller, bigger, male. He wore a hoodie so we couldn't see his hair, but he was scratching his covered neck, his hand the only body part you could actually see. His pace was just as quick, so he was in and out before you could blink.

I waited, expecting more, to see them come back into frame, both running this time. Something—anything—to live up to the promise the police chief had laid out. Instead, the screen just went black.

The camera focused back on Chief King as he spoke again. "We know it's short, but we think it's important. As I said, we'll be releasing the full video and we've taken a few stills we'll also be distributing. A number's been set up for anyone to call if they have information."

He read the number off, then motioned again to the monitor. The first still was already on the screen. I stood up, walked past Adore to take a closer look. It was of the woman glancing back. Now that she was frozen in time, it was clear she wasn't expecting someone to be behind her. She looked surprised.

She also looked like Janelle Beckett.

"The next still isn't as clear, but we're still hoping someone might recognize something about this man."

The monitor switched. As promised, this one was the man's back, his hand mid–neck scratch. With the black-and-white footage, you couldn't tell what shade of brown it was other than medium. And other than obviously being brown, there was nothing remarkable about it. No wedding rings. No tattoos. No missing digits.

My eyes moved to the hoodie. Behind me Adore spoke, but I barely heard her, her voice petering out like I'd turned down her volume. "The hand looks Black, but it's fine. I can call over now, let the police know that Ty hadn't booked the Airbnb yet. You know what hotel he was staying at? Maybe we can get one of the desk attendants to confirm he was in his room at whatever time the video was taken…"

She was fully on mute now as I continued to stand inches from the television. I stared. There was a lone image on the back of the hoodie. An illustration of a light-skinned Black woman in a jean top and large, thick hoop earrings. Her hair was pulled back into a long braid that was casually placed over her left shoulder. Both hands were crossed over it and the rest of her chest. I recognized her immediately.

Sade.

I recognized the hoodie too. Ty had told me his mother had it custom-made for him last Christmas.

I turned the television off. There was nothing else I wanted to see or hear. I wrapped my arms around myself.

Adore came up beside me. "You worried about the hand?"

I shook my head because I wasn't.

"Okay, good," Adore said. "Because it could literally be anybody."

I opened my mouth to speak, then closed it again, truly at a loss for words. Ty shouldn't have been there.

"Bree, what's wrong?"

If this were twelve years ago, I would've told her. Shared every single thought zooming around in my head. And she would've helped. But I wasn't ready to trust her. Not right now. I swiped at my eye. Shrugged. "I'm just tired. Gonna go to sleep."

She nodded, though I could tell she didn't want to leave. Not yet. But she had to. I needed to be in my safe space—and that was alone.

When she finally left, I didn't walk her out.

Billie Regan sits in front of the camera, crying. Her eyes are bloodshot. Streaks of black mascara run down her face. Her blond hair is limp. The #Justice4Janelle hashtag is still above her. Otherwise, she's the only thing on the screen.

"Hey, Billie Bunch. I only have a few minutes, but I had to post because I know you all are as devastated as I am right now. If you missed the press conference, the Jersey City police released a video of what just might be our Janelle's last moments of freedom. I'm not going to lie. It's hard to watch, but we have to."

Billie shrinks to the bottom right of the screen as a black-and-white video pops up behind her. A blond woman walks past the camera down what looks like an alley. She's alone. She walks a few steps, then suddenly turns, quickly looks back, and resumes walking again, faster. She does a quick double take behind her again before she exits the frame.

"Y'all see how terrified she looks," Billie says. "She's obviously scared for her life. And I'd be too. Look at *him*."

What looks like a male in a dark-colored hoodie with a drawing of a woman on the back of it enters at the bottom of the frame. He scratches the back of his neck as he rushes out of frame. We never see his face.

"He looks so . . . suspect. Let me play it again so you can see." The few seconds of video play again as Billie continues her talk. "He obviously wants to hurt her. It's warm out. Why would you have on a hoodie covering your face? Why would you be following some poor woman who's by herself down a dark alley? Unless he wanted to kidnap her to..."

She trails off, unable to finish her sentence. She takes a second to get herself together as the video continues to play on a loop.

"I know we can't see his face, but that has to be Tyler Franklin. It looks like his build. And I could be wrong, but the hands look...dark. This has to be when he took Janelle. And as hard as this was to see, I'm so glad the police released this footage.

"The Billie Bunch has been on it. I've been looking into Tyler Franklin and getting DMs from all of you. As per his bio, he works at JPMorgan in Baltimore. But if you call, they'll tell you that he's working in their Jersey City office this week."

She finally stops long enough to take a breath, then continues.

"But if you call the New Jersey office, they will tell you that he did not come in today. And his work email confirms it. He has an away message on saying he's unexpectedly out of the office and not checking email. He'll return your message when he's back in, *hopefully* this week."

She raises her eyebrows at that one.

"He's not answering his phone. Texts are delivered but not responded to. People in the area who've been camped out near Little Street haven't seen a single person fitting Ty's description cooperating at the scene. We've also combed video footage to see if he was in fact there the morning of Janelle's murder. We haven't been able to locate him in the crowd."

She pauses for dramatic effect, and this time when she speaks, her sentence is drawn out as if she's savoring every word.

"And I've been told even the police haven't been able to locate him *at all*." She nods as she continues. "That's right, it appears Tyler Franklin is on the run."

Another struggle for air before Billie continues. "Pause this video.

Screenshot every frame. Enlarge it. Go over each pixel with a magnifying glass. If you recognize him, or even think you do, let the police know. Better safe than sorry. If you don't, you can still help. There has to be something in this video that can help us get justice for Janelle. Maybe something on the ground. Maybe something on her. Maybe something on…him. I mean, look at the back of that sweatshirt. I know someone in my comments already did a reverse image search and nothing came up. But we can't give up. It has to be made somewhere, sold somewhere, right? If you know where, please let me know. If you don't want to leave a comment, you know my DMs are open."

There's a knock. Billie quickly glances off-screen, then turns back to her audience. "I gotta go. But please, stay vigilant. I'm not going to be able to sleep until we get justice for Janelle."

TWELVE

Adore was supposed to pick me up at 10 a.m. Normally that would be pushing it for me, but I barely slept. Every time I closed my eyes, I'd see it. *The hair. The hands. The jeans. The blood covering it all.*

And every time I opened them, I'd think about how I was in bed and Ty wasn't next to me. How I didn't know where he was—either last Monday night, when that video was taken, or now. But there had to be a good reason he'd been in an alley behind Little Street four days before he booked the Airbnb. And for him to have lied to me about never having been to Little Street before.

I wasn't going to be like my mother. Or that lawyer she'd hired. Or what felt like everyone who knew me before my arrest. I wasn't going to assume Ty was guilty just because that's what the cops wanted it to *look* like. I wasn't going to abandon him just like everyone had abandoned me.

WWTD?

He'd find me so I could explain everything and we could figure it out—together.

By 8 a.m., I was willing myself to get up, telling myself I needed a run. That it'd help me clear my head. Instead, I went to the business center.

Ty had been found overnight. Several times, in fact.

Billie had posted another video. This one chock-full of sightings. People had seen him everywhere, from grabbing a leisurely coffee at some Au Bon Pain in Jersey City to driving down the New Jersey Turnpike to a guy who looked "just like him" scurrying off the Amtrak in Boston's Back Bay. Someone had even managed to take a photo of that.

I was excited until I actually saw the pic and realized it was of just a random Black guy in a baseball cap. Not even close to Ty's skin color. Gotta love how we all look alike.

Billie had declared Ty as "on the run." Though I doubted any of those other sightings were him, I wasn't surprised he'd decided to keep lying low.

Ty knew the optics as much as I did. *Anyone* Black did. That some chance encounter with a stranger—a white stranger at that—would look like so much more. There was nothing on that video to make you think something bad was happening unless you *wanted* to think that. The only thing Ty had done wrong was be Black and in the same space as some pretty white woman. But that still didn't answer the more pressing question for me.

"Bree."

I jumped as a hand touched my shoulder, then calmed down when I recognized the stilettoed nails. Adore. Once again looking like a TV version of a lawyer. Pale pink pantsuit that managed to look modern and not like she was stuck in the twentieth century. She'd paired it with a black silk blouse, offering a hint of cleavage, and black stilettos. Her straight hair was in a sleek, high ponytail with hair wrapped around the band, and she had on the same shade of red lipstick. It must've been her signature.

I glanced at the computer's clock: 9:59. Adore was still punctual as all get-out.

"You could star in the next *Halloween* because you scared the hell out of me," I said.

But Adore didn't laugh. Instead, she leaned on the desk a few inches away. I smelled her same perfume. I was tempted to ask her about it, but the look on her face told me she wouldn't answer. She was too busy staring me down.

Finally, I spoke. "What?"

"It's him, isn't it?" she said. "In that video from the press conference."

I was about to open my mouth to lie like I had the night before, but she wouldn't let me. Not today.

"I can't help you if you don't tell me the truth, Bree."

I nodded, just as much to confirm she was right as to let her know I understood. "What gave it away?"

"You always wipe your eye when you aren't telling the truth."

She'd told me that before, but I'd forgotten. I pushed back from the desk. "He's a huge Sade fan. He loves that hoodie. His mother got it specially made for him last Christmas. He wears it all the time."

She didn't respond, just stared at the wall like some vision test.

"What are you worried about?" I said—because I still knew her too.

"That if he wears it all the time it will show up on his socials."

"Not this weekend. Weather was too nice. I didn't even know he'd brought it."

"He wear it on any other dates?"

I shook my head. "We always dress up. It's one of the things I like about him. The effort."

"You said he got it for Christmas. He take a pic then?"

"We weren't dating then. I don't know."

"What about some night out with his boys?"

I tried to conjure up his Instagram account. Instead, my mind went blank.

"Let me guess," Adore said. "You don't know."

"I'm not the type of girlfriend who stalks my boyfriend's Instagram." I hated how defensive I sounded.

She pulled out her phone. "Now's a good time to start."

We sat right next to each other. Adore already had Ty's Instagram up. I wasn't sure if she'd been checking it obsessively or she just hadn't closed it the night before.

"The front's pretty basic," I said. "Zip-up. Plain black. No writing. It's the only one like it he owns, though. Probably another reason he wears it so much."

I was talking too much—overexplaining—but I couldn't help it. I needed her to know I did know Ty. Just as well as I said I did, *better* than I said I did. Because it was only a matter of time before she asked the next question: *Why did he lie to you about being at a hotel?*

Adore started with the latest photo of our movie night, then scrolled back at rapid speed. In the photos rolling by like it was *The Price Is Right,* he looked happy and debonair—like the Ty I knew. The one who'd planned this trip for us. The one who would have a good reason for lying about last Monday night.

The most recent posts were hoodie-less—as much business as pleasure. NFTs and crypto and something called Web3. Posts I'd never read. Just had liked solely to be supportive. Others that predated me were all selfies and locations. A relief.

Just a few pics crowded in with his boys—all glassy-eyed from doing who knows what. We went back and back—in rows and weeks. Right as I was feeling confident, I saw it.

"Stop," I said.

There it was. The middle pic in the last row visible on Adore's phone.

Sade.

It was just her beautiful face. Close enough you couldn't even see her ears. Her name in all-caps red in the inky blackness of the bottom left. SMOOTH OPERATOR written sideways in gold in a long rectangle next to her photo. Her best album.

It wasn't the image drawn on his hoodie, but still.

"You think they'll put two and two together?" I wasn't able to pull my eyes away. "That they'll realize Ty loved Sade enough to own a hoodie with her on it?"

"They?" Adore said.

"The police."

"They probably already know, Bree. He had that hoodie with him. It could be in their evidence file right now. But they're not the ones I'm worried about. I care more about Twitter. TikTok. Instagram."

I rolled my eyes. "I'm more concerned about an arrest than a comment."

"What about a thousand of them?" She scrolled up until she reached the last photo. "At least the cops have rules and protocols. Instagram investigators do not."

She handed me the phone.

There were thousands of comments now with comments *under* comments.

You can't run forever. Stalking poor Janelle like that.

#Justice4Janelle

Someone needs to bash YOUR face in.

I was sick to my stomach watching you hunt Janelle down in that video. Your going to hell.

That last one had 388 likes and 46 replies. I clicked, only to find an argument.

You have no proof it's him. If he's going to hell, you'll be right next to him.

Who else would it be? It's him. You'll see. #Justice4Janelle

And what if it is? Is it a crime for a Black guy to walk down the street now?

Janelle is clearly scared!!! What else do you need to see?

It wouldn't be the first time a white woman was scared just because Black men exist. You're ready to convict the man without a shred of proof.

My hands were shaking so much it was like trying to read a book on a roller coaster, but still I kept going. Reading fight after fight, all saying variations of the same thing. I only stopped when Adore gently touched my hand to physically stop me from clicking. "Bree, it's going to be—"

I interrupted, not wanting her pity. "We need to go get my phone."

* * *

The ride over to Little Street was quick. We didn't run into any problems until we got to the cross street. The crowd had multiplied—squared, even. The police tape and barriers were still up, but now they needed four uniforms to keep onlookers at bay.

I could feel their energy from the car. Folks there to film, tweet, and post. I wondered if any of them had commented something nasty under Ty's post.

Adore took the next street and drove around to the other end of the block.

There were no crowds here—too far from the action to film anything good—and no barriers either. Just a lone cop leaning against his squad car. He was young, on the precipice of good-looking, like he'd wanted to play a cop on TV but had to settle for this. Adore put her blinker on and he ambled over, leaning down when he finally got to the car. I must've turned invisible on the ride over because he smiled right through me and at Adore.

"Sorry, miss, but this street is open only to locals." His voice was helpful. Cops never sounded like that with me either.

Adore already had her card out. "I'm A. Kristine McKinley and this is Breanna Wright. Detective Calloway's expecting us."

He eyed her card just as hard as he'd eyed her, then stood up and murmured something into the walkie on his shoulder. There was an even more muffled response before he bent down again. "Go right ahead, Ms. McKinley."

A few houses in, I was surprised to see a huddle of people coming toward us, led by a trio of various dogs. And once again it made me think of Janelle.

Everyone but the dogs turned toward our approaching car. I stared at them until they noticed and then I regretted not having slumped down. Though I searched for Ms. Morgane, I only recognized the blip of red in the middle. Krista.

And she recognized me too. Even still twenty feet away, her eyes narrowed to paper-thin slits. I turned away, but that didn't make it any better. I still felt the heat of her glare.

Though there was a spot directly in front of 110, Adore didn't dare park there. Instead, she stopped several houses down, like she was just dropping by a friend's.

"Probably best if you let me get your bag and whatever else," she said. "We can check that everything's there when we get back to the hotel."

"It's fine," I said, not wanting to think of random police officers pawing through my bras and panties.

Adore nodded before getting out and walking toward the house as if on a stroll. She left the car running. Calloway met her before she could even make it to the front gate. Even from half a dozen houses away, I could see the crowd perk up, more cameras rising like they were filming a concert.

Adore and Calloway exchanged a few words, then both turned to the car. I resisted the urge to wave. Just stared back until they turned around and disappeared inside a white tent now set up in front of the house, big enough to hold a small wedding.

With nothing else to do, I glanced at the house we were parked in front of. It was redbrick with white shutters and blinds drawn tight. I looked up and down the block. Other houses were the same—even though it was broad daylight. Krista and Company were gone. It was a stark contrast to the vibrancy of just a few days before. The street now felt deserted, even with the crowd. Like we'd all just dealt with a zombie apocalypse.

The pink Missing signs were still tacked on to every tree. Janelle looking so alive. So vibrant. Again, I thought about her life cut short. She had been a person with dreams. Hopes. Fears. Combinations of all three. And it all had ended because she encountered the wrong person at the wrong time.

And now all of us had turned her from a human to an *opinion*. A comment. An excuse to argue and judge. Even I was guilty of it—focusing on Ty. It made me wonder how many people truly cared about losing Janelle for who she was. I knew she had almost no family. Not a lot of friends.

I was so deep in thought, I didn't notice Randle until he knocked on the window. My breath caught, but I managed to force myself to breathe again by the time I rolled the window down. He smiled. "Ms. Wright. Figured I'd check in to see how you're doing."

Yeah, okay. He wanted something. When I didn't say anything, he kept on.

"You've had quite a twenty-four hours."

Had it only been that long? I kept my response short as I wiped my eye. "I had a good night's sleep. It helped."

"You're at that fancy hotel off Scott?"

Of course he was keeping tabs.

"It looks really nice. Sounds like it's nice too." He took a breath. "Did you have a chance to see the footage we released?"

And there it was. My voice was clipped. "Entire world's probably seen it. At least everyone with TikTok."

He smiled at that. "You recognize anyone?"

I nodded. "It looked like the missing woman. Janelle Beckett."

We stared at each other, daring the other to speak first. He lost. "What about the male?"

I shrugged, then chose my words carefully. "I didn't see his face. You have something else for me to look at?"

I convinced myself that the questions were actually a good thing. They meant the hoodie hadn't been in the house. Maybe Ty had taken it with him when he left yesterday morning.

If they needed someone to confirm that the person in the video was him, it wasn't going to be me.

"Detective Randle?"

The voice sounded like it was used to interrupting, and for once I didn't mind—happy for the respite. Randle stood back up, and from my vantage point, all I could make out was a set of white hands. A man.

"Sure am," Randle said.

"I asked the officer blocking our street what was going on. He said I should talk to you." The men shook hands. "Rod Stevenson."

"You own 108," Randle said. "We've been trying to reach you."

"The wife and I went out of town for a long weekend. Just got back to find all these police cars. Someone was killed?"

Must've been a good trip if he hadn't bothered to check the news. Though I didn't say it out loud, I must've thought it loud enough that they both glanced at me. Randle spoke next.

"You mind chatting at your place? I'm happy to share as many details as I can."

Randle didn't give me as much as a head nod goodbye. It took a good ten feet before I could finally fully see who'd been talking. The rest of Rod Stevenson was as sturdy as his hands—like he went to the gym but didn't spend hours there. The flecks of gray in his brown hair made me think he was in his forties, though his face had that smooth, well-rested look of a man who worked because he wanted to—not because he needed the money.

His voice carried back as they kept going. "My wife's asleep so we can't be too loud."

I didn't hear Randle's reply.

THIRTEEN

Randle and the neighbor guy were long gone by the time Adore emerged from the police tent, my seventy-six-dollar Kenneth Cole carry-on rolling behind her. My Target handbag bounced off her hip like a cranky baby. Neither looked right on her. Not next to the designer four-inch heels or the expensive makeup and hair extensions. On Adore Smith maybe, but not this A. Kristine McKinley.

I didn't get out to help her, just watched her make her way over. Part of me hoping she'd at least stumble a bit. Not because I wanted her to fall or hurt herself. Just so I'd know she was actually human.

But no, she maneuvered past the sidewalk's nooks and crannies like she did this every weekend. And she probably did, jetting off here and there for the job that let her get expensive-ass linen business cards.

She smiled when she opened the back door and deadlifted my suitcase onto the seat. She probably did some fancy workout program like CrossFit. "I hope this is everything because I don't think we should stay much longer. I'm sure some people got me on camera."

"Are they giving you Ty's stuff too?"

She shook her head. "I tried but 'he has to pick it up himself.'" Her voice mocked Calloway's peppy tone. "They're 'happy to hold it for him.'"

"That's complete BS." I leaned into the back and unzipped the suitcase.

She eyed the crowd off in the distance. "Maybe check it at the hotel. We can always come back."

I ignored that, too happy to have my stuff. Yet any reassurance I felt about this reunion up and disappeared by the time I had the suitcase open. They'd haphazardly thrown my belongings in like it was a washing machine—not even bothering to separate lights and darks. It did at least look like they'd gotten everything—even the homemade moisturizer I'd stored in decade-old Tupperware. I grabbed my handbag and repeated the entire process, noting everything they'd gone through. My driver's license was no longer in the first slot of my wallet.

But at least my phone was there and it still had plenty of battery power left. I tapped the screen, and there he was. Smiling at me. His arm casually slung over my shoulder as we stared up and at the camera. It was reassuring, even with his face covered by an onslaught of notifications. Proof at least that they hadn't been able to unlock it. Though I was sure they'd tried.

My mom had texted. And called. And apparently texted some more. So had Amina from work. Alyssa too. I hadn't even thought to tell any of them I wouldn't be back today. But that was a problem for Future Bree.

Present Me just wanted to check one thing. I scrolled, and there it was, all the way at the bottom.

Darius Lovehall

Audio message.

That was Ty. He'd sent it Monday at 1:17 a.m.

The only thing that stopped me from checking it immediately was the person who'd just gotten into the driver's seat. I didn't know what he was going to say. What I *did* know was that I didn't want Adore to hear whatever it was. I put the phone down and looked at her. "I didn't see my toiletries. I need my toothbrush."

"We can stop by CVS. Get you a new one."

"It's Sonicare. Removes up to seven times more plaque. Cost me fifty dollars plus tax." She put the car in Drive. I kept on. "That's not a lot for you, *Kristine,* but it is for me. I can't just leave that."

The car went back to Park. "Fine," she said as she got out. "Anything else you need to have?"

Just her to leave. I shook my head. Gave her a tight smile. Waited until she was two houses down before I finally tapped the notification and Ty's text thread magically reappeared. I immediately hit the Play icon, and just like with his outgoing voicemail message, my heart sped up at the sound of his beautiful voice.

"Bree. Baby..."

There was noise in the background like he was outside, and his voice was jumbled and out of breath, like he'd been running. But still. It was him. "I fucked up. I should've been honest with you from the get-go, and now—"

A horn blasted for way too long in the background. Once it finally shut up, Ty took in a breath. When he spoke, he sounded different, like he'd changed his mind about whatever he'd been planning to say. "And...now I'm so sorry. I've wanted to tell you: I love you so much."

And just like that, it was done. The world disappeared. The only things left, me and that message.

Oh no. Ty, what did you do?

The notification popped up in small letters. *Expires in 2m.* A second later it was followed by another option. *Keep.*

I didn't press it, just stared, silently counting the seconds in my head, until the message was gone forever—taking whatever Ty did with it.

But just when the countdown reached ten seconds, I pressed it. *Keep.*

It was the first time he'd said it. *I love you.* I'm not gonna pretend like I wouldn't have preferred it be under different circumstances. But the thing was, I loved him too. And it might've been silly to think that after everything that had happened, how he'd left me behind. But if he was in some deep shit, he needed me. I was going to find him. I just planned to curse him out first when I did.

I hit Play again. Ty's voice once again filled the car. "Bree. Baby...I fucked up. I should've been honest with you from the get-go, and now—" The horn blast. The deep breath. "And...now I'm so sorry. I've wanted to tell you: I love you so much."

That time I realized there wasn't just the horn. There was a voice announcement that went along with it. I hit Play again, pulling the phone right up to my ear. Because that made you hear better, just like turning off music helped you concentrate when you were lost.

The blast could mean only one thing: a train was coming. But which one? The area was nothing if not a hub of mass transportation. I'd taken the PATH and Amtrak in my short time here and walked past signs for others I couldn't name. Ty could've been heading to any of them. I pressed the message again, closing my eyes this time. And it actually worked. I could hear what the announcement said: "Next stop Essex."

I immediately went to Google: "nj train stops essex."

The first hit was an Essex Street New Jersey Transit stop somewhere in Hackensack. But that felt too far for Ty to be at 1:17 a.m. on Monday. Especially since the second one was much closer. A light-rail stop in Jersey City.

The stop before it was Exchange Place—near where we'd taken the PATH train into the city. The PATH station was right by the water and the 9/11 memorial was a couple of blocks away. So was something else. Ty's job.

I was staring at the map when the driver-side door opened and Adore got back in.

"Calloway says you don't want your toothbrush back. And I'm willing to trust her on that."

I looked up and forced a smile. "I'll send her my dentist bill."

But Adore wasn't looking at me. She was looking at my phone. "Everything okay? He call?"

I resisted the urge to wipe my eye. "No."

* * *

If this was some cop show, my brain would've been throwing out theories at ninety miles per hour about why Ty would've been at the Exchange Place light-rail stop at around 1:30 a.m. while his girlfriend was asleep and a stranger was possibly already dead three stories down.

But I didn't care about the why, not at that moment. I just knew he'd been there and I needed to know if he still was.

Adore hadn't said anything when I asked her to drop me off at the hotel. I made a big to-do of going to my room and waiting fifteen minutes before coming back down. Her car was long gone when I did.

The walk over to Exchange Place was shorter than one of my runs, but it felt like forever. Like I was running on a treadmill in one of those small, stuffy apartment-building gyms. I felt stuck and claustrophobic even as the sun beat down, my hand gripping my cell as Google Maps showed me the way.

It didn't help that my phone rang on the way over. I was so surprised I dropped it, staring in horror as it rolled a few times. I scrambled to pick it up, hopeful it was Ty and that I got to him before he hung up. But then I recognized the ringtone.

It was just my mother.

I'd put her on Ignore and put my phone in my bag. Though she could barely use talk to text and didn't even know her phone had emojis, she knew what going straight to voicemail meant. She called right back. I ignored her again. I'd have to deal with her eventually. It just couldn't be now.

Instead, I kept walking, tuning out the oodles of people taking advantage of the riverfront view. Some were there for the Manhattan skyline. Some were just there for exercise. None of them paid me the least bit of attention as they passed me by. There were no nosy neighbors staring at me with suspicion. No former friends acting like I was naive. No cops wanting to ask me questions.

I was anonymous.

I should've enjoyed it. Instead, I felt alone. Helpless. Unsure of what to do.

I'd barely paid attention to the light-rail when we'd walked by it on Saturday, too excited to get into New York City. But now I took in the station from across the street. It wasn't much. Just plopped in the street. The only hint that it was even a train stop were the tracks and long wires suspended over them. A handful of people stood waiting for the train, all donning the disinterested expression of New Yorkers despite being in New Jersey.

I looked at all their faces, hoping one of them was Ty. Like he'd just be standing on a nearby corner, waiting for the light to turn green—off to look for me like I was looking for him.

But he wasn't there.

Even though I'd known it was a long shot, I still felt disappointed. He had been here Monday morning. And I had to believe that he was *still* here. Somewhere. Waiting.

I looked up. It felt like there were just as many tall buildings as there were people. This wasn't like where I grew up or even like Little Street. Where you could tell what type of building it was just by the exterior. Some could have been offices. Others could have been condos.

I went to cross the street even though I now had nowhere to go. That's when the panic truly set in, the tears feeling imminent. I was closer to him than I'd been in days and yet I was still so far away. I felt like a baby trying to hold something in my hand for the first time and not able to grasp it.

I stopped only when I heard the horn, felt the stranger's hand grasping my arm. And that's when I noticed the car mere inches away. Pedestrians here never paid much attention to WALK signs, but they did notice cars passing by. In my panic, I hadn't realized that the cars were moving and the people weren't.

"You okay?" the man said, and for a moment I was tempted to tell this stranger how scared I felt. How lost I was. Physically and mentally. But instead I just nodded. Thanked him for essentially saving my life.

WWTD?

He'd force himself to calm down. Come up with a plan—even if it was a bad one at this point. The only thing I could think of was just going door-to-door. I decided to start with the door closest to me. The sign above it said HYATT HOUSE. It didn't look like a hotel, but nothing looked like it was supposed to here. It could've been a bank.

I couldn't remember the exact hotel he stayed at earlier this week. A Hyatt or maybe a Hilton. It would make sense for him to go back there. I just hoped it was this one. When I went inside, I was expecting a hotel lobby. Instead, I got a set of stairs going down and one guy in a stock security suit rocking an N95. He nodded when he saw me. "You checking in?"

I nodded. It seemed simpler than the real reason I'd come.

"Take the elevator all the way on the right," he said. "Hit 'TR.' Terrace rooftop."

It turned out "terrace rooftop" was their fancy way of saying thirteen. The lobby was on the top floor. A good thing. Maybe I didn't need to go up there at all. I could just start on two. Knock on doors until I found him. But then I hit the button for the second floor. Nothing happened. And that's when I noticed the black box. You needed a key card to get to the rooms.

I was heading to TR after all. The only things with me in the elevator on the ride up were the butterflies in my stomach. My smile was in place by the time the elevator doors opened. The front desk was closer than I'd thought it would be, about ten feet away. Clear dividers still up for COVID safety. They were the least glamorous thing in the place. Unlike downstairs, this looked how a hotel was supposed to. The rest of the lobby stretched out toward the left, but I laser-focused on the Latina woman staring back at me. She wore a face mask, but I could tell she was smiling by her eyes.

"Welcome to Hyatt House."

"Thank you." I walked over, talking fast as I did. Partly because I was so nervous and partly to not give her time to think. "Can you call Tyler Franklin's room, tell him Breanna Wright's here?"

"Sure." She picked up a phone. "What's the room number?"

I should've known I wouldn't be that lucky. My voice was slower when I spoke again, and for once, I didn't lie. "Look, I'm trying to find my boyfriend. I'm not going to insult you by expecting you to tell me if he's here when I clearly don't know myself. But can I just leave him a note? You can give it to him when he checks out."

She sighed, then: "The name does sound familiar. I will say that."

She slid me some hotel stationery. Grabbing a hotel pen, I left yet another version of the note I'd left at Ty's job. Then I folded it up, wrote "Tyler Franklin" in big bold letters, and placed it on the chest-level desk between us. "Thank you!"

I turned, ready to go back to my own hotel room and again wait to see if he'd call. But by the time I got to the elevator, there was another voice behind me. I didn't turn around, just pressed the Down button.

"Tyler Franklin's staying here?" This voice sounded younger than the first.

The elevator doors opened just in time. I practically leapt inside and quickly pushed the button for the ground floor, not daring to look at the pair even though they were directly in my line of sight.

"His girlfriend left that note for him," the first attendant said.

The doors started to close. And just as I was about to let out a sigh of relief, the second woman spoke again.

"Girlfriend? Janelle Beckett can't be here. She's dead."

A serious Billie Regan sits in front of the camera with the #Justice4 Janelle text covering her chest. Her makeup is subtle but flawless, as if she wants to look her very best but doesn't want you to know she does.

"Hey, Billie Bunch. I know I have that Live scheduled for later this afternoon, but I had to get this up immediately. For those new here, I'm Billie. This is my channel. Normally I do makeup tips, but lately I've been focused on the disappearance and now murder of one of my followers, Janelle Beckett, though the police won't even identify her poor body.

"When I went to check my DMs for that photo of Tyler Franklin in Boston, which I promise I'll still share, I had a message from someone else. This person and I had a nice long DM chat. And after I promised to keep their information private, they agreed to let me share what we discussed."

A screenshot appears behind her of a DM convo. Billie's sloppily blacked out the other person's photo and name. The light-gray bubble reads: *I was Janelle Beckett's freshman year roommate.*

There's more to the text chain, but it's blocked by Billie's upper body. She speaks. "She sent me this."

A photo's behind her now. This one is a close-up of a much younger but smiling Janelle Beckett next to an equally skinny woman. Her face has been blurred out, but you can tell her skin is pale. "They weren't close, but they got along. This is a photo of the two of them together. When she heard about what's been going on, she took a look at her Facebook albums from college, found this and some others, which I'll get to. You can only imagine how I felt getting this DM. How excited I was that someone was reaching out to share a bit more about Janelle's wonderful life. I couldn't stop smiling. Until she told me the rest."

Billie's face actually stops smiling as she gets serious. "Apparently, Janelle met some upperclassman. Fell in love quick. Spent a lot of time at his off-campus apartment. But the relationship was volatile. Janelle would come back to the dorm room every time they got in a fight. And she'd come back more and more as the semester went on. And then, finally, things came to a head. The roommate doesn't know what happened. Janelle never shared with her, but it must've been *bad,* because one day Janelle said she was dropping out. Packed up her stuff. And she never came back. The roommate tried to keep in touch, but Janelle never responded."

Billie shakes her head, as if she can't believe it. Tears form. "Our poor Janelle. She lived such a life of pain. I think that's why I connected so much with her. Because we're both the same in that, no matter what, we keep smiling. Always."

More tears. She wipes them away and gets herself together. "Here's where things take a turn. Let's go back to my DMs."

The DMs are back, except now Billie's shown more.

The light-gray bubble: *I was Janelle Beckett's freshman year roommate.*

Billie's response is now visible in blue. *At Montclair State?*

Their response: *No. College Park.*

Billie's positioned herself in the bottom right of the screen. She points to the words "College Park." "Before Janelle Beckett graduated from Montclair State University, she was at University of Maryland—College Park. I know you're wondering how we missed this, but it was just one semester. And as soon as I saw College Park,

I immediately recognized the name as where Tyler Franklin went to undergrad."

Tyler's Instagram page appears behind her; the *UMD Man* in his bio has been hastily circled in a thick red. "According to his LinkedIn, he graduated in 2011, which meant he would've been there fall of her freshman year. The roommate didn't even need to send me this photo, but I'm glad she did."

Another photo pops up. Janelle wears the same outfit from the previous picture. It's from the same night. Behind her, a few college-age kids are in what looks like an animated conversation. They're at a party. Janelle's hugged up with a Black guy.

It's a younger, chunkier Tyler Franklin.

"Janelle and Tyler Franklin dated her freshman year. He was the one whose apartment she was staying at, who'd kick her out every time they got into a fight. He was so horrible that poor Janelle had to leave campus and was afraid to speak to anyone there, including her old roommate."

Another screenshot pops up behind Billie. It's a comment from JayJay4321: *Today's #MakeupMonday got me wanting to hit up my ex.*

"When Janelle posted this on one of my Lives, I didn't think much of it at the time. But now I know that ex had to be Tyler Franklin. That would explain so much. This wasn't some random encounter. They knew each other. They were dating. Again. And I can't help but keep thinking about that comment and wondering if something I said pushed her back toward Tyler Franklin. It made me realize I need to be more mindful of what I say. How I use this platform. Because I would never be able to forgive myself if I played even the smallest part in what happened to Janelle."

She pauses. Contemplating. Truly torn. Finally, she shakes it off, smiles that fake smile to prove everything is okay. "If you know where Tyler Franklin is or can prove that's him in that video hunting down Janelle Beckett, my DMs are open."

FOURTEEN

A ding. The elevator doors opened, but I didn't move. Too busy crying.

No one was in the lobby, but I still didn't leave. Just stared at my phone blankly as the elevator doors shut again. Not ready to face the world, I didn't do anything. Just stood there in the safety of the elevator, and tuned back in. I wasn't the only one crying. On my phone, Billie was too.

I'd seen the video three times at this point—enough to know what was coming next, but it still felt like a slap in the face when I saw it.

Ty and Janelle hugged up. Looking happy as hell while at it. I would've recognized that smile anywhere.

Billie spoke again, and I could've mouthed the words with her. "This wasn't some random encounter. They knew each other. They were dating. Again. And I can't help but keep thinking about that comment and wondering if something I said pushed her back toward Tyler Franklin. It made me realize I need to be more mindful of what I say. How I use this platform. Because I would never be able to forgive myself if I played even the smallest part in what happened to Janelle... If you know where Tyler Franklin is or can prove that's him in that video hunting down Janelle Beckett, my DMs are open."

Billie was smart enough not to switch from the picture as she spoke from the corner. Unlike the Ring footage, there was no doubt it was him. A younger, thicker version, but him nonetheless.

I stared at him smiling back at me until the video started over again. The TikTok loop.

I still didn't stop it. Didn't press Pause. Just watched—alone in that elevator. Not daring to move. Staring at the screen once again, hoping that this time the video would end differently. That it was some other Black guy hugged up on Janelle Beckett.

But it wasn't. So I watched again. And again. And again. Until the elevator doors finally opened.

There were four of them. All male. All the same shade of brown, but different sizes, like Russian dolls placed side by side. They were as surprised to see me as I was to see them. The world had stopped. Now it was back moving again.

"Sorry." But I'd mumbled it and I doubted they heard me.

I didn't say it again. They parted and I barreled through, ignoring the security guard still standing by the entrance. He told me to have a good day anyway. I didn't tell him that ship had sailed.

Outside, the day was still beautiful. It shouldn't have been. It should've been thunder and lightning. A blizzard, even though it was already spring.

I tried to go through scenarios of how this information could make sense, because I didn't want to believe it. I wanted to believe in *him*. Even forced myself to think of the last audio message he'd left. He'd said he loved me.

But he'd also said he'd fucked up.

And as much as I wanted to go with my heart, my head was saying something else.

I quickened my pace, weaving through people on the street,

bumping into a guy who refused to get out my way even though I was on the correct side of the sidewalk. It didn't matter. I didn't feel it. Too numb.

I rewound back to the first day we'd met, when Ty told me my shoe was untied. Then I fast-forwarded through the rest of our relationship, searching for signs I'd fallen for a man who could do what I'd seen in that foyer.

I hadn't felt this naive—this silly—since the day I was arrested. And just like then, I got mad. I went to my phone messages, ready to delete his voice recording. Instead, I deleted the entire thread. Just as it disappeared, my phone rang. My mom. Once again, I was thankful to Past Me for giving her a special ringtone. It had been a good decision. Probably the only one I'd made in my life. Clearly.

I should've picked up. As unbearable as she was, she was still my mother. She had a right to know I was okay. We hadn't spoken in days at this point. It wasn't like me. But still, I ignored it. I couldn't talk to her. Not yet.

Not with the Billie video replaying over and over in my head as I bumbled about aimlessly, speeding up when I wanted to stop, stopping when I should've moved faster. The photo of Ty and Janelle hovering over me like a cloud.

Then I saw the crowd. I'd somehow stumbled on Little Street. Maybe it was instinct. Maybe fate. Maybe it was God having a sense of humor.

The police tape and barriers were still up on this end of the street. I stopped on the opposite corner. Watched the crowd watching the police. Thinking of Janelle lying there on the floor, blood seeping from what looked like every part of her body.

Yes, Ty had hurt me, but now there was a good chance he'd hurt her far worse.

Breathing heavy, I bent down, hands on knees like I had finally gone for my daily run. When I did catch my breath, I reached into my bag and took out my phone. Then I made a call.

I was surprised I still had the number memorized.

* * *

Adore still knocked like she was the police. Hard, quick taps that screamed, *I belong here,* meant to convey a confidence that she finally seemed to possess. My cell was in the bedroom by the time she got to my hotel. Thrown in the tangle of sheets I'd left that morning. I'd gone for the out-of-sight, out-of-mind approach and failed miserably.

A Brush With Billie's video still played on a mental loop.

Adore smiled when I opened the door, but it wasn't one like she was glad to see me. It was the one you give when your friend's finally realized you were right all along. That her boyfriend wasn't shit. We'd given each other that look a lot in college. But the look took on a different meaning when you were talking about a murderer.

"I brought sustenance," she said. Like this was just some average breakup bitch session.

Chunky Monkey. My favorite before I'd sworn off dairy. I grabbed it anyway, walking to the kitchenette to pick up two spoons. Screw a bowl. She'd beelined right for the table separating the kitchen from the living area. I was a few seconds behind, ripping off the top of the container like it was Ty's head.

Neither of us spoke at first, just shoved spoonful after spoonful into our mouths like kids anticipating Mom catching us at any moment. I ate until I felt it deep in my stomach. I'd pay for it tomorrow morning, but it wasn't like I could feel any worse.

She raised her hand to her mouth to wipe away ice cream that wasn't there. A. Kristine McKinley wasn't the type to have food on her face. "You okay?" she finally said.

And of course I went with the joke. "I did say it was always the boyfriend."

But then I started to cry. Again.

Adore immediately came around the table to hug me. "You need to be kind to yourself." She sounded like one of the corny memes my boss loved to send. "You found a body. Bludgeoned. And it happened when you were in the house. Upstairs. Asleep. That's scary, Bree, on its own."

"That's what I'll tell Janelle Beckett's sister. 'I'm so sorry I didn't do crap to help with catching her killer.' A woman died so horribly they can't even officially ID her, but I only cared about my boyfriend."

She ignored that. "You do realize that maybe the reason you were so focused on trying to find Ty is you didn't want to process how scary that was for you. You have nothing to apologize for. You didn't kill Janelle Beckett."

"What if Ty did?" I said. "What if by doing nothing I helped him get away? There's no way he's still in Jersey City. He could be in Mexico for all we know."

"Don't put that burden on yourself."

"You're being nicer to me than I deserve. I've been nothing but an a-hole since you saved me from the cops."

"We're both a-holes then. When I saw you in a video posted on Twitter, you looked so upset even from a distance. I recognized you immediately, knew you needed help. But I wasn't going to come. I was just going to sit in my apartment and think about how badly I messed up. How I wasn't there for you before when you needed me. But then I decided that even though I couldn't change the past, I could do the right thing now."

There was a pause then. It was like we were at the edge of the cliff, looking down, waiting for the other to say the word so we could jump.

"Bree, we need to—"

But then her cell rang. She pulled her eyes away from me to look at the caller ID. "I have to take this."

I stayed stock-still while she went into the bedroom to talk law-yer shit. Once again, I did a mental replay of everything that had hap-pened over the past two days, kicking myself for what I'd done wrong at each stage. Finding Janelle's poor body and not even calling the police. Then focusing on getting my cell, getting to Ty. Protecting him. I skipped forward, to the video from the alley. Me not telling Detective Randle immediately that I recognized the hoodie. I mentally pressed fast-forward again to a few minutes ago. Adore trying to make me feel better, broaching the conversation we should've had twelve years ago. It was silly and it was childish that we'd ignored each other for so long. It shouldn't have taken someone dying to bring us back together. But here we were.

Adore was right about one thing, though. Even if I couldn't change the past, I could change the present and make things right.

By the time she came back into the living room, I'd rehearsed what I was going to say a good ten times.

"I want to talk to the police."

* * *

After we made the call, I had no clue how long I pretended to nap. Adore had closed the blackout curtains and I'd unplugged the bed-side clock after I got sick of the red light taunting me. Still, I tossed and turned like someone had stuck a pea under the mattress. Except I wasn't some princess. I was just a fool.

And just like a fool, I still checked the hashtag. Some were brag-ging how they knew Ty and Janelle had a connection. How this had screamed a crime of passion from the jump. And now we just had proof.

Others were still on the lookout—posting "Ty sightings" with exact locations and times. Some had gotten braver. One group of teens followed a Black guy out of a drugstore, calling him a murderer until he made it to the safety of his car. The only thing he had in common with Ty was that he loved black hoodies.

That one had 14,000 likes and hundreds of comments from people saying they'd shared the license plate number with the police.

That was my fault too. They wouldn't have been harassing that poor man if I'd helped the cops find Ty.

There was a knock and I jumped, surprised Adore was still there. I hadn't been much company since I'd finished the ice cream. I felt sick to my stomach and I couldn't blame either Ben or Jerry.

Adore banged on the bedroom door again. Those police knocks. I just lay there, staring at a ceiling I couldn't see in the pitch-black. And suddenly there was light. I looked over, past the mess I'd made of my stuff even though I'd only just gotten my suitcase back. Adore was beautiful even in blacked-out profile. When she spoke, it was soft. "They're doing another press conference."

"You can turn on the light," I said.

She did but still stood there as I willed myself up, then scrambled to find where I'd left the remote. My hand patted aimlessly beside me before I finally found it under one of the pillows. "Come in," I said, and she did, sitting on the edge of the bed.

I turned the bedroom TV on. "What channel?" I said, then realized it didn't matter. It was on all of them.

It was just like before. Same podium. Same background. Same collection of white guys in what looked like the same outfits. Police Chief David Something or Other was already at the lectern. His face looked different. Better. It took me a second to realize it was makeup. Nothing fancy. Just a little powder. Made me wonder if he'd also been watching A Brush With Billie.

"Are they going to name me?" I said.

Adore glanced back. Shook her head. "I made that clear to Calloway after you spoke to her."

I didn't respond. Just took in a breath, the remote in a death grip as I waited for whatever came next.

The chief cleared his throat and once again began. "Good evening. I'm Police Chief David King. I'm here to give you an update on the deceased woman found at approximately ten thirty yesterday morning at 110 Little Street."

We all knew who it was. They needed to officially ID her already.

He continued. "Our department has been working around the clock on our investigation. Last night we shared a video of a woman being followed behind the house on the previous Monday evening."

I wanted to hit Pause then. Run out of the room. Instead, I sat back and once again found myself waiting. I glanced over at Adore, but her eyes were glued to her phone, the movement of her thumb hinting she was checking comments or tweets.

"We asked for the public's help in identifying the people in the video. And we were overwhelmed with the response. We must've had hundreds, if not thousands, of tips. So thank you to everyone who called the hotline."

He wasn't talking about me. Adore had Calloway's personal cell phone. She'd picked up on the second ring, even though I'd been hoping to be sent straight to voicemail. I'd thought maybe she'd be suspicious of why I suddenly was sharing the info about the hoodie. That she'd use her police Spidey sense to know it wasn't a coincidence my change of heart had come after Billie had gleefully shared that old photo. But if she did, Calloway hadn't said anything.

I'd figured Calloway would want a photo of her own, one of Ty wearing the hoodie, Sade's arms crossed casually over her denim shirt, staring expressionless right into the camera. But she didn't. Just asked me to stick around in case they had any other questions and then thanked me for my help. She hadn't mentioned what would come next. And now I was finding out along with the rest of the world.

"As many of you know, we've also been looking into the disappearance of a local woman who was last seen Monday night a week ago," Chief King was saying. "Her name is Janelle Beckett. Thanks to a reliable witness, we were able to identify Ms. Beckett as the woman in the video taken on that same Monday night, a few hours after her sighting in Journal Square."

He paused then, as if waiting for someone to come pat him on the back, like he wasn't just reporting information that had been already shared, liked, and commented on online. But hearing it from the police hit different.

"Although 110 Little Street is an Airbnb owned by a corporation, our investigation was able to confirm that it was rented out starting Friday by one Tyler Franklin of Baltimore, Maryland."

I didn't think it possible to hold the remote any tighter, but my hands were whiter than the 1,000-thread-count sheets. It was the first time the police had said his name. I didn't like how it sounded in the police chief's mouth, as if it tasted like black licorice or candy corn.

Chief King continued. "That was just one of many things that have come to light. We also were sent proof Tyler Franklin has a past connection to Ms. Beckett. And we just heard from another reliable witness who identified Tyler Franklin as the man in the video. Although we aren't ready to formally ID the victim from Monday morning, we do believe that crime is related to Janelle Beckett's disappearance. We believe Tyler Franklin to be a person of interest in both cases. We're asking that he contact us immediately. If you do encounter Mr. Franklin, please call the police. Do not try to talk to him or detain him yourself. We believe he may be armed and—"

The screen shut off. It was only after Adore turned to stare at me that I realized I was the one who had done it.

FIFTEEN

Not watching the rest of the press conference didn't help how I felt. It was like the shark in *Jaws*. Not being able to see it just made things worse. I was so busy imagining what else the police chief was saying, I forgot Adore was even in the room until her phone beeped. I jolted back to reality, looking over in time to see her checking her phone. "I have a meeting in a half hour. I'm happy to cancel it."

But I was shaking my head before she finished. "Go," I said. "I'll be fine."

I started to wipe my eye but caught myself. Just like that, I was back to lying. But fully committed, I got up to show her out, taking time to pat her shoulder as I walked by. "You've been with me nonstop. It's the middle of a workweek. You need to focus on your job. Otherwise, who's going to pay for the hotel?"

I turned when I got to the doorway and found her smiling. After a moment, she got up too. Followed me to the front door. She spoke just as I was opening it.

"Do me a favor, Bree. Delete your social media profiles."

I said nothing, but she could sense my hesitation.

"Only thing you're going to do is stalk the Justice for Janelle hashtag," she said. "I know you want to see what they're saying, but trust me, it doesn't matter. Janelle Beckett will still be dead. Ty will still be the one who did it."

I flinched hearing her say it, a part of me still wanting to object. To protest his innocence. Instead, I said, "Probably would be a good decision."

Adore hugged me, then was gone. I watched her until she turned the hall corner. Then I went back to bed and picked up my phone. There he was again. Staring at me. Smiling. Except this time it felt patronizing. I stared in pity at the photo of me next to him. Thinking I was happy when I was just naive.

I went to the Twitter app, all ready to delete my account. But instead, I clicked on the magnifying glass at the bottom. #TylerFranklin was already the number-four search topic on Twitter, the NBA Playoffs the only thing preventing him from being number one. His name was trending with two others: #Justice4Janelle and "person of interest." There were 11.6K tweets.

I wasn't the only one who had Ty on their shit list. But instead of feeling happy about it, I was pissed. Yes, still partly at him. I had a right to be. But the other part was just as mad at the almost twelve thousand people who felt they needed to share their opinion. Some sentimental. Some ridiculous. All attention seeking.

Eleven thousand six hundred of us may have been mad, but only one of us had come down those stairs Monday morning. Only one of us had found a bloodied and beaten Janelle Beckett a few feet from the front door. Only one of us had seen the blood seeping away from her like it was just as scared of her as I was of it.

Adore was right. Just like always.

And I still didn't listen to her.

Just like always.

Instead, I compromised and made my pages private.

* * *

I was up early yet again, which was how I knew that Janelle's sister had finally agreed to do an interview with one of the national news networks. They broke it up into two parts and teased it on their morning show. Her name was Denise, and she was an older, bigger version of her sister. In one snippet, she looked somber. "Janelle changed after our parents died. We each handled it differently. I had to get out of New Jersey, but she stayed as if stuck and kind of withdrew from everyone."

She spoke as they showed a childhood picture of the two of them, smiling while wearing Mickey Mouse ears, obviously happy to be at Disneyland. Once again I was struck by how alive Janelle looked.

Present-day Denise Beckett dabbed tears with a crumpled white tissue.

"Have the police contacted you?" the unseen voice said.

"Not yet."

"When is the last time you talked to your sister?"

And that's when she stopped mid-dab and stared directly at the unseen interviewer. "It's been months. We got into a fight over something I now realize was silly. I lost my parents. I wish we'd realized when they died how short life is."

I was thinking her words over when my phone rang. My mother, calling me at a time when she knew I'd be asleep. And normally I would've been if I hadn't been kept up by my brain thinking about Ty and Janelle—what had happened to them both.

I was tempted to not answer again, but I thought of the interview with Janelle's sister. She'd give anything to talk to her family again. I was ignoring mine. I accepted the FaceTime. It was 7:30 a.m., yet my mom had her "face" on. She sat on her side of our couch, my acne-covered high school graduation photo lording over her.

She flinched when she saw me. "You must be having a good time."

I was not, so I didn't say a word. Just wiped the tears-turned-crud out of the corners of my eyes before she said anything about it. "How's Grandma doing?" I said instead, realizing if I didn't get back soon my mom would need someone else to come take care of her.

"Yesterday was not a good day. She's still asleep, so we'll see how today goes. But I don't want to talk about your grandmother. How's it going? Your trip with your Mystery Man has to be going well if you decided to stay a few extra days. I've tried to be patient but couldn't take it anymore. I figured I'd catch you early before you two got on with your day."

She smiled then, full pink lips separating to show perfectly white teeth. For a second, I was tempted to lie.

"You hear what happened to that girl who went missing?" I said.

"That white woman? Janelle something or other? I know I sent you that. Almost called you too to tell you to be careful, but then I heard her ex-boyfriend did it."

My ex-boyfriend did it.

She spoke again. "Just goes to show you can't trust anyone."

She was right about that. My phone buzzed. Adore. I went to check the text.

"Why did the screen go black?" my mom said.

"Got a text from Adore." I had murmured it absentmindedly, then realized what I'd said.

I winced, not having to see her to know her expression. I quickly licked my lips to wait her out. It took only a few more seconds. "Adore Smith."

More statement than question. Neither of us needed a Google search to know that there was probably only one person with that name in this universe.

"Why are you talking to that woman?" My mother didn't curse, but then she didn't need to. She somehow had made "woman" sound like the synonym for female dog. "I warned you about her."

She warned me about everybody. She didn't like anyone, including me, though she'd never admit that. Loved me? Yes. Too much. Liked me? Completely different story.

"She's changed, Ma."

"How?"

The name was the most obvious, but I wasn't telling her that. She'd google her and be leaving Adore's law firm bad reviews on Yelp ten minutes after we got off the phone. I finally went back to FaceTime. My mother's face was stone. She wasn't looking at the camera. She was looking back. Twelve years ago.

"Has she apologized? For what she did to you, Breanna."

Not with words, no. But still. My mother kept on, though I tuned her out.

Maryland had voted to legalize recreational marijuana in 2022, the same year the president had pushed to grant pardons to anyone with a federal simple marijuana conviction.

I remembered how my boss had come to me on Election Day to tell me that she'd voted to legalize it because of me. I didn't have the heart to tell her it didn't matter. Making my record go away wouldn't magically make my life any better. It wouldn't take the shame away. It wouldn't make up for all the things I didn't do.

I never took the LSAT. Never moved out of my studio apartment. Never left the job I'd originally taken just for "spending money." Never moved to DC to live in a fancy loft like Adore and I had always talked about.

I said none of this, though—just thought it for the millionth time—as I watched my mother work herself up, always wanting to blame Adore's bad influence for what had gone wrong in my life. And that's when I made the decision: there was no way I was going to tell her about anything that was happening. Instead, I just continued to tune her out, offering the occasional nod and "You're right," because that was all I could say when she got like this. I didn't really tune back in until I heard my name.

"I'm sorry, Ma. What'd you say?"

"You need to come home."

She was right.

Calloway wanted me to stay, but she couldn't force me. It was time to finally go back to Maryland. I had family obligations, though I'd still want to go home even if I didn't. Ty had sprung for a round-trip train ticket. First-class cabin. The return ticket was open, so I could go whenever I wanted.

And it was only then I realized I *wanted*.

"I'll be home soon," I finally said. "Hopefully today."

We hung up and I checked the train schedule. Amtrak had a train leaving at ten. The good news was I didn't have much stuff to pack. If I rushed, I could check out and hopefully find my way back to the train station in Newark in time.

I'd just thrown one dirty-ass sock into my carry-on and was desperately searching for its twin when my phone rang. Adore. I put her on speaker.

"Morning," she said. "What are you doing? Figured maybe I could bring over breakfast."

"I'm not super hungry. How long does it take to get to Penn Station?"

"Newark? Twenty minutes." She paused, and then: "Why?"

The sock had crammed itself into my running shoe. I pulled it out, threw it into my bag, then sat down. "Just spoke to my mom. She wanted to know when I was coming back. I was afraid to tell her why I wasn't home already. I told my boss I needed to stay longer, but she's only going to be so patient. I need to get out of here."

"Okay...Did you tell Calloway?"

I deflated at the name. "No. Why would I have to?"

"She asked you to stick around."

"Right. Asked. But I'm not under arrest. I should be able to leave."

The panic must've been evident in my voice because Adore's words rushed out. "No, it's fine. You're right. But you should still just give them a heads-up. It might look bad if you don't."

I didn't say anything. Just stared at my suitcase, my belongings just as jumbled as my brain.

"What time's your train?" Adore said.

"Ten."

There was a pause as if she pulled her phone away from her ear to check the time, then she spoke again. "Great. I'll call Calloway. Let her know. And then I'll come drive you. I'll even stop by Dunkin' Donuts."

I hated her tone, like she was thirty minutes deep into negotiations with some petulant child about going to bed. But it was the adult in me who appreciated not having to do any of that myself. Adore would take care of everything. All I had to do was sit in a car and eat a Boston Kreme. "I'll be ready at nine fifteen," I said.

SIXTEEN

I was waiting on the street outside the hotel, checking #Justice4 Janelle on Twitter. A neighbor had been making the interview rounds. It was the redhead, Krista. Someone had thoughtfully pulled a highlight from her conversation with Anderson Cooper about how "aggressive" Ty was. The clip had 30,000 likes and close to 8 million views. I was giving it one more when Adore pulled up in her Tesla.

She didn't see me at first so I had to wave her down, happy for a reason to stop torturing myself with my Twitter timeline. Once I got her attention, she pulled over to the curb, ignoring the long and hard honk of the guy she'd cut off. I went to the back of the car, waited patiently while she popped the trunk, then threw my carry-on inside. Her trunk was spotless, like she paid extra at the car wash for them to dig all up in the crevices.

I opened the passenger door but didn't sit down. "We just need to check me out and we'll be good to go. Train leaves at ten. If I miss it, I gotta wait another two hours."

She said nothing.

I attempted a smile. "Everything okay?"

She looked at me. "I talked to the police."

No. "I cannot stay here, Adore."

I'd emailed my boss, apologizing for missing another day. Promised I'd be back since I'd switched shifts with Alyssa and was supposed to work tomorrow. And even if I hadn't, I couldn't stay here. I wanted to leave. Pretend none of this had happened, though I knew I'd think about it every day for the rest of my life.

"I told them you had to get back to work," Adore said. "That you'd be available 24/7 if they needed to talk to you. Even told them you'd jump on Zoom if need be. Video on."

"But…"

"They still want you to stay."

"For how long?" I said.

She shrugged.

"They want me to wait until they find Ty, don't they?" I took her silence as a yes. "Do they even have any idea where he is?"

"It shouldn't be long. They're getting a ton of tips."

"Right. From the Billies of the internet. They're probably calling in every Black guy in a hoodie in a ten-state radius. You saw that video she posted from the train in Boston? It could've been anyone's head."

"Give it a couple more days and I can make a case." She attempted a smile. "I did get the donuts. They're in the back seat."

I was quiet long enough that she finally looked at me.

"When's the last time you went on vacation?" I said, still talking to her from outside the car.

She looked confused, then resigned. "I haven't gone anywhere in a while."

"Christmas in Aspen? New Year's in Miami?"

"Mexico for my birthday."

August 2.

I didn't say anything at first. Just nodded. We were supposed to go to Mexico for graduation. She'd spent the entire year saving up. My mother was supposed to pay for my trip as a gift. "Cancún?" I said.

"Cabo."

She'd probably already been to Cancún. Several times. This was my first real vacation outside of a few family trips to Ocean City. I couldn't afford to go anywhere else. "How much underwear did you bring, Adore?" I said. "Four pairs? Eight? Twelve?"

"I don't remember, but then I don't remember a lot about that trip." She smiled, like it was the key to defusing a ticking bomb.

"Five days," I said. "I brought enough underwear for five days. I only needed two days' worth. That's how long I was supposed to be here. But you always pack extra, right? Because you never know."

I paused, the bomb three seconds closer to going off. "I'm out of underwear."

"We can buy you some more," she said. "Newport Centre is just a couple miles away."

"I don't want new underwear." I was crying again now. Big, watery tears that flew down my face. My breath sped up, faster and faster. Just as upset to be this panicked over underwear as I was upset about not having the underwear itself. By the time I did speak, I knew she wouldn't be able to understand a word I said. "I want to wear my own clean underwear."

"Two days, Bree. Just give it two more days and then I'll call them back. Remind them how cooperative you've been and that it's not your fault they can't find their main suspect. You've done everything you could to help. Now please get in."

I didn't say anything, just continued to cry as I finally got into the car and closed the passenger-side door. Adore checked for traffic, then pulled out.

"Where are we going?" I was not in the mood to walk past a Bath & Body Works like everything was okay.

"My place. I have a washing machine. Dryer too."

I was too tired to object.

She didn't live far. A left here. A right there. Half a dozen or so stoplights. And then she was home. I texted my boss on the way there with a horrible excuse for why I needed more time. I didn't want to mention what was going on. Her response was terse, but at least she didn't fire me.

On the outside, Adore's building wasn't much. I'd been expecting a high-rise encased in glass. Instead, I got three stories of brick. It was wide, though, taking up at least half the block. And it was fancy enough to have the building name on the awning.

The building also had its own parking lot with a single entrance. Gated, of course. Adore waved her key fob in the general direction of the sensor and the gate slid open like it was supposed to. Hers wasn't the only Tesla in the lot. She smiled after she pulled into a space marked 1B. "We're home," she said.

I hesitated only a moment before getting out, but by the time I did, Adore had her trunk open and my Kenneth Cole suitcase out. "I can take it," I said.

"I got it." She lifted the handle and started toward the door.

I didn't follow right away, just watched her and my bag, looking like the Odd Couple. Adore had brought a bag full of Kmart's finest with her freshman year. But this person, this A. Kristine McKinley, made that all feel like a literal past life. After a moment I rushed to catch up. She used the same fob to get us in the front door. The lobby was large, but it was also empty.

"No doorman?" I hated the way my voice had sounded as soon as I said it, the trace of bitterness in it like I had just swallowed a shot of cyanide. So I tried again. "Was just wondering how the Amazon deliveries come in."

"They find a way." She smiled then, playing along like she hadn't heard my tone as she wheeled my luggage through the hallway past the lone elevator. "I'm right here."

The inside was not what I'd thought it would be. I had been expecting one story. Low ceilings and not a lot of space. Instead, I got a two-story loft with an open floor plan. The kitchen was tucked in the corner closest to the foyer, leaving plenty of room for the oversized white couches and round marble dining room table. The place was a collection of muted colors—whites and nudes.

It was beautiful.

It was also exactly how she'd told me she wanted to live when we used to wax poetic about our futures. We'd talked about moving to DC, getting side-by-side fancy lofts with a view. Nothing like the house in the suburbs I had grown up in or the cramped two-bedroom apartment Adore had shared with her mom and three brothers.

And she'd done it, exactly what she'd said—*we'd* said.

She wheeled my bag to the kitchen, then left it to head to the stainless-steel fridge. My eyes took in the rest of the room, going up, up, up, until they landed on the second floor. More marble. This time on the wall. And two doors on either side of the short hallway. "Where's the washing machine?" I said.

"Bathroom. It's that door on the end."

I mumbled a quick thank-you, reclaimed my Kenneth Cole bag, and wheeled it across her beautiful hardwood floors while praying I didn't leave a scratch. Her bathroom was damn near bigger than my entire apartment. Even the washing machine was a thing of beauty. It had its own closet next to the glassed-in shower. It took everything not to slam the bathroom door.

I didn't dare put my suitcase on anything, so I just opened it in the middle of the floor, smack-dab on the fluffy white rug. My plan was to just throw everything into the washing machine, pour in some detergent, and let it rip.

But then I got stuck.

My building had a teeny-tiny laundry room in the basement. Two washers. Two dryers. All probably older than I was. This one was fancy. A front loader with too many buttons. It felt like the machine version of some foreign language. I pressed a button at random based on size. It beeped. Nothing happened. So I tried it all over again, only to get the same result. And just when I was about to start crying again, Adore knocked. "Need help? I can barely use the thing myself."

I stepped back to let her open it up, then handed her my clothes. She added a Tide Pod and pressed a few buttons until something beeped. I heard the water rush in. At least that was familiar. We both stood there, watching my clothes get more and more wet, before she turned to me. "I have wine."

I didn't even pretend like it was too early.

She chose a pinot noir. I knew because it said so on the label. She set it on the counter, then went straight to a cabinet. I figured there were wineglasses inside. I didn't figure on so many different styles. Wide. Narrow. Shapes I'd never seen. She selected two of the wider ones, then came back to me.

"How much do you drink?" I was proud I'd kept my voice light.

"The ex-husband fashioned himself a wine connoisseur." She didn't use air quotes. Just rolled her eyes. "And there are different glasses for different types of wine. When he asked me for the divorce, I asked for them in our settlement just to be petty. He had to buy all new ones for that bitch he cheated on me with."

I picked up my glass, swirling it around like this was some fancy restaurant. "So this is for reds?"

"Yes," she said. "I think. I mean, it tastes pretty much the same. It could be a paper cup and I'd still be buzzed after two."

"Gotta love marketing." I took a sip. It tasted delicious.

I swigged another, then took in her place again. It was the second viewing that made me realize something was missing.

Photos.

The ex-husband I could understand, but there weren't any of her mom or her brothers. She had three of them. There had to be some nieces and nephews by now. "Does your mom come up often?" I said. "Sorry I haven't asked about her."

Adore's mother was…a lot. So was mine, but in different ways. Ten minutes in a room with her mother and you could tell where the name came from. Adore wasn't just the only girl. She was also the youngest and the first in the family to go to college. There was no doubt Ms. Smith literally adored her child. Sometimes a little too loudly.

"She's good," Adore said. "Still in DC. I got her to move to a better neighborhood. But two of my brothers moved with her."

So one thing about Adore hadn't changed since college. Her siblings still weren't shit. "I'm sure she's proud of you," I said.

"Yeah. Also mad I don't drive down to see her. Wants to know when I'm giving her a grandbaby. I'm sure your mom's bugging you too."

But that was the thing. She wasn't. And part of me knew it was because she thought I'd mess that up like I did every other aspect of my life.

"How is she?" Adore said.

"Still trying to run my life. And I'm still letting her," I said, looking around at her fabulous place. Then at fabulous her. "Who'd you go to Cabo with?"

She literally jumped, and that's when I realized it had come out of nowhere. But I needed to know. "Girls' trip?" I said. It was probably some wonderful vacay with her Black Lady Lawyer Friends. "A date?" Some super-successful, super-rich older man she was dating. Maybe Bill Gates.

She gave me a tight smile. "It was a solo trip. I do one every year. It's easier to travel alone. You can do what you want. When you want."

She took another sip, then pushed her hair behind her ear. And that's when I remembered she wasn't the only one who could tell when one of us was lying. I could've called her out on it. But that would've been cruel. Even with the Louboutins and the Kelly. The loft and the law degree. It turned out Adore and I still had something in common after all.

"I'm proud of you, Adore," I said. "You always said you wanted a fabulous apartment in a big city."

She smiled again, this one genuine. "I did it." There was no cockiness to her words. She said it like the fact it was. "Can I say something I've been wanting to say since I first saw you?"

I paused. Were we finally going to have *the* conversation? I'd been so hurt and angry by her ghosting me when I'd needed a friend the most. If the roles had been reversed, if she'd called me from that jail cell, I would've come in a heartbeat. I would've stuck by her.

And even after all these years, when that anger was long gone, the hurt still remained. Holding my breath, I nodded, and she finally opened her mouth to speak. "Your skin is freaking amazing."

Not what I'd been expecting. I smiled anyway. "Thanks."

She continued, effusive in her praise. "Seriously, it's glowing. Meanwhile, I'm over thirty and still dealing with pimples and those dark spots I had in college."

Though I was disappointed, once again I took her lead. "Turmeric," I said quickly, then took my time with what came next because of how she was staring. "I'm a little obsessed with skin care. Make my own products and everything. Last year I gave them to my coworkers for Christmas. Ty thinks I need to start a side hustle."

I flinched at his name, even though it had come out of my own mouth. I needed to stop bringing him up. Stop thinking about him at all. Instead, I forced myself to think of the grant. The application was still in my bag. Crumpled up at the bottom but there.

"If you could get everyone's skin to look like yours, then definitely." Adore smiled. "What are you waiting for?"

I gave my standard excuse. "I still haven't thought of a good name."

"Bree's Beauty!" Adore sounded proud of herself.

It just made me once again think of Ty. Him jokingly telling me to call it Gunk. "I'll think about it," I said.

"Please do. You said side hustle, so what's your main one?"

"I'm still at the stationery store."

Her smile faltered half a centimeter. I wouldn't have even noticed if I wasn't looking for it.

"But I am happy to report that I no longer sleep in a twin bed," I said. Who needed to explain your stunted life choices when you could just make a joke?

And sure enough, she laughed. "How's your grandma? Isn't she living with your mom?"

I nodded, part of me satisfied to realize Adore *had* been keeping tabs. "She fell a couple of years ago, broke her hip. My mom converted the den on the first floor."

"The den!"

"The den!"

"Did your mom ever find out about that weekend when she went to the Bahamas?"

"I'm taking that to my grave."

"Me too." She finished her glass. "I think it's commendable you're staying close to home to help out your family."

I was about to make a joke but stopped myself because I realized she was right. At least partly. I was helping out family.

"A lot of people don't," she said. "Trust me."

I just nodded, let the lie hang that it was about them, not about me being too scared to become an actual, self-sufficient adult. That I wasn't still waiting to hit Play on a life put on pause when I got arrested.

I was sure people thought I should get over it. That I'd spent only ninety days in jail and it was twelve years ago at that. But I was curious how they would react if a cop planted drugs in their car, arrested them, and not even the people they loved most believed they were innocent. What they would feel if they had to relive it any time they looked for a new job or new place.

This country already wasn't kind to Black women, period, much less ones with a record.

I pushed Domingo's smirking face out of my mind, and when I tuned back in, Adore was still chatting away. "I honestly don't know if I'd be able to do it. My brother sure as hell—"

"Those weren't my drugs, Adore." I hadn't looked at her when I said it. Instead, opting for the fancy couch. Her designer bag. Her red-wine-only glasses. I was staring down her eighty-inch television when she responded.

"I know." She cleared her throat. "Breanna, look at me."

But I didn't and she still kept going anyway. At last. "I have to tell you something. Should've told you this a long time ago. I...I messed up and I can never forgive myself for what I—"

"Thank you."

"Bree—"

"No, let me finally get this out. Yes, I was mad at you for abandoning me. You ghosting me hurt as much as any man. Even more, if I'm being honest."

I thought of Janelle's sister. The interview with the unseen journalist. I kept going.

"But if there's something these last few days have taught me it's that I need to stop living in the past. There's nothing worse than never resolving things with people you love. Life is too short...So let's just finish this bottle." I held out my glass.

After a moment, she grabbed the wine bottle and topped me up.

I spoke right before I took another sip. "I appreciate you not offering me any marijuana, though."

There was a brief pause, then she laughed. It felt like an explosion, shaking the entire building. But instead of hurting us, it just made us feel better. "No problem," she said. "It helps I haven't smoked since undergrad."

"Same, girl. Definitely same."

Billie Regan sits in front of the camera sans makeup. It's way too early for it. Without it, she looks like she could be her own younger sister. She smiles, eager.

"Morning, Billie Bunch. I know it's not even 8 a.m. yet, but I had to go Live. When I woke up this morning, I had a DM from one of my longtime followers. Her name is Katherine and she lives in Jersey City. She found out about our poor Janelle from my account and has been following every video. Says I'm more up-to-date than CNN."

Billie tries not to smile even bigger at this.

"She messaged me to tell me there are cops combing some beach. I immediately messaged her back for more details. And asked her if she'd be willing to go Live with us."

There's a pause, then the screen splits in half. Katherine Powers appears in a square at the bottom. You can make out blue sky behind her with a few clouds.

She looks about seventeen with long red hair and green eyes. Freckles spread out over the bridge of her nose. She wears a purple tank top. Her facial expression is neutral until she realizes she's finally on camera. Then she smiles, as excited as Billie. She just isn't hiding it as well. "Billie! So good to meet you...I mean considering the circumstances. But I'm a huge fan. Your contour hack single-handedly saved my prom."

Billie smiles now, delighted. "Isn't it a lifesaver?" She remembers she's supposed to be breaking news. "So what's going on? Where are you?"

"Liberty State Park. My dad dragged me here this morning."

Katherine turns in a circle so we now see her dad behind her. He's the epitome of White Soccer Dad. They have the same hair and slim build. You can't see his eyes because he's got binoculars pressed to them.

"He likes to watch birds," Katherine says. "His name is Ernie."

Ernie speaks but doesn't turn around. "I saw a king eider here last week. Haven't seen him since."

Katherine rolls her eyes. "Anyway, when we got out here, my dad noticed the cops."

Billie perks up. "Where?"

"Over there." Katherine flips the camera.

There's an expanse of water, sweeps of marsh grasses, and in the distance what looks like a small beach. Billie cranes forward, her eyes becoming slits so she can focus better.

"You see them?" Katherine says. "There's two of them in uniform."

Billie nods, though it's impossible to see anything at that distance. "What area of the park is that?"

"Coven Point," Katherine says.

Ernie interrupts. "*Caven*. It's a bird sanctuary. One of the few left in this area."

Katherine ignores him, too intent on what she's about to reveal. "And get this. It's closed in the spring and summer."

Ernie speaks again. "It has to be. Migratory bird nesting."

Katherine keeps on, used to ignoring her father. "No one's supposed to be there."

Billie speaks. "So the cops have been searching the bird sanctuary? They find anything?"

Katherine shakes her head. "Not that I can tell, but it's a big place."

Ernie again. "Twenty-two acres."

Billie takes this in as we faintly make out the two cops padding along the patch of beach. One bends down to examine something in the grasses, but it's impossible to tell what from this distance.

"So someone could hide there for days if they wanted to," Billie says. "No one would find them."

"Nope," Katherine says. "Because no one's supposed to be there."

"How long could someone live in there?"

Katherine turns the camera back to her father. "Dad? Could someone live there?"

Ernie shrugs. "If they wanted to. It wouldn't exactly be the Four Seasons. It's all marshland, but there's a couple of paths. Mostly stretches of boardwalk over the marsh. The water in there is salt water. You couldn't drink it. So you—"

"Look." Katherine whips the camera back to the beach in the distance. A third figure has joined the two cops. They've abandoned their search and are all speed-walking back to the gap in the trees toward the bird sanctuary's entrance. "Dad, what's going on?"

Ernie still doesn't turn to the camera. "They found something."

SEVENTEEN

It had been a late night—Adore and I pulling a mid-nighter like we were back at Morgan. She sent me to the hotel in an Uber around 1 a.m. Luckily, my driver wasn't chatty.

I woke up to round two of the "It could be 5 a.m. or 5 p.m., thanks to these blackout curtains" game. The room was pitch-black, the only hint of color the red emanating from the alarm clock on the nightstand to my left that the housekeeper had plugged back in. My head hurt despite the Tylenol I'd dry-swallowed before falling into bed, so tired I hadn't bothered to put on my bonnet.

It took a sec, but my eyes finally focused: 12:34 p.m. I'd slept almost twelve hours yet still somehow felt like shit. I just lay there, willing my head to stop pounding. And just when it did, someone pounded on the front door.

Adore.

I got out of bed and bobbed and weaved to the bedroom door. Midday hit me so hard I stumbled back. It was bright in the living room. Too bright. Like walking-into-the-light bright. I protectively placed my arm over my eyes and tentatively made my way to the front door, praying I didn't stub a toe.

I didn't use the peephole. Just flung the door open and spoke as I immediately turned back around. I needed coffee. "Please tell me you're just as hungover as I am or I will be back to hating your very existence."

There was a pause. "I'm not."

I always said Adore knocked like the police. This time I was wrong. I turned back, moving my arm from my eyes to my braless shirt. "Detective Calloway. What's going on?"

She didn't ask to come in and I didn't object when she did. She didn't answer my question either, just walked past me. "I would've brought you coffee if I'd known you'd need it," she said.

I slowly followed behind her. "What's going on?" I said again.

"McKinley told me you wanted to head back to Maryland."

I said nothing, just swallowed, my impatience growing with each passing breath. I wasn't naive. I knew why she was here. Kind of. "Where did you find him?"

Ty had been gone for days at this point. Plenty of time to disappear—unless you were the number-four trending topic online. His photo had been retweeted, shared, hashtagged. The only thing that was surprising was it had taken this long. They could've caught him anywhere—even Boston.

Calloway swallowed. "Someone called in a tip about Caven Point last night. It's our bird sanctuary. Closed this time of year."

Ty was still in Jersey City? Why? If he hadn't left town right after he killed Janelle, maybe he'd realized it was too late.

"We sent a team," Calloway said. "They found a body this morning. Drowned in one of the tidal pools."

She didn't elaborate. I wouldn't have heard her if she did because all sound ceased to exist. Like we'd been teleported to outer space—or at least my heart had. Ty being found dead shouldn't have surprised me. It had been one of my first thoughts when he didn't turn up. But that had been a lifetime ago, when he was still nothing more than the first decent guy I'd dated in a decade.

I heard another voice then, but it wasn't Calloway. It was Ty. His last audio message.

I've wanted to tell you: I love you so much.

Emotions aren't like light bulbs, as much as we all want them to be. They aren't something you can turn on and turn off—dim or brighten depending on your mood. And despite everything that had happened, all the things I'd been through and learned since Monday, I still loved him. And it was just like I had said to Adore last night: there was nothing worse than never being able to resolve things with people you love.

"And it's him?" I finally said.

"Black male matching his description. He was fully clothed, but there was no license or cell phone on him. We don't have a positive ID yet."

So it was the same as with Janelle. "It was suicide?" I said.

Calloway hesitated. "You know I can't tell you the circumstances of his death, but I will say there was alcohol in his system and water in his lungs. He definitely was alive when he went into the water."

If I had any last doubts that he'd killed Janelle, Ty killing himself erased them. And in a weird way, also made me less mad at him. Like at least he'd felt guilty about it.

"When will you make the ID official?" I said.

Calloway stared at me until I met her gaze. Then she wouldn't look away. "After we get someone reliable to identify the body."

My heart was still in space but somehow managed to speed up. Me. They needed *me* to confirm that it was Ty. There was no way in hell.

When I didn't say anything, Calloway spoke. "We could call his mother again, though she wasn't really helpful last time we spoke. But Baltimore's only a few hours in the car. Hopefully someone else would be driving since I'm sure she'll be upset."

Even Calloway's frown felt manipulative.

I nodded, which she took to mean I was satisfied. She spoke again. "Can you come down to the ME's office? We can go right now."

"I need to get dressed."

"I'm happy to wait."

"It'll take a while." I wiped my eye.

"No problem. I'll figure out how to make coffee."

And then she actually went to the coffee machine. I looked around. Housekeeping had cleaned. The place was spotless minus the sneakers I'd left in the middle of the room. Anything worth snooping through was still in the bedroom. I went in there and locked the door.

I found my cell phone buried in the comforter. Six missed calls. All from Adore. The phone rang again just as I was about to call her back. "They found him," she said as soon as I answered.

My body instinctively clenched up, tried to fold into itself, like I was hearing the news for the first time all over again.

"I know. He must've been hiding out there." I tried to swallow all the air in the room. "Since he killed her."

She paused. "I was hoping you'd slept in. Hadn't seen he'd died on TikTok or something."

"Calloway told me."

"She called?"

I took a seat, not even bothering to straighten the comforter out. Just sat on the lump that had formed when I got out of bed. It wasn't like I could feel it anyway. "She came by. Still here actually. Wants me to come down. Identify the body," I said. Then: "He hates water. Can't swim. Won't even put his toe in. I tease him about it." My mouth slammed shut, realizing present tense was no longer applicable. Ty would forever be associated with things that ended *ed*. "Teased."

"Bree, don't do this."

"I have to," I said.

We were both silent, and when I did finally speak, I lied again. Pretended like I didn't know what she was referring to.

"Who else is going to ID him?"

It took her a second to answer, like she was trying to decide if she was going to play pretend with me. Like we were eight and sitting in front of a Dreamhouse. After a second, she picked up the Barbie. "He doesn't have family?"

"Not here. I'm not going to let his mother drive all the way up from Baltimore so she can spend three hours with false hope that maybe, just maybe, it's not her child."

"Fine. Tell Calloway you'll meet her. *We'll* meet her there."

The idea instantly made me feel better. I hadn't been inside a police station since I'd been dragged into one in cuffs. That was by design, making sure ever since that I followed every rule. And yet I was still here, in this situation. I shifted until the lump of blankets was no longer right under my legs. "She's gonna want to know when."

"Why? Not like he's going anywhere." She paused. "I'm sorry. Shouldn't have said that. I know you loved him."

Another *ed*.

"I did," I said, though the man I loved was far from the one Calloway wanted me to ID. "Let me go tell Calloway."

"I'll head to the hotel now."

We hung up.

Calloway was on the couch. She perked up as soon as I opened the door. "That was a quick..."

Her voice trailed off when she realized I hadn't been quick at all.

"I'm going to meet you there."

I made sure my voice was firm, and it must've worked because she just stood and nodded. "What time?"

I pulled a number out of the air. "Two."

"Great. I'll send someone to pick you up. I know you don't have a car." She attempted to smile. "Don't worry, it'll be unmarked. You'll be able to sit in the front."

"Adore—" I paused. "My lawyer's taking me. She's already on her way."

Calloway didn't like that. The fake smile disappeared. She just nodded, then headed toward the door. "You'll need to go to the medical examiner's office."

She rumbled off an address. I didn't even attempt to write it down. That's why Google was invented. I didn't show her out, didn't even watch to make sure she left. Just stood between the bedroom and living area until I heard the door close. It was only then that I realized she'd actually made coffee.

* * *

Adore didn't ask how I was doing when I got in the car. She didn't ask anything at all. That's how I knew she and I were finally back on good terms. The silence. The lack of a need to fill the space with noise. No voices. No music. Nothing at all except for the knowledge that just being nearby was enough.

I stared out the window, until I heard a familiar voice. Adore had put on Beyoncé's *I Am...Sasha Fierce*. "Halo" played over the fancy speakers, sounding so crisp it was like the singer was in the car. We'd loved that album, almost as much as we'd loved each other.

It turned out the medical examiner's office wasn't at the police station. It wasn't even close to it but in a whole other city. When we got there, it looked like any old redbrick building. I'm not sure what I had been expecting. Maybe a rain cloud permanently hanging overhead? But the day was gorgeous. Ty would have suggested we go for a run.

But Ty was dead. And I wasn't sure I'd ever run again.

The parking lot was behind the building. Adore pulled into a spot, then we hiked to the front door. We were five minutes early, but Calloway was already waiting, looking as impatient as if we'd been on CP Time.

I wanted to bolt. The only thing that stopped me was how my feet had somehow managed to fuse themselves to the cheap linoleum.

I'd already seen one dead body this week. Now that I was here, I wasn't sure I was ready to make it two.

It had sucked not knowing where Ty was the past three days. But now that I did know, it didn't make me feel better. Instead, I wished it *had* been him they'd seen in Boston. In Baltimore. All the way down in Mexico. Because then he'd be alive, not dumped on some cold metal slab waiting for me to make an ID.

I took a step back, forgetting Adore was behind me. She placed both her hands on my waist to steady me. "It's fine." Her voice was a whisper.

Those two words played on repeat in my head, getting louder and louder as Calloway checked us in and we followed her down a long hall of doors. I flinched as she reached for the last handle. I figured she'd say something to me or at least to the person on the other side. But she didn't even bother to knock. Just opened the thing. I instinctively closed my eyes, like I was watching the horror movie that this was.

Ty was on the other side of the door.

No, Ty's *body*.

I took a breath, bracing for impact. I looked in front of me, ready to see him laid out like on TV.

But it was just a sitting room. An eight-person conference table in the middle of it.

Calloway motioned for us to go in first like she was some gentleman. "Dr. Diaz will be here in a few minutes."

It took him ten. I'd been too nervous to sit, just did miniature laps around Adore and Calloway. I only stopped when the door opened. Again, I was expecting Ty's body. Like Dr. Diaz would roll it in or something. But he came alone.

He was younger than I'd expected. More attractive too. He smiled when he came into the room, like any other doctor—especially if they were bringing bad news.

"Thank you all for coming," Dr. Diaz said. "Let's have a seat."

Our seating arrangement felt like a game of musical chairs. It was clear everyone was waiting for me to make the first pick. I chose the side facing the door, so I'd see Ty when they finally brought him in. Adore immediately sat next to me. The medical examiner chose the opposite side. Calloway should've been next to him, but she chose to sit on our side, like that would make her part of the team.

"Ms. Wright, thank you so much for helping us out," Dr. Diaz said. "I'm assuming it's your first time doing something like this."

I nodded. "Hopefully my last."

"Understandable. Well, it's not like what you see on television," he said, but that was already very apparent. "We understand how traumatic it is to possibly identify a loved one, and we don't want to add to that pain. We've taken some photos of a few distinguishing marks on the deceased. All you'll need to do is take a look and let us know if you recognize them. Is that okay?"

I immediately glanced down at the manila folder he'd placed on the table when he came in. I'd barely registered it, but now I couldn't stop staring. It was like the anxiety had leapt from my brain and landed between the folder's pages.

"Ms. Wright?" Dr. Diaz tried again.

"That's okay."

"Great. I do have to tell you that although we tried not to take any troubling photos, you will see some discoloration. Unfortunately, that's what happens when a body has been submerged for days."

I glanced up. "How long?"

Calloway was looking at me as hard as I'd been eyeing the folder.

"How long was he in there?"

"We're not sure yet," she said.

But I already knew. *Days*. Not day. The ME had said *days*.

This whole time.

Ty'd been dead this entire time. Had he intended to kill himself when he'd left Janelle in the house—*us* in the house? Or did he just run and then make a split-second decision when he saw the water?

Dr. Diaz spoke again. "Are you okay, Ms. Wright?"

"Yes." I rubbed my eye.

He slowly opened the folder. The photos were face down. He slid the first one toward me, then flipped it over. The gesture wasn't dramatic in the slightest—just a flick of the wrist—but I gasped as if he'd made something disappear and ended with a ta-da.

It was a tattoo. Diaz hadn't been exaggerating. The skin around it was murky and puffed up with a greenish tint. But I recognized the *K* in the diamond all the same. I'd spent what felt like hours tracing it on Ty's chest.

I stared hard, not seeing it as it was but how it had been that first night I slept over, feeling how I'd felt then too. How I'd felt every second of every day until this last one.

"That's his chest," I finally said. "Left side. It represents his fraternity."

Dr. Diaz barely nodded, just slid another photo toward me, but I already knew what it was going to be. Ty had a scar on his stomach. I'd been waiting to ask him about it, but now it would just represent how I hadn't known Ty at all. Not really. We'd never discussed if he wanted kids. And if so, how many. Never discussed what he'd wanted to be when he was younger—or how he'd gotten that mark.

Dr. Diaz turned the photo over and there it was. "That's him," I said.

Then I sat back in my chair, more exhausted than when I pushed myself to run an extra two miles on a Saturday.

"Thank you, Ms. Wright." Dr. Diaz gave Calloway a nod.

I'd done what they wanted, what they expected. It was over.

Adore was the next to speak. "When are you going to announce the case is closed?"

Calloway's voice was clipped. "When the case *is* closed."

Adore quickly glanced back at me before speaking. "He killed himself."

"We need to do a complete investigation," Calloway said. "We won't be sharing any details until we've done our due diligence."

Dr. Diaz was up at that point and had the door open. He waited for Calloway and Adore to walk past as Adore kept on. "But people already know you found him. That he killed himself. You have to say something. Otherwise people are going to be creating all kinds of outlandish theories online."

Again, she glanced back at me. I had lagged behind. Dr. Diaz didn't look put out in the slightest, like he wanted me to hurry it up. Instead, he looked kind. Patient. The type of person who was used to seeing grief each and every day. I stopped right when I got next to him, at the door. "That scar. How would Ty have gotten it?"

"Appendectomy."

EIGHTEEN

My running shorts still smelled of Adore's laundry detergent. It'd been only five days since I'd last worn them, but they still felt foreign. Like I was some kid playing dress-up in my mom's closet. I laced up my black ASICS, threw my cell into my running belt, and headed outside. It was early, but it was hot for April. The air felt stifling, like all the oxygen had up and left—leaving us to deal with the carbon monoxide. But I wasn't sure I could blame Mother Nature for that feeling.

I could make out the Manhattan skyline in the distance so I headed in that direction. Too fast. The first half a mile tricked me. Had me feeling way too comfortable. But then the exhaustion set in just as I got to the water. I kept going anyway, past Exchange Place and Hyatt House. Still pushing myself too hard—weaving past people out for a leisurely stroll on the waterfront's walkway.

It took getting to Liberty State Park to remember that pain was a good thing. That there was something to be said for being so tired you can't think of anything other than breathing in and breathing out. The stubbornness of my legs took me another mile, hugging the metal rails that separated the stone walkway from the Hudson River right next to it. Past two sets of parking lots and many more people. I kept going, not even bothering to wipe the sweat crowding both eyes. Past a pavilion and more grass. Curving to the left to pass some fancy silver two-story building and a narrow wooden bridge.

I kept going until, ten minutes later, I finally found the sign I'd googled the night before. The sign I'd thought about all night when I couldn't sleep yet again, hugging my pillow because Ty wasn't where he was supposed to be, next to me. The sign that said two words:

CAVEN POINT.

I paused more than did a full stop because I wasn't alone. A handful of youngish-looking white kids had set up shop across from the roped-off entrance and empty parking lot. Each with their phones up. Taking selfies like this was the Grand freaking Canyon. They whispered to their phones as I passed, casually slinging the words "murderer" and "suicide" like this was some Netflix movie and not my real life. How many likes would their "on the scene" posts get—5? 500? 5,000? Would they go viral, be viewed millions of times? Or would no one really care?

They were gone by the time I got to Port Liberté and circled back, but two new people had replaced them. Same excited looks. Same iPhone models. Same whispered words hurled carelessly about. I said nothing, just went from a run to a brisk walk. Still not stopping, just occasionally glancing at the landscape until my running belt buzzed around the time I returned to that first parking lot. I pulled my phone out.

Adore.

"What's up?" My voice was thick with exhaustion.

"Something tells me you're not at the hotel."

"I went for a run."

"Good. I'm happy you're trying to return to a routine. When will you be back? I can meet you at the hotel."

I needed to check one more thing. "Give me an hour and a half."

* * *

Adore had made a pit stop at Dunkin'. It was the first thing I noticed when I finally walked into the hotel lobby. I was hot and sweaty, but I also needed coffee. We met in the middle of the lobby and she handed me a cup as we made our way to the elevators. I pressed the Up button.

"How was the run?" she said.

"Gonna be sore tomorrow. Already sore now."

"Nice. Where'd you run?"

"Caven Point."

"Bree." She glanced around as if the lone desk attendant all the way on the opposite side of the lobby could hear us.

"Technically, I only ran there. I actually walked back to Little Street. Well, a few blocks away. People are still camped on the corner."

"Breanna."

"Have you been there?"

"Breanna Grace Wright."

"Caven Point. Not Little Street." An elevator dinged. The doors opened and we got in. "Have you?" I said again.

Adore shook her head, resigned. "I'm not a bird person."

I pressed the button for Four. "If you were, you'd know it's closed during the spring and summer. Something about bird migration. Anyway, it would've taken him over an hour to walk there from Little Street."

"So he took a car. Got dropped off."

"Dropped off where? There's one entrance. You can get to it from two directions. If you're coming from the path on the other side, it's through this fancy-ass gated community. Like a place that calls itself Port Liberté would let a bloody Black guy in a hoodie just stroll through in the middle of the night. Of course he could've come the other way, the path along the waterfront. But it's still a good ten-to-fifteen-minute walk from any place he could have got dropped off."

"So he walked ten to fifteen minutes."

"Right. Along a path that's literally right next to the Hudson River. I mean, it has that rail, but that's what? Four feet high? It's just there to stop kids and dogs from accidents. If you really wanted to jump into the Hudson, you could. Not to mention him hating water." When we got to my floor, I exited first. "It doesn't make any sense," I said at last.

Adore followed close behind, her voice reduced to a hiss. "What doesn't make sense is you trying to rationalize the thought process of someone who'd just beat a woman to death."

I turned to face her. "But what if he didn't?"

She took in a sharp breath. I could practically hear her counting to five in her head. "Ty couldn't swim," she said. "I haven't been to Caven Point, but a lot of people like to hike there when it's open. I looked at some pics online. Those paths are scary in the *daytime*. No handrails over the marshy bits. I can't imagine how it must've been at night. Would've been easy for him to step off the boardwalk. Get lost. Fall into one of the pools of water. Not be able to get out."

"Or someone could've pushed him."

"Please, just let this go. Ty did it. He killed Janelle Beckett, then he freaked out, roamed around for an hour, and decided it was better to die by suicide than face the consequences of his actions. I'm just glad he didn't decide to kill anyone else."

My eyes turned to slits. Ty may have been a cheater, seeing Janelle again, and I'd have to deal with that, but he wasn't a murderer. "Call Calloway. I want to talk to her."

"It was a murder-suicide, Bree. Crime of passion. It happens every day in this country."

"I'll call her myself." I pulled my phone out from my running belt. "Siri, what's the number for the Jersey City police?"

"What are you gonna tell them? That you timed your morning run? You just sound like an in-denial and now guilty-feeling girlfriend. You'd need proof."

I didn't have a response to that because she was right. At least about the guilt. I'd let Billie and the rest of the internet convince me to doubt him. *I'd* been the one to give the tip that cemented him as the main suspect.

I walked to my room, trusting she was behind me. Neither of us said anything until we were both inside. She sat on the couch as I leaned against the lone desk, gripping the Dunkin' cup. "Can't we just talk to them, Adore? See if they're at least considering it?"

"Just let it be a murder-suicide."

"Why?"

"Because if someone killed them both, the first person anyone is gonna look at is the in-denial girlfriend. Also the only person in New Jersey who knew he couldn't swim."

She was right. And I knew firsthand that cops didn't always give a shit if you were actually guilty or not.

"I didn't do it, though," I finally said. I wasn't going to be passive this time. I had to fight—for myself and for Ty. "And if I didn't do it and if Ty didn't do it, then who did? You said it yourself. This was a crime of passion. Everyone's been so focused on Ty, but who else in Janelle Beckett's life might have done that to her? What if someone actually dangerous is getting away?"

Adore said nothing. After a moment, she took out her phone. Not the response I had been expecting. "What are you doing?" I said.

"Background check on Janelle Beckett."

That was definitely more like it. "I'll dig deep into her socials," I said. "See if anybody was tagged who suddenly stopped making appearances."

We worked in silence for the next hour. Thanks to A Brush With Billie, I had Janelle Beckett's social media handles committed to memory. She'd used the same one for all her platforms. Her Twitter and TikTok weren't much. She was clearly an Instagram type of person. The recent IG posts were much more curated. Lots of selfies and cute videos of dogs. I recognized the small brown dog belonging to Ms. Morgane in more than one.

But the more I scrolled back, the less filtered it got. The account had started in 2020, which was weird in itself, considering she was just a few years younger than me. A photo of the Manhattan skyline was her first post. Again, strange for someone from the selfie generation. She'd been fascinated with New York City architecture for a while. No photos of other people and no one even tagged. So I got to checking early comments. Unlike the most recent post with the space buns, the first year's photos still had only five or six comments at a time. Guess no one wanted to go that far back to leave their RIPs and promises of #Justice4Janelle.

Adore's voice sliced through my research. "Well, the good news is she's not a sex offender. Or on any terrorist watch lists. No legal judgments. She hasn't filed any civil cases. I also searched New Jersey, New York, and Maryland criminal records. No arrests."

"I'm glad one of us can say that," I said. I wasn't too upset about it, though. It was what I had been expecting. "What about restraining orders?"

"I can't find any taken out on her."

"What about ones she took out?"

"That's a civil matter. Wouldn't show up. Any luck with her socials?"

I shook my head. "Unless it was a dog attack, then no. She wasn't really the type to put all her business on social media. And if she did at one point, it's now been deleted. I can check the folks she followed. Maybe comb Billie's TikTok to see if she mentioned any personal stuff in comments."

"Don't waste your time. We need to talk to someone who knew

her. Who'd know if she was having problems with anyone." For once, Adore looked defeated. "But no one like that is going to talk to either of us. Even if we ask nicely."

I thought about Janelle's Instagram. The pics of the dogs. "I might know someone who will."

Luckily, I'd saved Ms. Morgane's number.

NINETEEN

Ms. Morgane hadn't gone the revamp route with her row house. Number 106 was still all dark woods and walls, but I liked that it looked like a house meant for people and memories—not something created solely for pretty pictures.

She'd sounded happy to hear from me when I called, immediately inviting us over. The only caveat was to come in through the back. She didn't have to tell me why. I'd seen the people and the teddy bears and the candles. It would be a while before Little Street was able to morph back from a memorial to a neighborhood.

Adore and I came through the kitchen, each stopping to grab a small bottle of Poland Spring before continuing into the dining room and finally the main living area—Ms. Morgane's small dog, Chelsea, leading the way like we were on some expedition. The place was clean but cluttered, a heaping pile of half-opened mail in permanent residence on the coffee table. No one spoke until we'd all downed at least two sips of water and then Ms. Morgane kicked things off.

"I've been thinking about you a lot."

"Well, it's been a lot."

"I'm sorry," she said.

She could've been referencing anything—finding Janelle's body, learning Ty had died, having my entire existence upended. I didn't ask her to elaborate.

"Me too," I said instead. "I apologize for not contacting you earlier. I know you and Janelle were close."

She nodded. "I'll definitely miss seeing her on my morning walk." She glanced toward the front door. "Whenever I can get back to it. What exactly happened that night?"

I inhaled. "I don't know." Then took a long sip. "I was asleep. I just know I came downstairs. Ty was gone and she was there—"

The hair. The hands. The jeans. The blood covering it all.

I looked down but still saw Janelle in front of me.

Adore jumped in. "Bree would like to share condolences with anyone else who was close to Janelle. Like her family?"

Ms. Morgane didn't answer at first. I could sense her staring but was afraid to look up. Like she'd know I hadn't done enough. That I'd been more concerned with Ty than with Janelle. Finally, she spoke. "Her parents passed away. One sister, but I only found out about her through the news."

"What about friends?" Adore said.

"A few. I got the sense a lot of her high school friends had moved away and she was one of the few who'd stuck around. She mentioned a Brenda occasionally, but they hadn't spoken a lot since Brenda'd had a baby."

"Exes?" Adore said.

Ms. Morgane shook her head.

Adore kept trucking. "There had to be someone."

"She never mentioned anyone. Not even Ty." That made me look up, only to find her still staring right at me. She didn't look away, not ashamed at all to be caught. It was only then she spoke. "I didn't know they were seeing each other."

"Me neither." I said. A comedian.

No one laughed. Adore just kept on with the cross-examination. "She seemed to spend a lot of time online. Maybe someone there."

Ms. Morgane finally tore her eyes away from me to look at Adore. "What's going on? You clearly have an agenda." She glanced back at me. "If you tell me what it is, maybe I can help."

I finally was ready to rejoin the convo, my voice tentative yet pleading. "I'm not saying Ty didn't do it. One thing I realized is that three months is not a long time to get to know someone. I obviously couldn't tell when he was lying to me. But I also just want to make sure we're not so focused on him that we're ignoring other possibilities. That we're not so quick to condemn, we don't notice the more dangerous person sneaking out the back door."

"I will say there hasn't been much investigating going on, at least not here," Ms. Morgane said.

"They haven't spoken to any of the neighbors?" Adore said.

"They chatted with Drew, Krista, Rod and Lori, Jeff and Carl. Basically the folks who live on either side and across the street. Guess that was good enough for them because they didn't even make it this far down, and I'm only two houses away."

"No one saw anything?" Adore said.

"Jeff and Carl didn't. Lori and Rod were out of town. I'm sure they've spoken with Drew the most."

I piped up again. "That makes sense. He happened to be walking his dog when I found Janelle. He was the one who called the police."

Ms. Morgane nodded. "He also was the one who made the flyers. He was Janelle's first client on the block. Was probably why everyone else used her. He said Puffy loved her."

Adore jumped on that. "So they *were* close?"

She pulled out her phone as Ms. Morgane shook her head. "I don't know if I'd describe it as that. She never mentioned him other than saying he tipped well."

"Did he say anything to you about finding her?" Adore said.

Ms. Morgane shook her head again. "I haven't seen much of him since, which is why I know he's taking things hard. Usually he's always out, giving people hell for lawn length and noise like we have some HOA. He's not the friendliest, but he's consistent."

"Maybe he hates the crowds?" I glanced over at Adore, but she was too focused on her phone.

"They're nonstop," Ms. Morgane said. "It was worse a few days ago, but it's thinned out considerably since…" She trailed off, not wanting to remind me Ty's body had been found. Good thing I didn't need a reminder. She finally picked up the convo again. "Anyway, I think he's been letting Puffy out in the backyard. But then we all are. You try to walk outside and all you see are people with their phones out."

I was about to respond when Adore's phone rang. She finally glanced up. "Sorry, but I have to go. Meeting. Thank you so much for letting us stop by."

Adore barely looked at me as she stood, just assuming I'd follow her, and of course I did. But only after I flashed an apologetic look at Ms. Morgane. "I'm sorry. I really do appreciate you talking to us. I know it hasn't been easy."

"I can only imagine what you're going through." She stood and placed her hand on my arm. "I'm here whenever you need to talk."

I nodded. "You don't have to walk us out."

But, of course, she did.

* * *

Adore was already in the car by the time I got through Ms. Morgane's back gate. "What was that about?" I said as soon as I closed the passenger door.

"That was about Andrew Martin, owner of 109 Little Street, Jersey City, New Jersey, 07302."

So much for a meeting. "You looked him up that quick?" I said.

She turned on the car. "You've clearly never stalked someone. It's not too hard to find who owns a house. Background checks are a bit harder. We need to do that back at my place."

"What did she say to make you think Drew is involved?"

"I just found it interesting how he's been taking the murder. Didn't she say he's been hiding out?"

He'd also seen the body. Maybe it was haunting him like it was haunting me.

I waited until we got to the corner before I spoke again. "The few times I met him he was a jerk, but he also helped me that day. He had the wherewithal to call the police. I just stood there in shock."

"So he wasn't surprised?"

I sighed. "Of course he was. He immediately went inside to check on Janelle. He looked spooked when he came out. I'm sure I looked the exact same way."

"It seems like he took an extra interest in her, but she clearly wanted to keep it professional."

"Ms. Morgane literally said he liked her because she was good to his dog. Puffy," I said.

"And that he was the one who's been the most upset since she went missing. It's just notable he happened to be outside the exact moment you came running out."

We'd just covered that. "Maybe he was taking a walk. In his neighborhood. Like he probably did every morning—until he found someone bludgeoned to death."

The hair. The hands. The jeans. The blood covering it all.

She pulled the car over. "This is why we went to visit Morgane, Bree. To see if there was anyone else the police should be looking at. It was your idea."

Adore was right. I was the one who'd wanted to rush over, but now it felt too quick. Too out of the blue. "I don't want to point fingers at someone else just so they're no longer pointed at me and Ty."

I couldn't do that to anyone, not after what had happened to me.

"And I would never do that." Adore put on her blinker, then waited for a car to pass before pulling into traffic. "Let's go to my place. I'll look him up. You can check out his socials. And if we find nothing, we find nothing. It can't hurt."

I wasn't so sure.

TWENTY

A ndrew Martin didn't have Twitter or Instagram or TikTok or Snapchat. He didn't even have a Facebook account I could find. He was not on social media of any kind. But luckily for us, Puffy was. He had one of those Instagram accounts that pretends to be from the dog's point of view. The type with cute pics and corny captions along the lines of "Rawr, had so much fun with my dad at the dog park today."

It hadn't taken off. There were just 30 followers—but one of them was Janelle Beckett. And that was the only reason I saw the account. "Puffy" had left a comment on one of Janelle's photos of the two of them together. I had to travel fifty-four weeks back to find it.

"How's it going?" Adore said.

We'd been quietly working side by side on her couch since we'd gotten to her house a couple hours ago.

The sofa was so white I'd been afraid to sit on it, and I definitely had turned down her offer of a glass of red. "I can't find any other Puffy comments," I said. "He doesn't like any of her pics, though she liked all of his. No comments from her, though. You?"

She motioned to the MacBook on her lap. "His background check's more boring than watching paint dry. Not even a parking ticket."

"Well, we tried." I put my phone down and thought about how hungry I was. "Want to order pizza?"

"I don't know," she said, but it was clear she wasn't talking about food options. "It's still giving me 'He was such a nice neighbor, we're so surprised he was a psychopath' vibes. Who doesn't have parking tickets?"

"I don't," I said. Just had much worse.

"There has to be something here."

"Or maybe there isn't, Adore. Maybe he's just a boring white guy who always obeys the speed limit and loves his dog way too much."

But she didn't answer. Too busy looking something up.

She was still a fast typer. One of the million and one things she had always been good at. We used to get together to write our essays, all ten of her fingers flying across the keyboard, me going much slower with the two-finger method. I still hadn't learned how to type properly. Yet another case of arrested development.

"You wanna order pizza?" I said again, but she still ignored me. "What are you doing, Adore?"

"Morgane Porter has a DUI."

I reached for the laptop, but she wouldn't let me take it. "You're looking up Ms. Morgane?"

"I'm looking up everybody on that block. She's just first because I know her full name."

This was not going how I'd thought. I sure as hell wasn't going to look up Ms. Morgane's socials, even if she had any.

Instead, I typed "110 Little Street" and "Airbnb" into my search. The first hits were just as I'd expected. Stories about the murder. I quickly kept scrolling past link after link—all with the same photo of a happy and alive Janelle in her space buns.

I only lifted my thumb when my eye caught on another pic. This one was of the house itself. The link was to the Airbnb listing. I'd never seen it—just the screenshots Ty'd sent, as he had taken care of all the reservations—back when his secrets had been fun.

Beautiful Row House in Jersey City (Directly Across the River from NYC)

It was a surprise the listing was still up.

I clicked. The price wasn't cheap. Ty had really gone all out. Now I wondered if he'd found it through Janelle. I shook off the thought, flinging it across the room like it was some spider. There was work to be done. It wouldn't do to get distracted thinking of Ty and Janelle's relationship—what it had been or what it hadn't been. It didn't matter right now. What mattered was finding out who had killed them both.

I went back to the listing. One hundred percent of guests had given the location a five-star rating. The first from someone named Tula. *Great for families!*

There was also Nathan, who highly recommended staying there.

And Roselle, who just adored the location.

I was jealous of them all. They had been able to have an amazing experience. I should've had one too. Just like I should've been back at home right now, counting the days until Ty came home while I shared my own ratings with my coworkers—even Perry, who I usually couldn't stand.

I became a woman obsessed. Reading every single word of every single review. It wasn't until I got to number thirty-two that I saw it. Sonia'd left something at the house. When she'd called the company that owned it, they'd asked her to speak to a neighbor. Apparently, one watched the place for them and would get it when they let in the cleaning crew.

"Adore." I practically shoved the phone in her face.

It took her a second to read the review, another five to process what it said. I helped her along. "A neighbor has access to the house."

Adore nodded. "Text that to me."

"I wish she'd said a name. I'd love to contact her, but 'Sonia' isn't much to go on."

"It doesn't matter. It's definitely Drew."

She was probably right, but still. "I'd feel better if she'd said a name," I said.

She didn't answer. Just put her laptop on the square pleather ottoman doubling as a coffee table and picked up her phone.

"I'm calling Ms. Morgane again," I said. "She might know."

I called her on speaker. She sounded happy to hear from me so soon. It was nice. Unfortunately, I didn't have time for small talk so I got right to it. "I was calling because I had a quick question. Have you heard of the company that owns 110 paying a neighbor to watch over the place?"

Ms. Morgane was quiet. "No one mentioned it to me. Why?"

"Nothing. If it was someone on the block, any idea who it might be?"

Adore yelled out. "Maybe Drew?"

"That would make sense. He's across the street and nosy as hell." Ms. Morgane squeaked out a laugh to let me know she was joking.

Adore gave me an I-told-you-so look, but it still wasn't enough for me. "Can you ask around?"

"Sure."

"Thank you," I said.

I zeroed in on Adore as soon as I hung up. "Adore, I mean it. Don't do anything until we know it's Drew."

She still said nothing, but her face changed as she looked at her notifications.

"What?" I wasn't sure I could take any more news.

"The police are doing a briefing," she said.

"Now?"

I looked around for the remote, but Adore found it first and turned on the television.

If it weren't for the word *LIVE* some CNN employee had thought-fully put in big red letters, I would've thought it was footage from any of the other briefings. Same office. Same setup. Same collection of older men—and one woman—in the exact same order.

We were late enough that we'd missed the briefing part, but they were taking questions. I couldn't see the press, but I could tell from the cadre of voices that there were a lot of reporters present. More than at the first briefing or the second. The voices in the ether shouted over each other as if the Ravens had just scored. But one was louder than the rest. "And who identified Mr. Franklin's body?"

It must've been something they all wanted to know because the voices stopped so quickly I thought Adore had hit Mute. But then the chief spoke. "We're not at liberty to say, but it was someone close to the victim."

"The girlfriend?"

I inhaled so quickly I surprised myself. So far, I'd evaded being named. Even Billie had barely paid me any attention. It was a streak I wanted to continue.

"Again, we're not saying. Next question."

"Is there any truth to the rumors Franklin had narcotics in his system?"

The chief didn't hesitate. "There were traces of alcohol."

"And that the ME believes he was dead for days when he was found? That he probably died sometime Monday morning?"

"Yes, but it's impossible to provide an exact time of death. Next question."

Another cacophony. Another voice that somehow rose above it all. "Why were you able to identify Mr. Franklin's body but have yet to make a formal ID on the initial victim?"

The chief shook his head. "There are several factors to identify a body. We're making sure we're thorough before we make any announcements. Dot every *i*. Cross every *t*. Next question."

But the voice immediately spoke again. "So you're saying Ms. Beckett's body is currently beyond recognition?"

Chief King ignored that, motioned to someone on the other side of the room. "Next question."

"Do you consider both cases to be closed?"

"No, though I'm very proud of the progress my team has made. From everything we've gathered so far, we do believe these cases are related and we're treating them as such. Next."

The next voice sounded older. "Do you watch A Brush With Billie?"

He did. You could tell by the way he flinched at the name. He clearly found her as annoying as I did. "We are aware of the channel," King said. "She needs to stick to doing makeup."

"Did you see her last video?"

"No, my makeup technique is fine," King said.

Adore and I shared a look. As far as I knew, Billie had gone silent since this morning. Her last video had been some makeup hack I'd stopped watching as soon as I realized she'd moved on from Janelle and Ty. I'd been hoping she would be hacking away from here on out. But it sounded like I wasn't so lucky.

"She found a witness who saw Tyler Franklin near Caven Point before 2 a.m.," the reporter said. "From my sources, that could be as much as two hours before Janelle Beckett was killed. Do you have an exact time when the initial murder occurred?"

I leaned forward so quick you'd swear I'd been catapulted.

Chief King rolled his eyes. "We haven't spoken to that witness. They haven't contacted us. I can say we're extremely confident in our investigation and believe the Little Street victim was murdered sometime between 4 and 10 a.m., when the body was found."

Someone yelled out. "By the girlfriend?"

There it was again. Perhaps I should've been grateful I was still just a description and not yet a name. Instead, I was more concerned about what I'd just heard. Ty had been seen that far away hours before Janelle died? He hadn't come back to the house after he'd left me that audio message.

"That's all we have time for today," King said. "I do want to close by reiterating what I said at the beginning of this briefing. If you believe you have information regarding either of these two cases, please reach out to our department. We're happy to talk to anyone and take every call seriously. You can rest assured your tip will be looked into. Please don't attempt to investigate yourselves. Don't harass the residents of Little Street. And don't trespass in Caven Point. We've already arrested two people and don't want to arrest any more. Let the police do their jobs. You may think you're helping, but you're just hindering our investigation."

The officers all filed out—one by one by one—accompanied by the orchestra of voices still wanting their questions answered. CNN waited until they were all gone before jumping to Anderson Cooper in studio.

I didn't hear a single word he said. I was too busy opening TikTok on my phone. A video I didn't want to see immediately started playing. Some skinny white chick doing a dance I'm sure had gone viral. I didn't wait to see the moves. It wasn't like I was going to attempt it myself.

Instead, I clicked Discover and typed in Billie's handle. And there she was. I pressed the most recent video and started watching. Adore didn't come closer to me, didn't try to look too. But I knew she was paying attention by how quiet she was. Billie started by plugging some vigil she was planning for Janelle before finally getting to what I wanted. Her witnesses were teenagers—two siblings of South Asian descent. They lived in the fancy gated community I'd run by earlier. The older one had seen him, Ty. Had just walked by him, around 2 a.m. They didn't mention anything about blood. Or say he was acting erratically. Or that he seemed upset. Just Ty was looking at his phone, like he had somewhere to go. Ty hadn't said anything. Billie was just as confused as I was about the timing. Her face could've been turned into a bewildered meme. All it needed was someone to superimpose mathematical equations all over the screenshot.

Yes, I hadn't known Ty for long, but in those few months, I'd occasionally seen him upset. And I knew his home training trumped his anger. He would've spoken even if he was mad. Just like he would've spoken if he'd been drinking—*especially* if he'd been drinking. He didn't turn into Mr. Hyde. Just an amped-up Dr. Jekyll—louder, funnier, friendlier.

Not to mention the optics. A Black guy walking alone that late at night? He'd go out of his way to be friendly to strangers—hands easily visible so they wouldn't think he was going to rob them. It was sad, but it was also true.

If he didn't speak to them, it was because he was distracted—like they'd said. When I finally spoke, it was just two words. "Two o'clock."

"Bree," Adore said.

"It doesn't make sense for Ty to go all the way to Caven Point, then back to the house, then back to Caven Point—to kill himself. I don't think he ever came back to the house."

"Maybe she was already dead when he left."

"Uh-uh. There was someone in the house when I woke up. They turned off the light."

"Are you sure it wasn't a timer? My Alexa can do it."

"Why would anyone time a light to turn off at four in the morning?"

"To make you think someone is there."

I'd stayed there for three whole days. Never saw an Alexa. Never saw any directions for timers. Never saw any lights randomly going off and on. *Someone* had been there. The killer—and they'd heard me.

I opened my mouth but thought back to our earlier convo. Adore wasn't going to listen to me. I had to find someone who would. "You have a point." I resisted the urge to wipe my eye. "I didn't think about that. I'm just tired."

She smiled. "Guest bed's already made up if you want to stay here."

"Tempting, but sadly, the hotel is kinda feeling like home."

I stood and she followed. "Yeah, not gonna pretend like I went all out on the guest-bedroom mattress."

"Definitely going to the hotel, then. That bed's really comfy."

She giggled, and I could tell it'd worked. She believed me. The car ride was short. I was proud of how normal I acted, nodding along to Beyoncé's "Diva" like I wasn't consumed with thoughts of Ty.

I didn't pull out my phone until after I watched her drive off. Then I looked up the number for the nearest Jersey City police station.

I took in a breath, held it for as long as I could. I'd do this. I'd click on the Call option Google gave in its search results. Once they answered, I'd ask to speak with Calloway—Randle if she wasn't there— and share my suspicions.

Finally letting the breath out, I pressed Call.

It was busy.

I hung up, paced the lobby a few times, then tried again.

Still busy.

I sat, gave it five minutes, and called again. Same damn result.

I went back to my room and tried again over the next half hour. The busy sound taunting me each time. Part of me wanted to take it as a sign that I'd tried and clearly something somewhere didn't want me to talk to them.

It hadn't been a lie when I'd told Adore how comfortable the mattress was. I could get in bed, burrow under the covers like I used to do when I was afraid as a kid. Of course back then it'd been all make-believe. Now I knew real life was much scarier than any monster hiding under the bed.

But when I hung up the last time and swiped to make my phone app disappear, I found Ty smiling at me. My wallpaper was still the photo of the two of us. A time when I'd thought the worst thing that could happen to us was him taking a work call during our romantic carriage ride.

His smile had always been my favorite feature. He knew it was a winner too, which is why he spent so much time on it. White strips. Cocofloss. Brushing after every meal. Carefully applying the ball of Eos he stole from me under the guise of wanting his lips to be in tip-top shape for *my* benefit. Up until a few days ago, he'd been the man of my dreams.

He still was.

I glanced at my phone, but it'd already gone black. Tapping it, I checked the time. Not even close to 5 p.m. There was a good chance Calloway would still be at the station. Before I knew it, I did another search, then opened the Uber app I'd used only one time before. They found me a driver—Ralph—and promised he'd be here in five minutes. I went back outside to wait for his gray Camry with Jersey plates. He got there in four.

He was super friendly, rushing out of the car to open my door like some rich-people chauffeur. I smiled through the face mask I'd brought with me, a convenient disguise. The Camry was spick-and-span. A bottle of water and a tin of unopened Altoids were in the seat back in front of me. Guess if I was going to get laid, Ralph wanted me well hydrated with breath smelling fresh.

"So, Breanna, you been visiting long?"

"Little over a week."

"Practically a native. Where from?"

I glanced at the app. Like going everywhere in Jersey City, the ride was less than ten minutes. "Baltimore."

"Oh, I love Baltimore!"

"You've been?"

"No, but I've seen *The Wire*. You're probably too young to remember that one."

"I've seen it. You should visit Baltimore. Actually see other parts of the city. It's really a great place to live."

"I bet. It's cool you even have a show set there. You never see anything set in Jersey City."

"There has to be one." I racked my brain, which for once wasn't filled with thoughts of Ty and Janelle.

Ralph glanced back at me in the rearview. "See, you're trying to think of one and can't."

I laughed. "Guilty. There are shows set in Jersey. *The Sopranos*. Best show ever."

"Yeah, after *The Wire*."

"Touché. You also have reality shows," I said. *"Jersey Shore. Real Housewives."*

"Not claiming those, and not just because they aren't filmed anywhere near Jersey City."

I laughed again and it felt good to mean it. I wasn't normally one for small talk, especially not with strangers. But this time I was happy for it. It took my mind off where we were going, what I needed to do: walk into a police station of my own accord to convince them to at least look into the idea Ty was a victim, not the perpetrator. I tuned back in to our conversation. "There has to be some show set in Jersey City," I said.

"Nope. Most people don't even know it exists. I bet you only came here because it was so close to the city."

I said nothing at first and he smiled.

"I'm right, aren't I?"

"You are," I said.

"PATH or ferry?"

"PATH," I said. "I was surprised how clean it was."

"You gotta try the ferry next time. Just don't drop anything into the Hudson. Of course everyone knows who we are now, thanks to that guy killing that woman. Bet you they probably won't even shoot it here when they make the movie about it."

And just like that, my smile disappeared—because to him we were still doing small talk. Instead of responding, I went to grab the water—solely for something to do. I didn't even realize my hands were shaking until I struggled to pick it up.

Ralph was still yammering on up front, not even noticing I'd checked out. I'd just managed to get the bottle open when we pulled up to a beige building with JERSEY CITY POLICE written on the wall by the entrance stairs.

"Please don't tell me you got robbed," he said. "Believe me when I say we're normally a very quiet area."

I said nothing, just opened the door, even though he'd barely pulled to a stop.

"Breanna," Ralph said.

But I was no longer interested in talking to him. I mumbled a goodbye, then hurried past a parked car and the covered outside seating for the restaurant next door. I was about to head toward the entrance when a woman in uniform came out.

Muscle memory kicked in. My throat tightened like it always did around cops. I'd figured since I was going voluntarily, I'd be mentally prepared. My body obviously felt otherwise.

This was not a good idea. At all. I took a big step back, then another. I was about to take a third when I bumped into someone. Ralph.

"You left your cell," he said.

He handed it over. Ty smiled at me from my screen saver.

"Thanks," I said, but he was already hurrying off. Nowhere near as friendly as he'd been on the ride over. But then his car was still double-parked—outside a police station. I'd hurry too.

Sneaking another glance at Ty's pic, I put my cell into my pocket, then went up the station's steps and through the door. Inside looked nothing like the police station in Baltimore, but it still had all the same ingredients. Most of the office was safely behind a door with a lock on it. The lobby was small, bookended by a counter on one side and some cheap-looking hard-backed chairs on the other. They were all occupied, holding a United Nations of folks. A lone older white guy in a uniform manned the counter.

He cradled an old-school landline phone in the crook of his neck, rolling his eyes at whatever the person on the other end was saying. He spoke loudly as I approached. "If you have the number, I suggest you use it." And with that he hung up.

The phone immediately rang again. He acted like he didn't hear it, opting instead to just stare at me. "Help you?" He hadn't said it like he meant it.

"I can wait until you answer that."

"You gonna be waiting a long time. Been ringing nonstop all day. Night too. Now, how can I help you, ma'am?"

"I'm looking for Detective Calloway."

He rolled his eyes, like I'd called his mom a ho. "If this is about the Little Street case, then you need to leave and call the tip line."

He rattled the number off so quick, it was clear he'd been saying it a lot. I waited for him to finish before I spoke again. "No, I don't think you understand. I—"

"Have important info. Yeah, I know." He motioned to the ringing phone. "They probably do too. And I'm gonna tell you the same thing I tell all them. Call the tip line."

"I'm Breanna Wright."

His expression didn't change. I suppose I should've been happy I wasn't a household name here.

I glanced behind me, at the people sitting in the lobby. None of them paid me any attention, but I still whispered when I spoke. "The witness in the Janelle Beckett murder."

"Huh?"

"Can you just call Calloway? Give her my name. She'll want to speak to me."

"Right, because you're a witness."

I nodded. Finally, he got it.

But then he kept on. "Excuse me for being rude, but there have been a lot of witnesses."

The phone stopped ringing and for a moment it was blissfully silent. Then it just started up again.

"Would I know Calloway's name, though?" I said.

"Yep, because everyone does. I think someone put it on Twitter or TikTok or something. One of those."

I was about to name-drop her partner, but he beat me to it. "They know Randle's name too. And I'll tell you what I also tell them: if you were a witness, you'd have Calloway's direct line."

I did. Well, Adore did. But there was no way she'd give it to me. "Can I just leave her a note?"

He put his hands up in mock surrender. "If that'll get you out of here." He pushed over a blank police report. "Use the back."

The video starts with a flyer. *#Justice4Janelle* is up top with *Candlelight Vigil* right below it. Two photos are in the center: One is the familiar picture of Janelle Beckett in her space buns. The other is a professional glamour shot of a perfectly made-up Billie Regan. They're equal size and side by side.

At the bottom: *Join activist and influencer Billie Regan from A Brush With Billie in a special vigil to honor the life of Janelle Beckett.*

It's on for just long enough to read it before it's replaced with the real live Billie Regan. She sits in front of the camera with no makeup. Her hair is in a loose topknot that looks like it hasn't been touched in hours. It's early, but she looks invigorated.

"I know it's the middle of the night, Billie Bunch, but we found her." She's so excited, she's completely forgotten her normal intro. "Us. Not the cops. Us. The ones who just want justice for Janelle. The cops sure didn't give a shit when she went missing. We were the ones who made them pay attention. We were the ones who practically handed them Tyler Franklin on a platter. If they'd just listened to us, he'd be alive right now in jail instead of getting to take the easy way out. Without us, there would be no investigation to even *hinder*."

Billie takes a deep breath and tries to compose herself. "I got a DM last night. Not going to tell you from who, but as soon as I saw it, I immediately had to call them. They had information on Tyler's girlfriend. The one who found the body but *didn't* call 911. The one who's the *sole* reason the police think our Janelle died when she did—though it was hours before the police were called. The one who's been in *hiding* ever since."

She gives the camera a look. "I always thought it was curious how she never came forward, but I'll admit I was so focused on Tyler, I didn't really pursue it. I assumed she was also a victim of his. But now that I know who she is, I'm not so sure.

"Apparently, the police think the same thing because they haven't let her leave town. She's been staying at some hotel a few minutes from where Janelle was murdered. They even spoke with her at the station *last night*—after my interview with Sarah and their brother revealed Tyler wasn't in the Airbnb a couple of hours before Janelle allegedly died. After I spoke with my source and got the girlfriend's full name, I went down a rabbit hole. I wanted to be sure of my suspicions. And you'll never believe what I found."

A screenshot appears behind Billie. It's a mug shot of a brown-skinned, college-aged Black woman with a tangle of kinky black hair. She's pretty despite the grim expression. "Let me introduce you to Breanna Grace Wright. Tyler's other woman and a *convicted criminal*. This is from the time she was pulled over for erratic driving after running a red light. Police found a *significant* amount of marijuana in her car. And get this: she was charged with both possession *and* resisting arrest."

Behind her the screenshot changes to a newspaper article. LOCAL WOMAN CHARGED AFTER TRAFFIC STOP. Billie glances back as if she can see it behind her. "Breanna Wright pled guilty. Was sentenced to three months in prison. Two years of probation."

Billie is silent for the next minute, contemplating. "I can only imagine how she must've reacted when she learned Tyler and Janelle were still seeing each other. Were in love after all these years. You never forget your first love, right? There was no way this Breanna

Wright could compare to our Janelle. *What she could've done.* I mean, look at her."

The screen flashes back to the mug shot. Breanna Wright's eyes look more angry now than scared. "I'm sure you're just as shocked as I am. Asking yourselves the same questions. How was this woman, this Breanna Wright, not a suspect from the get-go? And was she working with Tyler—or was he also a victim?"

She lets that settle before speaking again. "I'll be back as soon as I have more info—and possibly a pic of her at the Jersey City police station."

TWENTY-ONE

It'd been so long since I'd woken up to a landline, I almost didn't recognize the noise it made. I'd been asleep but not dreaming. It took three rings to cut through the haze and another two to realize what the sound was. I glanced at the alarm clock, wanting to know why the front desk was calling me so early. It was just past 7 a.m.

"Morning." I made sure not to say "good."

"Breanna Wright?"

"That's me. Everything okay?"

"It would be—if you hadn't killed Janelle Beckett."

And just like that I was awake. Except I couldn't speak. Couldn't even move. I just lay there, listening as the voice continued. It sounded young—probably a teenager, which made it even more horrible.

"You deserve to go back to jail—for life this time."

Finally, I got it together enough to hang up. My first coherent thought was *I need to talk to Adore. Immediately.* My second was *I, of course, have no clue where I left my cell.*

I started with the bed, frantically tapping it here and there like I was trying to get its attention. I gave up after a couple minutes and decided to search the floor. It'd been known to fall in the middle of the night.

But there was nothing. So I went to the living room, flinching at the bright morning light. I was moving toward the couch when the landline rang again.

I paused practically midstep like they could see me. Then I stayed like that while the phone rang and rang and rang. I stopped breathing at five rings, stopped counting at ten. When I realized they weren't going to hang up, I decided to do it myself. Walking over, I picked the phone up and immediately slammed it down. Then I breathed.

I was two breaths in when I finally saw my cell on the counter. I'd never been happier. I was about to rush over to grab it—when the landline rang again. This time I didn't hesitate. Just picked it up. Slammed it down. Picked it up again, leaving it off the cradle this time. Ignoring its faint noise of protest, I walked over to my cell, but the notifications let me know they'd found that number too.

Crap.

I ignored the litany of missed calls, just like I ignored the litany of texts—people I knew interspersed with people who'd decided I was now America's Most Wanted.

My hands shook as I tried to pull up Adore's number, only to be interrupted by my phone app appearing again. This person was smart enough to hide their number. It came up private. I hit Ignore, then called Adore.

She picked up right away. "You've been doxed."

"They've been calling the hotel nonstop. They know I'm here."

"I'm two lights away. Meet you in the lobby."

My knight. "I just need to pack."

"What—"

But I'd already hung up. At least I knew where my Kenneth Cole was. I made it two steps before I went back to my phone. This time I turned it off.

I didn't fold shit, just grabbed things from where I'd randomly left them and threw them all into the bag. Then I flashed on the people who'd gathered outside Little Street and Caven Point. Police tape and steel barriers had been the only things stopping them from getting closer. They'd obviously found me, but there would be no police tape or barriers downstairs. Nothing to stop them or their cell phone cameras. I couldn't hang up on a hotel lobby.

Hands still shaking, I reached for a face mask, then went back into my bag to find the sunglasses I'd forgotten I'd even brought with me. I put them both on. It wasn't until I stared at myself in the mirror that I remembered the Ty "sighting" in Boston. It didn't matter if I covered up my facial features. They were just looking for skin tone. It didn't even matter if it wasn't remotely close to my color.

There was probably some poor Black woman mistakenly being told she deserved to rot in hell at this very moment.

It took me five whole minutes to open the hotel-room door. No one waited for me. I sprinted down the hallway, my bag doing its best to keep up behind me as my ASICS made only brief contact with the carpet. The elevator came quick, even though I was the only person on the planet who wanted it to take its time. Thank God it was empty. I'd made it this far. I just had one more thing to deal with.

The lobby.

And that's where my luck ran out. There was just a handful of people there but more than I'd seen since I'd checked in. Most of them were too old to be internet sleuths. But there was also a family, two of them teenagers. Both looking at their phones. No doubt scrolling TikTok or Twitter or Instagram. Or somehow all three at the same time.

I stopped short when I saw them, then glanced out the front door. The Tesla was double-parked. I wanted to sprint. Instead, I forced myself to walk. Cool. Calm. Collected. I made it to the door before the voice came behind me.

"Have a nice day, Ms. Wright."

I glanced back at the front attendant, only to find both the teens staring. I didn't say a word. Didn't stop moving. Just left and got into Adore's car, throwing the Kenneth Cole in the back.

"Billie?" I said.

"Of course."

"Someone called my room. Several someones."

Adore didn't respond at first, just pulled out into traffic. "I'm sure we can call and check you out," she said. "You can stay with me."

"I need to go home."

Adore glanced at me. "You don't think they're calling there too? Don't have your address already?"

I thought of my mom. Prayed they hadn't reached her. Though if anyone could give as good as she got, it was Beverly Anna Wright.

"How'd they find me?" I was afraid to check for myself.

"Billie mentioned you were staying in a hotel. Doubt she even knew which one."

"So they called them all." I leaned my head back. "I need a new phone number too."

"You can probably change it on your provider's app."

"That would require me to turn it back on."

"Online then."

Both options sounded like a pain in the ass. "What did she say about me?" I said.

"A bunch of things we can sue her for."

That didn't make me feel better.

"She showed your mug shot," Adore finally said. "Basically implied since you were a criminal you had to have at least helped Ty kill Janelle, if not done it yourself. She also said the police hauled you in for questioning. Claims there's some photo."

Ralph.

The Uber driver was the only one who knew where I was staying. The only one who saw the screen saver with Ty on it.

And now it was all out there. I'd spent the last twelve years lying low. Not causing any drama. Doing everything I could to avoid my past. Because I didn't want anyone to use it against me. To judge me. Only to end up here, right back where I had been at twenty-one.

"Bree, where are you?"

"Sorry."

"I was saying the pic's probably some poor Black woman who doesn't even look like you."

"It does, though," I said. "Exactly like me."

Thank God we were at a light because her head swung in my direction. "The police hauled you into the station last night?"

"I went there to talk to Calloway."

She didn't say anything but didn't have to. I'd seen that same expression on the face of my mother. Disappointment.

"She wasn't there, though." I spoke quickly, just like I had done as a kid. As if saying something fast enough would negate the words themselves. "So I left a note."

"Why didn't you tell me?"

"Because you would've tried to talk me out of it. I'm pretty sure my Uber driver's the one who ratted me out. He's definitely getting zero stars."

"This is not funny."

I spoke. "You knew I was gonna get doxed." *Adore. Always right.*

"Doesn't mean I'm happy about it."

"But it does mean you've thought about what to do." I sounded hopeful.

She finally turned away from me. "I already DMed Billie."

Good thing I wasn't driving because I would've slammed on the brakes. But the car kept going, slow AF too. Adore didn't say more, just kept her eyes on the road like she really had to concentrate.

"You sent the Airbnb screenshots?"

She nodded but didn't say any actual words.

"And?" I prodded her along.

"And I haven't checked to see if she responded. It's only been a couple hours. I'm sure she's swimming in DMs."

She'd left her cell in the cup holder. I reached for it. "What's your passcode?"

"I can do it when we get back to my place."

"That's like a whole five minutes away." When she didn't crack a smile, I kept on. "I'm not gonna check any other messages."

"Fine, I'll do it at the next light."

But God had a sense of humor. We cruised past two consecutive greens before hitting a yellow. I took in a breath, thinking Adore would stop. Instead, she sped up, hitting the intersection just as it turned red. Something was up.

"You just sent the screenshots?" I finally said.

Nothing.

I tried again. "No mention of anyone else who lived on the block?"

"You said yourself that Drew guy was most likely to have access to the house."

"And then I said we needed actual proof before we brought his name up."

"No one's better at getting that than Billie."

"You should've run it by me, Adore."

"Like you should've run it by me before you went to the cops."

"You would've told me not to do it."

She looked at me again. "Exactly."

"I know what it's like to be accused of something you didn't do. Have your life ruined."

We finally hit a red.

"I know. Which is why I'm trying to stop it from happening again,

Breanna. Billie probably has millions of DMs to get through before she sees mine. If you really want me to, I'll unsend the message."

But she kept both hands on the wheel like she was mid–driving test.

"Unsend it."

"Fine. I'll do it right now."

She was in the right lane, so she was able to pull over. Neither of us said anything as she picked up her phone. I even played it cool as I watched the lock screen disappear out of the corner of my eye. By the time she'd opened Instagram, I'd already turned away, staring blithely at a McDonald's.

"Crap," Adore said.

I whipped my head around, leaning in even though my vision was still damn near perfect. Billie hadn't just seen it. She'd responded: *Interesting.*

*   *   *

Like everything else in my life, I hadn't changed my cell number in over a decade. T-Mobile made me call them, then had me hold a good fifteen minutes before I finally reached a human. Once I did, I was scared to say my name. But if Jared did think I killed Janelle Beckett, they didn't say anything. Just walked me through each step until everything was taken care of.

None of my voicemails or audio messages were saved.

The only thing that would've stopped me from changing my number was Ty. I thought of that last message. Him telling me he loved me. But it was already long gone. Deleted when I'd believed he'd murdered Janelle Beckett. In that sense, the messages were right. I was a horrible person.

The T-Mobile rep warned me my call log would only stay on my phone until the next billing cycle. I'd also need to update all my accounts related to my number, which Jared threatened was better done sooner than later—otherwise I'd lose access to anything with two-factor authentication. But judging how things were going, that probably wasn't a bad thing either.

I should've called my mother as soon as my phone rebooted. Let her know I was okay. Given her my new information. But I didn't. She hadn't believed me the last time. I was afraid how I'd react if she didn't again. When I did talk to her, it would be to tell her they'd made an arrest—of someone else.

Instead, I opened TikTok. They'd found the account—not surprising—and had started tagging me in their own comments and videos. I ignored each and every one. Instead going straight to why I'd come: Billie's account.

She'd posted nonstop since Janelle was first reported gone. Often several times a day. I was fully expecting her to have at least two posts in the time I'd gotten a new number and she'd responded to Adore's DM with just one word. But there was nothing new. The last post was still the one where I'd been doxed. The comments, however, were World War III. And apparently there'd been a break-in at 110 Little Street. Another internet detective on the loose, no doubt.

I begrudgingly went back to my home page, then, in a masochistic moment, tapped, tapped, tapped, until I found my mentions. There were hundreds, maybe thousands. I clicked one at random, then immediately thought better of it. It was too late, though. The word "killer" jumped out at me like a jack-in-the-box. So did "drug addict." "Psycho." Combinations of all three.

I leaned on Adore's kitchen counter, staring at comment after comment as they somehow came together to form one oversized monster that felt like it would haunt me forever. I had just zoomed in on one when Adore's hand covered my screen. She hadn't spoken much since we'd gotten to her place. "You're safe. Internet comments are just that."

I nodded. "I survived three months in jail. I can survive Prancer-Dancer1873542 condemning me to hell." Of course knowing that still didn't make me feel better. So I said it again, hoping to mean it. "I'm okay."

Adore had called the hotel and checked me out over the phone. Now, at least, no one knew where I was.

"Your mom left a message on my work line." Adore finally removed her hand from my phone.

"If my mother could find your number, it must not be that hard."

"She's the only one who's been blowing up my work phone. No unknown numbers have called my cell. Not even spam. You're safe here, Bree."

"For now."

"I didn't mention your name when I DMed Billie. There's no way for her to connect us."

"Unless one of her 'police sources' gives it to her," I said.

"If they do, I hope it's because she's calling about Drew. She hasn't posted a video—yet."

I pretended like I hadn't checked myself. "Good. Of course if you do need to change your number, I know exactly what to do."

She didn't laugh. "Call your mom, please. Tell her I passed along the message."

I sighed. She was right. As much as I wanted to not talk to my mother until all this was in the past, I couldn't avoid it. She had a right to know I was at least okay. I owed her that even if her comments would be the ones that hurt most.

Adore's loft was beautiful but not exactly ideal for privacy. She must've noticed me looking around for a door because she spoke. "You can go upstairs if you want. Room on the left's yours."

I hadn't been to the second floor yet. There wasn't much to it when I got up there. Just a small hallway open to the rest of the apartment with two doors off it. Both were closed. I did as instructed and went left into the guest room.

Adore had downplayed it the other day, acting like it wasn't as nice as a hotel. She was right. It was nicer, decorated in white with silver accents and a mattress so thick I'd probably need a step stool to get into bed. I could only imagine how she'd done up the room she actually slept in.

My mom's cell was another of the few I knew by heart. But now I wished I didn't. It took me five minutes to call, hanging up at least twice when I got to the last digit. I wasted time by turning on the television. Found CNN. But it was a commercial.

Finally, I ripped the Band-Aid off—hitting all ten digits, then waiting. Normally she was quick to answer, happy to launch into whatever complaint she had this time. Because that's what the world was for her: one big complaint. Traffic. Work. Me.

All existing solely to make her life miserable.

But this time the phone just rang. And rang. And rang. And when it did pick up, it was voicemail. My message was quick and to the point. "Hey, Ma. Had to get a new phone. I, uh, lost mine." I wiped my eye. "That's why I haven't called. This is my new number. I'll try to call you back later."

Another lie. I couldn't do it, explain that I'd once again gotten myself into a mess. That I was once again being blamed for something I didn't do.

I hung up, but not before I said a prayer my mother didn't check her messages today.

Who knows how long I sat on the bed—and it wasn't because it was so comfortable.

There was a knock. Adore didn't wait for me to say, *Come in*. Just opened the door and said two words. "She posted."

TWENTY-TWO

"F inally."

Adore and I were so close, her whisper sounded full volume. She held her cell so we could both see it as we sat at her kitchen island.

"Shhh," I said, but it was gentle, not like the ones your grandma would give you at church two hours deep into service.

I wanted to hear what *interesting* news Billie was finally going to share. But first we had to hear about the vigil that night. Billie flew in from LA and was clearly posting from a hotel room. Others were coming from all over the US—and even at least one person from Canada.

Billie was planning to go all out—thanks to thousands of people who'd contributed to her GoFundMe. They'd found someone to donate candles, and everyone needed to wear pink. It was Janelle's favorite color. Billie made sure to remind us it was *hers* as well.

Once she got that out of the way, she brought up the break-in. "Yes, I've heard about it," she said. "How? Because someone DMed me saying it was my fault. That I have been causing hysteria and encouraging people to, quote, take the law into their own hands, unquote. Which we all know is the furthest thing from the truth. I'm just as upset as you all are that someone tried to break into a crime scene. Even the idea that one of my millions of followers would do that is simply heartbreaking. And I disavow it."

Billie stopped to wipe away a nonexistent tear. "I get a lot of ridiculous DMs with really out-there information and accusations—and I *do* make a point to be careful with what I share."

Beside me, Adore sighed. "She knows the break-in was one of the Billie Bunch; otherwise she wouldn't be so triggered."

I didn't respond, too focused on the tiny screen.

"Now, let's get back to this DM I got," Billie said. "I almost missed it since it was from someone who's never reached out before. But this one seemed credible. He obviously knew what he was talking about."

He.

"What's your Instagram handle?" I said to Adore. Maybe it was just initials. Billie could be making an assumption.

"My name."

Or maybe not.

I got up to head to the fridge a few feet away. Adore didn't move, didn't acknowledge I was no longer beside her.

"It's about Breanna Wright's arrest," Billie said.

Of course it was. I got to the fridge and just stopped. Listening.

"I heard from someone who'd dated her best friend in college," Billie said. "Was there the night of the arrest."

Adore was my best friend in college and she'd dated only one person junior year. Keith.

"That asshole," Adore said.

It wasn't the first time she'd said it. She'd used it so much in college, I almost thought it was his middle name. She was right, though.

He *was* an asshole. One who'd apparently still use any opportunity to get some shine—especially since his football dreams never worked out.

"He says Breanna Wright was partying it up that night."

I'd barely stayed an hour.

"Had a lot of alcohol."

Half a glass.

"Left the party in a huff."

Because he'd insulted Adore. Again.

"Turn it off," I said.

"But—"

"Please."

Billie's voice disappeared. I didn't bother to say thank you. Just finally opened the fridge and stood there, the cool air washing over me.

"Bree, I'm so sorry. I haven't spoken to Keith since we broke up right before graduation."

I would've cared about that back then. But now it was inconsequential. I tried to reason with myself. Tried to tell myself the same BS I would tell Adore in a few minutes. That this was a good thing. Exaggeration aside, good old Keith hadn't shared anything new. Folks had probably already googled my arrest enough that I was up there with Jesus himself in most-searched phrases. That it was good poor Drew wouldn't be subjected to the treatment Billie had given Ty and now me. No one deserved this.

But I couldn't lie to myself as easily as I could lie to the rest of the world. Because now that I was standing here knowing Billie wasn't going to move her spotlight from me on over to Drew, I could admit it was what I'd wanted.

Behind me, Adore had her phone on speaker. "I'm calling Calloway," she said, even though I hadn't asked. "Maybe she got your note. She could already be asking the neighbors about that Airbnb review. All of them. Just not Drew."

"Maybe."

"Calloway." The detective's voice rang through the air, and I finally closed the fridge door. Still didn't turn around, though.

"It's A. Kristine McKinley. I'm here with Breanna. We wanted to see if you got the note we left." I ignored Adore's sudden use of "we," but only because I was just as curious about the answer.

"I did." Calloway followed it up with silence.

After what felt like an eternity, Adore spoke again. "So you saw the screenshot?"

"I did."

This go-round, Adore waited only a few seconds before realizing Calloway wasn't going to elaborate. "I'm assuming you're looking into it. It's quite damning a neighbor would have access to the house like that, especially since we know someone brought Janelle Beckett there in the middle of the night while Breanna slept upstairs."

"They change the code after each guest. The neighbor wouldn't have had access to it."

"And you know this how?" Adore said.

"Because he told me."

Again with the "he." This time I was happy to hear it.

"Andrew Martin?" I made sure my voice was loud enough to carry.

"You know I can't tell you that." Calloway sounded amused.

Over the games and the BS, I went back to the couch to grab my newly numbered cell, then ran up the stairs to the spare bedroom. Ignored Anderson Cooper, muted on the TV.

I was surprised when Ms. Morgane picked up.

"I tried to call you when I saw the news," she said after I identified myself. "Got worried when that voice said your number was no longer in service. How you holding up?"

She sounded like she really wanted to know. It was a nice reminder that the entire world didn't hate me. So for once I didn't even attempt to lie. "Not good. I had to check out of the hotel because the entire internet found where I was staying. They found my cell number too. Reason I had to change it."

"Oh, Bree. I'm so sorry."

It didn't help that I looked up to see my mug shot. CNN's scrawl underneath it. It took everything not to cry.

"You there?" Ms. Morgane said.

"My mug shot is on television."

There was a pause, then Ms. Morgane spoke. "Okay."

I pinched my nose as if that would create a dam in my eyes. But they still overflowed.

Ms. Morgane spoke again. "That mug shot doesn't define you."

But it did. It had for the last twelve years. "Everyone thinks I did it."

I wasn't sure if I was talking about now or then—or even if it mattered.

"Did you?" Ms. Morgane said.

"No." My voice was quick. Emphatic.

"Then honestly that's all that matters. You hold your head high regardless."

I didn't say anything, but I heard her. Just like I heard what she said next.

"Screw all those people. Screw the ones on TV. Screw the ones on the internet. Screw the ones out here all time of night, even trying to break in."

I wiped the tears away, exhausted. Happy to talk about something else. "I heard about that. What happened?"

"Beats me. I woke up at about 3 a.m. to flashing lights outside my window. Didn't even bother to put on real clothes. Just rushed out in pajamas to see what was going on, but one of the neighbors already had called it in."

My hand dropped. "Drew?"

"No. I'd been trying to call you because I found out who watches that house when it's empty. It's Rod and Lori right next door. Guess he's been super vigilant since they got back from their trip. Heard some noise and immediately went outside."

I remembered Rod from when we went to pick up my stuff. He and his wife had been out of town when Janelle was killed.

So much for Andrew Martin.

I deflated, surprised at how disappointed I was. Again, I tried to talk through my emotions. "Well, I'm glad they stopped the person. Whoever it was."

She agreed. A dog barked in the background. "I gotta go, Bree. You're going to be okay."

That was still to be decided. "Thank you," I said. I'd never meant it more.

We hung up and I just sat there, enjoying the quiet. Pretending it meant everything was fine. It was five minutes before the phone went off again. I recognized my mother's number. The phone was on silent, but it didn't matter. Somehow it still sounded harsh.

I let it go to voicemail. I couldn't talk to her now, not after that comforting conversation with Ms. Morgane.

The text came soon after. All caps. BREANNA WHY ARE PEOPLE SAYING YOU KILLED SOME WHITE GIRL?

The news had finally made it from TikTok to the Baltimore suburbs. I was contemplating the best way to respond when Adore came upstairs. She stood in the doorframe like she was afraid to get too close.

"I have an idea, but you have to promise me you won't say no right away," she said. "That you'll take at least an hour to think about it."

"What is it?" I said, though I didn't want to even ask.

"You should talk to Billie. She's honestly more important than the police at this point. We need to get her on our side."

I shook my head. *No way.*

Adore finally came in. Sat down beside me on the bed, way more put together than I was. "She's the best way to let people know you didn't do it. She's got a bigger audience than CNN."

I stared at the text from my mom. Flashed back twelve years, when she came to get me at the police station. Heard the words like she was saying them to me right now. *What did you do, Breanna?* I wasn't going to let her say that to me again.

"DM her."

TWENTY-THREE

A nything from Billie?"

I'd said that phrase a billion times over the past couple of hours. To her credit, Adore didn't sound annoyed when she responded. "Still just says *Sent*."

I leaned back on Adore's couch. My cell phone was upstairs, where I'd left it after six unanswered texts in a row from my mom. "What are the odds she'll see it today?"

"Don't know," Adore said. "She's busy doing a tour of—and I quote—'Janelle's Jersey City' while claiming she's doing all this work for the vigil. So far she's hit Janelle's favorite dog park and coffee shop."

"It's all so performative. Like she cares about Janelle's death when it's really all about getting her own profile up."

"If it makes you feel better, she tried to go Live from Little Street. Morgane and some uptight—but cute—old white guy ran her off."

I wondered if that was Rod. I smiled. "Of course you'd notice how attractive the man was."

"Older men are my weak spot."

"That was your husband?"

"Fifteen years older than me. And honestly that was too young."

We laughed and it felt good—both to have a light moment and to hear more about the life of *A. Kristine McKinley*. But this wasn't a girls' trip, as much as I wanted it to be. "Billie mention me in that one?"

"Nope."

I felt surprise as much as relief—until Adore kept going.

"Folks in the comments, on the other hand…Someone called you and Ty the new Bonnie and Clyde. And the hotel put out a statement on their socials. Let me pull it up so I don't misquote them."

She tapped the screen until she found what she was looking for. "'There's no guest by the name of Breanna Wright staying at any of our facilities. All of us at the Crown Hotel support the efforts to find #Justice4Janelle.'" She put her phone down. "Translation: 'Stop clogging our switchboard.'"

"This is ridiculous. I just need five minutes to talk to Billie, convince her to stop making people think I had something more to do with this."

I flashed on the blood, the hair, the hands, but this time it was quicker to push it away.

"I'm a victim here. Ty is too." I realized what I'd said. "*Was. Ty was a victim.*"

I'd been so focused on myself that it felt like I'd forgotten about him. But he was still being vilified. We needed to figure out what had happened, to clear his name as much as mine. I owed him that, since he was no longer here to do it himself.

"I can message her again," Adore said. "It'll bump the message to the top of her queue at least. Better odds she'll see it."

But I was already shaking my head. I needed to be seen—in real life. Not in some DM. And that meant only one thing. "The vigil's at sunset?"

"No." Adore's voice was sharp.

But my mind was made up. "So that's, like, 7:30?"

She had her phone again. "'Breanna Wright deserves to fry.'

'Breanna Wright will rot in hell.' 'Someone should kill Breanna Wright the same way she killed Janelle.' And you want to go to where these people are?"

But that last comment just made me think about Janelle's body. The pictures of Ty that the medical examiner had shown me. "Yes."

She said nothing. I went to my handbag, pulled out my sunglasses and face mask. It only took a sec to put them both on. I tried to keep it light even though I felt like I was sinking to the bottom of the ocean. "Look, a disguise."

"And when it gets dark?"

"I'll be one of those jerks who wear their sunglasses at night. They'll think I'm some celebrity." It was a struggle to sound unbothered. Images of Janelle and Ty were still on my mind.

"These are the people who harassed some random Black man just trying to pick up a prescription at CVS."

"So you'll come with me. Give them only a fifty-fifty chance of thinking the Black girl is me." I took off the glasses and mask. "I can't spend the rest of my life hiding in your very, very, very nice guest room, Adore. You're the one who suggested I talk to Billie. Those threats just prove it needs to be as soon as possible."

It took a moment for Adore to speak. "Okay, but let me get you a hat. You look ridiculous in the sunglasses."

I called after her as she walked away. "But they're from Target."

* * *

"Remember what I said. No matter what she says, keep your cool."

Adore still wasn't happy about the vigil logistics, only agreeing to help me if we spoke to Billie before it started, then hauled it back to her place. Now she was acting like we were preparing for a cross-examination in the court of public opinion.

I nodded. "Yep, and if there's something I don't want to talk about,

I just look at you and you'll save me." I gave her a smile as we stepped into the crosswalk. "It'll be fine."

It turned out Hamilton Park was just a ten-minute walk from Adore's apartment. I would've thought the fresh air would make me miss my morning runs. Instead, I just felt stifled, sweat clinging to me like I was fresh out of the shower. The mask and hat didn't help, but I didn't dare take either off. They were already right up there with my childhood blankie when it came to emotional-support objects.

We were almost to the corner when I saw the first of them crossing the street. Just two initially. One with a poodle. They all wore pink—even the dog. I instinctively slowed, not wanting to literally cross paths. It worked too because none of them looked in our direction. Canine included. And by the time we got to the corner, they were pink dots in the distance.

I felt better—until we actually got to the cross street. A steady stream of pink was making its way into the park, and another handful of attendees were stationed at the entrance next to a set of tables. Volunteers. They handed out unlit pink candles as skinny and tall as strippers' stilettos and plain pink balloons as round as their asses.

Someone brushed my arm as she pushed past.

I cursed myself for not listening to Adore, for thinking a face mask and droopy hat would be enough to feel protected. To feel safe. I could've been at her apartment at that very moment, drinking red wine out of a stemmed glass until I was ready to sleep it all off on white Tencel sheets. Instead, I was here.

"Guess we shouldn't have ignored the pink memo." Adore looked at me, expecting a laugh. I couldn't even manage a smile. "You okay?"

I wiped the sweat from my brow. "Yeah, it's just the heat." Another lie.

"Then we shouldn't waste any more time. Just stick with the plan. Find Billie. Talk to her. Leave. We'll be in and out before you know it."

I nodded but didn't budge. Though I also didn't object when she pulled me toward the conga line snaking its way to the vigil. Everyone else was way more excited to be here than I was, their animated voices overlapping. I didn't look at any of them too long, much less make eye contact or say hello.

We'd made it two steps past the entrance when the voice came. "Excuse me."

It was clear they were talking to us. I didn't stop. Neither did Adore. It spoke again. Louder this time. Closer. "You in the hat."

It was followed a few nanoseconds later by a hand on my arm. It felt hot enough to brand me: *Killer*. It took everything not to wrench away. Instead, I just stopped. Slowly turned around to look at the woman. White with brunette hair in space buns, she'd written "#Justice4Janelle" across her cheeks.

"Excuse me?" Adore must've used her court voice. Strong. Self-assured. Not here for any mess.

It worked too because Brunette stepped back as if our breath stank. There was an awkward moment when none of us said anything as pink shirt after pink shirt eagerly wound past us. A dog barked a few feet away.

Finally, Brunette smiled, nervous but trying not to show it. "You two didn't get your candles or balloons."

My shiny armor disappeared. "Right." I turned to Adore. "We need our candles."

"And balloons. How could we forget?" Adore was all smiles now.

We followed her back—she was hurrying so we couldn't walk next to her—until we were at the entrance. Original Brunette quickly grabbed a candle—then handed it to Brunette Part Deux, more than happy to let us be someone else's problem. Part Deux smiled as she passed me my candle first. "We're doing a balloon release, so you should wait until Billie gives the go-ahead."

Despite the steady stream walking in, the park wasn't as crowded as I'd thought. There were a lot of people, sure. But more low hundreds than thousands. And they all seemed to be taking selfies.

No one even gave me a first glance, much less a second or third. We kept going to the gazebo up ahead. Tonight's stage.

I felt stronger with each step. More confident. These people weren't here to hunt down a killer. They were here to tell people they'd come. And as long as I didn't jump onstage and scream, "I'm Breanna Wright," I'd be okay.

Fingers crossed.

"It's like a cult." Adore watched a group rush past us. "A clone cult."

She was right. There was now just one problem. Everyone looked the same. White and pink and space-bunned, from what I could see behind their balloons. It made it impossible to figure out which one was Billie. They all had her carefully crafted aesthetic as if they'd watched and paused and rewound her makeup tutorials one right after another.

Grazing Adore's arm, I whispered into her ear. "Which one is Billie?"

"Damned if I know."

We did two loops with no luck, only a couple of false alarms. Adore wanted to start lap three, but I was tired and hot and had to pee.

"You still have the world's smallest bladder," Adore said.

"And you still love to give me crap about it."

She rolled her eyes but was already heading in the direction of the bathrooms. It looked like half the crowd was in line. "At least I'll have a good seat for the vigil," I said. "It'll be on the toilet, but still."

Adore turned to me. "Race for the Cure sophomore year."

The memory came back instantly. "Let's do it."

We both made our way to the men's room on the other side of the building. It was empty except for a lone woman standing outside. She clocked us coming, then stepped protectively in front of the door like a bouncer.

"I'm sorry. Billie's doing some last-minute prep for her speech.

So you can't talk to her right now," she said as soon as we got within earshot.

She spewed it off automatically, like she'd been saying it over and over. She followed it up with more of the same. "She's happy to chat as soon as the event is over."

Adore and I exchanged a look.

"She'll want to talk to us," Adore said.

"What media outlet are you with?" the woman said.

"None, but she'll want to speak with us."

The woman stared Adore down. "Why?"

Adore was not impressed or intimidated. "I'd rather tell her directly."

"Then you can wait."

"That's fine." Adore moved to stand right next to the woman, but I lightly touched her arm. The last thing we needed was to bring attention to ourselves.

"No problem," I said. "We'll just come back later. Thank you."

Adore let me drag her away but muttered under her breath as she did. "Asshole."

"Last thing we need right now is to cause a scene," I said.

"I was the one being nice," Adore said as we skirted the back of the crowd. "And I wanted you to pee."

I was more than fine holding it now.

"What do you want to do?" Adore said.

The plan had been to talk to Billie before the vigil and get out of there.

"Wait," I said.

We'd come this far.

TWENTY-FOUR

Adore and I were on the outskirts when the crowd went silent. A lone figure walked up the set of stairs on the gazebo's right. It wasn't easy to see her with all the balloons, but there she was. In real life, Billie didn't look much different than she did on my phone—it didn't help that we were so far back she was probably the same size. She held a megaphone and a candle. No one said anything until finally a random voice yelled out. "Justice for Janelle!"

Billie smiled so wide even I could see it from way back as the crowd all started to yell and clap. She said nothing for what felt like an eternity. Finally, she brought the megaphone to her mouth. The crowd quieted once again as she spoke. "Justice for Janelle!"

More applause. This time she didn't let it go for more than a few seconds.

"I just want to thank you all so much for coming here, wearing pink. Making sure to get your candles. I've already been seeing your great posts. But it's important to remember why we're here. Janelle Beckett. I have so much I want to say about her. About how society treats women. But before we do that let's send these balloons to Janelle up in heaven."

Billie was the first to let hers go, but it was soon joined by many more. It was only after Adore nudged me that I realized I still had mine. By the time I let it go, its peers were a good twenty-five feet up. It was as alone as I felt.

It was still slowly trying to catch up when Billie finally spoke again. "And now it's time to light our candles."

The woman who'd been guarding the bathroom door came up the stairs. Billie smiled at her gently as the woman whipped out a lighter. After her candle was lit, they hugged. I could hear her whisper "Thanks" as the crowd started to glow with spreading candlelight below her.

And it was then I realized we were the only ones who'd forgotten to bring a lighter. I glanced at Adore helplessly as the woman next to her smiled. "Y'all need a light?"

I nodded.

She leaned over and lit both our candles. Then she looked me dead in the face. For a moment, I thought she recognized me. But then she spoke. "Justice for Janelle."

I paused, then nodded. "Justice for Janelle."

Up ahead, Billie started to speak. "Four thousand nine hundred seventy." She paused just long enough for us all to figure out what she was talking about. "That's the number of women who were murdered in the United States last year. That's almost two thousand more than two years before. I want to have a moment of silence for Janelle Beckett and for the thousands of women who've been killed and those who are missing. There's also Kimberly Iron, Faith Lindsey, Sabrina Rosette, Cecelia Barber Finona. I could go on and on. I wish I could name them all. Because their lives are just as important."

The crowd started to cheer, but Billie stopped it immediately. "Let's bow our heads."

They hushed.

I spent the time thinking about Janelle—how I'd found her. The blond hair. The blood. The jeans. And that made me think of Ty. The color of his skin in the photo from the medical examiner. And how

I'd meant it when I'd told our neighbor, *Justice for Janelle*. Because she deserved it. But Ty did too.

The crowd was silent until Billie spoke again. "We miss you, Janelle."

I was the only one who kept my head down. And that's where I kept it for the rest of Billie's speech. Catching stray words here and there, my mind consumed with Janelle and Ty. My candle was as burnt out as I felt by the time the crowd applauded. Billie was done. I looked around. I wasn't the only one who'd been crying.

"We should go try to talk to her." I'd forgotten Adore was next to me.

We headed toward the gazebo, but everyone else had the same idea. The mass moved forward, all aglow from their cell phone screens. I had a vision then. Billie pointing at me, screaming. In my mind, she'd added my middle name for posterity.

Breanna Grace Wright.

They'd burn me at the stake, then hashtag their selfies with my body.

I grabbed Adore's hand. "I can't."

Her response was barely a whisper. "They have cell phones, Bree. Not pitchforks."

"I'd prefer the latter," I said. "Less dangerous."

Adore looked past me, smiling at something or someone. I said nothing more, just stood there as space buns and pink shirts moved past.

"You made me stand through all that and now you want to leave?" Adore said at last, but she was teasing. Her delivery wasn't any better than mine usually was.

"I still want to talk to her," I said. "Just not in front of this crowd."

Adore's voice was barely above a whisper. "You can't have it both ways. I don't know how long she'll be here, or where she'll be when she leaves. You either talk to her now or we go home."

I glanced toward the gazebo. It was fully dark now. I couldn't see Billie in the crowd of pink, but I could assume she was still there, holding court. Likely describing herself as an Angel and me as the Devil incarnate. "I'll go," I said.

But I didn't move. Just stared at the crowd.

Finally, Adore spoke again. "You stay by the exit. I'll go talk to her. See what she says. I'm not going to say you're here, but if she's receptive, I'll text you. You can come over."

I smiled, liking that, then remembered she couldn't see it under the mask. I was still smiling when she patted me on the arm and walked away.

Not knowing what else to do, I finally went to the bathroom. I couldn't immediately find Adore when I got out, so I headed to the exit and sat on the closest bench. Adore was radio silent for twenty-three minutes. I didn't do any of my usual things to pass the time. No YouTube. No Candy Crush. Definitely no social media. Too afraid of what number I could be trending at. I did nothing but stare at the photo of me and Ty, waiting for a text that would never come.

I missed him. I wanted him next to me, holding my hand, making jokes, giving me Muddy Buddies even though he hated the taste on my lips. I owed it to him to clear his name.

I was so busy thinking about Ty, I didn't see Adore until she was right up on me. I glanced behind her, half expecting to see Billie. But there was no one. Even the most dedicated of the Billie Bunch had gone home.

Popping up, I spoke. "So…"

"She's prettier up close. Also looks older without the filters."

And with that Adore started moving toward the exit. I caught her in less than two strides. "And?"

"She assumed I wanted a selfie, then assumed I wanted an autograph. I said no to both."

"Adore, this is not the time."

She removed the hint of a smile. "Fine. I went up, whispered I was the one who told her about that neighbor. She nodded even though it was clear she had no clue what I was talking about. I could see her already looking past me, but she gave me her full attention when I mentioned you. I showed her a pic. That one of us from the Que party sophomore year."

I motioned with my hands to get on with it just as we got to the street corner. Adore stopped talking long enough to look both ways and then crossed the street.

"Based on the fact we're heading back to your house, I'm assuming she didn't want to talk," I said.

"No, she did. With me. She was upset I turned her down. But then I mentioned I could probably arrange for her to talk to you."

"And?"

"And...she thought it over. I reminded her she'd be the first person you spoke to. That got her interested."

My heart sped up. "So are we meeting her somewhere?"

"Yep. The Regency. She's being interviewed for some news segment so she'll text me once she's done."

*   *   *

Like Hyatt House, the Regency was another Hyatt hotel. But whereas Hyatt House looked like a bank, this one looked like a beached orange cruise ship, more wide than tall and jutting out into the greenish Hudson River so it could charge extra for "views of Manhattan." It wasn't until I heard the train horn that I realized I'd seen it before, when Ty and I took the PATH into Manhattan and again when I went to look for him that first day afterward.

It had taken Billie two hours to reach out. Adore had suggested I try to nap, but it was pointless. I just tossed and turned. Then picked at my food when she tried to get me to eat. I had known I wouldn't have been able to keep it down anyway. But now we were finally here. It was so late Adore was able to find a parking spot on the street. She spoke softly as the escalator took us up to the lobby. "You remember what to do? Give her Perky Black Girl. Smile no matter what she says. Take time to answer. Remind her you're a victim here too. She needs to remember you're human."

I could only nod. The nerves were back. So was the anxiety. The feeling like I was on a roller coaster making its initial climb. Up. Up. Up. Taking so long, I felt exhausted—like I'd already experienced every rise and fall and upside-down loop de loop.

"Bree, look at me." Adore stopped right as we got off the escalator in the lobby. She pulled me into a hug. I could smell her expensive perfume. "This is going to be great," she said. "She's going to love you. Then she'll let her followers know there's no way you could've done all of this."

I tried to believe her. I'd had no idea what to expect when we got to the second floor, but it wouldn't be Billie. She hadn't given Adore her room number, instead telling us to text when we got here.

The lobby was practically deserted. A night attendant smiled blankly in our direction as I looked around. "Can I help you?" he said.

Luckily Adore answered. "We're waiting for a friend. Just texted her."

"Great. Feel free to have a seat until she arrives."

He glanced at me for the first time and I jumped, feeling completely naked even with 90 percent of my body covered.

I sucked in a breath so hard the material of my mask went an inch into my mouth. Despite the hotel's artificial arctic feel, like that of most commercial buildings, I was sweating so much my mask was wet and my phone slipped out of my clammy hand.

When I went to pick it up, I saw him. Ty smiling at me from my lock screen.

And that's when I knew I could stay. I could do this. That I shouldn't have to spend even a nanosecond longer freaking out every time someone looked in my direction. I'd been there already. Done that. My sentence had lasted way longer than the actual three months I'd spent in prison. And the only way I could put all this to rest was to finally meet Billie face-to-face.

"She's here," Adore said.

There was no one in the hall. "I don't see her."

Adore nodded in the other direction and there she was. Billie. I couldn't make out much since she was still so far away. As she got closer, more of her came into focus, like a YouTube video going from 144 to 720 pixels. The blond hair was still in her vigil style—space buns—and she was wearing all pink. I still couldn't make out her expression, thanks to a pair of oversized sunglasses and a patterned face mask. Incognito wasn't much fun when you were on the other side.

"Take your mask off and smile." Adore's voice had been a whisper.

I did, then tried to smile so hard I was surprised I didn't blind the entire lobby with my white-stripped teeth. I stayed like that until Billie stopped a few feet away. I wasn't sure if she was social distancing or just afraid to get too close to me. We all stayed like that longer than I cared for, none of us saying anything. Me because I wasn't sure how to play it. Maybe her the same.

After a moment she removed her mask and sunglasses, taking me in with her blue eyes. Then she smiled, the corners of her eyes crinkling as she did. Adore was right. She looked older in person, but that just made her more attractive. She looked like a human, not some AI created version of the "perfect woman."

Billie stared at my ASICS just long enough that I was tempted to lift my foot to show her the pink sole. But I didn't, and she slowly continued her once-over. Then finally—thankfully—she spoke. "Breanna Wright...you're even prettier than in all the pics I've seen."

I wasn't sure what to make of the compliment. It sounded nice. Sincere. But still, I couldn't help but zero in on the subtext. *All the pics.*

I'd made my social media private. That meant someone—someone I knew—had posted them, or at least sent them to her, and she wanted me to know.

I was still trying to figure out the best response when Billie spoke again. "Are you all hungry? I know it's late, but I made sure to get us some food."

Her eyes crinkled again, but she turned before either of us could respond. Then she walked back the way she'd come. Adore's eyes were wide, not any more sure what to make of the onslaught of charm than I was.

"Y'all coming?" Billie called over her shoulder.

And that's when we both followed her.

"Sorry it took so long to text, but I fell down a rabbit hole trying to edit video from the vigil." She glanced back, this time at Adore. "Wasn't it amazing? So many people. CNN covered it and I did a quick interview with MSNBC."

And there it was. The Billie I had been expecting. The one who was self-involved.

"Anderson Cooper shared the sound bite of other women missing. Hopefully that brings more attention to their cases."

And once again I was surprised. Even felt bad about stereotyping her.

"You really put together a great event to honor Janelle's life," Adore said.

She was right.

An older couple was coming toward us. They both stopped their chitchat when they saw Billie. I highly doubted they recognized her—not exactly her target audience—but they still looked at her like they knew she *had to be* someone. She must've noticed too because she spoke. "Evening. Hope you both had a great night."

They smiled, happy to be acknowledged, still beaming as they passed by Adore and me without so much as a glance.

The hallway seemed to stretch forever, with only the occasional door to break up the monotony. I'd assumed Billie would take us to her room. Instead, we were clearly in a conference area.

"Breanna, you a coffee person?"

I jumped at my name, even though I'd heard Billie say it a million times at this point. This time was nicer, curious. Adore's eyes bore into me, willing me to channel Perky Black Girl—the woman I used to be when Adore and I had first met. The one who laughed and made friends easily and wasn't afraid to share things about herself.

"Yes." I smiled.

"Decaf?"

"No. What would be the point?"

She laughed. "Exactly. I also don't get the folks who just take it black."

Billie slowed down so the three of us could walk in a line like grade school best friends.

"Me neither," I said. "Four sugars. If I don't get a jolt from the coffee, I'm gonna hedge my bets. Get one from the sugar."

"My kind of girl. But then my mom used to feed me Pixy Stix before I did pageants as a kid."

"I bet you always won," I said. It explained the charm.

"Yes, except that one time I lost to Jennifer Woods. That bitch." But she laughed when she said it. She looked me over again. Up and down. But when her eyes came back up, they had kindness in them.

"How are you holding up?" Said like she meant it. Said like she hadn't played a part in making my life hell.

I opened my mouth to respond, but Adore's arm brushed against mine purposefully.

Perky Black Girl.

"I've been better," I said. "I miss Ty. He was an amazing person. Doesn't deserve any of this." I caught myself. "Didn't deserve any of it."

I met her eyes. And she stopped. This time she opened her mouth like she was going to be honest for once.

"Here we are." Billie motioned at some random door I didn't even realize was there. "Like I said, I already got us food, but I'm happy to order anything else you want. I think we have an hour before the kitchen closes. It's my treat. I really appreciate you both coming out so late."

Adore jumped in. "We appreciate you taking the time to talk to me as well. You didn't have to."

"Of course," Billie said.

She opened the door to a medium-sized conference room complete with a standard-issue deep brown table for eight. I was only two steps in when I saw the ring light and the cell phone set up facing the far wall. Billie glanced back, smiling all innocent-like. "Figured we could go Live here."

Billie Regan sits in front of the camera. Behind her isn't her usual setup but a large television and some generic artwork. She smiles, fresh-faced and glowing. Her blond hair's in two space buns, and she wears a pink T-shirt she's tied in the back to make more formfitting. "Hey, Billie Bunch. I'm Billie. This is my channel and, yes, I'm uploading this video late AF, but, you all, look at this view."

She flips the camera so we're staring at downtown Manhattan through a window. It's an unobstructed view of One World Trade Center surrounded by smaller skyscrapers, all lit against the night.

The camera flips back to Billie, still beaming. "The vigil tonight was amazing. Janelle would've been so happy. The only thing that would've made it even more perfect is if she could have been there.

"I'm truly humbled by seeing so many people come out for Janelle both in person and online. Seeing all of us together, united. We definitely sent a message to the police—and to all the men out there who keep hurting women. If you missed it, don't worry. We're uploading the entire thing. Of course there are lots of other videos from all the folks there too. Please check the Justice for Janelle hashtag."

The photo disappears and we're back with Billie in the hotel suite. "I've finally had a chance to check my DMs again. And, of course, read your comments. So many of you are asking me what's next. Well, the fight continues. And I've decided to stay here to keep putting pressure on the police to identify Janelle's body for her sister. She couldn't make the vigil, and although I'm bummed, I totally understand why."

She pauses, appropriately somber.

"Someone else reached out to me. And I'll be honest, at first I was hesitant when I found out they wanted to talk. But then I realized I needed to do this. Because they are the only person alive who can give us the answers we need. Who can tell us about Janelle's last moments."

She pauses again, dramatically.

"Later tonight, I'll be chatting with Breanna Wright. We'll be going Live around 1 a.m. I know that's late, but I want to make sure we get all our questions answered as soon as we can. So please comment with what you want me to ask her."

TWENTY-FIVE

I never told you Bree wanted to be filmed." Adore's eyes shot daggers.

Her target sputtered for a few seconds before finally getting a sentence out. "But, Kristine, you said she wanted to talk."

"Correct. There was no mention of it being on camera."

Billie faced us, the glow from her oversized ring light causing an almost ethereal cast behind her. "How else would we do it?" Billie looked genuinely confused.

Adore and I were side by side. I was quiet—shocked—as she spoke. "You knew exactly what I meant when I spoke with you tonight. You're trying to use her for views."

"Of course," Billie said. "But don't tell me you aren't doing the same thing. That's why you're here and not with the police. It won't take long. She's looking a little washed out, though. No offense. I'd love to make her a look a little more camera-ready."

"How nice of you." The sarcasm dripped from Adore's voice.

Billie turned from Adore to me, having decided I was the reasonable one. "You're fine with it, right?"

Now they both looked in my direction, each wanting me to tell the other they were wrong. "Billie, I really do appreciate you letting us come," I said. "But, honestly, I'd rather just talk to you first."

"Oh yeah, of course. We can get to know each other. Then go Live."

Adore cut in, her words sharp. "If you had brought up anything about being filmed, we would've left sooner. Just like we're doing now. Come on, Bree."

She immediately followed through on her words, heels gliding so fast on the carpet I was surprised there weren't sparks. But I was too stunned to move. So I was right there when Billie called out. "That's a shame, Kristine. I've already told my followers we'll be speaking."

But Adore was gone. I stared at the open door, then turned to find Billie staring. "I can't tell your story for you, Bree. You need to do that yourself. That's the only way they're gonna be on your side."

I practically recoiled. "Billie, I watch your channel. I've seen every post. Every Live. Every dramatic reveal. Every shocked expression. Every fake tear. You're the one who turned them against me."

She shook her head, and when she spoke, it was with pity. "No, I'm the one who made people care about Janelle. The police weren't doing shit. And if I had to get all pretty and do some theatrics to get the world to tune in, I am okay with that. Because it made them care too. Do you want the person who did this to be caught?"

The hair. The hands. The jeans. The blood covering it all.

I pushed the thought away, but Ty's voice just replaced it. *I've wanted to tell you: I love you so much.*

My mouth went dry.

Billie was still going. "People talk about how big the internet is. It isn't. It's small. Full of people looking for connection. Herd mentality at its best. If you do this, they'll believe whatever you want them to. You just have to present it in the right way. But if you don't do it, what do you think they're gonna believe?"

I swallowed. "Let me go talk to Adore," I said.

"Take your time," Billie said. "I'll get the mascara out for you."

She smiled. Eyes crinkling.

I'd underestimated her.

* * *

Adore was in the bathroom. It took me ten minutes to find her, and when I did, she had both sides of a porcelain sink in a death grip, staring at herself, barely blinking and not smiling at all. I'd never seen her this way.

I leaned against the sink next to hers and of course tried to lighten the mood. "If you were my lawyer twelve years ago, I would've gotten off."

She just shook her head.

I spoke again. "I need to do this, Adore."

"She tricked us. Me."

"Yes, but she also told her millions of followers we're going to talk tonight. If I bail, it'll look like I'm trying to hide something."

"Not if we go to a *real* outlet. Let you talk to them on camera. CNN. CBS. MSNBC. They'll all want to talk to you. I just need to contact them."

"And while you're doing that, Billie's 'Breanna Wright has something to hide' TikTok will gain a kabillion views."

She made me wait before she gave her answer and then it was just one single word.

"Fine."

We turned to go. "She was right about one thing," Adore said. "You do look washed out. You can't go in there looking like a mug shot."

"She's seen my mug shot."

"I know. You actually look better in it."

* * *

As soon as we went Live, I was reminded this wasn't a regular interview. Billie had insisted we sit side by side—something about angles—like we were filming a YouTube reaction video instead of discussing the most talked about murder in the United States. We were so close I could smell Billie's vanilla-scented perfume—as we stared at a tiny iPhone smack-dab in the middle of an oversized ring light.

It should've made me uncomfortable. Instead, it had the opposite effect: reminded me we weren't in an interrogation room or on some morning show. Billie ran through her usual introductions (*Hey, Billie Bunch*) and purpose (#Justice4Janelle) before turning to me. Not literally, though. She'd already told me she hated the angle.

"Breanna."

I immediately interrupted, turning to speak to her. "Only my mother calls me that. Please call me Bree."

After a moment, Billie nodded. "Bree."

She smiled, though her eyes didn't crinkle. Then she reached out to rub my shoulder. I'm sure on camera it looked warm, like she was welcoming me. But in reality, she maneuvered me back to the angle she wanted.

"I want to thank you for coming on my channel," Billie said. "It's very brave of you."

My laugh was soft. "I wouldn't call it brave. I wanted to come on because you *are* the person who's been getting justice for Janelle Beckett."

Billie smiled at the compliment.

I kept on. "And having been there. Having seen what happened to that poor woman, I want justice served as much as anyone else." I took in a breath. "Even if it means going through this phase, where people are calling me with death threats."

Billie had the nerve to look shocked. "Death threats? That's completely unacceptable—just like everyone blaming me for spreading rumors when we're getting to the truth."

I nodded. "And that's also why I'm here. I wanted to share what actually happened that night…"

The hair. The hands. The jeans. The blood covering it all.

For once, I didn't push the thought away. Instead, I focused on it. Janelle Beckett lying in a pool of her own blood. Beaten beyond recognition.

"Bree, you okay?" Billie gently tapped me with her elbow, her eyes still focused on the phone in front of us.

"I'm sorry. I just…It's hard to think about seeing her body, lying there like that. It was the last thing I expected when I came downstairs that morning."

"I can only imagine. Take us through the night."

I took a breath, and then I did, the words tumbling out without much thought. "It started with playing hooky from work. Me and Ty. I was supposed to leave last Sunday, but we decided I should stay longer since he'd had to work so much while I was here. Our last conversation before bed was about breakfast the next morning. And I thought he was going to say he loved me. We hadn't said it before. But he stopped himself."

Now I wished he'd said it if only so I could say it back to him. It would be a lifelong regret no matter how this all turned out.

I kept on. "Finding Janelle wasn't the first time I woke up. That was around four thirty. Ty wasn't in bed. I assumed he'd gotten up to work. I went to get him. I know you've seen the pictures of the house, but it doesn't do justice to how big it is. The main bedroom is on the fourth floor, and you couldn't hear anything below. I didn't know what was going on when I went down the first set of stairs. Could barely make out a light on in the kitchen. I called out—and the light went off. And I figured he was coming to bed, so I went back up to the bedroom. I realized later that this was when she was dying. And that maybe, just maybe, if I had gone downstairs, I could've saved her life."

The first tear hit then, rushing out of my eye like a waterfall and making its way down my cheek. I didn't wipe it away. Didn't touch my Billie-powdered face at all. Instead, I just kept talking, staring at the iPhone but not really seeing it. "But I didn't. I went upstairs and I went to sleep again. For hours. While she lay there. Bleeding. And when I did finally wake back up and go downstairs, I found her. But it was too late. I noticed her shoe first. Then I noticed the blood. The hair."

I felt like if I reached out right then I could touch the body. The waterfall had turned into an ocean and it was only then I attempted to wipe my face. I realized Billie was finally looking at me as if no longer caring about angles or the best way to manipulate an audience of millions.

I struggled to get the next bit out. "Her hands were by her head, and I'd like to think Janelle fought back. That she was brave until the end, fighting for her life while I slept upstairs—instead of helping her. And even after I saw her, I didn't help. Didn't think to even call for an ambulance just in case. No. I just freaked out. Managed to somehow get outside, where I ran straight into a neighbor, who was able to call 911."

"Drew." Billie knowing Drew's name is what brought me back to the present. "Where was Ty during all this?"

"I don't know," I said. "I didn't wake up again until ten, and he'd told me he was going to work. So that's where I thought he was—until the detectives told me he hadn't gone in."

"That must've been a shock."

I nodded. "I also thought he'd never been to Little Street until the day I got there."

Billie's eyes widened. "So he lied to you as well. You think he did it?"

I took Adore's advice and didn't respond right away. I'd been expecting this question, but still it was hard to answer. Ty wasn't perfect—he'd lied to me over and over, and he'd even admitted he *fucked up* in that last message.

But he wasn't a murderer.

I didn't care how intimately he had known Janelle. He didn't kill her. I opened my mouth to say so too when Adore cleared her throat so loudly we both looked over. Billie turned back to me. I finally spoke.

"I think the Tyler Franklin I thought I knew wouldn't do it."

TWENTY-SIX

The rest of the conversation was a blur, but it must've gone well. Adore didn't feel another need to interrupt, and she was smiling when Billie finally stopped recording and turned the ring light off.

"Two hundred thousand people watching," Billie said. "Not bad at all."

The crinkle was back.

I didn't say anything. Didn't do anything. Just sat there, face still placed at the perfect angle. I'd done it.

Finally shared what had happened. Spoken from my heart. I didn't know what I'd been expecting—to feel accomplished? Victorious? Empowered?

Instead, I felt exhausted on all levels, and like all the water had left my body. My throat felt dry and my eyes itched.

And I was ready to go home. "Thank you again," I finally said.

I went to grab my handbag when Billie spoke once more. "You know that jerk who told me about your conviction tried to contact me again."

Adore and I exchanged a look. Keith. "About what?" I said.

"The night you got arrested," Billie said.

I cringed. Having just relived the worst night of my life, I didn't also want to rehash the runner-up.

"He said you were insistent they weren't your drugs, but he had proof," Billie said.

I rolled my eyes. No such proof existed. Still, I wasn't gonna get into it. But when I turned around, she was shoving her phone at me. I recognized the photo immediately. I wasn't in it, but it didn't matter. I knew it. It *was* taken that night. The photograph was of a living room with a HAPPY BIRTHDAY sign strung on a wall. People were splayed out on any available seating. I didn't see myself, but I didn't expect to. I'd gotten there after all the seats had been claimed and thus been relegated to leaning on the kitchen counter.

I did recognize Adore, though—not the A. Kristine McKinley version of today but the Adore I knew. Loved. The one who was pretty despite the cheap clothes and cheaper makeup. She was leaning over the coffee table, rolling a blunt. Next to her was a baggie of weed. Orange, with pumpkins drawn on it.

I recognized it just as easily as I recognized her.

What in the entire fuck?

"You okay?" Adore was across the room now, too far to see the photo but close enough to see from my face that something was wrong. She turned to Billie. "He's my ex," Adore said. "Still mad I broke up with him."

Billie spoke. "Men."

They both laughed, but I didn't join them. There was nothing funny about this situation. "I have to go," I said, already aiming for the door.

Billie mumbled something behind me—probably goodbye—but I didn't hear her. Didn't respond. Just took off.

* * *

I was finally running again, my heart pounding so loud it sounded like a drum solo as my legs took me down the hall, then the escalator. And finally into the inky blackness hovering outside the hotel exit. It was then and only then I stopped, and even that was only because my brain didn't know where to go next. I couldn't go back to Little Street. My hotel room was long gone. I sure as hell wasn't going to Adore's house just as I sure as hell wasn't going back in *there*.

I was trying to figure out what to do, where to go, when Adore came rushing out. "Bree." She went to grab my arm, but I swatted her away.

I walked up on her—not stopping even when I was just a centimeter away, forcing her to step back. Once. Twice. It took a third step before I spoke. "It was your marijuana."

I expected her to deny it—even hoped she'd act like I didn't know what I was talking about. But instead she said just one word.

"Yes."

I felt myself implode, then was shocked when I looked down to see my body intact. I took inventory. Hands. Legs. Heart. Destroyed but there. She didn't say anything more. Just watched me. I counted my inhales. The first were too short and so sharp I was surprised I didn't stab myself. I tried again, but those were too long, as if trying to suck up the entire world. Finally I found one that was just right. And it was only then I spoke. "That orange baggie ruined my life."

I expected her to apologize. Again I was wrong.

"You're just gonna stand there?" I said.

"What do you want me to say, Bree?" Her eyes were pleading.

"I'd start with 'I'm sorry for being such a coward,'" I said. "'For letting my best friend take the fall for my marijuana.'"

"It fell out of my bag." She sounded insistent, like that would make it okay.

And she wouldn't glance at me when she spoke—even though I'd never wanted anything more in my life than for her to look me in the eye. To see what she'd done to me. Instead, she stared to her right, so I took a step in that direction to stay in her eyeline. But she just turned her head left.

"So it was an accident?" My voice was little more than a hiss. "Were the twelve years of radio silence an accident too?"

I was crying again even though I would've sworn it was impossible. That I had no water left in my body. "Why?" I said.

"I would've lost my scholarship."

"Yes, you would have. I know because I lost *mine*."

"If I didn't finish school, I would've gone back home. Been sleeping in bed next to my mother. I would've had nothing. Been nothing."

Again I nodded because I knew. "You would've been stuck."

"Your mom came to get you. I heard she brought a lawyer."

"She did," I said. "Because she didn't believe me. She still doesn't."

"I thought you were going to be okay," she said.

"And when you found out I wasn't?" I said, but she didn't respond. I kept on. "At least now I know why you kept tabs on me. Why you suddenly appeared the other day, going out of your way to make amends. Being so sweet I felt like an asshole for being mean to you. You felt *guilty*."

I gave her a once-over, taking in the Louboutins. The designer jeans. The Hermès holding the business cards touting a profession she'd never even wanted. "You ruined my life—and then you fucking took it."

Adore's head turned. When she finally looked at me, her face was stone. "I wasn't the one who ran that light. Or resisted arrest."

The words sounded rehearsed—like something she'd repeated to herself each night instead of counting sheep.

"Because those weren't my drugs," I said, not even wanting to think about how many times I'd blamed Domingo. He was still an asshole, but he hadn't planted those drugs in my car.

"If you hadn't mouthed off, you would've been okay," she said.

Once again, it sounded like this was something she'd told herself a million times and had convinced herself was true.

"How would you know?" I said. "You weren't there. *During or after.* Even if you didn't tell the cops, you could've at least told me."

"I can help you get your record expunged," she said, as if that would erase the past twelve years.

She was back to not looking at me. I tried to calm myself down by attempting to take in air. It didn't work.

"Fuck you, Adore."

I took off running again.

*   *   *

I got all the way back to the light-rail before my body betrayed me, my breaths as ragged as a piece of old clothing. When I went to check the time, I saw Adore had texted. I was naive enough to still expect an apology. But I'd already forgotten this wasn't Adore. This was A. Kristine McKinley, born the day she let me take the fall for her drugs.

Your stuff is still at my house.

She could burn it all for all I cared. I'd change my underwear once I got to Maryland. I just needed to figure out how to get there.

It was well after 1 a.m. I still had my return ticket, but the last Amtrak train was probably long gone, having departed back when I didn't realize how deep my best friend's betrayal ran.

The light-rail was deserted, not even a homeless person setting up shop on a bench. Suddenly I felt vulnerable. Being Black and a woman in someplace strange so late at night was dangerous.

That's when I saw the sign for Hyatt House.

I took inventory of what I still had with me—even if my wits weren't one of the items. Just the clothes on my back, my handbag, and my cell phone. I'd brought my debit card but didn't have to open my bank app to know I didn't have enough in my account to purchase a hotel room.

It was fine. I could find an all-night diner. Nurse a cup of coffee like I was on call at a hospital. But when I googled, the search came up empty. Only places that were still open were take-out. Blame post-pandemic life for the new operation hours.

So I did what I had to do.

My mom picked up on the second ring. "Breanna?" She made her voice sound tired even though we both knew she was a night owl. "You're finally calling me back."

"Mommy." I hadn't used that word in twelve years. "I need—"

But she cut me off. "Are you at the police station, Breanna? You've been arrested again?"

Her tone hurt worse than a blow to the stomach. I waited for the lecture followed by the onslaught of questions about Janelle Beckett and my involvement. Part of me wanted to scream out that she was right about Adore, had always been right. Adore was the reason I was arrested, so my mom could forgive me now. But I wasn't sure she'd believe me. Still.

"No," I said. "Because I didn't do anything. I didn't hurt that girl. Ty didn't hurt that girl. And I'm going to explain everything to you soon as I get back home. But for now I just need your help." I paused. "Not your judgment."

There was a moment of silence. By the time she spoke, it felt like her words had walked all the way from Maryland. But then: "Okay, baby. What do you need?"

I exhaled. Maybe even smiled a bit. *Okay.* It was just one word. Two syllables. But it was exactly what I needed to hear. "A hotel room," I said. "Hyatt House. Jersey City."

"What's the number?"

It took me only a second to google it and five minutes more for her to get me a room. She didn't call back when she did. Just sent a text

that an open-ended reservation was under my name. I'd still been flying high on our exchange, but that's when I had the next mini crisis.

My name.

It wasn't just mine anymore. It had been shared everywhere, from
comment sections to dinner tables—synonymous with "missing,"
"monster," and "killer." And now I was supposed to use it for a hotel
stay. It hadn't gone so well the last time. I had the changed phone number to prove it.

But still, it wasn't like I had much choice. I couldn't stay out here
alone in the middle of the night. I needed a place to hunker down for a
few hours until I could catch the first Amtrak home.

I took a deep breath, then willed my legs to walk in. There was
no security in the downstairs lobby this time, but it was okay. I knew
exactly where to go. The elevator ride to the lobby on the top floor was
just as long as before. I spent the entire time hoping the woman who
had been there before hadn't picked up a night shift.

The door opened. I don't know what I had been expecting, but dead
silence was not it. Not a single soul was in sight. The person on the
clock probably napping somewhere sight unseen. Possibly a good thing.
Maybe they'd be too tired to recognize my face or name.

The front desk was only ten feet away, yet I milked the walk for all
it was worth. I still got there way too soon, so I just stood. Patient for
once because I was in no rush for someone to be of service. I didn't call
out. I barely let out a breath. Still, they must've had some sort of camera
because a door opened somewhere in the ether.

It took just a second for them to appear. A man. Black and
older—the specks of gray hair a dead giveaway because the skin never
was. I squinted at his name tag. PETER. He smiled when he saw me.
Alert.

I smiled too but still only felt half out of the woods. Sure, he probably wasn't a member of the Billie Bunch, but my name had made it to
both CNN and MSNBC. Probably Fox News too.

"I need to check in," I said. "I believe you already have a credit card on file."

My ID was at the ready, so I just slid it across without saying anything.

He nodded, clearly sensing my silence though not seeming put out about it. But it was very late and he probably was used to dealing with cranky folks. His mouth moved slowly as he read my name to himself. "Breanna Grace Wright." He looked up and after a moment smiled. "Pretty name."

"Thanks," I said. "Can I change it?"

Better safe than sorry to put the room under a different name.

"Permanently?" But he laughed when he said it.

"And risk the wrath of my mother?" We both laughed at that one. "I'd just prefer to have a different one in the system."

"Got it." He sounded like he'd heard far worse, and once again I was happy this was the night shift.

I gave him the name of my favorite coworker. We didn't speak again until he was handing over my key card. "We're all set with your suite. Please let me know if you have any issues once you get to the room. Kitchen's closed, but I put you on the Manhattan side to make up for it. It's quieter there."

He could've put me in the basement for all I cared, as long as he didn't do one thing.

"Can you also not transfer any calls to my room?"

*　*　*

Peter did, in fact, put me on the Manhattan side. The view was gorgeous, from the two-second glance I took before closing the curtains. I texted my mom to tell her I'd checked in, then tried to figure out what to do next.

I decided to go with what I could control first. My hunger. Except my brain couldn't process what to get. It just knew I needed food ASAP. It didn't matter how many stars the place had on Google or if some guy from Montclair thought the chips were stale. I'd eat cardboard at this point. It took a second to remember I'd done this before. Ordered food in Jersey City.

Only that time I had been ordering for two.

I pulled out my phone to distract myself from thinking about Ty and scrolled the call log. The last vestiges of my old number. The Before times. Even though I was starving, I still deleted all the unknown numbers in red. Missed calls from assholes who thought it was cute and brave to call people who'd been doxed. I didn't need the reminders taunting me. My brain was doing a good job on its own.

Finally, I got to the taqueria place I'd ordered from before. I'd been in Jersey City long enough to recognize the area code. The first three digits matched the location—201—but there was a different 201 number right underneath it. Another I didn't recognize, but it couldn't be one of the assholes. The timing didn't match. And it was black, which meant it'd come *from* my phone. But I hadn't called anyone in Jersey City.

Then I remembered: Ty had. We'd been in Central Park and I'd been annoyed he was still dealing with work. Now I wasn't so sure. There was just one person it could've been.

Janelle.

It shouldn't have mattered—not after everything that had happened. Everyone who had *died*. I'd been so understandably consumed with the murder that I hadn't allowed myself to think about Ty's cheating. Even now, I felt like it shouldn't hurt that my deceased boyfriend might've been calling his deceased other lover from my phone as I sat blissfully unaware in a carriage a few feet away.

And yet it suddenly did.

I'd seen what Janelle looked like—in photos as Billie talked over her and even in videos as stoic news anchors turned her life into the lead story. But I'd never heard her voice. And until then I hadn't realized I needed to. Was it cutesy like Jennifer Tilly's? Deep like Scarlett Johansson's? Something in between? I needed to know. Now.

I pressed the number.

It went straight to voicemail. When I heard the outgoing message, my breath caught so quick I was surprised I didn't unravel.

"Hi. You've reached Lori Stevenson. Sorry I missed your call, but leave me a message—with your number—and I'll get back to you as soon as I can. Thanks."

I hung up.

Maybe he'd been working after all. Ty never told me his clients' names—confidentiality—but still it sounded familiar. I tried to imagine it coming off Billie's lips and got nothing. Same with the police and the news anchors.

So I did what I needed to do. The Google app was open and her name in the search bar before you could pronounce all five syllables in it. Lori Stevenson pulled up too many hits. I took it a step further, adding Jersey City to the mix.

A people search was the third result. Something I'd normally find intrusive—the idea of the internet giving your contact info to anyone with a keyboard. But that all changed as soon as I saw Lori Stevenson's address: 108 Little Street.

She was a neighbor.

TWENTY-SEVEN

The night felt longer than a one-minute plank. Same with me. I was rigid, shaking, but still determined to not give up. Sitting there frozen in place, eyes focused on my phone, as I desperately tried to find anything I could on Lori Stevenson.

But for once, Google had let me down. Other than the few people-search hits, Lori was an internet ghost. No Instagram or Facebook. No Twitter or TikTok. Not even a LinkedIn. It made me doubt she'd ever even had a MySpace account.

It was weird and suspicious. Why had Ty been calling her? It had to have been for work, but what if it wasn't? Had he been cheating on me with this Lori instead of Janelle? Or just in addition to her? I spent the 3 a.m. hour searching my brain for mentions of the name as either a client or a friend. Digging in crevices I'd forgotten I had in there. And finding nothing.

The closest my brain came up with was a Lauren. The only other Black person in his office. Ty had claimed she would come bitch to him when their mutual boss was showing his ass. But her last name wasn't Stevenson and there was no way she'd own a whole row house in Jersey City.

No, this Lori was new and unrelated. And yet he'd called her on my phone when we were supposed to be taking a romantic carriage ride in New York City.

The four o'clock hour drove me back to Janelle's Instagram account, desperately searching for any photos with some untagged woman, even lurking in the background. But there were none to be found.

A ghost.

Around five is when I remembered the connection to the husband. Ray. Roy. Rod. Something like that.

The neighbor who'd been tasked with keeping an eye on the place for whatever unnamed corporation actually owned the Airbnb. The one who came over whenever there was an issue. The one the police had dismissed as unimportant because the key code was supposedly always changed.

It took until the six o'clock hour for me to realize there *was* a connection to Lori Stevenson—and it turned out it was me. I'd seen her. Briefly interacted. The glam blonde in the bedazzled face mask, my first night. The one who'd been so rude. I'd assumed it was because she didn't know me. But now I wondered if it was because she did.

And I'd seen her going up the stairs at 108. Disappearing inside.

She'd been home. But hadn't Ms. Morgane said she and her husband were at some convention?

I needed to find out more about Lori Stevenson other than the fact that she liked sparkly face masks and even sparklier luggage. And if Google wasn't going to help, I'd have to go old school: phone a friend.

I didn't know if Ms. Morgane was an early riser, but I was tempted to roll the dice and call her anyway. Instead, I texted. It came up green. No iPhone meant no telltale signs of it being read or telltale dots indicating it was being responded to. Instead, I was forced to wait it out. Much like a pot, a watched text never gets responded to.

I told myself I'd wait until 8:00 a.m. and I somehow managed. It wasn't easy. I did a half marathon in that suite, walking around the bed and out to the living room—then back again, glancing at the otherwise unnecessary alarm clock every few loops. I made it to 7:59 a.m.

She picked up at 8:00 a.m., her dog barking up a storm in the background. "Bree?"

"Hi, Ms. Morgane."

"Been thinking about you. I heard you did some interview."

"Guess you could call it that." It felt like a lifetime ago when it'd only been a few hours. "It was on TikTok."

But that last bit was drowned out by her dog barking. "Shush, you," she said, thankfully not to me. "We're going out. Give me a second."

It was a perfect transition. "I don't want to keep you. Just wanted to ask about Lori Stevenson."

"She's probably my favorite human on the block. Of course that's not saying much with this group."

"Have you seen her lately?"

She didn't answer right away and even her dog got quiet. "No." She kept on before I got too excited. "Just a couple of texts after everything that's been going on. None of us have been out much and Lori's a homebody anyway. I have theories about that..." She trailed off as if she was about to change the subject, then went right back to it. "Let's just say the only time I know she's home is because I can hear them arguing when I walk Chelsea."

I wasn't sure what to say next. I wasn't some crack detective. This wasn't *Law & Order*. I was just someone trying to figure out how a neighbor was connected to two dead bodies. "I remember you mentioning a trip..." I finally said.

"Yeah, but they're back. He has some work convention a couple times a year he always makes her go to. She never wants to, but she also won't tell him no."

"That doesn't get in the way of her job?"

"She doesn't have one. Rod's the type that likes to keep you financially dependent." Her tone made it clear what she thought about that.

There was another bark. "Give me a minute." But her voice was farther away, like she wasn't talking to me. When she spoke again, it was louder. More clear. "This dog's brought me her leash."

"It's no prob. I should let you go."

After we hung up, I did another few laps around the room, ignoring my stomach growling so loud it could rival a pit bull. I wasn't sure what to make of any of it.

I glanced back at the alarm clock for the billionth time. It was only 8:05 a.m. Lori Stevenson was probably at home at this exact moment, looking at her own alarm clock.

Maybe there was a legitimate reason why she'd been talking to Ty. Maybe the family had been looking for a new financial planner. Maybe I could just go and ask her myself.

*   *   *

The walk over to Little Street took only ten minutes, but it wouldn't have mattered if it was ten hours. There was no way I was risking another nosy Uber driver with a TikTok account and no fear of a bad rating. I put on my disguise—mask and sunglasses—and headed over, careful to keep my head down and stay out of people's way.

The barricades were still up when I got there, but the crowd was long gone. The street was deserted. No one walked a dog or headed to their car. I refused to even glance at 110. Just seeing it out of the corner of my eye was enough. Folks must have come over right after the vigil because I recognized some of the candles.

I forced myself to focus on the next-door neighbor. The house was just as intimidating as it had been the first day I'd gotten here. I needed to talk to Lori. Instead, I stayed rooted to my spot, looking so suspicious I'm sure at least two houses called 911. But still I couldn't move. Too afraid. I wanted answers. But now that I'd found the one person still alive to give them to me, I balked.

Because what if she didn't just know what happened? What if she *did* it?

I didn't know how long I'd been there when a hand touched my shoulder. It wasn't much. So faint that the first time I thought it was a breeze even though the rest of the world was stock-still. But then it happened again.

I screamed, all the while stumbling forward without even looking at who the hand belonged to. A neighbor? A Stevenson? A cop? Each option worse than the last.

"Bree." Ms. Morgane's voice followed behind me as I kept walking. "Bree."

That time I turned to find her exactly where I just was. Chelsea wasn't with her. She'd clearly come to see me. But still, I didn't head back toward her. I just didn't move any farther away. We stared at each other for a few moments.

"Bree, what is going on?"

I flicked the sweat from my brow. "Nothing." The lie was automatic, a longtime favorite from back when my mom would catch me doing something I wasn't supposed to. But of course Ms. Morgane didn't buy it any more than my mother had.

She glanced around—at windows, not the street—then came over to me. "Walk with me."

She touched me again, but this time I was ready for it so it felt comforting when she linked her arm through mine. I tried to speak, but she shushed me and we walked in silence until we got off her street.

It was another block before she finally said something. "I called a few neighbors after that weird phone call of yours. I'm not the only one who hasn't seen Lori. I tried to call her this morning. No answer. Made me think about how long it's been since we talked in person. It was definitely before what happened."

"I saw her. First night here. She had a suitcase with her, but she was coming," I said. "Not going."

Ms. Morgane thought it over. "That's weird. I distinctly remember her telling me the convention started on a Thursday. You think Lori or Rod are involved in what happened?"

I told the truth. "Ty called her from my phone a couple of days before I found Janelle. Maybe that's who he was having an affair with."

"No." Ms. Morgane sounded resolute.

"You made it seem like they aren't happy."

"Because they aren't. But she wouldn't have an affair. Or be responsible for what happened."

When I spoke, my voice was quiet. "I used to say the same thing about Ty."

She didn't say anything. We got to another corner, where we had to wait to let two cars pass. Her eyes followed the first, then doubled back to follow the second. "I know Rod goes to the gym Sunday morning. Always out the door by eight thirty."

I glanced at my phone, then realized it was off. I'd forgotten to charge the battery. "What time is it?" I said.

Ms. Morgane smiled mischievously. "Eight thirty-eight. Let's go."

I put ten-year-old "My mother is calling me because dinner is ready" me to shame in how fast I booked it. Ms. Morgane was neck and neck with me too, like it was some race. She won. The Stevenson house was one of the few on the block protected by a wrought-iron fence. Ms. Morgane pushed the gate open so quick you'd think she was Superman, then we walked side by side along the ten feet of sidewalk and up those eight stairs.

It felt good to have someone with me—someone I could actually trust. She knew exactly where the doorbell was and had it rung before I even knew she'd pushed the button. I almost jumped as it played a few bars, then went silent. So were we.

"It can take a while if you're on the fourth floor. Drives me nuts when Amazon doesn't want to wait," Ms. Morgane said.

I just nodded, not wanting to think about the last time I'd used the stairs next door.

But no one came. There were no windows anywhere near the front door. We had no clue if Lori Stevenson was four floors, four feet, or four inches away. There also wasn't a Ring camera. Just an old-school peephole.

Ms. Morgane repeated the entire process three more times to the point even I was sick of hearing the doorbell ring. Finally, she took her hand off the button. "Someone's coming."

She smiled then and I recognized it. *Perky Black Girl.* I pasted on the same grin myself. We might as well have been selling Girl Scout Cookies. Finally I was going to get some answers.

There was that familiar slight crack of a door opening. We waited as the door slowly made its way inside the house. My smile faltered.

It was a man.

Rod Stevenson wasn't on his way to the gym. He wasn't even wearing workout clothes. I glanced at Ms. Morgane out of the corner of my eye and could see she was just as surprised as I was. The house was up a step, which made his tall figure loom over us even more. He took us both in, making no effort to open the screen door.

"Hi, Rod." Ms. Morgane's voice was butter soft. "Sorry to bother you, but I figured you'd be out and about already."

"I'm not." There were no smiles on his end. No attempts to be sweet or charming to put us at ease. He didn't need to activate any Perky Black Girl.

"Well, we all need a day off." Ms. Morgane was still smiling. "I'm here to chat with Lori." As she spoke, her hand went to the screen's knob. She pulled it. It didn't budge. Locked.

"Lori's busy." He smiled even though he sounded the polar opposite. Like a man used to his words being heard. Listened to. Respected.

But Ms. Morgane wasn't deterred. "It'll only take a minute. I just haven't seen her in person since everything happened next door."

"I'll tell her to call you."

I could recognize a lie when I heard one. It helped he didn't even try to sound sincere.

"Can't you just tell her I'm here? She's expecting me."

"Yeah?" he said.

She nodded. "Yeah."

"Well, then I'm sure she'll call you to reschedule. Have a good day."

He closed the door, never so much as glancing in my direction.

Ms. Morgane didn't look at me either, just made her way down the stairs toward the sidewalk. This time I trailed behind her.

"He knew you were lying," I said.

"Then that makes two of us."

We got to the sidewalk, then headed to her house next door, her muttering the entire way. "What a miserable human being. That was him being nice. We all hate how he treats her. We all want her to leave him—though we'd never say that to her. She's too afraid to leave. Especially with him 'preferring' for her to 'not work and stay at home.'" She'd used air quotes as we walked up to her door. "Just code for 'I want you to be completely dependent on me so you'll be afraid to leave.'"

"Wouldn't she get half?"

"He has to have a prenup. That's what these rich folks do."

She had a point.

I couldn't see the woman Ms. Morgane described as a killer, though I could see her going outside her marriage to find the affection it lacked. And if there was one thing Ty had been good at, it was affection. Once again, I was surprised at the emotions that bubbled up. And just like I'd suddenly yearned to hear Janelle Beckett's voice, I needed to at least see what Lori Stevenson looked like. "You have a photo of her?" I said.

Ms. Morgane didn't seem to think it was weird, but then she wasn't in my head. "I'm sure I do on my phone. There was a quick group trip a few of us went on last year when Jeff and Carl got married in Mexico. Come in and I'll find it." She looked me up and down. "And you can eat something."

I nodded, more so for the photo than the food—though I still hadn't eaten.

I followed her inside, ignoring Chelsea as she excitedly jumped up on us both. I was afraid Ms. Morgane would make me wait for the picture until she'd cooked enough food to feed an army. Instead, she casually motioned to the cell phone she'd left on her coffee table as she continued on to the kitchen.

There was no password and it didn't take long to find her photo app. I didn't have time or desire to be nosy—and Ms. Morgane mainly had dog pics anyway. I swiped as I walked, like I was horny and this was Tinder. By the time I made it to the kitchen, Ms. Morgane already had four eggs in a bowl. She was still mumbling. "The nerve of that man. But it would be him holding her hostage in her own house. I should call the police."

I stopped when I saw a photo that looked familiar. Blond hair. Sculpted build. Red bedazzled face mask. Some random trees behind her.

Lori Stevenson.

"Think I found her." I walked over and flashed the photo as Ms. Morgane stirred eggs. She glanced at it, then looked at me all puzzled.

"That's not Lori. That's Janelle."

TWENTY-EIGHT

Ms. Morgane was right about having a photo of Lori Stevenson somewhere on her phone. I kept swiping until I found her—ironically in a set of photos with Janelle. The first was of just their faces and upper bodies. Up close and side by side, their features weren't that much alike. Lori was all hard lines to Janelle's soft edges. But their height and physique were similar and so was their hair.

I swiped again. This one was a group shot taken at a distance to get all four people. Ms. Morgane. Lori. Some woman I didn't know. Janelle. They were all packed and ready to go, their luggage waiting patiently next to them. Again: the rose-gold suitcase.

It was next to Janelle.

The one near Lori was dark blue and patterned. I zoomed in. Alligator. Probably real.

Breakfast was so quiet we could've been eating in a library. Ms. Morgane ate at her kitchen sink, watching out the window the entire time, hand moving from plate to mouth like she was hooked to a conveyor belt.

I was more than fine with her being a bad host. Happy for the silence as I tried to make sense of it all—like looking at a blurred photo taking too long to load into focus. I replayed the things I knew for a fact.

Lori Stevenson was supposed to leave town with her husband on Thursday.

On Friday night, I'd seen a woman going into 108 Little Street like she owned the place. She'd had a key and a very distinctive face mask. One that looked like it cost more than my luggage.

On Saturday, Ty called Lori without letting me know.

On Monday, I found a body in the foyer.

Now Ty was dead, no one had seen Lori Stevenson, and I'd just discovered the person I saw on Friday night was a supposedly missing white woman named Janelle Beckett.

And if that was Janelle Beckett I saw on Friday...did that mean it was Lori Stevenson's body I found just a few days later?

It scared me how much sense it made. It explained why the cops still wouldn't commit to formally identifying Janelle as the victim.

Because she wasn't.

And yet it brought up even more questions. The first being: How was Ty involved?

I relived our last moments together over and over—searching for signs of an affair. He'd been distant at times, way too focused on his phone. There was that fight because he'd had to work, thanks to some needy new client. I'd decided he'd been lying then, covering his tracks.

But what if he'd been telling the truth? What if the client *was* Lori Stevenson?

Ty worked in finance, helping people find the best ways to save money. He'd been the first person I knew who was into crypto—even with all the ups, downs, and uncertainty surrounding it. He'd make jokes about how it'd buy him a house one day. Had even tried to get me to invest. And I probably would have if I had any money to do so.

Maybe he'd told Lori to do the same.

I knew jack about crypto except for one key thing. The initial appeal was in the anonymity. You didn't need any type of proof to buy it. Just some complicated passcode and a way to access it. What if Lori had been planning to leave her domineering husband—take the family fortune with her?

It was what *my* Ty would've helped her do. The one I fell in love with. The one I still loved. And it would explain all the secrecy. The stress—especially with Janelle suddenly missing. He wasn't cheating on me. He was trying to help someone. And he'd paid for it with his life.

It all sounded so ridiculous—and there was so much I didn't know. Didn't understand, and Ty wasn't here to explain it all.

But still, it made sense.

Janelle Beckett was the common link. She could've connected them. And she could've decided to kill them both and take the money for herself.

Maybe she wasn't missing. She just wanted people to think that so they would think it was *her* body in the Airbnb. Maybe she was on the run—with Lori's identity. It would explain why "Lori" had texted Ms. Morgane a few times but never picked up the phone.

It all fit—except for one thing. If Lori Stevenson was dead, why was her husband pretending otherwise?

It felt melodramatic, like something you'd find on a daytime soap—"stories," as my grandmother called them—circa 1986. But still. I needed to run it by someone—and Ms. Morgane would definitely tell me if I was living in a fantasy world. I started to open my mouth, but she spoke first.

"He left. Come on."

It had been only twenty minutes since I'd heard someone speak, but I'd already forgotten what words sounded like. I jumped, then took a full minute to comprehend what Ms. Morgane was saying. By the time I did, she already had her back door open.

I finally put down the fork I'd been holding in the general vicinity of my mouth. "What are you doing?"

"Going to talk to Lori."

I rushed to follow her down the tiny path from her back entrance to the gate in her fence, still thinking. Once we got out Ms. Morgane's back gate, we walked over to the one belonging to the Stevensons' house next to it. Ms. Morgane yanked on the gate like she'd done this a million times before. Maybe to borrow sugar. Maybe to just say hello. She was so confident she knew the gate would open that it was a shock to both of us when it didn't.

Ms. Morgane tried again. Still no luck.

"They never keep this locked during the day," she said.

I glanced around. "You're not gonna try to jump the fence, right?" We were Black.

Ms. Morgane shook her head. "Of course not. You know how quick someone would call the police?"

I almost started to share my theory but then thought of a better option: checking online. I could see if I was the only one floating the "What if Janelle is still alive?" theory. What if there were already sightings? Maybe even in Boston.

I looked at my phone, only to be reminded the battery was dead. "What now?" I said.

Ms. Morgane started back toward her house. "I'm going to talk to some neighbors. If no one's seen Lori, we need to do a wellness check."

It was what I would've wanted a neighbor to do for me. It was also the last thing I needed. If Janelle Beckett *was* indeed alive and using Lori Stevenson's identity, I couldn't have cops announcing Lori was missing. Janelle would just chuck Lori's ID and use whatever money Ty had put in that crypto account to buy another one. And she'd never be found.

I didn't have much time. I called after Ms. Morgane. "Do you have an iPhone charger?"

* * *

She didn't—but my phone was the only way I could get online. I left Ms. Morgane talking to some neighbor named Carl and making plans for him to call Rod himself.

The walk back to the hotel was swift, as by now I knew exactly how to get there. A good thing since I was on autopilot, my brain still focused on my theory.

Ty could've told me. I would've helped him. We could've figured this out together. Why Janelle had suddenly disappeared. What Lori needed to get away from her husband. We would've taken care of it as a team—and he'd still be alive.

I found myself getting mad that he'd kept it all secret, dealt with it all on his own. But then I remembered I'd kept my secrets too. I hadn't given him the chance to help me.

I was so lost in my thoughts, I didn't notice Adore until it was too late. It wasn't the first time I'd unexpectedly encountered her in my hotel lobby. This time she looked every bit as surprised as I was.

She'd just stepped out of the elevator when I walked into the building. We made brief eye contact, then I looked past her at the elevator bank. We were the only ones down there. The lone security guard was probably somewhere downing coffee from the Dunkin' around the corner. For once Adore looked small and unsure of herself. It wasn't a sight I was used to, but I couldn't even revel in it. I'm sure I looked small and unsure of myself too.

"I…" she started, took a breath, then tried again. "I just dropped your stuff off."

My home training kicked in before I could stop it. "Thanks." The only solace was that I sounded sarcastic.

"Your mom…" Again with the inability to get out a thought. "She still has the same landline. I called her to find out where you were."

The last thing I needed was my mom knowing what Adore had

done. She'd make my anger seem like a good mood. As if I didn't have enough to deal with: the Janelle-Lori revelation, my own feelings about Adore's betrayal, being the world's most hated woman.

I didn't ask Adore what they'd talked about, just did a wide arc past her until I was close enough to jab at the elevator button. I willed it to come back quick, as my ears strained to hear Adore walking through the exit. Instead, I heard breathing.

"Breanna, I…"

And this time I was thankful for the hesitation because it gave me enough time for the elevator doors to open. A lone woman was inside, her white blouse and brass name tag saying KITTY letting me know she worked here. She did a double take when she saw me, then quickly looked away before I could smile at her and let her know I was a friendly.

I still tried anyway, but she refused any more eye contact, just like I'd done with Adore not even two minutes before. And it was only then I realized I'd forgotten to put on my mask.

What was the saying? "When it rained, it poured"? This was feeling like a whole entire hurricane. Kitty didn't bother to come out of the elevator, and I couldn't afford to wait her out. I just got in. When I turned around, Adore was still there.

Kitty finally got herself together enough to exit. At the same time, Adore came forward, like I'd asked her to join me. "Breanna," she said again as she got inside.

The employee must've heard because she slowed her gait.

I finally spoke. "You need to leave."

But Adore stayed put and the elevator doors slid closed, trapping me with the last person on the planet I wanted to be close to. At least anymore. I tried again. "Leave. Me. Alone."

I backed up as I said it until I was literally trapped in a corner. Adore stayed still. Not coming toward me. Not pushing a button. Not doing anything but staring. I didn't know what to do. What to expect.

And then, suddenly, the elevator opened. Kitty placed her perfectly manicured hand on the door to prevent it from closing again.

"Is there a problem, Ms. Wright?"

It took me a second to realize she was talking to me and another to realize her tone was friendly—at least until she spoke to Adore. "We don't allow loitering on our premises and we surely don't allow any harassment of our guests. So you'll need to do what Ms. Wright suggested and go."

Adore looked at me, as if she truly thought I'd defend her. And when I said nothing, she didn't put up a fight. Just walked out of the elevator, being sure to brush past the woman as she did. We both waited until Adore disappeared outside, then the woman removed her hand from the elevator door.

"Thank you," I said, and this time there wasn't a lick of sarcasm.

"Of course." The doors started to close. "I'm so sorry this happened."

I knew she was talking about more than the past few minutes.

I nodded just as the doors finally closed, then started to cry.

* * *

I got my shit together on the ride to the tenth floor but still didn't want to risk going to the lobby to pick up my things. Clean underwear could wait another half hour. I needed to get online.

I grabbed my charger when I got into my room and plugged my phone in. As soon as it had enough juice, I opened Twitter first. My account was private, but it didn't stop me getting tagged. I ignored the Notifications button, but Twitter didn't care. Someone I followed had tagged me. A singer I liked. Her tweet was simple:

Watching the #BreannaWright interview. In tears at how a Black woman is once again being treated as a suspect and not the victim she is. #BelieveBreanna

It had over 80,000 likes.

And I couldn't help it. I clicked the hashtag, expecting one or two more tweets. There were thousands. People all upset about how I'd been treated. How Billie and her Bunch had made me a scapegoat. And of course the hashtag had also been co-opted. Both sides going back and forth, throwing daggers 280 characters at a time.

Hundreds of thousands of folks had watched my conversation with Billie, and each and every single one of them had *thoughts*. Thoughts that sometimes had to be expressed with a meme here. An acronym there. There was many a Twitter thread. I counted one with 46 tweets. Even I didn't read that one.

Once again, it was odd to see strangers with such strong opinions about my actual life. But this was what I wanted, right? Folks on my side. People willing to go to bat for me as others were ripping me to shreds. But now that I had the fan club?

It still sucked. I would've given anything to be anonymous again. For whoever that woman had been in the Little Street foyer—Janelle Beckett or Lori Stevenson—to be alive. Ty too. For us to still be arguing over him working on vacation.

I wanted it all to go away—and there really was only one way for that to happen.

I needed to figure out the real killer.

If Janelle was alive, I wasn't going to just walk by her on the street. She'd had days at this point. She'd be long gone from New Jersey. My guess would be across the river in Manhattan. Millions of people, and they all minded their own business. It was the best place to be anonymous.

I was back on the main #Justice4Janelle hashtag, looking for anyone who may have seen her alive since her "disappearance." But it was just folks arguing for likes and retweets. Throwing out theories about who was to blame: Me? Ty? Billie?

Maybe that was it. I'd be proactive. If Janelle Beckett was still alive, I could make it hard for her. I thought of what Billie had told me before our convo. Then my mind flashed on the Ty "sightings." How internet sleuths had managed to come together to make it hell on brown-skinned Black men in hoodies. How it didn't matter if it was South Jersey or the South of France, folks just knew Ty had traveled through their town. All because someone with a platform and a hashtag had put it out there that they should be on the lookout.

I thought it over. I had a hashtag of my own now.

And I had a platform.

Breanna Wright stares at the camera in confusion. It isn't well lit so you can barely make out most of her features. She leans in, then disappears out of the frame. We hear the scrape of curtains opening, and the room lights up. It's only then we realize we're in a hotel room.

After a moment, Breanna comes back into the frame and sits down. We can finally see what she looks like. She's Black and brown skinned. Her kinky hair is up in an Afro puff on top of her head. She doesn't wear a lot of makeup—a bit of lip balm and some mascara—but she doesn't need it. Her skin is smooth and oil-free. Breanna doesn't say anything at first, just glances toward the bottom of the screen. "Wow. Three thousand people in here already. Okay."

She says nothing more for a moment, eyes still watching the number tick upward as more people enter the room. Finally, she shakes her head, as if waving off whatever negative thoughts are in there.

"Hello. I'm gonna be honest. I debated doing this. As I'm sure you know, after...Janelle's death, I made my accounts private. I planned to keep it like that, but then I saw my phone log."

She holds her hand up. "I should probably explain better. This was Saturday before...Janelle died. Ty and I were in Central Park. We'd spent the entire day together. Saw all his favorite spots in New York. And we ended up in the park. But he kept getting phone calls. And one thing about Ty. Never kept his phone charged. I don't know if he even brought a charger. So his phone dies. And he needs to call someone back. A client.

"He uses my phone. The call was so quick, I forgot about it completely until last night. And only then because I saw it while looking for something else. But there it was. And I was curious. So I called it. Honestly, I thought maybe he'd called Janelle. That maybe they were planning some rendezvous after I left. And I don't know why, but I needed to know if what everyone was saying was true. That he'd been lying to me and they were together."

She shrugs.

"I call. No answer. Finally, the voicemail kicks in. A woman's voice. But it's not Janelle. The voice tells me who it is and she's not in. I hang up, but I also think the name sounds familiar. It's because she lives on Little Street. Right next door, actually."

Breanna lets that settle before continuing.

"I have a friend who lives on the block. Knows all her neighbors. And she tells me no one's seen this woman since before Janelle died. She's disappeared. No one knows where she's gone. Though her phone's still on. I called it myself yesterday. And I don't know what's going on. But I can't help but think that maybe, just maybe, her disappearance is somehow connected to Janelle dying. And I know it's a long shot, but I figured I'd share this and see if maybe someone knows her. Maybe she's not involved at all. But then maybe she is. Her name is..."

Breanna's voice trails off. She wipes her brow before continuing. "Lori Stevenson."

She looks down as if reading from an unseen piece of paper. "I don't have a photo of her, unfortunately. But she's got long blond hair. It kind of reminds me of Janelle's in the photos I've seen. Probably around five foot six. One hundred ten pounds. If you know anything or have seen her, please contact the police. I'm happy to share the number."

Breanna gives out the tip line number for Janelle Beckett's disappearance. "And if you don't feel comfortable, you can always DM me directly or tag me in a video. I've been chatting with the police—*a lot.* I'm happy to share this with them directly. I just... It's just there's been so much tragedy. And I just want it to stop."

TWENTY-NINE

I asked the front desk to bring the luggage Adore had left to my room, then spent most of the day hiding in the living room, glued to my Instagram inbox. I didn't even bother to open the curtains again, the only light peeking through cracks and coming from my phone. My iPhone Screen Time app would not be happy at the end of the week.

It was strange watching my DMs update like some stock market ticker. It felt like I was gambling with each message. Not knowing if it would be kind or cruel. Helpful or just someone using their anonymity to be a full-on schmuck.

But I kept reading, alternating between DMs, comments, and Twitter hashtags—just in case. I'd made sure to give a description that matched Janelle. The Missing flyer was quite helpful with that. Lots of folks were eager to help, sharing blurry photos and long-winded explanations of someone they'd seen briefly but they didn't get a name or even a close look. The closest they came was somebody with the same exact name in Illinois, but a quick Google search disproved it was her. There were no sightings in New York City.

I was just about to give up when the DM came. The message was simple.

This her?

By that point I doubted it. It felt like I'd been sent photos of every blond woman in the continental United States.

But I still clicked anyway. The angle was sloppy, the camera aimed low, and the shot was taken from a distance, as if the photographer was backing away. It was of a brown take-out bag on a front porch. Delivery. Whoever had ordered it was caught mid-snap—blond hair cascading over taut, tanned shoulders. Muscled arms accustomed to much heavier weights bending down to grab one of their three suggested meals for the day. But it wasn't the hair or body that made me take notice.

It was the face mask.

Red. Bedazzled. Familiar.

Bingo.

The message had been sent a good twenty minutes ago, but there was no indication of where—or when—the photo actually had been taken. I wrote back immediately, afraid to allow myself to get too excited.

When was this?

I pressed Send, saying a prayer the response would be quick. Thankfully they were as attached to their cell as I was.

Last night.

My heart sped up and I couldn't type the next word fast enough. *Where?*

Another lightning-quick response. *Here.*

Here.

One word. Several meanings. Several places. There were no landmarks. No telltale backgrounds. Just a close-up of a bag of food. There wasn't even a restaurant name on it. It was just a generic greasy brown paper bag. It could've been Manhattan, but with my luck this was the other side of the world. Janelle-Lori would've had enough time to walk there at this point.

I responded. *City?*

I was still hoping for New York.

Them again. *Sorry. Thought you knew. Here. JC.*

And if the other responses had my heart racing, that made it stop. *Here.* Janelle or Lori was here. I didn't respond right away. Too busy scrambling around for a pen and paper so I could write the address down when they gave it to me. But when I got back to my cell, they'd responded anyway.

Almost there.

It took me a minute to connect the dots. First here. Now there. Because of me, someone was on their way to confront what could be a killer. And I didn't even know their real name.

My first response was to freeze. My heart. My breath. My hands. Nothing moved except the fear. It started at my toes and slowly snaked its way up until it got to my head. And only then did my brain jump-start. It was too late to freak out.

This was not what I'd wanted at all. This harshest of reminders about the consequences of saying crap online. So I did what I had to. Pushed the Camera button and waited as it rang.

They picked up. The face was as young as I was afraid it would be. A cute white brunette cheesing it up like she'd finally beat her mom in Connect Four. But it made sense because this was all a game to her. She giggled. "This needs to be quick because we want to film us pulling up."

We. Of course there were two of them.

I skipped all pleasantries. "You can't do this."

"Of course we can. Gonna live stream it. Kara is too since she has way more followers than me."

"That woman—Lori Stevenson—is dangerous," I said, but I might as well have been mouthing the words.

She didn't hear me, too busy looking past the camera at the street. "No. Don't stop. Gun it." There was a pause, then she glanced down at me, disappointed. "Kara stopped at a yellow."

"You hear what I said?"

"Yep. The woman is dangerous."

But it was obvious that dangerous to her was reserved for movies and true-crime podcasts. And it had never crossed her mind she could be the subject of one of them. The world was a safe place for her—and I wanted it to stay like that. So I tried a different tack. "What's the address?"

I'd call the cops as soon as I had it. Beg them to send someone over. "We're here!"

I tried again. "This is a horrible idea. Stay in the car. Call the police."

But she just opened the door. "Gotta go."

She hung up, booting me back to our IG DMs. I called her back, but it just rang until finally Instagram told me to give it up. She wasn't going to answer.

Crap.

I wasn't Adore. I didn't know what to do. Had no idea how to handle this—the situation and the guilt that I'd sent two naive young women to confront a killer. I hadn't been thinking when I did that Live. I already regretted it. This time I'd deserve all the hate and hashtags.

I tried them again and still got ignored. So I DMed. *Please don't go to that house.*

It wasn't even marked seen.

Then I remembered why she was doing this: the Live stream.

I went to her profile. Finally found the name of the woman I had put in danger. Layton. Sure enough, the word "Live" was in small letters under a profile pic of her enhanced by both makeup and filters. I clicked. Layton had the camera flipped as another thin, long-haired brunette walked ahead of her, the door I recognized from the photo in the distance. They were indeed *there.*

There were only nine people watching. I commented.

Stop. Please head back.

But Layton wasn't even looking at the screen. "We're two seconds away from finding the woman who killed Janelle Beckett. And I bet you're wondering how we know. Well, you probably know Kara does DoorDash. She's been to this place a couple of times, including last night!"

A voice spoke from off camera as they made their way up a short walkway to what looked like a row house, but there were a billion of those in Jersey City. "Yep," what had to be Kara said. "And I only remember her because she used the same name as my mom and she's a *horrible* tipper."

They got to the first step. "Of course she is." Layton didn't sound surprised.

I pulled my phone closer to my face. Maybe I could make out a house number or some landmark. Anything to give to the police I was finally willing to call.

But there was nothing.

Instead, I watched Kara press her face against the window next to the door, both hands cupping her eyes for a better look.

"You see her?" If Layton's voice got any higher, only dogs would be able to hear her.

Kara turned around dramatically and just stared directly at the camera. And I found myself holding my breath. *Please don't ring the doorbell. Just go. Please just go.*

Finally, she spoke. "No one's in there. She's gone."

The tension instantly lifted, bringing my shoulders and the sides of my mouth with it. I'd never thought I would be *happy* Janelle was nowhere to be found.

My first thought was another lecture, but it'd be nowhere near as effective via comment as in person. Even if I used all caps. Instead, I just left the Live. It took fifteen minutes for my brain to focus on anything but my breathing. The inhales sharper than my uncle dressed for our last family cookout. It was almost an hour before I got my breath back right—and that's when I realized something crucial.

She'd stayed in town. Holed up in much nicer digs than I was and probably ordering better food too, but she was still in Jersey City. That alone made me think it was indeed Janelle. I'd had a lot of experience recently with not wanting to be recognized.

Janelle should've been long gone, just like I wanted to be. But I'd been forced to stay. She probably had been too. And it couldn't be because the police were making her. It had to be something else. I could think of only one thing that could keep someone from leaving a town where everyone was looking for them.

She couldn't afford it. She didn't have the money that had cost Ty his life. Lori Stevenson's too.

Ty and I hadn't discussed his work much, but still some of it had seeped into my brain. Call it osmosis. If Ty had helped Lori move her money into crypto, he wouldn't have emailed her any account info or even risked putting it in the mail. He would've wanted to get it to her in person. And it wouldn't have been just handing over a piece of paper.

He would've used a crypto wallet.

The first time I saw one, I thought it was a USB drive. The last time I saw one was during our final argument. I might've assumed that if he did give it to Lori, or even to Janelle to give to Lori, it would've been during that earlier Monday encounter before I got there, but I saw it on Sunday morning—in the house.

I didn't see it the rest of the day, but that didn't mean it wasn't still there.

Ty and I had been together the entire time minus one thirty-minute argument. Janelle could've swung by, but why risk her "disappearance" to come by in the middle of the day? Especially on a street where everyone knew her—was *looking* for her, in fact.

Of course the police could've taken it with Ty's things. It could be sitting in some evidence drawer collecting cobwebs. But I hadn't heard anything about Calloway releasing his stuff, and even if she did, it wouldn't be to me. Of course Adore could probably get it, but I wasn't that desperate.

Besides, there was one other thing that made me think it was still in that house.

The break-in attempt.

Everyone had assumed it was #Justice4Janelle groupies, but what if it had been Janelle herself?

It would explain why she was still here. She was just biding her time to try to get back into the house. Unless someone else got there first.

THIRTY

It wasn't that I wanted the money. I just didn't want her to have it. She'd used Lori Stevenson. Her abusive relationship. Her desperation to leave it. Her desire to be safe. Janelle literally took her life in more than one way.

She'd also used Ty. His knowledge. His kindness. His desire to help. She'd used society's prejudice to her advantage. Because she knew how this would play out. And then she'd *killed* him.

She'd used me. My circumstance. My past. My *love*.

She'd thought she could get away with it all. And so far she'd been right.

She'd planned to ride off into the sunset with a shit ton of money to keep her company.

Now she just needed to find it.

Ty would've told me what a bad idea it was. That I needed to let the cops handle it. But he wasn't here because she'd taken him away from me—and his good name too.

I didn't have much black to wear so I had to settle for the darkest workout gear I'd brought with me when this had been just a quick romantic getaway. Ty was on my mind hard from the moment I'd decided to do this.

Besides learning about crypto wallets, I took lessons from Ty's illicit visit the Monday night when he first arrived. Because of him, I knew where the Ring cameras were. I wanted to rush out immediately, just to get the entire thing over with. But it was too light out and I didn't want to get caught because of impatience.

So I waited. And waited. And waited.

I passed the time doing my hair. It'd been loose and I'd barely given it a thought since I'd been here, not doing much more than barely putting it up in a pineapple each night before bed. Now it was long past wash day, if I was honest. I didn't want to look like the me that Calloway knew. Or Ms. Morgane. Or everyone who'd tuned in to TikTok and Instagram.

As any Black woman will tell you, there's an intricacy to the Black Hair Experience. It takes time and patience, and that was exactly what I needed at that moment. Something to take my mind off what was to come.

I went to work. Detangling with the wide-tooth comb I always had in my handbag. Washing with the hotel shampoo clearly not provided with our hair in mind. Carefully parting and twisting until I had a head full of twists—ones I could take out tomorrow and I would look completely different if need be.

By the time I was done, I still felt like myself but better. Stronger. Clark Kent right after he took off his glasses but before he ripped open his button-down. I was ready to go by the time I walked out of my room at eleven that night—in my own costume. Face mask included.

It was a Sunday night. A good day for a break-in if there ever was one. Nobody was out late on a Sunday. The partiers were recovering. The worker bees mentally and physically preparing for another Monday. The streets were deserted, which somehow put me on higher alert.

I was tempted to run the entire way, but I still wasn't quite ready to exercise. It felt too much like before. Instead, I kept my hands by my sides and my head low the entire ten-minute trip. The barriers were still up, guarding against an inky blackness. There weren't even any lights on in the row houses. It was as if the whole block was too exhausted to stay up late. It should've made me feel better. Instead, it just made me more scared.

I kept walking past the main block, until I got to the alley. It was so black I could've sworn my eyes were closed. I had to remind myself I'd been here before—earlier that day, in fact. The first step was tentative, crossing a literal line. A point of no return. But then I just went for it, quietly counting houses and sticking close to fences to avoid the Ring camera across the street.

A keypad lock was on the back gate at 110 Little, just like on the front door. And I was banking on them not having changed the code. It wasn't like they'd be able to rent it out anytime soon—though I'm sure there would be some sickos jumping on the chance as soon as they did.

I'd found a spare pair of cheap knit winter gloves in my handbag and thanked Past Me for not spring cleaning. I knew, wearing them, they'd be hot, but it wasn't like I wasn't already sweating. I put them on before quietly inputting the four numbers that had started this whole thing—1018—then said a quick prayer before I hit the Key button.

It worked. Both literally and figuratively.

The gate creaked open, feeling as loud as in a horror movie. Like some sound guy had put a boom mic mere centimeters away for the entire block to hear. I wiped the pad off with my T-shirt—gloves be damned—then pushed until the gate gave enough space to allow all my 135 pounds through. Then I waited.

For lights to come on.

For dogs to bark.

For neighbors to creak their own doors open to see what was out there.

But it remained pitch-black and silent.

I race-walked through the yard, then up to the back door, and repeated the entire process. Code. Clean. Creak. I stepped inside—noting they'd left the stove light on—then immediately regretted it as soon as my eyes adjusted. I don't know what I'd been expecting, but stepping back into a time capsule of one of the best days of my life was not it. The police hadn't cleaned up anything. Not even the jug of orange juice we'd left on the counter that last night.

It was still there. So was the Nature's Own bread and the glasses in the sink, my nude lipstick still visible on one rim. Even the Muddy Buddies Ty had given me were still half closed on the counter by the back door. I almost expected him to appear behind me at any moment, pressing against me while whispering naughtily in my ear.

But then I remembered it wouldn't happen because he'd died. And there was a good chance Janelle Beckett had killed him. I did a cursory survey for the crypto wallet and promised I'd come back for a better inspection if I didn't find it in the office or bedroom.

I left the time capsule for the living area, and at least I was prepared for that. I hadn't turned on any lights, banking on remembering enough of the place to make my way through the first floor and up to the second.

That too served two purposes. Protecting both my body from folks passing by and my mind from actually seeing the blood that had consumed my brain. But that didn't work either. I hadn't accounted for the streetlights being bright enough to give the place an eerie, almost ethereal glow—even through the closed gauzy white curtains.

The blood was still there, dried up but still there. Another time capsule. This one of the worst day of my life.

I didn't stop when I saw it. Didn't allow myself to think of that poor body. Just arced around it, then rushed up the stairs like I was still in a horror movie and making a bad decision.

When I got to Ty's office, it was clear the police had been just as interested in it as I was. It was the first time I could see their presence.

Things were missing. His laptop. His files. Even the glass of Coke I'd spilled. All gone. The desk as clean as the first day of school.

I opened a drawer. Empty. So was the next and the ones on the other side. They'd taken everything. There was no way they would've left the drive.

I was tempted to leave then and there. Go back downstairs, ignoring the sound of my heart pounding as I rushed past the bloodstains and out the back door.

But then I remembered the safe upstairs, hidden in the walk-in closet. The police probably knew about it. Had called around to find how to unlock it without the code. Maybe even used brute force to split it open like someone's head. But I still needed to check anyway.

Up I went.

The owner's suite was another time capsule. I hadn't made the bed. Hadn't had a chance, though I probably wouldn't have anyway. It looked like I'd just gotten out of it. The pillows were still how I liked to sleep, bookending me where I could press my back against one of them.

I went to the closet. The police knew about the safe, all right, but they hadn't wasted time trying to bust it open. Instead, they'd just taken the entire thing out of the wall, leaving nothing more than a gaping hole.

I wanted to cry.

I'd been scared. I knew it was a ridiculous plan. But up until that moment I didn't realize that I'd also been hopeful.

She was gonna get away with it. Janelle Beckett was going to kill two people—including my Ty—and get away with it. And there was nothing I could do.

I made it down the three flights in record time and was prepping myself for the blood in the foyer when I heard them. It sounded like there were two people outside the front door. One must've had a flashlight because a tiny beam bounced around the walls and the floor.

They knew someone had broken in.

I froze—just like I'd done that night. Still resisted the urge to go back up the stairs. Once again, I found myself running, this time as if someone was about to give chase. The front door buzzed just as I made it to the one in the back, and I instinctively looked behind me—cursing whoever had decided an open floor plan was a must.

I barely felt the counter when I damn near bounced off it, knocking the bag of Muddy Buddies over. I turned just in time to watch powdered-chocolate Chex Mix shoot out in all directions across the marble counter. But that's also when I saw something else, the small plastic object half out of the bag.

The drive.

The front door began to open. I didn't have time to think. Just shoved the drive back into the bag so I could take it with me and yanked the back door wide—not bothering to close it behind me.

I didn't look back until I'd run all the way to the hotel.

* * *

I'd never been happier to have a hotel lobby on the thirteenth floor. There was not even a security guard at the front entrance to watch me rush into the building and up to my room. I made a call as soon as I got there, immediately recognizing the voice of the man who'd checked me in the night before.

"You're up early, Ms. Wright." He paused. "Or late."

I laughed like he wanted. "Is there a business center?" My voice sounded anxious. I didn't have a computer with me, but the hotel did.

"Right behind me."

"What are the hours?" I needed to check the drive. Confirm it was real.

"Usually nine to five, but luckily I know someone with a key."

"I'll be right up."

I got to the room's door before I thought better of it. Realized what a bad idea it was. Ty—my Ty—had gone out of his way to hide the drive. That meant he knew how dangerous it was.

We hadn't been dating long. We hadn't discussed much from our past or even much about our future. I clearly hadn't known him like I'd thought. But one thing I did know was that he believed in me—even though I didn't always believe in myself.

I couldn't risk ruining it all by checking the file in public—especially since I didn't even know what to check for. It would be better to wait. I called the front desk and claimed I was too tired to come up after all.

I got in bed, but it was impossible to sleep. I was too wired, tossing and turning. Even hugging my pillow didn't help. I just wished it were Ty.

I eventually passed out from exhaustion, not even bothering to take off my sneakers. I didn't open my eyes again until a good ten hours later, too tired to even dream.

I kept my eyes closed when I woke up. My eyelids a movie screen showing the replay from last night. The break-in. The crypto drive. The sound of the front door creaking open. It had been close, but I'd done it. And I was confident no one had seen me—even if they knew I had been there.

I was ready for the credits to roll and to finally be able to ride off into the sunset.

I opened my eyes, determined. The first thing I saw was the Muddy Buddies bag lying next to me. I couldn't check the drive upstairs, but I could at least know what to check for when I found a safe computer. And that research was something I could do on my phone.

As usual, it was playing a game of hide-and-seek. I eventually found it on a table by the front door. Pretty much no one had my new number, but the ones who did were making good use of it. There were a couple of missed calls from my mom to add to the running tally. I was back to promising to call her "soon." I didn't have the same thought for the missed call from Adore.

She'd texted as well.

Police called me looking for you.

My heart threatened to stop, but it was momentary. The police had been wanting to ask me questions for days at this point. There was no reason to believe it had to do with last night. I deleted the text immediately, but she popped back up a few seconds later with a new message.

Calloway wanted to know if we were together last night...

That one stayed.

There was only one reason the police would want to know where I was.

I forced myself to breathe in. Then out. In. Out. Of course the break-in would be news. But I'd been careful. The gloves. The hair. The mask. Someone had heard me but not seen me. I was out before they had the door open. And there wasn't anyone when I ran out into the alley.

I didn't write Adore back. Just went where I always did for breaking news: Twitter.

"Break-in" was trending, along with "Janelle" and "Little."

I clicked, though I didn't have to read it to know what it was about. Someone had broken into Little Street last night. It was the second attempt, but the first to be a success. Hearing something, the next-door neighbor called the police, but the suspect got away before they could arrive.

The fourth tweet down finally shared info I didn't already know. The police were holding a press conference later today with more details about the robbery and the suspect.

My first inclination was to call Ms. Morgane. See if anyone had theories. If anyone had actually seen anything or if the headline was just clickbait.

But my call went straight to voicemail.

Like I was blocked.

And that's when the panic set in.

I immediately went to Billie's TikTok, but she hadn't posted. It hadn't stopped folks from going wild in the comments section of her last video. Theories abounded—from an evil robber knowing the place was abandoned to an overzealous "fan" who'd been too obsessed with the case online. No one seemed to see the irony in that one. The good news was, it seemed like the only person they didn't suspect was me.

I expected relief to wash over me, but it barely reached my toes. The cops weren't the internet. And for the first time in a while, I was more scared of them. No one had chased me last night or even yelled anything when I heard the front door open. I'd assumed it was because I'd been too quick. But maybe they hadn't because they didn't have to.

They knew who I was.

They just didn't know where to find me.

Yet.

There was only one person in Jersey City who knew where I was staying.

I checked the time. Less than an hour left until the press briefing. Not for the first time, I wondered if it would be best to get gone. Leave now under the twin-sized cover of goodwill I still had. I wouldn't make it far, but maybe I could make it far enough. Get to Newark. Get on a train. Keep my mask on and my head down until Amtrak deposited me in Baltimore.

But when I got back on the Amtrak app, I was quickly disappointed. The next train was leaving in ten minutes, then I'd have to wait four whole hours for the one after it. There was no way I'd risk sitting out in the open at the train station for that long—mask or not. It was better to stay at the hotel. I didn't pack just yet, just busied myself, pretending like I didn't have a care in the world. Like this was the vacation it hadn't been since I'd come downstairs that Monday morning.

I didn't watch the press conference. Instead, I did something much worse—watch the clock and imagine what was going on. At 11:01, the line of officers would stroll in like a frat when their step song comes on. The police chief would take the lead, Calloway relegated to the back despite doing all the work. At 11:04, Chief King would say my name along with "person of interest." The crowd would gasp in unison like someone had said, "Action," while a lone person screamed out, "I knew it!" At 11:06, I'd already be trending number one worldwide, and at 11:07 Billie would go Live. Reporters would start asking questions around the same time. Police Chief King sharing that I was missing and asking people to keep an eye out—but not to approach me because I was considered dangerous. But it would be too late. Twitter and Tik-Tok would have combined to be on that case.

The good thing was that my mind wrapped it all up by 11:15, and according to the unwanted text Adore sent with a link, I was right. I still didn't respond, but I sure as hell clicked on it. Someone had already posted the good stuff on Twitter.

Chief King was front and center, but he'd let Calloway stick close enough behind to be in the camera frame. She stared impassively as he spoke.

"...don't believe anything was taken, but it could be because the perpetrator was interrupted. A neighbor immediately called the police after seeing someone suspicious walk into the alley. Our first patrol car arrived at the scene approximately eight minutes later, but the perpetrator had already fled. We were able to interview all four witnesses and believe that we're looking for a brown-skinned woman between 100 and 150 pounds and somewhere between five foot two and five foot six inches, wearing a dark T-shirt, leggings, and sneakers with bright pink on them."

I wasn't sure who I wanted to curse out more: myself or Eric at the ASICS store, who had convinced me highlighter-colored soles were "giving." I glared at them now from across the room, then tried to remember all the times I'd had them on when Calloway had come to see me.

THIRTY-ONE

The unknown number's first attempt was a little after 1 p.m. I let it ring.

The second was five minutes later. This time they left a voicemail. It went unchecked.

I already knew what Calloway was going to say. What she wanted. But there was no way I was talking to her without a lawyer, and I no longer had one of those.

The text came right before 1:30, long enough for Calloway to realize I wasn't going to call her back. The message was simple.

Hey.

I'd had enough booty calls in college not to fall for that one, so I ignored it. Too busy panicking, pacing so hard I felt bad for the person staying in the room below me. It only took Calloway another ten minutes to realize I wouldn't respond.

That's what I was doing when the second text came through.

It's Billie.

Oh.

I retroactively checked the voicemail. Sure enough, I recognized her voice, even from the tinny confines of my phone app. "Hi, Bree.

It's Billie. I'm still in town, so just wanted to check in on you. You left so abruptly the other night. I saw your Live too." She paused for a moment, and when she spoke again, her voice was teasing. "We gotta work on your camera angles and lighting. But overall it was great. Anyway. Call me back."

She picked up on the first ring. I was so surprised, I didn't say anything at first.

"Bree... You didn't butt-dial me, did you?"

She was friendly, and I was appreciative. It was what I needed—to hear someone happy to talk to me. The last person had probably been Ty.

"Sorry," I said finally. "It's just been a day."

"I bet. Are you still in town or did you finally get back to Baltimore?"

She didn't bring up the break-in and I sure as hell wasn't going to either. "Still here," I said. "Leaving today."

I needed to see what was on that drive.

"Glad I caught you, then," she said. "I wanted to send you something. I called Kristine to get her address, but she said you weren't staying there anymore. She didn't know where you were. I had to beg her to give me your number. Hope you don't mind."

"It's not the worst thing she's done to me," I said.

"Where are you staying? So I can have someone deliver my gift."

It was a sweet offer but not one I wanted. "It's fine," I said. "You don't need to send me something."

"But I want to. I need to. It's part thank-you, part apology."

A friendly voice wasn't the only thing I hadn't heard in a long time. An apology was right up there on the list. And although I'd expected it from Adore first and foremost, I would take this one too.

"Hyatt House."

"And you're leaving when?"

I quickly checked the alarm clock. "Couple hours."

"I better hurry up, then. Please text if you leave early."

Again, I could hear the smile in her voice, so I smiled too. "I will."

* * *

I was surprised when my room's landline rang even though I'd been waiting for it for over an hour. I'd been staring at the clock, anxious to get home.

The voice was deep and male. "Hello. You have a visitor."

Billie's surprise. "Thanks. They can leave it up there."

When the voice spoke again, it was muffled and not speaking to me. I didn't bother to try to make out the words. Just waited until they came back to the phone. "They're insisting on dropping it off."

Maybe they wanted a tip. "Okay," I said. "You can send them down."

I went to check my handbag to see if I had a spare five dollars. I hadn't packed yet so my empty luggage waited by the door, underneath the entry table, where I'd plopped my handbag and my room's key card. It wouldn't take long, though. I wasn't a good packer on my most stress-free day, so I'd just shove everything inside, including the bag of Muddy Buddies. I hadn't even taken the drive out.

A quick search in my handbag turned up a couple stray bills. Not much since I also had to tip housekeeping, but fingers crossed it would do. I wasn't even sure what Billie was sending. If it wasn't travel friendly, I'd have to take a pic for a thank-you text, then leave it.

My room was close enough to the elevator to hear the ding when the doors opened. Pressing my eye against the peephole, I waited until the world's biggest floral bouquet came into view.

The flowers were so gorgeous that I wished I could take them with me.

They got closer. Closer. Closer. My hand gripped the door handle, waiting for the appropriate time to open it and shove the few dollars

I'd scrounged up at the unseen person holding their hands out before I closed it again.

I had the door open when the bouquet was about five feet away, a smile plastered on my face.

"Surprise." The bouquet spoke, its voice familiar.

"Billie?" I said.

Her perfectly made-up head peaked out from the side. "In the flesh!"

"You didn't have to come." I made sure to keep my voice light as I reached for the flowers. At least I could save the tip to give more to housekeeping. But she didn't hand them over. Instead, she pulled back slightly as if beginning a game of keep-away. It could only mean one thing. She wanted me to be social. And I just wanted to get out of here.

Still, I took a step back. I'd give her ten minutes, then say I had to leave. "I'm going to the train soon, but come in for a few. I don't have much more than tap water, but at least the glasses are clean."

But she was already pushing past me. "You sounded so depressed on the phone. You were trying to hide it, but it was there. I had to come see you." She mistook whatever expression was on my face because she spoke again. "Don't worry. No one recognized me."

She set the flowers down, then looked around. "It's cute." She sounded as if she was trying to convince herself. She slowly walked around, taking in the plate on the couch, the cups on the coffee table, all of what I'd haphazardly thrown about.

I stole a look at the clock. *Ten minutes.*

I turned back in time to watch her disappear into the bedroom so quick it felt like actual magic. "I gotta pee," she said.

My unmade bed flashed before my eyes, followed closely by my mother's voice admonishing me for being such a pig. One should both always be ready for guests and never allow them into your personal areas. I rushed into the room to find Billie staring at the mess of sheets. I quickly spoke. "I was in a rush earlier."

"Same. We've all had an eat-in-bed-type morning."

And with that, she headed to the bathroom.

I did a piss-poor job of straightening up while she was in there. Tossing the comforter over the bed. Throwing away the remnants of snacks I'd raided from the minibar. By the time she'd washed her hands and opened the door, I had the bedroom looking semi-decent.

"Thirsty?" I said.

She followed me back into the living room, where I poured us each a glass of water. It was tap as threatened, but she didn't say anything. Just took the glass without so much as a thank-you. I took a big gulp, hoping it would encourage her to do the same. Instead, she just held it.

Neither of us knew what to say next. It was weird. I'd spent so much time staring at this face since I got to Jersey City. I wasn't used to it staring back. It was as awkward as a first date, both of us searching for neutral topics and common ground—and coming up short. Finally, Billie must've stumbled onto something because she opened her mouth. I leaned in, eager to smile and nod and agree how it had no business being this hot even though it was spring and we'd just finished complaining about how cold it was.

"Aren't the flowers just gorgeous." She pretended not to notice me nodding eagerly before she'd even gotten the first word out.

"Stunning," I said.

"I asked the florist to make the biggest bouquet they could."

I kept nodding, thinking about how I'd leave a note for the housekeeper to take them home. "Definitely the biggest I've seen." I stole another glance at the clock, even though I knew no time had passed.

She glanced at her phone, as if stalling. Once again we were at odds. "How you getting home?"

"Train."

"Kristine taking you to the station?"

I damn near recoiled at the name.

She noticed too. "Guess not," Billie said. "I figured something happened the other day. And then when I spoke to her today, she said something… You know what? It doesn't matter."

But it did. "No. What did she say?"

"That she'd made a mistake."

I rolled my eyes. "A mistake is putting the wrong answer down on a test. Those were *her* drugs the cops found the night I got arrested. And she never told me. Just let me go to jail. Ruined my life."

I didn't look at Billie. I regretted it as soon as I'd said it. Hated that I'd been so vulnerable. The emperor after they realized they were butt naked.

"I'm sorry, Bree."

"It's not your fault."

"I'm not just talking about Kristine. I'm talking about me. What I did to you. Even the other day, tricking you. Using you as a pawn and pretending like it was okay because I was bringing attention to someone's murder. It sounds like a lot of people have betrayed you. And you don't deserve that. Again, I'm sorry."

I was no longer staring at the clock. There were so many ways I could've reacted. Anger. Sadness. Fear. So many things I could say. *You're right. You're all monsters. Fuck off.* Instead, I said, "Thank you."

Again, it felt like a weight lifted.

But Billie was right about one thing. She had brought attention to what happened. If it wasn't for her, Ty's body would still be in that water. No one would care what happened to him or the woman I found in the foyer. And it made me realize that she might be the one person I could still trust.

It made sense looping her in. Not even just from an emotional standpoint. Forget Calloway. Billie was still the chief investigator of this case. The one folks listened to. The one folks shared theories and sightings with. There was no way she could read them all. And I knew from my own experience that she didn't always share them publicly. Anything could be hiding in her DMs—including someone who could confirm Janelle was the person behind this all. Billie just needed to know to look for it.

"You're a victim—just as much as Janelle was." Her cell beeped and she instinctively checked it.

"But what if she wasn't?" The words tumbled out my mouth so fast I could practically see them sprawled out all over each other on the floor.

Billie's thumbs paused mid-text response. She didn't say anything or even look up, so I kept going.

"Did anyone DM you with the idea that Lori Stevenson is the body I found? It makes sense. She lived next door. She and Janelle had similar hair. A similar build. Apparently, she had a horrible husband she was about to leave. Taking a ton of his money—*their* money—with her. And think about it. The police still haven't confirmed the body was Janelle. And it can't just be because they're being careful. It has to be because they're still not sure, right?"

The entire world froze on its axis as Billie looked at me. And just when I thought I was about to go extinct, she spoke. "You make a lot of sense. And that would mean…" She was quiet. "That would mean it's not connected to Janelle at all. Just a horrible coincidence. She could still be alive."

Billie looked excited at the very thought. Since I was in it up to my neck, I figured I might as well wade the rest of the way in. "What if Janelle *is* involved? She's the common link in all this. She was friendly with Lori. We all know she used to date Ty. Like I said, Ty had a client that had him unexpectedly working overtime that weekend. It *had* to be Lori. Janelle could've introduced them."

"Then why would Janelle be hiding?"

"Because she was the person who turned the light off downstairs when I woke up that night."

Billie grabbed me by the arm, her touch so light it felt like a fly landing. She pulled ever so slightly to lead me to the couch. She didn't speak until we were both sitting, then she smiled at me, her blue eyes kind. "Like I said, Bree, you're a victim in this. And I get it—you are trying to make sense of it. Make all the pieces fit. But here's the thing. You can't force it into place."

"You also had doubts about Ty killing someone."

"Yes, but it's like I said before too. It's easy to just say stuff. But even when you look at the facts, Bree, he probably did it. And I'm sorry about that. It's not easy to imagine someone you're dating is a monster—even one who buys your favorite snack or makes you laugh all the time. But there's only one way to know for sure if he did it. You would've had to keep going down those stairs that night. And I'm glad you didn't."

"But…" I trailed off, suddenly unsure of myself, as she stood.

"I have to go," she said.

We walked to the door, then hugged in the small foyer. Her phone pinged again. She paused to check it as I went to open the door.

"Let me know when you get home, okay?"

The way Billie had said it made me think that maybe—just maybe—we'd actually become friends, bonded by this bizarre week. I nodded and stepped back to let her pass. If nothing else, she'd definitely gained another follower.

After she left, I just stood there. Replaying the entire conversation, because she was right. This wasn't AP Calculus. This was life. Often the simplest answer was the right one. And maybe that was the reality—I'd almost interrupted my boyfriend killing Janelle Beckett in a rage. He was a monster who'd tried to cover up his nature with gifts and snacks.

Except there was just one issue. The snack. It felt like a throwaway comment—but it was too much of a coincidence. I'd never mentioned Muddy Buddies to anyone but Ty—not even my mother. The only way someone would've known that was because they'd heard me make a joke about them.

And the last time I'd done that was Monday at Little Street when I almost interrupted a murder. And only one person could have heard.

The killer—Janelle.

And anyone she'd told.

Like Billie.

I'd been right when I said Billie knew everything—and now I realized that could include the fact Janelle was both alive *and* a killer.

And Billie hadn't said anything. Just let the rest of us believe in her lies.

I needed to confront Billie. Make her tell me where Janelle was. It'd been only a few minutes since she'd left. I could catch her. I threw the door open, running into someone waiting right outside. Except it wasn't Billie.

"Ms. Wright, we've been looking for you," Calloway said.

THIRTY-TWO

I hadn't been in an interrogation room since I'd been dragged into one in cuffs twelve years ago. It didn't look anything like that one, but it didn't matter because it felt the same—like the walls were closing in. Calloway hadn't cuffed me, but muscle memory had me rubbing my wrists anyway.

She came in after an hour holding two paper cups. "I know you like your coffee."

She set both down, then settled in across from me, smiling all the while. "I see you've been busy."

She paused then, as if that was all it would take to get me to confess to the break-in. But the one advantage of being a convicted criminal is you already know how things go. I said nothing, and after a moment she spoke again. "I saw your Live. Lori Stevenson?"

I didn't even nod.

"You screwed us over, by the way, with that. Bree, you're a smart woman. But we're smart too. We've already been looking into Lori's disappearance and the strong possibility she's the person you found. It's just taken longer than we wanted to get a sample of her DNA. You want to know my theory? I think she was planning on disappearing while her husband was on his trip. Had been planning it for months. Maybe even years. Knew her husband had too much pride to report her missing. And she must have had help with it."

Janelle.

"But she got help from the wrong people and paid for it with her life. And your Live just let Janelle Beckett know that she can no longer use Lori Stevenson's identity."

There was what I'd been waiting for, desperate to hear. Someone was onto Janelle—the cops at that. I should've been relieved, and yet. "She's still here," I finally said.

"*Was* still here," Calloway said. "She's moving from place to place. We don't know where she is now."

"Billie can tell you."

"The chick on TikTok?"

"Yep. I'm sure she's the same one who told you where I was."

Calloway thought it over. "Someone called my direct line with a tip. Woman's voice."

"Exactly. You need to talk to her. She's been in contact with Janelle. Probably helping her. She's staying at the Regency. You should go now."

But Calloway didn't budge.

I, on the other hand, got fidgety. "Who knows how long she'll be there?" I said.

"What was in the house, Bree?"

I didn't answer.

She kept on. "Janelle has to be sticking around for some reason."

"You can ask her yourself once Billie tells you where she is."

"I'm sure you found it," Calloway said. "Because you're the only one of us who knew what she was looking for. I don't care that you broke in. I just need to know what you took."

Cops didn't care about a lot of stuff, but that didn't mean they wouldn't arrest you for it anyway. I couldn't just magically hand over the drive without admitting where I'd gotten it—and I wasn't sure I even wanted them to have it in the first place.

"So what was it?" Calloway said again.

"Go talk to her. Now. Or send somebody. I'll stay in this room all night if you want. But just send someone to the Regency to talk to Billie Regan. We can be in side-by-side interrogation rooms."

"Fine." Calloway pulled out a set of cuffs. "Stand up."

"Thought you didn't care," I said, but I sure as hell stood up as I said it.

"Turn around." Calloway made no attempt to be gentle as she put them on, squeezing them tighter than necessary. "You have the right to remain silent. Anything you say can and will be used against you in a court of law. You have the right to an attorney. If you cannot afford an attorney, one will be provided for you. Do you understand the rights I have just read to you? With these rights in mind, do you wish to speak to me?"

Needless to say, I invoked my right. Just plopped down in the seat, staring at Calloway all the while.

"I can stay here all day too," she said, then sat back down as if trying to prove it.

Putting her feet up, she started scrolling through her phone. I resisted making a crack about TikTok. We stayed like this for a while, stretches of silence that Calloway occasionally interrupted to ask one simple question: *What was in the house?*

I ignored her each and every time, too focused on Billie. She'd visited me only to stall until the police came to arrest me. But why? Payback for ruining Janelle's stolen identity? Or was it because she knew I might have taken something from the Airbnb? It would explain why she was trying to look around the suite.

But she hadn't taken anything. I was with her the entire time except when she went to the bathroom and there was nothing in there for her to take.

It just didn't make sense. I was replaying Billie's and my conversation for the millionth time when the knock came. Both Calloway and I looked up as Randle poked his head in. "We need to talk," he said.

Calloway didn't look at me as she left, but I didn't want her to—still focused on trying to figure out Billie's visit. I replayed it over and over again. I didn't know when Calloway eventually came back, but she looked grim when she did. "Stand up," she said.

I didn't rush, taking my time, until I saw her pull out what had to be the handcuffs key. "What's going on?" They were the first words I had spoken in at least an hour.

"Someone confessed to the break-in."

You'd think she would sound more excited about solving a case.

I managed to hide my surprise. My first thought was someone from TikTok claiming it as some sick bid for attention. But it didn't matter. I'd take it if it meant getting out of here.

"You need a ride back to your hotel?" Calloway said.

"I'll walk."

I had nothing with me. Calloway hadn't even let me take my cell. But I didn't care. I'd rather walk to the ends of the earth than get into another squad car. Besides, I wasn't going back to the hotel. At least not mine.

Calloway opened the door. I didn't look at her as I walked into the hallway and toward the exit. I had to pass Randle to do it. He held the door open for what had to be Interrogation Room 2. The one I'd been so desperately wanting Billie to be in.

I couldn't help it. My head turned as I passed the door, twisting to look beyond Randle's burly frame to see who was sitting inside. Who'd confessed.

It was Adore.

She was staring at her manicured, cuffed hands, but she must've sensed me because she looked up just then.

I hesitated when we made eye contact. Time seemed to once again stand still as we just stared. She gave me a single nod. I gave her one back. Then I kept going.

@ABrushWithBillie TikTok
534 Following 4.1M Followers 14.3M Likes

The screen is just a black image with words on them.

I'm taking some much needed time off.

—Billie

THIRTY-THREE

Billie was gone. I went straight to the Regency as soon as I left the police station. It wasn't hard to find. Just walk toward the skyline and look for the orange blob. But when I got there, I was too late. The front desk attendant told me she'd checked out that morning.

She'd disappeared. Probably heading home.

I needed to finally do the same. Adore had given me a literal get-out-of-jail-free card. I needed to stop being hung up on the past—be it twelve years or twelve days. I needed to be like her: use this as an opportunity to stop being scared to follow my dreams. I owed it to Adore. I owed it to Ty. And I owed it to myself.

Let Calloway find Janelle—do her *job*.

I was going home.

I went back to my hotel. It didn't take long, and when I got there, the first-floor entrance was empty. Not that it mattered. I was over hiding behind my mask. Since I didn't have my key, I was only able to get to the hotel lobby on the top floor.

It was there that my solitary confinement ended. An older blond white lady in short shorts and a hot-pink tank that matched her manicure was saying something to yet another in a long line of front-desk attendants.

I stayed a respectful six feet away, barely listening as they discussed important room-related business. When it was apparent the woman and attendant weren't going to be finished anytime soon, another employee popped up from the back room and waved me toward her. I managed to muster a smile. "Hi. I need a room key. And I don't have my ID."

"Sure, Ms. Wright. What's your room again?"

For once, I was happy to be known. "Suite 1042," I said.

She nodded, then began pressing keys.

Out of the corner of my eye, I spotted the blonde staring me down. Normally, I'd ignore her. But instead, I looked her dead in the eye. Then I smiled. "Hello."

She lit up. "We're neighbors!"

I nodded, expecting her to ask about my earlier police-escorted exit. I was sure the entire metaverse was talking about what had happened. It would explain Adore's well-timed confession.

Instead, the woman said, "I just checked in about an hour ago."

So she'd missed it. For the best. "I'll try to be quiet," I said as the attendant handed over a key.

"No prob," the blonde said. "You're both so nice, I wouldn't mind."

My head began nodding before my brain processed exactly what she'd said. "Both?"

"I met your friend earlier when we were both going into our rooms. I would love to get my hair that color."

I asked a question even though I already knew the answer. "Pink highlights?"

"Yes! Do you know how she did it?"

But I didn't answer. I was already at the elevator, jamming the button like I was Bob Marley. Billie had somehow gotten into my room after I left. Billie who had called the police. Billie who knew Janelle was alive. Billie who probably knew about the damn crypto drive.

And if she knew about the drive, she had to be in on it with Janelle. She'd always said Janelle was one of her first followers. Always commented on her posts. It would make sense that they could've developed a relationship. DMed each other. Had it been Janelle's idea and she roped Billie in later? Or could they both have planned the whole thing out together?

What had Billie called it? "Herd mentality"?

"Everything okay?" The joy had left my neighbor's voice. She sounded concerned.

"Yeah, I just forgot I left the stove on."

The elevator doors opened before she could respond. I jumped in, jammed the button for Ten until the doors closed. The descent was slow, but just as scary as the beginning of a carnival ride.

I hadn't done anything to hide the crypto drive. I should've at least put it in the room's safe. That's what they were for. Instead, I couldn't even remember where I'd left the bag of Muddy Buddies. Housekeeping probably would've thrown it out if Billie hadn't broken in first.

It had been a mistake, but that's how it always was with me. Not doing what I was supposed to, then asking God for help later on. I said a quick prayer now, repeating it a few times until we got to my floor. I tried to wrench the doors open. It didn't help, but it made me feel better. Gave me a place to discharge the energy that had built up over just a few short minutes. I sprinted down the hall, banging into my door and somehow managing to get it open.

Billie was long gone. Not a surprise, but still. The place looked... normal. I'd been expecting something more. Like you see in movies. Overturned cushions and cutlery hastily thrown out of drawers. But the only thing I saw was the mess I'd left myself.

For a moment I thought maybe the woman upstairs had been mistaken. That she'd misheard my room number. Got confused about what floor she was staying on. Maybe had some encounter with some other blonde who'd dyed her hair in honor of Janelle's vigil. But then I saw it.

My key card was gone.

Billie must've taken it when I wasn't paying attention, maybe that last time she hugged me like she gave a crap about my life—like she wasn't still actively destroying it.

I couldn't remember where I'd left the crypto wallet. It didn't jump out when I searched the room, so I started looking everywhere. It wasn't on the couch. Not stuck between cushions or kicked underneath it.

Next up were the tables, both coffee and end. The coffee table in particular had a lot of shit on it. None of it the drive.

For once I wanted to curse myself for being so messy.

I moved to the bedroom, a bit less than a disaster scene thanks to my quick cleaning attempt when Billie was over earlier. But it wasn't on the dresser. Or either end table. And it wasn't in any of the drawers the first or second time I checked each one.

She'd taken it. It was gone—and Billie and Janelle would be gone too.

And it was all my fault. I'd been so close. Ty had made sure I would find it. Only for me to fuck it up. Dejected, I sat on the bed and felt something crinkle.

The Muddy Buddies bag.

And just like that, I was thankful for my laziness. That I hadn't bothered to move it before "making the bed." It was still there.

The comforter was on the floor and the bag was in my hand before I could think. I dumped the entire thing onto the bed—saying sorry to the poor housekeeper who'd have to clean it up—and watched powdered sugar rain down like snow. The plastic-wrapped digital wallet looked like hail.

It was there.

Thank you, God.

* * *

"Here you go. It'll come on track 4." The agent gave me the ticket, the one I'd wanted in my hand for so long. "You still got some time, so feel free to wait in the lobby."

I hadn't checked out of the hotel or called anyone to tell them I was leaving—or coming. I hadn't even taken my suitcase with me. I never wanted to see the name Kenneth Cole again. The same with my work-out clothes and my one nice dress. I also left the mask.

Besides my handbag, cell, and the crypto wallet secured in a hidden pocket in my pants, I'd brought only one thing.

The grant application.

I found a seat on a hard wooden bench and pulled it out of my handbag, along with a pen I'd swiped from the hotel. The application wasn't much. Just two pages front and back asking for standard information.

I started with my name, address, date of birth, filling in things I'd known since I could write. My hand only stopped moving when I got to the part that had already stopped me before: *Do you consent to a background check?*

I checked yes and kept going until I got to the next question, which stumped me.

What's your company's name?

I thought about it for a minute and then wrote.

Gunk.

By the time I finished, I had fifteen minutes until my train.

I followed a mass of people into the hallway, then took the stairs up two at a time to my track. The station was busy, and all the trains from New York seemed to stop on the same track. The first train to come belonged to New Jersey Transit. A double-decker—split-level from the looks of it. It came to a gradual stop, then the doors opened. People spilled out. None of them looked in my direction. Just instinctively moved around me like I was a wall. I didn't move.

"New Jersey Coast train," the conductor said. "Next stop Union."

Folks got off. Folks got on. The process was quick and efficient, and they were gone in two minutes, leaving me with nothing to stare at but the train platform across the way. I was hyperalert. I'd gotten this far, was just a train ride away from home. And I wasn't going to let some internet sleuth ruin it by recognizing me. Or attempting to take my pic.

I stayed like that, watching as a train came in and the entire process was repeated. People in. People out. The only difference, the conductor screaming out this was the Northeast Corridor Express. The next stop was Princeton Junction.

Once everyone was on, the train dinged and the doors started to close.

At first, I thought I was dreaming. I had to look three times to know it was real. That *she* was real.

But there she was.

A woman. She sat in a window seat on the bottom level. Blond. White. Slim. Wearing a red crystal-encrusted face mask and leopard-print sunglasses. I hadn't seen her in over a week, yet she looked just like I'd pictured so many times since.

Even through the dirty glass, I knew it was her. I should've done something. Yelled her name. Called for the police. Run to the nearest train door so I could pry it open and try to catch her. Instead, I just stared. Frozen. Not able to move. Unable to look away. Just watching as she impatiently looked down, as antsy as I was.

She must've sensed me, because suddenly she looked up, her face shifting to my direction. And I could feel it even if I couldn't see it. She was smiling. Not at me but at the irony of the circumstances that had all led to this—the two of us separated by a closed train door. Both of us finally leaving town.

But only one of us had the crypto drive. And that's when I finally was able to move, walking closer to the platform edge. I walked right up to the window, ignoring the bumpy yellow stripe at the edge of the tracks, and bent down so she saw me.

Eye to eye.

And that's when she did it. She took off her sunglasses and the mask. Finally showed her true face. The one I'd seen on so many pink posters. So many tweets. So many TikToks. The one that looked so sweet and kind.

In person was a completely different story. There was a hardness about her. A bitterness. Then she smiled and it disappeared. A mask donned even though it wasn't red and bedazzled.

I'd hoped for this moment for days now. For Janelle to be alive. But seeing her in person... I wasn't impressed at all. She was still smiling, obviously taking me in too. And whatever she saw made her grin wider, like she was accepting some recognition.

Like she'd won.

After a moment, she put up her right hand, fluttering her fingers into a wave.

I reached into my pocket before putting my hand up too. Waved back. And then I put my other hand out palm up and opened it. Her smile faltered because she saw it and knew exactly what it was—the reason she'd killed Ty and Lori Stevenson. The reason she'd tried to break into Little Street. The reason she'd sent Billie to my hotel and called the cops on me.

The horn sounded again, and I could hear the train gearing up to move.

Then I stood up and walked away.

Behind me, the train took off, but it didn't matter. My phone was already out. Calloway picked up on the second ring. I didn't even let her say hello.

"I know where you can find Janelle Beckett."

The conductor had said the next stop was Princeton Junction.

EPILOGUE

Yasmin Cole sits in front of the camera, brunette hair in a sloppy bun. Her makeup is flawless, perfectly lit, courtesy of an unseen ring light. Behind her is a white wall with photos of her favorite celebrities. When she speaks, there's a Midwest accent. She's reading comments and responding.

"Yes, Rae Rae, I did see that article about that domestic abuse charity getting a crypto drive mailed to them with no note. It had to be some rich lady who sent it."

She reads some more. "You know I already got my tickets for Taylor's new concert. Had to refresh like twenty times on the site to get them. Drop a note in the comments if you're going."

Yasmin pauses to read again. "Yeah, I figured that lawyer would get off for breaking into the house on Little Street. Agree—Breanna Wright looked good sitting in court behind her. Someone said they were best friends."

She smiles at another comment. "Okay, we have a bunch of folks going to see Taylor too. Maybe we can do a meetup at the Birmingham show—"

She stops abruptly at another comment. Her eyes narrow. "There's no way Billie Regan's dead," Yasmin says. "I know so many of y'all think it's suspicious that she posted that hiatus message the same day Janelle Beckett got arrested on that train in New Jersey three months ago. That Janelle killed her like she killed Lori Stevenson and Tyler Franklin. But Billie's not dead. And I can prove it. Give me a sec."

She stares intently as we hear her tapping on a phone or tablet, as if she's looking for something. After a moment, she smiles. "Found it."

She holds up her iPad. There's a blurry photo of a couple standing in front of the Eiffel Tower. Behind them is the back of a blond head. The ends highlighted pink.

"She's in Europe right now, spending the millions of dollars that Janelle stole. And I'm gonna find her. If you spot Billie in Paris, let me know. My Instagram DMs are open."

ACKNOWLEDGMENTS

It always feels like writing acknowledgments is just as hard as writing the book—and this book was really hard to write.

Like most folks, I'd have to say that the last few years have been a lot. One of the key reasons for me was that I lost my paternal grandpa in July 2021 after a prolonged illness. He was the last elder on my dad's side, having already lost his wife and two stepsons years before.

So this book is for William Ellis Stewart, who loved his yard, puzzles, reading, and most of all his family. I could fill an entire book with why he was so great but will just share this: I got him a Fire tablet a dozen years ago. We shared an account so every book I bought would also show up on his tablet. For the most part, he would just read what I read, but the only times he asked me to get him a book was a Joe Pike novel by Robert Crais and *Fifty Shades of Grey*. You know a book is truly everywhere when ninety-year-old Black grandfathers are itching to read it.

Next I need to thank my agent, Michelle Richter, and my editor, Helen O'Hare, for their patience and always having my back during the long, arduous process of turning this idea into a book. I know sometimes it felt like a covert *Mission Impossible*–sized Tom Cruise running down a hallway mission to get me to finish, but you both somehow did it!! (Smile)

Also, thank you to the entire Mulholland team, including Alyssa, Danielle, Liv, Karen, Josh, Dianna, and everyone else who isn't included on annoying emails from me for putting in so much work to make my dreams come true. And I need to thank Katherine, Genevieve, Laurie, and the Simon & Schuster UK team as well.

I also need to thank my mom, Valerie, for passing on her love of books, especially mysteries, and always being supportive, as well as my entire family. I love you and I'm sorry that I didn't have enough freckles in this book. I will do better next time.

The one family member I do need to specifically call out is my uncle Tim Calloway, a retired cop who would patiently answer all my really random law enforcement questions. Calloway is named after him, though she is nowhere near as cool.

Uncle Tim's not the only person who'd get really random texts from me like "Where is the best place to hide a body in Jersey City?" and would calmly just answer because they were probably too scared to confirm it was for a book. Thank you to Katherine Reddington, Jennifer Rawley Lloyd, and folks I can't name. Let's pretend it's for your own protection and not because I forgot to thank you.

There are other friends I need to thank as well. First and foremost, Laura for letting me stay at her place in Baltimore to start what would become *Like a Sister*. It was there that my overactive imagination gave me the idea for this book. Next, I need to thank Liz, Alyssa, and Valerie for the sprint sessions. There literally would be no book without you all being like "Want to do another session?" Also, a huge shout-out to my super-talented friends who inspire me every day, like Alex, Amina, Alafair, Yasmin, Shawn, and Mia.

And if I didn't include your name and I should have, please know that it's not because I don't appreciate you. It's because this is due tomorrow and I, of course, have waited until the last minute to write it.

ABOUT THE AUTHOR

KELLYE GARRETT is the author of *Like a Sister*—an Edgar and Anthony nominee for Best Novel and a Lefty Award winner for Best Mystery—as well as *Hollywood Homicide*, which won Agatha, Anthony, Lefty, and Independent Publisher "IPPY" awards for Best First Novel and was named one of *BookBub*'s Top 100 Crime Novels of All Time. She is also the author of *Hollywood Ending*, which was nominated for both Anthony and Lefty awards. Prior to writing novels, Garrett spent eight years working in Hollywood, including a stint writing for *Cold Case*. She is a New Jersey native, a cofounder of Crime Writers of Color, and a former board member of Sisters in Crime.